*Anything can happen if you
dare to break...*

THE *Rich*
Man's
RULES

Three fabulously sexy reads from

LUCY MONROE
ANNE OLIVER
SUSAN NAPIER

THE *Rich* *Man's* RULES

LUCY MONROE
ANNE OLIVER
SUSAN NAPIER

M&B™ and M&B™ with the Rose Device
are trademarks of the publisher.
Harlequin Mills & Boon Limited, Eton House,
18-24 Paradise Road, Richmond, Surrey TW9 1SR

THE RICH MAN'S RULES © Harlequin Books S.A. 2010

The Rancher's Rules © Lucy Monroe 2006
One Night Before Marriage © Anne Oliver 2006
Just Once © Susan Napier 2007

ISBN: 978 0 263 87057 2

027-0110

Harlequin Mills & Boon policy is to use papers that are
natural, renewable and recyclable products and made from
wood grown in sustainable forests. The logging and
manufacturing processes conform to the legal environmental
regulations of the country of origin.

Printed and bound in Spain
by Litografia Rosés S.A., Barcelona

The Rancher's
Rules

LUCY MONROE

Lucy Monroe started reading at the age of four. After going through the children's books at home, she was caught by her mother reading adult novels pilfered from the higher shelves on the bookcase... Alas, it was nine years before she got her hands on a Mills & Boon® romance her older sister had brought home. She loves to create the strong alpha males and independent women that people Mills & Boon® books. When she's not immersed in a romance novel (whether reading or writing it), she enjoys travel with her family, having tea with the neighbours, gardening, and visits from her numerous nieces and nephews. Lucy loves to hear from readers. E-mail her at LucyMonroe@LucyMonroe.com, or visit her website: www.LucyMonroe.com

Look for *What the Rancher Wants,* the second in Lucy Monroe's fabulous Modern Heat™ duet, coming in *His Cinderella Housekeeper*!

For Myra...a dear friend and heart sister
for more than two decades. You are and will
always be a very special part of my life.
Much love, Lucy

CHAPTER ONE

GRANT took a swig from his beer and set the long-neck bottle on the familiar oak surface of the kitchen table. He grimaced. It tasted like swill, and didn't smell much better in his opinion, but it was all part of the ritual.

"Damn it, Bud, this is the third one in two months." His date last night had ended the evening with a *Dear Grant* speech, and he hadn't even been able to work up enough remorse to make her feel properly appreciated.

He'd been too busy trying to control the urge to follow Zoe and the guy on the Harley. He'd been looking after Zoe Jensen for as long as he could remember. Too long to take seeing some leather-clad joker with his hands all over her with any kind of equanimity.

Bud did not answer, and Grant took no offense. He stared morosely into his new friend's beady but understanding eyes.

"Guess you understand, *amigo*. You got dumped too."

Bud wiped his face and stared silently back at Grant.

Grant nodded. "Women. Who can understand them? Even Zoe is like a puzzle with a piece missing lately. You should have seen the loser she was with last night."

Just remembering the thick-necked biker-wannabe who wore more leather than one of his bulls made Grant's jaw ache. He knew Zoe had been going through some kind of emotional crisis since her dad had sold Grant the family ranch, but he hadn't thought she would take it so far. She did not belong on a cattle ranch and she had to know it. He had expected her to come to terms with that truth by now.

If her recent behavior was anything to go by, she hadn't.

He moved the hamster's cage so that he could put his booted feet up on the already scarred oak tabletop. It was the oldest piece of furniture in a house that had been home to four generations of the Cortez family. Surprisingly, it had survived the decorating efforts of his grandmother, his mother, and then his stepmother.

Looking at Bud, he sighed.

A man who talked to hamsters probably had no room to criticize Zoe's choice of dates. On the other hand, a hamster would make a better companion for her than the guy last night.

Grant stood up and put his now empty beer bottle on the counter. He could not stay still and he did not enjoy the feeling. Zoe had him tied in knots and she was not even his woman. But he felt as possessive of her as if she bore the name Cortez. He only wished he saw her as a sister.

His image glistened in the window behind the sink. He glared at his reflection. Disgusted blue eyes glared back. Almost black hair left a little too long brushed the collar of his denim shirt. For once, he looked like the rancher he was. He spent most of his time in suits, overseeing the Cortez conglomerate, but at heart he was every bit the rancher his Spanish great-grandfather had been.

Ramón Cortez had left his aristocratic roots and the country of his birth to make a new life for himself, and every generation after him had built on his efforts. There was no conceit in Grant's belief that he'd increased the Cortez empire more than any man before him, only simple truth.

His father was a millionaire; Grant was a multi-millionaire. Unlike the rich and famous who had winter homes in the area, his family had their roots in this small town. And, as wealthy as he was, he preferred the slow pace of life here to that in the big city, though his business interests dictated that he spend a fair amount of time there.

In fact, he had a business trip coming up he could not get out of. And maybe that was a good thing. He needed to get away from Zoe before he did something they would both regret. He wanted her, but his daddy had a saying and it made a lot of sense: "Don't piss in your own backyard. It kills the grass and gets your boots muddy."

Giving in to his desire for Zoe would be a very stupid thing to do, and Grant Cortez was not a stupid man.

He swung around and faced Bud's cage again. Opening the door, he reached in and took the hamster out. The tiny furball started climbing up his arm. "Do you know what my problem is?"

The hamster did not pause in his ascent up Grant's arm to answer.

"I need sex."

Saying it out loud didn't help, and neither did the idea that Zoe's date might be getting more in that department lately than Grant was.

The hamster shifted his path to climb across Grant's chest, unimpressed with the man's problems. After all, the little rodent had gotten cut off too.

Grant petted the hamster curled up near his breast pocket. "Don't worry, Bud. Zoe'll take you in."

She had a soft spot for animals that resembled a *Double Tuffed* down pillow.

He'd never forget the look on her face the day they'd met. He'd saved her life from a mountain cat, only to find out the reason the six-year-old had been wandering the range was that she had been trying to save her pet cow, Flower, from a stock sale. Her dad had been furious, but had reluctantly agreed to sell the cow to Grant instead.

At eleven, he had given up the money he'd been saving to build a soapbox car to buy that cow. He had learned the lesson well, and he'd been taking care of Zoe ever since.

He put the hamster back in its cage as he heard the back door open. Zoe came into the kitchen with a blast of cold air and a flurry of snow. He hadn't realized it was snowing.

He frowned. "You should have waited to come until tomorrow. Just because your truck has four-wheel drive is no excuse to risk the ride over in the snow."

Zoe pulled off her stocking cap, revealing the silky length of her pretty brown hair. The ridiculous bobble on her hat bounced when she tossed it on the counter.

"I'm not driving my truck." She yanked on one glove with her teeth and shivered. "Something went wrong with the doo-hickey and Wayne has it down at the garage. I borrowed my landlady's compact." She shivered again. "The heat's broken."

Grant grabbed her hand and pulled off the other glove. "What the hell were you thinking? You could have frozen on the way over here." She nearly had. Her small hand felt like an icicle. He chafed it between his own much larger and warmer ones, enjoying the smell of spring she carried with her, even in the dead of winter. "Angel, you need a keeper."

Zoe smiled up at him and her chocolate-brown eyes twinkled. "I already have one. You."

He did not smile back. "I'm not doing a very good job if you're out driving in the snow in some broken-down car without a heater, *niña*." No way was she driving home in that death trap.

She pulled her hand from his grip and started unbuttoning her coat. Her fingers trembled. "I'm not a child, and the car isn't broken—just the heater. What's the emergency?"

He picked up the hamster cage. "This is the emergency."

Zoe's eyes narrowed and she crossed her arms over her chest, pressing the swell of her breasts against her loose knit sweater. "No."

Ignoring his body's blatant reaction to the subtle stimulus, he forced his gaze to her less than welcoming expression.

She stomped her foot and snow fell onto the kitchen floor. "Do you hear me? I'm not taking him."

Grant opened the cage and pulled the hamster out. He extended his hand to her. "Look at those sad little eyes. He's already been rejected by one woman. Don't do this to him."

She did not take the animal, but stood defiantly silent—all five feet two inches of her.

"He was a gift to my foreman's daughter, along with another hamster. The pet store said they were both female."

Zoe's eyes widened in comprehension. "They weren't, and your foreman did not want a zillion hamster babies running around the house?"

Grant nodded. "Little Sheila had to choose between her two hamsters. She chose the female. Bud got left out in the cold."

Zoe unclipped her long brown hair and smoothed it back, clipping it again. Grant recognized the gesture. She was thinking. She looked at him, her expression unreadable, and then shifted her gaze to the hamster. She reached out to take Bud and cuddled the little furball close to her chest.

Her nicely rounded, high-breasted chest. He ground his teeth at the thought. He hadn't noticed Zoe's feminine attributes since the summer she was nineteen—he'd made sure of it—but lately his body had been going haywire around her. He definitely needed an outlet for his libido.

"What's his name?" she asked.

"Bud."

"Why didn't they just take him back to the pet store?"

"They tried, but the store owner wouldn't take the older hamster along with the babies."

Zoe's gaze shot to his. "They already had babies?"

"Yep. That's how they figured out they weren't both females."

Zoe raised her brows at this. "They couldn't figure it out before that?"

Grant shrugged. "I guess not."

"Why can't you keep him?"

"Get real. I don't do small furry animals. That is your domain. I do not begin to have time for a pet." Not even a hamster. "Besides, I have to fly out for a business trip tomorrow."

"So, me coming tomorrow would not have worked?"

"No, but had I known you planned to take your

life into your hands to make the trip, I would have come to you."

"Bringing Bud, no doubt."

He did not bother to answer. That was a given.

Her eyes skimmed the kitchen, another indicator that she was thinking heavily, and her gaze lit on his empty beer bottle. "Get dumped again?"

"Don't sound so cheerful about the prospect."

"The woman last night? Linda?"

"Yes."

Zoe smiled. "She take exception to you turning your evening into a double date at the last minute?"

As a matter of fact, she had. But Grant wasn't about to share that with Zoe. He shrugged instead.

She laughed. "You didn't have to join me and Tyler. He's a sweetheart under all that leather."

"Sweethearts do not get tattoos of naked women in chains on their biceps."

Zoe had got that *I'm going to protect the underdog* look on her face. "He got the tattoo when he was a lot younger. You shouldn't judge a man by the vagaries of his youth."

Grant couldn't help it. He laughed. Zoe leaping to the defense of an abandoned kitten made sense. Zoe protecting the reputation of the guy she had been out with the night before did not. He had looked like someone who could take care of himself and Zoe besides. That was why Grant had insisted on joining them. He hadn't liked the way the other man had looked at her.

"You going out with him again?"

She shrugged. "I don't know. Maybe."

"Come on, *niña*. He's not your type."

She looked at him, and something in her eyes made his body tense, ready to do battle. "Just what *is* my type, Grant?"

"It's not that clown from last night."

She walked over to the table and gently put Bud back in his cage. "His name is Tyler."

"I don't care what his name is. He is not the right man for you."

"Yeah, well, according to you, neither are any of the other men I've dated since I was sixteen."

It was an old argument and Grant knew he'd lose. Zoe dated who she wanted, driving him crazy in the process.

She grabbed her coat. After she'd put it on, she yanked on her gloves and hat. The bobble bounced wildly from her harsh tugging. "I'm really not in the mood to argue about this. I've got forty little yellow bells to cut out for tomorrow's craft project. I'd better be getting home."

Grant grabbed his car keys from the drawer by the sink. "Take my truck. You don't want Bud to freeze."

She considered his suggestion silently. He could tell she was warring with her desire for independence and her concern for the hamster. "What about my landlady's car?"

"I'll follow you and drive my truck back."

She chewed on her lower lip. "It's a cold ride.

Mrs. Givens doesn't need the car right now. It belongs to her son and he's away at college. Just bring it by when you get back from your trip. I assume you are flying out in the morning?"

"Yes."

"You could have one of your hands make the transfer tomorrow, if you like."

"We'll see," he said noncommittally, knowing he would not do so. He would rather she kept his truck until his return, when hopefully her own vehicle would be repaired. He was careful not to let the satisfaction he felt show in his face, however.

If she thought he was getting away with being "overly protective", as she called it, she was stubborn enough to insist.

That Sunday, Zoe rushed around her apartment before Mrs. Givens arrived for tea. She had invited her landlady the previous week and didn't want to cancel at the last minute. It would make the older woman suspicious. Zoe didn't want Mrs. Givens to realize that she had taken in another stray. Even this close to Christmas, she had the feeling that one more pet would prompt an eviction notice.

She led her German Shepherd, Snoopy, into the back bedroom and shut the door, and then tucked Bud's cage into the cubbyhole above the sink in her tiny bathroom. That should do it. With luck Zoe would find a new owner for Bud before Mrs. Givens was any the wiser. The hamster's exercise wheel squeaked as Bud's short rodent legs trod a constant rotation on the plastic device. Princess, one of Zoe's cats, watched with a hungry look. Zoe tapped the acrylic cage and smiled. Even Princess could not get into the hamster's haven.

Just to be safe, she shooed the cat out of the bathroom and shut the door. The doorbell rang and Snoopy let out a shattering series of barks. She hushed the dog before opening the front door, and almost fell backward as she came face-to-face with Grant's imposing six-foot-two-inch frame.

He reached out to steady her. "You okay?"

"Sure." She'd just been expecting a rather short, rather round older lady rather than his well-muscled, ultra masculine person. She'd done a pretty good job of sublimating her body's response to Grant since that awful night when she'd been nineteen, but every so often feelings she'd rather not acknowledge leapt past her defenses. Like now.

"What are you doing here?" Her breathless voice gave her away, but if Grant followed past patterns he wouldn't notice.

Sometimes she wondered if he thought she was as sexless as he wanted her to be. Not that she wasn't, but she shouldn't be, darn it. And that wasn't going to change any time soon. Not as long as her body still thought Grant was *the one,* even if her mind and her heart now knew better.

"I have come for my truck."

"I thought one of your hands would come for it."

She frowned in consternation. She hadn't been mentally prepared for a confrontation with Grant right now, even a pleasant one. Not when she needed all her wits to make nice with her increasingly annoyed landlady.

"Still mad I called your boyfriend a clown?"

"I'm not mad, just busy." She forced a smile.

She hadn't been angry the other night either. Not really. Grant couldn't help being overprotective. Besides, she wasn't really dating Tyler, just trying to fix him up with a friend of hers from school. They were both skittish. "Mrs. Givens is coming for tea."

Grant leaned down and scratched the silver fur on her cat's neck. His lean, tan fingers moved in a mesmerizing rhythm, a rhythm Zoe had an overwhelming desire to experience herself. She tamped down the feeling, just like she'd been doing with similar desires for the past four years—longer if you counted how long she'd wanted Grant before *The Night*.

He straightened and dropped a set of keys in Zoe's hand. "She'll be happy I brought back her son's car."

His fingers brushed her palm and she jerked her hand back at the contact. Darn. She needed to get some perspective here. She turned around too quickly and nearly went sailing when her feet got tangled with Alexander, Princess's brother. She yelled. Grant gripped her shoulders and pulled her toward him. She landed against his chest. Still standing, but barely.

Snoopy's barking, the parrot's screeching and Grant's laughter faded as Zoe became aware of the feel of Grant's hard chest against her back. What would he do if she turned around and kissed him?

Would he open his lips over hers and let her taste his tongue like he had that one time when she'd discovered passion included a whole lot more than the rather innocent dreams she'd been weaving around Grant since she was sixteen? More likely he'd think she'd gone nuts. And she had if she was contemplating giving Grant another run at her heart.

She trusted him with her life, and always would, but her emotions were a different matter entirely.

The sound of another voice alerted Zoe to her landlady's arrival; she jumped away from Grant. This time she watched where her feet landed and managed to stay upright. "Mrs. Givens. Grant was just returning your son's car."

The elderly woman smiled and patted Grant's cheek with her fleshy pink fingers. "Dear boy. You are so very thoughtful. I'm sure we would not have missed the car if you had waited until the weather improved before returning it."

Grant turned his smile on Mrs. Givens and Zoe was able to collect herself enough to find his truck keys. "Here." She handed him the keys. "We won't keep you. I know you have better things to do than stay and have tea with us."

For whatever reason, her hormones were in overdrive today, and no way could she handle Grant's presence at her tiny dinette table. Mrs. Givens frowned at Zoe.

Grant just winked. He really wasn't fond of Zoe's landlady. "As always, my schedule is full."

She knew it was true, and didn't understand why he had come to bring the car back himself. "Then I guess you had better go." Zoe pushed him out the door. "I'll talk to you later."

She closed the door on his rather astonished expression and turned to Mrs. Givens, who was trying to avoid stepping on one of the cats and frankly doing a better job of it than Zoe had earlier.

She smiled at Zoe. "That Grant Cortez is such a nice boy. I remember we all worried when his daddy put him in charge of the ranch at such a young age, but he's certainly made a success of it."

"Yes, he has." Not to mention his other business interests. She often marveled at the fact that their friendship had survived childhood.

Zoe wasn't in a league with the Cortezes of the world any more than she was with the famous actors who now made up a good part of the winter and summer population of Sunshine Springs. It was the new Vale—only more exclusive in some ways, since many of the families had lived in the area for generations and land was hard to come by.

Grant had been forced to pay her father premium rates for the ranch when it had been sold because an actor, a rock star and another cattle conglomerate had all been bidding on the property at the same time.

"Still, a young man at twenty-two should have

been dating, not running a spread the size of the Double C." Mrs. Givens tsked her disapproval.

Zoe agreed, knowing better than anybody what it had cost Grant to take over the ranch at age twenty-two, leaving his dad and stepmother free to move to Portland like Lottie had wanted. He'd given up his plans for a career on the east coast and lost his fiancée all in one devastating blow.

He'd resurrected the career, on his own playing field...but not the relationship. And he hadn't had another serious once since.

"Not that he hasn't done his share of dating these past six years. He's very photogenic." Which was the older woman's way of alluding to Grant's many pictures in the press with the supermodels and actresses who graced his arm socially.

Linda was the daughter of an aging rock star who'd breezed into town and thought nothing of dating the area's most eligible bachelor...until he'd gone into "protect Zoe" mode.

Mrs. Givens smiled conspiratorially with Zoe. "I'm sure you know more than the tabloids even..."

The woman was an inveterate gossip, and Zoe had no intention of responding to the thinly veiled hint to share what she knew of Grant's lovelife.

"It's to be expected, I suppose." She ushered her landlady to the table, where she had already laid out the tea things. "I'm trying a new apricot blend tea. I hope you like it."

"That sounds lovely, dear." Mrs. Givens was a

true tea connoisseur. She went to sit down and an ear-splitting yowl assaulted Zoe's ears. Alexander must have been sitting on the chair again.

Mrs. Givens shot up from the chair, stumbled one step forward, and fell over Princess. She gasped and crashed to her knees on the carpet. Her blond wig went askew and her thinning gray hair stuck out on all sides. Her polyester dress rode up so that the tops of her knees were exposed, and nausea climbed up Zoe's throat.

Not today. The tea had been an attempt to stay on the good side of her landlady, but now disaster loomed darkly on Zoe's horizon. Feeling doomed, she rushed to the woman's side and lifted Mrs. Givens to her feet. "I'm so sorry. Are you all right?"

The older woman took several gasping breaths. "I... I..."

Zoe pushed her into the now empty chair. "Sit down. I'm sure you will feel better in a few minutes." She patted Mrs. Givens shoulder, not at all sure the older woman would feel better in the next millennium. Her expression was not promising. "Let me pour you a cup of tea."

Mrs. Givens nodded, causing her wig to tip further over her left ear. "A cup of tea. Yes. That would be nice." She rose unsteadily to her feet. "But first I think I'll freshen up in your powder room."

"Certainly." Zoe helped Mrs. Givens to the closet-sized bathroom—remembering the hamster hidden in there only when a truly awful sound emerged from behind the closed door.

The landlady came tearing out of the bathroom, her eyes wild. She pointed a trembling finger at Zoe. "You have a rodent in your…your…"

"His name is Bud. He's a hamster. While technically still rodents, hamsters are domesticated and quite safe as pets."

The expression of horror convulsing Mrs. Givens' features didn't auger well for Zoe's chances of explaining her way out of the situation. She tried anyway. "Please. It will be all right. Bud is harmless."

Mrs. Givens shook her head violently, causing her wig to fall to the floor. Princess and Alexander immediately attacked it with all the fervor of hunting felines left in a cramped apartment for too long.

"My wig," Mrs. Givens wailed. Her hands flew to her head as she tried to hide the gray and white hair.

Wanting to cry, Zoe jumped to the rescue of the wig. She wrested it from the two cats and handed it to Mrs. Givens, who yanked it back on without much improvement in her appearance.

She stood up, trembling with indignation. "I have been more than tolerant."

"Yes," Zoe hastened to agree.

"I have put up with large dogs, screaming parrots, annoying cats, and even allowed you to keep your goat in the old chicken coop. But I will not stand for rodents."

Zoe didn't know what to say. Everything her landlady said was true. "I'm going to try to find a home for him. It won't take me very long. Children love hamsters. I'm sure one of my students will be happy to take Bud home as a pet."

Their parents would be even happier to get the paraphernalia that went along with a hamster for free.

Mrs. Givens sadly shook her head. "I know how much you love your animals, dear. But I simply will not abide a rat living in my home. Even if you found a home for him today, I would not feel safe. Who knows what you would bring home next?" She shuddered delicately. "You might even take it into your head to adopt a snake."

"I truly am sorry. I didn't realize you had such an aversion to rodents. I won't bring any more home. I promise. As for snakes—even I draw the line at reptiles."

Well, that wasn't strictly true, and she was hoping Mrs. Givens had forgotten the iguana incident. The landlady's narrowed eyes told her she hadn't.

"I seem to remember a very reptilian creature living in your bathtub not a month ago. I'm very sorry, Miss Jensen, but you are going to have to find another place to live."

"Please give me another chance," Zoe pleaded, "It's so close to Christmas. It's almost impossible to find living quarters in Sunshine Springs." Especially those that allowed pets.

Mrs. Givens' expression softened, and Zoe would have been home free if Snoopy hadn't perpetrated his trick of opening doors and come bounding down the hall. Mrs. Givens was not fond of large dogs, and she found Snoopy intimidating. Unfortunately, Snoopy adored her. He jumped up on Mrs. Givens to give the landlady a kiss goodbye.

Zoe shouted, "Down, Snoopy."

The dog obeyed, but the damage was done.

Mrs. Givens wiped the dog slobber from her face, her expression murderous. "The time has come for you to find a home more amenable to your soft spot for animals."

CHAPTER TWO

ZOE rang Grant's doorbell.

It was a new experience.

So was coming in through the front door. She took in the different perspective of the imposing portico while she waited for Grant to answer. Snow covered the ground around the impressive Spanish-style mansion with Christmas-card loveliness. The house was old for the county, probably the oldest one within a hundred miles, and still the most impressive. Wrought-iron grillwork decorated every window and doorway, while the stucco glowed in the moonlight.

She took a deep breath of the frosty air, the faint scent of wood smoke teasing her nostrils. Grant must have built a fire in one of the many fireplaces. Probably the study. She could certainly stand being in front of that fire right now. She shivered and clapped her gloved hands together. *Where are you, Grant?*

She heard a bump and a muffled curse. The door opened. Grant's dark hair stood on end, and the imprint of three fingers marked his cheek. He'd been asleep, but he wasn't undressed so he hadn't gone to bed. He'd probably fallen asleep in front of the computer again. The man worked much too hard.

His comical look of disbelief nearly sent Zoe over the edge into hysterical laughter. Although nothing about this situation was even remotely funny. She lifted her hand and wiggled her fingers in a quick wave. "Hi."

Brilliant. *Hi.* That was really going to convince him to let her stay. She had to look pathetic. She tried.

Grant squinted at her. "Something wrong with your face?"

She sighed. Of course she couldn't do a good job at pathetic. It wasn't in her nature. Grant was the only one who thought she needed a full-time keeper.

"Mrs. Givens evicted me."

How was that for pathetic?

Grant did not say anything. Zoe tugged at the ends of her wool scarf. "She detests rodents. Who would have guessed?" This time she tried for a look of innocent confusion. When Grant just stared at her, she gave up. Frustrated, she demanded, "Say something."

"You rang the front doorbell."

Zoe looked into Grant's eyes. Were they bloodshot? She didn't think so, but it was hard to tell with the hall light off. The outside light was on a timer, but its glow didn't reach far into the entry hall.

"I know I rang the bell." She sighed. "It seemed appropriate."

Grant rubbed the back of his neck. He always reminded Zoe of her father when he did that. She frowned.

"Why?"

"It just did." She chafed her arms and stamped her feet. "I thought you should have some say in the matter, after all."

"Some say in what matter?"

"This matter." Hadn't he heard her say that she had been evicted? "The *I brought one too many animals home and my landlady evicted me* matter."

Grant straightened. "I heard that part. But why ring the front doorbell?"

Couldn't he think of anything besides the stupid doorbell? "Grant, I need a place to stay until I can find a home for me and my pets. I've tried everywhere in town and no one would even consider renting to me."

It hadn't been easy coming to Grant. Not that she didn't think he'd want to help. She knew he would. But she'd been making it on her own, proving that her parents selling off her home and defecting to Arizona did not matter. She'd refused Grant's offer to let her continue living in the family home. Even paying rent it wouldn't have felt right. She couldn't afford the kind of rent the place would have gone for on her salary as a kindergarten teacher, and wouldn't allow Grant to offer it to her for less than the going market rate.

She'd come very close to regretting that decision today.

"One apartment manager laughed so hard when I told him how many pets I had that I'm sure he had a seizure." Zoe's lips were getting numb. "Doesn't it cost an awful lot to heat up the outdoors with your one little furnace?"

He got the hint. Stepping back, he waved her inside. "Come on in. We can talk about your situation in the house."

"I've got to get everyone else." She turned around and headed to her truck. Wayne at the garage had fixed the doo-hickey and it ran better than new. She lifted the canopy window and called back over her shoulder. "The cats are in the cab. Would you get them, please?"

She ignored Grant's less than pleasant rejoinder.

He came out of the house just as Zoe led Snoopy inside, carrying her birdcage and Bud's home. Grant took one look at her pets and grumbled, "I thought you would take care of Bud, not show up on my doorstep with a zoo."

She smiled. "Consider it a return on your investment."

He frowned at her before opening the cab door. He pulled out the cat carrier. Zoe went around to the back of the truck to get Maurice. The goat had not liked the ride out to the ranch. She pulled him toward the house. "Come on, Maurice, you're going to like Grant's place. It's warm and cozy."

"And it is not open to goats. He can stay in the barn."

"But Grant..." Zoe let her words trail off at the

implacable set of Grant's features. At least he wasn't sending *her* to the barn. "Let's go, Maurice. I'll get you some nice, snuggly hay to curl up in."

Grant snorted.

Zoe led Maurice to the barn and settled him in as quickly as possible. She didn't even stop to visit with the horses on her way out. Coming in through the back door, she felt warm air blast her. She looked around the kitchen. Grant had already put the teakettle on to boil. Smart man, not to mention self-sufficient. He kept a minimum of domestic staff, and none of them stayed over in the house.

Though the foreman's wife did most of the housework and cooking, she lived with her husband in a house on the ranch.

Grant turned toward her and she nearly went back out the door. His expression could have tamed a grizzly. It didn't take long for Zoe to get miffed herself. *Some friend.* She could not help it that she did not have a place to live. A tiny voice reminded Zoe that she could have refused Bud. *It was Grant's idea,* she retorted to her conscience.

"I put your suitcases in my old bedroom." He did not sound nearly as mad as he looked.

"Thanks." She gave him a tentative smile. "I really appreciate this, Grant."

"What happened? When I left, you and Mrs. Givens were sitting down to tea. I can't believe she would evict you this close to Christmas."

"Mrs. Givens hates rodents."

Grant's expression did not lighten. "Bud is a hamster."

He was annoyed with *Mrs. Givens.* Zoe should have realized sooner, but she'd been in panic mode ever since her eviction notice.

"Hamsters *are* rodents."

"Why didn't she just tell you to get rid of the hamster?"

"She hit the end of her rope with me, I guess. Said she thought the next thing I'd bring home would be a snake. She never got over the iguana in the bathtub."

Grant narrowed his eyes. "What about your classroom?"

Zoe pictured the look on her principal's face if she showed up with another animal and laughed. "I already have more class pets than any other kindergarten teacher this side of the Cascades."

"I still don't understand why she would just kick you out like that. You have rights. Besides, Mrs. Givens likes you."

"Snoopy kissed her."

Grant's eyes widened, and then he laughed.

Zoe smiled, feeling hopeful for the first time since getting evicted. "I'm glad you find it amusing. Mrs. Givens didn't. She thought it was time for me to find a place to live that would accept my weird need to have so many pets."

Grant's laughter dried up like a creek bed. "She said your tender heart toward animals was weird?"

The teakettle whistled. Zoe scooted around Grant

to move it off the burner. "No, she didn't call me weird. She didn't have to. Grant, most people think my tendency to collect pets like other people collect dust bunnies is a bit strange."

"There's nothing strange about it. You have a soft heart, that's all."

"Tell that to my dad." She hadn't meant to say that. She didn't like to dwell on her relationship with her dad. He had never understood her, and she was not sure she would ever understand him.

Grant squeezed her shoulder. "I did."

"Yeah, I know. Always my protector."

Grant brushed a finger down her face. It took every speck of self-control she had not to lean into his touch.

"Always." The warm promise in his voice soothed her.

"So, I can stay?"

Grant stepped back. "We'll start looking for a new place for you tomorrow."

Zoe frowned. "What's the rush? Can't we wait until after the holidays?"

It would be perfect. She and Grant could entertain their parents together, and she would not have to spend any time alone in the company of her father. With Grant around, even Zoe's mom would not be able to finagle such a meeting.

Besides, finding a place wasn't going to be all that easy. Hadn't he heard what she'd said about already looking? She hated facing it, but she'd have to get rid of the goat and the parrot. Someone might rent to her with a dog and two cats, but even that was pushing it.

Grant shook his head. "This is Sunshine Springs, not Portland. Among the year-round residents, kindergarten teachers don't cohabitate with men—not even their best friends."

"We wouldn't be cohabitating. I'm just staying here until I can find another place."

He reached around her and started mixing two mugs of hot cocoa. "You and I know that, but the busybodies of Sunshine Springs don't."

"But—"

"No buts." He handed her a cup of hot cocoa. "I know what we'll do."

Zoe took a sip of sweet, steaming beverage and waited for Grant to tell her about his brainstorm.

"Frank and Emma Patterson went across the mountains to Portland to visit family for the holidays. My ranch foreman is keeping an eye on the place. I'm sure they won't mind if you stay there while you're looking for a new home."

Zoe rolled her eyes. "Yeah, right. Grant, most people wouldn't let me stay at their home with all my pets. Why do you think it's so hard for me to find a rental?"

She also didn't know how she felt about staying in her old home, now occupied by the Pattersons, a wealthy retired couple who rented the place from Grant.

"I'll call Frank in the morning," he said, just as if she had not spoken.

"If you are that intent on getting rid of me, go

ahead and call." She set her half-finished mug by the sink. "I'm going to bed. It's been a long day."

Grant frowned. "I'm not trying to get rid of you. The Patterson place is a lot closer to town, and you won't have to drive so far on icy roads to work."

School let out in a couple of days, and Grant knew it. "So, we don't tell anyone I'm staying here. If they don't know, their overstimulated imaginations won't have any fodder. And with school letting out soon, how is anyone going to know?"

Grant's granite-like features twisted into a cynical smile and his blue eyes mocked her naïveté. "Mrs. Givens."

"You think she'll tell?"

His derisive laugh was answer enough.

"Okay. Call the Pattersons."

Grant savored the quiet of the predawn darkness. He'd wanted to make some international business calls before waking Zoe. They needed time this morning to take care of her homeless situation. If she had let him rent her old home to her, none of this would have happened. But Zoe's pride was only exceeded by her stubbornness.

When he walked into the kitchen, not only was the coffeepot on and giving off a terrific aroma, but Zoe was making breakfast. She flipped a golden pancake off the griddle onto a plate. A pan of eggs warmed on the back of the stove. He knew better than to look for bacon.

Zoe was a vegetarian. Ever since she was sixteen

and had told him that every time she bit into a hamburger she saw the soft brown eyes of a cow. When she'd said it, he'd come close to giving up beef too.

A vegetarian rancher. Right.

Her dad had gone ballistic. Jensen had never even considered leaving the ranch to Zoe, and when he'd decided to retire early he'd sold the ranch to Grant to add to the Cortez holdings. Her dad had not believed that she would be able to raise cattle to butcher or sell. Grant did not doubt the older man had been right.

Zoe did not belong on a working ranch and that was a fact.

At least she still ate eggs. His stomach rumbled at the sight of the fluffy yellow pile of scrambled eggs on the plate.

"Mornin'."

She turned around and smiled at him. "Mornin'. I made breakfast."

"I see. Are you saying that if I let you stay here I can figure on the services of a housekeeper?" He teased. "That might make me rethink calling Frank Patterson—especially since I gave my housekeeper time off from now until Christmas to get ready for her children's visit."

"I cooked breakfast." She pointed at the sink with the spatula and smiled. "I didn't say anything about washing dishes."

She stretched across the counter to pour him a mug of coffee. Her nightshirt rode up creamy thighs and Grant's gaze glued itself to the sight while his fingers itched to reach out and touch the soft skin. Would it be as smooth as he remembered? Would she shudder like she had that one fateful time he'd allowed himself to see her as a woman?

He bit back a curse. He wasn't about to give in to carnal urges where she was concerned again. Their friendship meant way too much to him. It meant more than any other relationship in his life, and he wasn't about to put it at risk for something as fundamental as sex.

"Don't you have some sweats or something to wear with that thing?" He grimaced at the question, hoping she didn't hear the tinge of desperation in his voice.

Zoe stopped stirring the coffee and gave him a quizzical glance. "Why? I'm not cold. Does my nightgown bother you?"

Nightgown? It looked more like a T-shirt to him. "Of course not. I just thought you might be cold."

She shrugged. "I'm not."

"Good." What else could he say? That the sight of her sexy legs had sent his male hormones raging?

She would run screaming from the kitchen. Or, worse, she would stay.

He'd call Frank right after breakfast.

The call started off fine, but took a dive like a 747 with engine trouble when Grant brought up the subject of Zoe staying at the Patterson place. Apparently Frank's wife and Eudora Givens were good friends, and Zoe's ex-landlady had already given her

version of events. Frank wasn't about to cross his
wife by letting Zoe and her "menagerie" as he called
it, stay in their home.

Grant hung up and sat staring morosely at the
phone. How was he going to help Zoe find a place
if even Frank Patterson wouldn't let her stay in
her old home?

Grant ran his fingers through his hair and rubbed
the back of his neck. What was he going to do? Who
would let Zoe and her pets move in?

No one. That was who. The only way she'd find a
place to live would be to give up most of her animals.
That was never going to happen. But...she could leave
her pets in the barn with his livestock while she stayed
at the Patterson place and looked for a new rental.
Frank would not object to Zoe living there alone.

Now Grant just had to convince Zoe.

After returning from school, Zoe went straight to the
barn. She wanted to check on Maurice. He was used
to living in a chicken coop, so the barn should be an
improvement. However, she didn't know how he'd
respond to living with horses. They were so much
bigger than him. He might be nervous. As it turned
out, Maurice seemed perfectly content. He accepted
Zoe's petting with an expression of goat disdain.

"I talked to Frank."

Zoe jumped at the sound of Grant's voice. She
whirled to face him. "I didn't hear you come in."

He smiled. "You were busy."

Zoe gave a final pat to Maurice. "What did Frank say?"

"His wife is a good friend with Mrs. Givens."

Zoe couldn't say she was sorry. She'd prefer staying with Grant until after the holidays. After the visit from her parents. "And?"

"She won't let you and your pets stay."

Zoe shrugged. "Guess you're stuck with me for a while at least."

Grant smiled. "Not necessarily."

"What do you mean?"

"I'm a problem solver, remember? It's what I do. If I can figure out the logistics on shipping beef to Japan on a scale large enough to keep my investors happy, I can figure out the living arrangements for one small kindergarten teacher."

"Watch the size cracks," she warned teasingly, but she was nervous. He was a problem solver, and she could see her plans for handling her parents' upcoming visit with aplomb going up in smoke. "So, what is your solution?"

"You can stay at the Pattersons' and leave your pets here with me. When you find a place, you can take them with you." His cat-that-found-the-cream-pitcher grin said that he thought his idea had merit.

Zoe's stomach tightened in a knot. Her day had been emotionally wrenching enough. She'd forced herself to put an advertisement for Maurice, Bud and her bird in the local weekly paper, along with sending flyers offering the animals free of charge home with her students. The last thing she wanted to do was to leave all of her animals behind and go live in the sterility of a pet-free household at the Pattersons'.

"You have too many responsibilities already. I can't expect you to take care of my pets too. You're the one who said you didn't have time to take care of a hamster."

"I don't. My hands will take care of your pets, and the real problem was that I didn't *want* a hamster. I'm not the small pets type and you know it."

No, he was the tycoon type, with a strong attachment to the land.

"I feel responsible for you being evicted and I am doing my best for you now."

She didn't need that reminder of his guilt. She'd much rather think he was helping her because they were friends. She really wished he didn't want to get rid of her. "They'll miss me."

"You can visit, Zoe. You're not going to be living in another state. The Patterson place is only about ten minutes away. Besides, I'll help you find a place and you won't be separated all that long."

Zoe dug in her heels. "No."

Grant leaned over and petted Maurice. "Be reasonable, Zoe."

"No."

He straightened, and his conciliatory smile was gone. "You're an unmarried grade school teacher. Neither your principal nor the school board are going to think highly of you living with a man."

Grant had a point and he knew it. She did too, which was why she hadn't argued too fiercely with him the night before. "It isn't going to be that long. I'll explain to my principal about getting evicted. He'll understand."

Grant shook his head. "He might, but other people won't. Do you want everyone in town talking about you?"

Zoe laughed, but it was hollow. The specter of gossip was all too real. "I don't care what anyone who doesn't know me well enough to know better thinks," she said, with more rebellion than truth.

"What about your students' parents?"

Why was he pushing so hard? "What about them?"

"Don't play dense, Zoe. You don't want your children's parents to think you're living with some man."

"You aren't *some man*. You're my best friend," she muttered.

He smiled. "Yeah. And because I'm your best friend, I'm not going to let you ruin your life, *niña*. What do you say? Should I call Frank back? The sooner you get moved to his place the better."

Zoe could not stifle the twinge of pain that Grant's eagerness to get rid of her caused. It reminded her too much of her dad's attitude when he'd moved her mom to Arizona. "Will you ask him if I can bring Princess and Alexander?"

Grant smiled, obviously relieved. "Sure."

"Great. You'd better do it right away. You wouldn't want me to have to stick around any longer than absolutely necessary." She could not help the bitterness in her voice.

Turning on her heel, she headed out of the barn. Grant couldn't have made himself clearer if he had shouted through a megaphone. He did not want her around. She should have expected it. She'd worn out her welcome with her dad before she'd ever been born just by being a girl.

Grant snagged her coat and stopped her mid-step. "Hold it."

She refused to turn around.

"I'm not trying to get rid of you."

Zoe snorted in disbelief. *Right.*

"Okay, maybe I am. But it isn't because I don't want you around. Come on, *querida.* You know it's for the best; you're just too stubborn to admit it."

She heard his words. In one part of her mind they made sense, but they did nothing to dislodge the lump in her throat. She wasn't sure why she was feeling so emotional. Perhaps the words hurt so much because they were almost identical to the ones her dad had spoken when he'd told her he was selling the family ranch rather than let her oversee it.

Heck, Grant probably had some convoluted reason why his actions on *The Night* had been best for her too. She'd hurt then and she hurt now.

She shook her arm loose from his grip and headed up to the house. Her happy reserves were all used up and she was in no mood to discuss why it was better for her for Grant to kick her out too.

CHAPTER THREE

GRANT tapped his pen against the desktop. He'd been working the figures on their most recent Japanese export deal, but he couldn't concentrate. The image of Zoe's hurt expression when he'd convinced her to leave her animals on his ranch and move into the Pattersons' was burned into his brain.

It didn't help that she'd been avoiding him ever since. She'd been by to care for her animals twice yesterday. Both times she had made excuses not to stick around and talk. Not that he had time for it, but it bothered him that *she* didn't.

Which made him what? Contrary, if nothing else. He should be grateful she was avoiding him with the way his hormones had been behaving around her lately, but he wasn't.

He missed her.

She could be so damn stubborn sometimes. Like when her dad had sold the ranch. It had been the only move that made sense.

The Jensens had had Zoe late in life, when her dad

had been in his early sixties already. He'd wanted to retire. His only son had died a year before Zoe had been born. With only a vegetarian daughter who would no more sell the cattle for beef than cut off her own right arm, he hadn't had anyone to leave in charge of the ranch—so he'd decided to sell.

He'd been doing Zoe a favor, and Grant still wasn't sure what she had been so upset about. Certain times of year, like during the stock sale, she'd been miserable living on the ranch. He'd tried to talk to her about it once, but she'd changed the subject. He hadn't pursued it, not wanting her to realize he'd been the one to encourage her dad to sell.

They argued about enough lately.

Mrs. Patterson needed to vacuum under the guest room bed. Zoe sneezed for what seemed like the hundredth time while she pleaded with her cat to come out. "Alexander, you can't stay under the bed while I'm at school. The litter box is in the bathroom, with Princess."

Zoe was afraid that was the problem. She had left the cats in the bathroom with the litter box the last two days while she went to school. Alexander had not liked the confinement. Smart enough to realize that today would require more of the same, he had run under the bed and wasn't coming out.

Zoe had already tried her most coaxing voice and offering kitty treats, but Alexander would have none of it. Darn it. She was going to be late for school if she didn't hurry.

"If you don't come out from under there, I'm giving Princess your play mouse."

Who said cats couldn't understand plain English? Alexander dashed from under the bed and made a bee-line for the bedroom door. Zoe would have lost him if two male hands had not shot out to catch the desperate feline. Zoe saw fancy tooled Spanish cowboy boots from her vantage point under the bed. Grant.

She scooted out and lifted her gaze to him. He was wearing jeans and a flannel shirt under his coat. So today he was working the ranch with his hands. It surprised her he still did it. He was a man of contradictions. A smart business tycoon who could ride herd on a horse or fly a helicopter to do it equally as well.

And he looked equally yummy in both business and ranch attire, which was not a comforting thought in their current relationship.

Jumping to her feet, she dusted her hands off. "What are you doing here?"

"Bad morning?"

"Not if you discount that I woke up late, had to skip breakfast and my cat hid under the bed. Now, even without breakfast, most of my students are going to arrive before I do."

"I'm glad I came over, then."

"Why did you?" She smiled so he'd know she wasn't being snippy.

Her annoyance with him had worn out sometime after dinner last night. It wasn't his fault she was feeling so vulnerable since her dad had sold the

ranch. It had been a final slap in the face. The ultimate confirmation that Zoe wasn't the son he'd
wanted and hadn't made much of a daughter either.

"The roads are bad." He smiled that killer smile
that had been doing strange things to her insides since
she was sixteen. "I'm going to drive you to work."

She sighed with exasperation. "Grant, you may
not realize this, but there are women all over the
county who are driving themselves to work today.
Some are driving busloads of children to school and
even more are driving their own."

He shrugged. "Better get a move on. You're already late."

"You aren't going to listen to me about this, are
you?"

"No."

"I could refuse to ride with you."

"I'd just follow you all the way into town. Why
deny yourself my scintillating company?"

Why indeed? It was pretty sweet he wanted to
drive her himself, considering that even if he was
concerned he could have asked one of his hands to
do the chore. "Fine. Put Alexander in the bathroom.
Check their food and water too, please. I'm going to
get myself something to eat on the way, since you'll
be driving." Grant was not the only one who could
give orders.

He tipped his Stetson. "Yes, ma'am."

The fake drawl shivered through her, doing things
to her heart and her desire. She forced a casual smile

and squeezed past him, her breath quickening as her breasts brushed against his arm. She rushed into the relative safety of the kitchen.

When they were in the truck, she started to peel the banana she'd grabbed along with a yogurt for her breakfast. "How are my pets?"

"You know they are fine. You just saw them yesterday afternoon. Snoopy is sleeping out in the barn, though. He prefers it."

Zoe felt a pang in her heart. Snoopy didn't belong being cooped up in an apartment. He was a ranch dog. Grant had offered the big German Shepherd a home when Zoe had moved from her parents' ranch, but she'd refused. Maybe selfishly. But Snoopy had been her dog since he was a pup and she couldn't let him go.

Considering the results of her calls on apartments the day before, she might not have any choice. Sunshine Springs wasn't a big town, which was why the rich and famous seemed to like it so much as a getaway destination. It helped that it was close to the ski slopes on Mt. Bachelor as well. But rental space for year-round residents was limited, and the rates could be astronomical.

No one she'd spoken to, no matter what kind of rent they charged, had been willing to rent to someone with a large dog like her German Shepherd.

Grant frowned. "Your bird is one of the loudest, orneriest parrots I've ever seen."

"You get used to his singing after a while."

He slid her a disbelieving glance before focusing on the snow-covered road. "*Singing?* The bird squawks loud enough to wake the cows in the pasture."

"I'll have you know that my parrot is a highly intelligent bird. He even says my name."

"Zoe, that parrot does not talk."

"Sure he does. You just have to understand his dialect."

Grant snorted.

"What about Bud?"

"He rolls all over the house in his exercise ball. I think he likes the living room best. I'm really not into small pets, but I let him do the ball thing a couple of hours each night."

Zoe smiled. "Thank you. Just think of it as training for when you have kids and *they* have small pets."

"I'm not getting married anytime soon. Ergo... no kids."

A sudden image of a little boy with Grant's dark coloring swam into her mind, making her long for things she could never have with him. "Do you have to drive so slow? I'm already late for school."

"It's a good thing I stopped by this morning to drive you. You'd probably have ended up in a ditch, driving too fast."

Zoe did not appreciate his comment. "Listen, Grant, I drive myself to work every other day of the year and I do not end up in ditches."

"So, your guardian angels work overtime? I knew that the first day I met you."

"Then I guess I don't need you doing it too, do I?"

"Maybe you don't, but you're stuck with me." His set jaw let her know that he found her flippant answer annoying.

It amazed her how quickly small disagreements escalated into full-blown arguments with him lately. This time she was going to remain calm. She gave him a conciliatory smile. "I've noticed."

He didn't return her smile. In fact, his frown grew more intense. "I promised your parents I'd watch out for you when they moved and I will."

Just like that, her resolution to stay calm went up in smoke. "Don't let a promise to my parents stop you from finding someone else to tyrannize. They gave up on me a long time ago."

He swore.

The rest of the drive to town was mile after mile of charged silence.

She unbuckled the minute Grant pulled up in front of Sunshine Springs Elementary School. Pasting a fake smile on her face, she unlatched her door and hopped out. "You don't need to bother picking me up. I'll catch a ride with someone else."

His jaw could have been hewn from canyon rock. "I'll be here at three-fifteen."

"Fine." She forced herself not to slam the truck door.

Grant waited until she was safely on the sidewalk before backing up. He exited the parking lot at a much faster speed than he had driven into town.

Zoe swallowed her frustration and headed into

the building. The last thing she needed to deal with a roomful of five-year-olds was a bad attitude.

When he pulled up in front of the school that afternoon, Grant half expected Zoe to be gone. She wasn't. She stood talking to a couple of other teachers in some flowy cotton thing that flirted in the wind, with her legs encased in tight leggings. Didn't she know any better than to wear stuff like that in this weather? And where was her coat? At least she was wearing a turtleneck under the flowy thing.

Wasn't that the tattoo man from the other evening? If she thought Grant would let Mr. Leather drive her home, she was in for a shock. No way was she going home on a Harley in these conditions.

Zoe looked up and met his eyes. Grant breathed a sigh of relief when she said goodbye to her friends and headed toward his truck. At least that was one battle they did not have to get into. Not like this morning. He still couldn't figure out what had offended her so much. Did it really bother her that he had wanted to drive her to school?

A small, still voice chided Grant. It hadn't been Zoe's response that had escalated their argument. It had been his own. He was edgy and he knew why. Her dad had called him the previous evening, after she had taken care of her animals and left. He and Mrs. Jensen weren't coming for Christmas.

They had been invited last minute to join a group of retirees on a cruise for the holidays. Heaven knew why they accepted, but they had. Zoe would be devastated. He had given the number for the Patterson place to Mr. Jensen, but the older man had asked Grant to relay the news—said they were too busy packing to make another phone call, which was a load of manure. The man just didn't want to have to deal with his daughter when he told her they weren't coming back for the holidays. He'd probably dealt with enough grief from his wife, but Mrs. Jensen was an old-fashioned woman. She might argue with her husband, but she wouldn't outright say no to him.

Grant could have refused to tell Zoe, but that would not have improved the situation. Mr. Jensen did not know how to talk to his daughter. He would hurt her with his pragmatic attitude. He might even go on about Zoe's pets and the new mess she'd gotten herself into because of them, as he had to Grant on the phone the previous evening.

Much better for Zoe if Grant were to break the news. First he would have to get her speaking to him again, though. He was going to have to apologize. The thought did not lighten his mood.

She opened the passenger door and climbed in, shivering. "You're late."

"I got caught on a phone call to New York on the landline." If he'd been on his cell, he could have left on time.

She harrumphed like only Zoe could. He imagined her little kindergarteners knew just when they had upset Miss Jensen without her saying a word.

She had a look when she was mad or disappointed that left no doubt how she felt.

"What were you doing talking to that joker?" He hadn't meant to ask, but now that he had Grant wanted an answer.

Zoe's head snapped toward him and she gasped. She turned back and looked out the front windshield. "I do not know to whom you are referring. None of my friends are jokers."

He ground his teeth. "The guy in all the leather."

"I told you, his name is Tyler."

"So, why were you talking to him?"

"I talk to lots of people, Grant. Do you expect me to keep a record and report back to you?"

"Of course not."

"Good, because I would have to disappoint you if you did."

He had not meant to get so off track. "Are you going out with him again?"

"That's none of your business."

"It sure as hell is. I promised your parents I'd watch out for you."

"So you said this morning."

Grant cleared his throat. The thermal shirt under his flannel suddenly felt like one too many layers. "About this morning…"

Zoe gave him a sideways glance. "Yes?"

"I'm sorry I came on so strong. I know you're a good driver and I should not have implied otherwise."

Zoe's tense stance deflated like a pierced balloon. "Thank you."

He nodded. "Do you forgive me?" He knew with Zoe that once she gave the words it would be a reality.

She knew it too. She inhaled, and then let out a long, protracted breath. "Yeah, I forgive you. Are you sorry for calling Tyler a joker too?"

Grant smiled. "Don't push it."

Zoe laughed. "He really is a nice guy."

Grant just snorted. He wasn't about to say something to start another fight with her.

"You'll be happy to know that he's going out with my friend Jenny now. She was the redhead talking to us when you drove up."

He liked hearing that, but wasn't it awfully damn fast? Less than a week ago Tyler had been going out with Zoe. "What happened with the two of you?" he couldn't help asking.

Zoe's laughter filled the cab with more warmth than the heated air blasting from the vents. "Nothing happened with the two of us. We were never more than friends. I wanted to fix him up with Jenny all along, but both of them were shy to begin with."

Grant could imagine Jenny being nervous about dating Tyler. Most women would be. "Uh...Zoe, there's something else I need to tell you."

"Another apology? I don't know if my heart can handle it."

"No. Your dad called last night."

"Really? Did you give him the Pattersons' number? I didn't hear the phone ring."

"I gave your dad the number, but he was real busy."

She couldn't quite hide her disappointment. "Oh."

"They got invited on a seniors' cruise for the holidays."

"That's wonderful." She smiled. "I'm glad they're settling in so well. I was a little worried about Mom. She's so shy around strangers. I'm sure it disappointed her to tell her new friends no. There will be other cruises, though."

Zoe's concern for her mom's feelings made the news that they weren't coming even more obscene in Grant's mind. "They didn't say no. Your parents aren't coming out for Christmas."

"What do you mean? Of course they are coming. We've been planning the trip since before I visited them at Thanksgiving."

He reached across the seat and pressed his fingers around her arm. "They changed their minds."

"They changed their minds about spending Christmas with me?" She made it sound every bit as bad as it was.

"It's not the end of the world, Zoe. Just think, you get to avoid the yearly Christmas argument with your dad."

"We don't have those anymore." He grunted, and she said, "They aren't as bad as they used to be anyway."

"You won't be alone. My parents are still coming, and Mom's expecting your help with dinner." It was a small stretch of the truth, but he was sure that his stepmom should be expecting Zoe's help for dinner.

There had to be things besides the turkey that Zoe could help prepare. And since his stepmother would insist on doing all the cooking, so the foreman's wife could be with her family, his comment wasn't a real stretch at all.

Zoe did not answer.

Grant decided to change the subject. It wouldn't do Zoe any good to dwell on her strained relationship with her parents. "Do you want me to swing by the Patterson place, or take you to the Double C first?"

"Just drop me off at the Pattersons'. Your hands are doing a great job taking care of everyone. I'm sure Snoopy wishes he could live over there permanently. He was never meant to leave the ranch. I should have taken you up on your offer to give him a home a long time ago. I've been too stubborn."

Grant hated the dejected tone in her voice. "I thought maybe you would come over for dinner tonight. I won't even make you cook."

She smiled at him briefly, and then turned to look out the window. "No, thanks. I have work to do, and I don't want to leave the cats cooped up in the bathroom."

"We can stop and pick them up." He ignored her comment about having work to do, sure it was just an excuse.

Grant would not let Zoe get out of the truck when they arrived at the Pattersons'. "I'll just run in and get the cats."

Zoe watched him walk away and reminded herself that at least she had him. Although she had told him that morning that she did not need him, nothing could be further from the truth. For as long as she could remember, Grant and his folks had been filling an empty place in Zoe's heart left by her parents' disapproval. She should not be surprised that her mom and dad had opted to join their new friends on a cruise. They'd never made it a secret that she didn't live up to their expectations.

How could she? She wasn't the dead brother she'd never even known, who by all accounts had been the perfect rancher's son. She didn't think her dad had ever forgiven her for being born female, maybe even for being born at all after he'd lost his precious son.

Grant opened his door and a blast of cold air whooshed into the cab. She shivered while he tucked the cat carrier in the extension behind the main cab.

"If you thought Alexander was unhappy about spending time in the bathroom today, you should have seen him getting into the cat carrier."

Zoe grinned. "That bad, huh?"

"I just hope we can find him later, when it's time to bring you home."

"We've only got one more day of school, and then I'll be there and he can be out of the bathroom and roam free."

"Except when you're looking for a place."

She said nothing to this reminder of the monumental task before her.

* * *

Twenty minutes later, the fragrance of melted butter and popping corn filled the kitchen, and soon the subtle aroma of brewing coffee joined it. Grant had suggested watching a DVD when they arrived, and she'd accepted gratefully. She knew he had stuff to do—he always did—but somehow he also always managed to make time for her when she needed him.

Grant Cortez was a really special guy.

When the popcorn and coffee were done, they went together to the entertainment room. "Want to watch an *I Love Lucy* episode?" Grant asked, knowing the old black-and-white comedy was one of her favorite shows.

"Sure."

She sat down on the couch. He popped in the DVD, then turned around to sit down and hesitated. What was the matter with him?

She patted the seat beside her. "The popcorn is over here."

After another short hesitation, and an unreadable look, he sat down, leaving a few inches between them. She scooted over to sit up against his side and rest her head against his shoulder. It was how they always watched DVDs. Grant sighed and put his arm around her shoulders.

The image of Lucy trying to stuff chocolate candies into her already full cheeks faded as Zoe became intensely aware of Grant's arm where it touched her.

This kind of thing had been happening with increasing regularity over the past year, and Zoe had always forced herself to ignore it. She'd thought *The Night* had well and truly cured her of any lingering romantic feelings toward Grant, much less any lust for his hard-muscled body. She'd been wrong, as the past year had too frequently shown…at least about the lust part.

She couldn't believe that she still wanted him after the painful rejection he'd dealt her when she was nineteen.

She'd been home from college for the summer, and they'd spent tons of time together, like always. Only there had been something different about that summer. It had been as if Grant had finally woken up to the fact she was a woman. He'd taken her places he'd previously only taken dates, and she'd caught him looking at her, his blue eyes darkened with what she'd been sure was desire, on more than one occasion.

She'd realized he was the embodiment of every romantic fantasy she'd ever had or would have when she was sixteen. Only he'd been engaged and living the majority of the year on the east coast then.

He'd gone to college near his real mother, so he could get to know that side of his family. It hadn't worked out the way either he or his dad had hoped. Grant's grandfather had died his sophomore year of college and he'd left his grandson the majority of his wealth, making Grant's mother angry and driving another wedge between mother and son.

Grant had started dating "the witch" that same year, and they'd been engaged ten months later. The engagement had ended when Grant had agreed to return to Oregon to run the ranch, after his dad had told him he intended to move with Lottie to Portland and oversee his business interests there.

To give Roy Cortez credit, he had offered Grant three options: hire a foreman with full decision-making authority, sell the ranch that had been in their family for four generations, or come home and run it himself.

Considering the fact that Grant had planned to live and work on the east coast, it had come as quite a shock to most everyone when he had agreed to move home. Everyone except Zoe. She'd known he wouldn't leave the ranch's running to a foreman, and that he would never sell it. He was a business tycoon through and through, but he was also connected to the land in the same way his great-grandfather had been.

His fiancée hadn't liked it, and had given Grant back his ring. He'd started dating lots of different sophisticated women then. There were always plenty to choose from, both in the winter, when ski bunnies showed up, and the summer, when supermodels lazed by their swimming pools in barely-there bikinis.

Zoe had been sure he would never look at her that way. She was too smalltown, and not exactly centerfold material, with her petite frame and mousy brown hair. But she'd been wrong, at least for a little while, and it had all come to a head one night that summer, when one of their many playful arguments had turned into a wrestling match.

She'd found herself pinned beneath his hard body

and his even harder erection. She could still remember the shock she'd felt as his hips had settled into hers, making her intimately aware for the first time of the effect she had on a male body. And not just any male body. That hardness had belonged to Grant.

He'd kissed her and it had been incredible. So incredible that she hadn't noticed him removing clothes until they'd both been naked from the waist up and his mouth had settled on one of her nipples. The pleasure had been so intense it had shocked her right out of her passionate haze and she'd panicked.

She'd never even been French kissed before. She hadn't wanted to experiment with anyone but Grant, and he hadn't been available. She had pleaded with him to let her go. She'd thrown her shirt on and run from the barn and from the feelings he'd evoked in her. Later, she'd wanted to kick herself for being such an idiot. She could have trusted Grant not to hurt her.

She'd loved him all her life, and if it wasn't him it would never be anyone. So she'd decided to give him her virginity. He'd been supposed to escort her to a town dance, and she'd planned to offer him both her love and her innocence that night. Her plans had ended in her private humiliation when a model from New York had convinced Grant to drop Zoe off at home before taking her for a nighttime flight in his private plane.

The only consolation she could take from that night was the fact that Grant had not known her plans, or of the love that had been burning inside her for most of her life.

She would never give him the opportunity to stomp on her heart that way again.

Even knowing that the friendship they shared was as close to intimacy as they should ever get, she still desired him—and now it was getting worse. Like that summer four years ago, she sensed that Grant had become aware of the air sizzling between them as well. His breathing had turned shallow and his heartbeat thundered in her ear.

Zoe pulled back and looked into his eyes. Their normal blue lights had darkened with unmistakable desire. Zoe's lips parted involuntarily. His gaze zeroed in on her mouth and it tingled as if he'd touched it. The sound of tinny laughter came from the TV screen, but he didn't look away from her mouth and she couldn't look away from him. In a gesture born of nervousness, she flicked her tongue out to wet her suddenly dry lips.

Grant made a growling sound deep in his throat.

"Grant?" Her head was screaming, *Not again*, but her body was refusing to listen as she leaned just one centimeter closer.

"This is not a good idea." He said the words even as he cupped the back of Zoe's head and pulled her forward to receive his kiss.

CHAPTER FOUR

THE feel of Grant's lips against hers was so overpowering Zoe almost forgot to respond. Her body knew what it wanted, however, and she found herself arched against him, kissing him back for all she was worth. Her hands dug into the flannel covering his chest and she tried to eat his lips. He groaned and dragged her onto his lap, deepening the kiss.

At the first touch of his tongue Zoe lost whatever sense of reality she'd had left. Her mouth opened and she invited him in with little flicks of her tongue against his. His mouth was hot, his taste utterly masculine. How had she gone so long, forgetting how this felt?

Grant's body shuddered under her, and Zoe felt more than just his hard thighs against her backside. A responding wetness warmed her inner thighs and she clamped them tightly together in an effort to assuage the ache in her most feminine place. She squirmed against him, exultant when he bucked under her.

She licked the salt and butter from the popcorn off his lips, tunneling her fingers into his hair, awed by the feel of its silkiness against her skin. His hands were locked on her hips and she desperately wanted to feel them move. Then they did. Right up her body to her breasts that longed for his touch.

He brushed her already erect nipples as they strained against her top. She wanted more. She wanted to rip off every layer of cloth between her burning skin and his hands, and she wanted those talented lips that were wreaking havoc with her mouth to do the same to the needy little buds jutting against his palms.

She rocked harder against him and he groaned deep in his throat. He bucked upward, pressing his hardened penis against the juncture of her thighs, and she almost came apart.

It was too much.

It was too wonderful.

It was over.

Grant had torn his mouth from hers and yanked his hands away from her breasts. She kept her eyes shut and waited for him to resume the kiss, to go on to something better.

Seconds moved in slow succession.

She opened her eyes and could have screamed at the look of horror on Grant's face. He stood abruptly and she fell on the floor, landing hard on her bottom.

So much for their first kiss in four years.

He moved to stand near the recliner.

Zoe climbed up off the floor. "Ouch." She rubbed her backside. "What was that for?"

Grant ran his fingers through his hair. "Sorry. I…"

She waited, but Grant never finished his sentence. He just stared at her, like she had grown a couple of antlers…or worse. Her body ached from wanting, not to mention her unceremonious trip to the floor. Grant's dismayed features were not helping.

"Stop looking like that. It was just a kiss."

"*Just a kiss?* Zoe, you're my best friend. A man does not kiss his best friend."

This was getting out of hand. "Grant, I don't know if you have noticed or not, but your best friend happens to be female. There is no cardinal rule against kissing me."

"*I* have a rule against it."

Had he written that rule before or after their hot and heavy session in his barn when she was nineteen? She felt her face crease in a frown. "Well, you broke it."

"I know."

He looked so genuinely dismayed that she fought with dual desires. One to comfort him and the other to smack him. What was his problem? Being his best friend, she decided on comfort and leaned forward to pat his arm. He jumped back.

She glared at him. "Stop acting like kissing me was tantamount to cattle rustling." *She* was the one with all the reasons to keep their relationship platonic. He'd walked away from their last encounter with mutual passion heart-whole.

She hadn't.

He frowned. "This is serious, *niña.*"

"I know." Seriously disturbing. She might not

think getting involved with Grant was up there on the list of her one hundred most intelligent life choices, but she sure as certain didn't understand his melodramatic reaction. "Why do you have a rule against kissing me?"

He looked at her like she'd lost her mind.

"It's a reasonable question. I liked kissing you." She knew it couldn't go anywhere, but it wasn't exactly the crime of the century.

Grant glared at her. "Get over it. It won't happen again."

"*Get over it?* No wonder women break up with you by the truckload. If you treat them all like mass murderers for liking your kisses."

"Stop dramatizing. We have enough to worry about without you getting theatrical."

Her theatrical? She wasn't the one turning a simple kiss into a federal offense.

He folded his arms across his chest, his stance defensive. "For your information, the women I date rarely break it off with *me,* and I don't mind them liking my kisses."

Okay. He was mad. That was pretty obvious. And he looked pretty confused too, but the words still hurt.

"What's the matter with me?"

She had not meant to shout.

Grant winced, then rubbed the back of his neck.

"Stop doing that. You remind me of my dad," she accused, out of all patience.

"Good. That's good. Just remember, I'm a lot like your dad. You don't want to kiss me again."

Zoe pinched herself. It hurt. "Ouch."

Grant looked at her with that dumb cow stare that men got sometimes when faced with a *relationship* discussion. "Why did you do that?"

"I wanted to know if this was some bizarre dream. Unfortunately, it's not." She rubbed at her arm where she had pinched it. She could not understand Grant's reaction. She had a good reason for avoiding a relationship with him, but what was *his* problem with *her*?

She needed some time to think—away from the maddening man trying to convince her that he was just like her father. No two men could be more different. Grant had never made Zoe feel like she needed to be something or someone different to earn his approval. He'd hurt her when she was nineteen, but he hadn't known how much. After all, as far as he was concerned she was the one who had run from the barn.

He didn't know that she'd changed her mind and been prepared to take their relationship to a deeper level. But that didn't excuse him turning to another woman so quickly, or the fact he hadn't talked over what had happened with her before doing so. Zoe wasn't the only one who had seen her and Grant as a couple that summer.

"I'm going to check on Snoopy and Maurice."

"Great. I'll start dinner."

His obvious relief set her teeth on edge. "Fine."

She left, stopping briefly to don her coat. When

she opened the door, cold air and flurries of snow blasted her. She made her way to the barn, glad for the guide rope Grant kept during the winter between the barn and the hacienda. Her hands were numb in no time, and she berated herself for forgetting her gloves. She pulled her hands inside the sleeves of her coat and used the ends like mittens, holding onto the rope through the down-filled cotton. When she finally reached the barn, she yanked open the door and rushed inside.

She pushed the door shut against the howling wind and swiftly falling snow. She leaned against it, trying to catch her breath. One of Grant's horses neighed. Zoe's head snapped up at the sound. Snoopy came bounding toward her, barking a greeting.

"Hush, dog." Zoe sank to her knees to hug him, and scratched him behind the ears. Snoopy crooned low in his throat at her affectionate scratching.

"Grant has a rule against kissing me. Can you believe it?" She patted Snoopy and stood up. She wanted to check on Maurice as well. "In fact, he would rather kiss just about anyone but me. He made that perfectly clear." She walked over to the goat's stall, talking to Snoopy all the way. "My best friend and self-proclaimed protector has a rule against kissing me. The man's got a screw loose. I never noticed it before. I'm not exactly a candidate for the lead role in *Fatal Attraction*."

She entered Maurice's stall and leaned forward to pet the goat. He ignored her. Maurice had never really accepted Zoe. The only person he had ever shown any affection for was Mr. Givens. Zoe sighed. She checked Maurice's food supply and then left his stall.

Snoopy danced around her. "Well, screw loose or no screw loose, after that kiss I've got some thinking to do." Her body still tingled in places where he had touched her—even places he hadn't. The dog barked once loudly. Zoe smiled. "I'm glad to see you agree."

She sat down on the barn floor, glad for Grant's penchant for cleanliness and his ranch hands' follow-through. Snoopy nuzzled her neck before settling down beside her and laying his head in her lap. She scratched behind his ears again while she contemplated both her own and Grant's reaction to the kiss.

The one relationship in her life she knew she could count on was her friendship with Grant, and she didn't want to do anything to jeopardize it. She didn't want to get hurt again either.

It had been a whole lot easier when she'd been living in Portland and going to college, and then doing her teaching practice. Maybe coming home had been a mistake in more ways than one. She'd wanted to mend her relationship with her father, but that hadn't worked out. He'd sold the ranch and moved away.

Now, instead of being a blessing, like she'd thought it would be, her constant proximity to Grant was sending her libido out of control. While out of sight hadn't exactly been out of mind, without his constant physical presence she'd been able to convince herself that this passionate encounter in the barn had been an aberration and she didn't want him anymore.

Right.

Her body was still aching from a simple kiss. What would happen if they got even half of their clothes off, like they had that fateful night? And, more importantly, did she want to find out? Could she give him her body without giving him her heart, and if she did would it help her to dismiss this aching need pulsing through her once and for all?

She didn't know the answer to those questions, but she did know it irritated her that Grant had a rule against kissing her. It brought out a primitive, competitive side to her nature, and a speculative look settled on her face. It was a look that Grant knew well and one he'd learned to be very wary of.

The smile that tipped her lips was one that had sent him into damage control mode on more than one occasion too, but he wasn't there to see it now. Poor guy.

Grant could not believe that he had kissed Zoe. Talk about sheer male stupidity. Memories he'd fought hard to suppress rose to the surface, reminding him of how it felt to hold his best friend's delectable body in his arms. A nuclear meltdown would have been cooler.

After filling a pot with water, he placed it on the gas range to heat, and then moved to the fridge to pull out ingredients for the cheese sauce. He wasn't a fool, so why had he behaved like one? Zoe was his best friend. She was younger than him and needed to be protected, not seduced. He'd almost done that once when she was nineteen. He wouldn't have stopped, and he'd had her half-naked before she'd come to her senses and done so herself.

Letting her go had been one of the hardest things he'd ever done. It was right up there with trying to live with himself after seeing the look of horror on her face when she'd run from the barn after he'd all but taken her innocence. At twenty-four, he'd had a lot more experience than her, and she hadn't known what to do with the feelings their kisses had inspired but he had. And he'd tried to do it.

It was not a memory that made him feel good about himself. He'd moved fast to get their friendship back on track, and to do it had gone so far as to flirt with a woman from New York a few days later at the town dance. It had worked. Until now. He wasn't about to repeat his mistake of the past and risk losing Zoe's friendship, but, *damn*—she had tasted good.

Grant swore soundly. Remembering how good she tasted was not going to help him keep their friendship on the right footing. He didn't need to remember how good she'd felt in his arms either. She belonged to another part of his life. The permanent part.

Any physical relationship between them would have to be transitory. He didn't *do* permanent. He didn't even try to anymore. Besides, she would be no happier as a rancher's wife than she had as a rancher's daughter. And he'd learned that leaving the ranch was not an option for him. He belonged here.

But she didn't. That left her place in Grant's life pretty well defined: friend.

And friendship was good, especially with Zoe. She didn't care about his money, his holdings, or his mother's connections on the east coast. Zoe only cared about Grant, and that kind of friendship wasn't something he'd ever willingly risk. Not even for soul-shattering sex.

He pulled out a block of Tillamook cheese and started grating it into a bowl.

"It's freezing out there."

He swung around to face her, still holding the cheese in one hand and the grater in the other. Snow stuck to her hair and jacket. Her hands were red from the cold. He wanted to grab her and take up where they had left off on the couch.

He yelled at her instead. "What the hell were you doing outside without gloves?"

She smiled teasingly. "Glad to see that you are in a better mood."

He ground his teeth together, in no mood for her joking. "I mean it, *niña*. If you had the common sense God gave a cat, you'd know this is not bare-headed and bare hands weather."

Her smile withered and died. "I was going to offer to help you with dinner—but without the common sense that God gave a cat I'm sure I'd do myself damage. And, since you persist in seeing me as a child, I can't imagine being of any real help to you either."

She turned around and left.

Had he offended her into going back to the Pattersons'? No, she would not do so without the cats. He continued grating cheese, listening for a cat's yowl or a door slamming, but heard neither.

She came back into the kitchen moments later, this time without her coat.

He stifled his relief and said nothing as she got herself a glass of water.

After a few minutes, Zoe's continued silence got to him. "Okay, I'm sorry." He hated apologizing. So why did he always end up saying he was sorry to Zoe?

"For what? Speaking the truth as you see it?"

"I do not think you are senseless and, while I use the term *niña* as an endearment, I do not think you are a child."

"Are you sure?"

"Positive."

She sighed. "All right, then. I forgive you."

Grant stifled a demand that she promise not to go outside without gloves again. He'd had enough arguing for one night.

She hopped out of her chair and started gathering the rest of the ingredients for dinner. The water came to a boil and he dumped the pasta in. "We'll have to wait until the snow lets up for me to drive you home."

Zoe's eyes widened. "You've got to be kidding. No way are you going to be able to drive me back tonight."

Was that why she had not stormed out? Because she thought she was stuck there? "My truck has four-wheel drive."

She stopped measuring ingredients into the saucepan on the stove. "Four-wheel drive won't do a thing for low visibility. It's a good thing we brought the cats with us."

Someone had sucked all the air out of the kitchen, and Grant regretted giving his foreman's wife time off for the holidays. At least if she were here to prepare dinner they would not be alone. "You can't spend the night."

"Don't be silly. Of course I can."

He was drowning. "You don't have any clothes with you."

She gave him a cheerful smile. "You can lend me something to sleep in."

Zoe sleeping in his clothes? The image of her wearing one of his T-shirts as a nightgown caused an uncomfortable sensation in his groin. A mental picture of her wearing *him* made his jeans feel like a pair of Speedos two sizes too small. "The snow will let up."

"I hope so." She tasted the cheese sauce by dipping her finger in a spoon of sauce and licking it off. Slowly.

He itched to copy the action, her finger in his mouth.

"I don't want to miss the last day of school tomorrow." She took another tortuous lick of the sauce, this time off the spoon.

He needed better ventilation in the kitchen. He could not get enough air.

She turned toward him and offered the spoon. "Want to try it? I think it's done."

"N-no." His voice hadn't cracked like that since middle school. He cleared his throat. "I trust you."

She shrugged. "You're missing something. It's really good." Then she proceeded to lick every last drop of melted cheese from the spoon.

The pasta boiled over and he jumped forward to save it. He grabbed the pot, inwardly cursing his earlier inability to look away from Zoe's tantalizing lips on the spoon. The noodles looked cooked. He tested one and burnt his tongue. "Ouch."

She handed him a glass of water. "Drink. It will help."

He grimaced, but didn't argue.

"You do this every time." She combined the noodles and sauce. "All you have to do is be a little more patient."

He did not interrupt her tirade. He was not about to explain that the image of her tongue on the spoon had all but robbed him of his senses. Hell. He had almost kissed her again. He tossed asparagus spears into a pan with butter and sautéed them.

They chatted about Zoe's class at school over dinner. The kids were involved in the Christmas program at the Sunshine Springs Community Center the following week. "You'll go with me, won't you?"

He wanted to refuse, figuring that any time spent around her right now would just lead to further tortured urges, but he'd hurt her feelings enough for one day. "Sure."

"Thanks." She took a bite of her pasta and then licked the fork. The temperature in the kitchen shot up. "You know how nervous I get when my kids are performing, and I'm not even on the program committee this year."

"Yeah." He smiled, trying to hide his reaction to her innocent actions. "One year you'd unraveled an entire knit scarf by the end of the program."

She laughed, her head going back to expose the creamy column of her neck. He wanted to reach out and touch the smooth skin. This was nuts. He stood up.

"Where are you going?"

He stared. Where *was* he going? "The bathroom." What could she say about that?

When he got to the bathroom he turned on the cold water and bathed his face. Looking in the mirror, he glared at his reflection. "Knock it off. Zoe's off-limits."

The man staring back at him looked unconvinced. He splashed cold water on his face a second time and dried it. He felt marginally better. Now, if Zoe would just refrain from licking her fork, all would be well.

He went back into the kitchen and sat down across from her again. She smiled. He smiled back and nearly choked. She'd picked up a piece of asparagus and was systematically licking all the butter off the vegetable.

"This is really good. You sautéed these perfectly."

Her guileless comment mocked his randy response. He mentally chastised himself for his unruly thoughts, but it didn't make his jeans any more comfortable. By the time Zoe had finished the fifth prong of asparagus he was sweating and hard as a rock. At this rate he wouldn't be able to get up from the table when dinner was done.

She looked at him, her eyes darkened with concern. "Are you okay? You're perspiring. I hope you aren't coming down with something."

"It's too warm in here. I must have the thermostat set high." He knew it was a lie. He hadn't changed his thermostat in days. But what else could he say? Watching his best friend eat her dinner had him so hot he was melting?

He breathed a sigh of unfettered relief when Zoe did not take a second helping of vegetables.

Later, he got the longest T-shirt he could find for her to wear to bed and then headed for his office. Why bother going to bed? He wasn't going to get a wink of sleep, knowing Zoe's too tempting body was down the hall nestled in his old bed. She was going back to the Pattersons' tomorrow, even if he had to drive her in a blizzard.

Zoe snuggled down under the quilts on Grant's childhood bed. Dinner had been very entertaining. Grant might have a rule against kissing her, but he sure wanted to. His gaze had strayed to her lips twelve and a half times. She'd counted. One time he had only looked at her neck before looking away, thus the half. She was certain that he'd wanted to look at her lips.

She'd made it interesting for him, trying her best

to eat her food as provocatively as she could. At one point, she'd almost felt sorry for him.

Almost.

He deserved it, making that crack about kissing anyone but her.

The following morning, Zoe woke up to chattering teeth and the smell of bacon cooking. It took her a moment to realize the person doing the chattering was herself.

Had they lost power last night in the storm? She could not believe that Grant or the foreman hadn't started the generator yet. She gritted her teeth and tossed back the covers. She yanked on the sweats Grant had lent her, which she had refused to wear to bed with the oversized T-shirt. She also donned a pair of thick socks, and went searching for a flannel shirt in Grant's closet.

After pulling on one of his shirts, that hung down to her knees, she went to the kitchen to find him. He stood at the stove, turning bacon. She wrinkled her nose at the smell of pork cooking and made a beeline for the coffee.

"It's freezing in here. Did something happen to the furnace?"

Grant slid a mug for her coffee across the counter toward her. "No."

"Then why is it so cold?" Zoe wrapped her hands around her mug, letting the heat seep into her chilled skin.

"Is it cold? Doesn't feel bad to me."

Grant wore a sage-green turtleneck under a black flannel shirt, faded jeans and cowboy boots. Of course he wasn't cold. The man was dressed to work outside. He did a lot more work on the ranch this time of year, so his hands had time to do the holiday thing with their families. But could he really be that dense? She walked into the hall and checked the thermostat.

"*Fifty-eight degrees?* Grant, are you nuts? No wonder I'm freezing."

She went stomping back in the kitchen and came to an abrupt halt at the look of satisfaction on Grant's face. Evidently he had a few little surprises of his own. "This is about your kissing rule, isn't it?" *And dinner last night.*

If grown men could look as innocent as newborn babes, then he should have had a pacifier.

"Isn't it?"

He placed two plates on the table. One piled high with bacon, eggs, hash browns and apple slices. The other identical except, without the crispy strips of bacon. "Sit down and eat before the food gets cold."

She sat. "It can't get any colder than I am."

"Stop whining. If you don't eat and get a move on, you'll be late for the last day of school."

Her gaze skittered to the window. Bright sunlight reflected almost blindingly off the snow. "You're right."

She took a big bite of her hash browns and nearly spat them out. Groping for her coffee, she took a huge gulp, scalding her tongue in the process. She stood up, knocking her chair back, and weaved like a drunk toward the sink.

Grant looked up from his own rapidly disappearing breakfast and asked, "Are you okay? Something wrong with the food?"

Her hand gripping her throat, she choked out the word "water."

He jumped up and grabbed a glass from the cupboard. He filled it with water from the tap and handed it to her. She gulped it down and took several deep breaths before turning to face Grant. "What did you use to season the potatoes? Dried jabañero peppers?"

"A little of this, a little of that. You know I cook by the seat of my pants."

She wasn't buying it. Giving him a look that had sent five-year-olds scampering for cover, Zoe advanced on Grant. "What did you put in my breakfast?"

He did not appear intimidated. "It's a little spicy, but you don't have time to savor your food this morning anyway."

"What does that have to do with...?" She let her voice trail off. Understanding came like air rushing from a balloon. "You didn't *want* me savoring my food?"

His cheeks took on a wind-burned look, although he had not yet been outside. "Like I said, you don't have time."

Right. It had nothing to do with his response to her

and the asparagus the night before. "Whatever you say. Are the eggs similarly spiced?"

He shrugged.

Great.

Grabbing the apple slices from her plate, she carried them to the sink and rinsed them off. She was not taking any chances. She left the kitchen, munching on her apple, without another word.

CHAPTER FIVE

GRANT watched Zoe leave the kitchen and his appetite went with her. He'd woken that morning thinking she needed payback for dinner the night before. He'd worked out around two a.m. that there'd been nothing innocent in the way she'd eaten. He'd known her practically her whole life, and she did not eat that sensually.

He didn't know what had gotten her dander up— maybe the comment about him not minding other women liking his kisses—but whatever it had been, she'd set out to prove she could make him uncomfortable. And she'd succeeded. In spades. This morning it had been his turn, but now he felt like a skunk.

He picked up the plates and scraped the food into the garbage. Feeling guilty, he toasted her a bagel and slathered it with her favorite blackberry honey. He finished cleaning up the kitchen, washing the dishes. He had just rinsed the last plate when Zoe came storming in.

White terry cloth barely concealed the curves he had spent the entire night trying to forget. Her hair still had soap bubbles in it. Water trickled down her neck to disappear in the cleavage at the top of her towel. Grant thought seriously about opening a few windows. He needed air—cold air—and he needed it now.

Nothing competed with the expression in her eyes, though. He could see murder, mayhem and his own demise in her usually sweet-tempered eyes.

She slammed her hand down on the counter next to him. "So it's not enough that you set your thermostat to arctic temperatures and freeze me to death." She moved so close he could see the sudsy foam drying around her temples. "And then you spice my food with enough hot stuff to permanently maim my tastebuds."

She reached around him, but the sight of Zoe nearly naked had Grant paralyzed. If she was going for the cast-iron skillet, he was powerless to stop her. Her hand came back around and she waved a recently washed plate in his face.

"*This* is the last straw."

He stared down at the plate and could not fathom what had her so furious she would come storming out of the shower with soap still in her hair.

"I cannot believe you would stoop to washing the dishes while I was in the shower." She punctuated each word with a shove to his midsection with the offending plate.

Sudden comprehension made him smile. Big mistake.

"You think this is *funny?*" She nearly shrieked the words.

"Calm down. I forgot about the water-shower thing." The hacienda had had many updates over the years, but the interior plumbing had last been seen to before he was born.

"You expect me to believe that? You have lived in this house your whole life." She slammed the plate down on the counter with enough force that it should have broken. "First hot, then cold, then hot again. My skin is still trying to decide if you were attempting to scald me or freeze me to death."

Tears sprang to her eyes and she swiped at them. "Damn it, Grant. I was not the one who started the kissing last night. You broke your own rule, and taking it out on me is not going to make that fact go away. You don't have to torture me to within an inch of my life before I promise not to attack your manly virtue. I promise already."

With that she pivoted and headed out of the kitchen. She stopped at the doorway. Turning her head, she pinned him to the counter with her stare. "If you run so much as a teaspoon of water while I finish my shower, I'm feeding your favorite boots to Maurice."

He really had forgotten about the water thing. She was never going to believe him, though. She was right. *He* had started the kissing last night. She had responded with enough passion to keep him sleepless with longing for the next several nights, but she had *not* started it. However, he had not been the one to go all sexy in his eating habits.

She had to take responsibility for her actions. Well, actually, she had. So why did it bother him so much that she had promised to keep her hands off him? That was exactly what he wanted. Damn it. He needed to get his libido under control before he risked losing the one person in his life he would never willingly let go.

This morning hadn't been a good example of how to maintain friendship in the face of desire hot enough to melt rock.

What he needed was a diversion. Something or someone to keep his mind off of Zoe's delectable lips and even more delectable body. An image of Linda popped into his mind and he grimaced. Okay, so it hadn't worked with her, but he was a problem solver by nature. One small setback did not justify junking an entire strategy.

His mind skimmed through the possibilities and settled on Carlene Daniels, the bartender at the Dry Gulch. He played poker with the owner and a couple of local high rollers every few weeks, and she always served their table.

She had a sense of humor, and dressed like a walking commercial for prophylactics, but she didn't date much. She seemed to have a reputation, all the same, which was exactly what he wanted. A woman who knew the score and would help him get his desire for Zoe under control.

If he hadn't given his ranch hands so much time off he would have left on a business trip, but that wasn't an option right now. Which left Carlene.

Never one to wait when he'd decided to act, he grabbed the phone book to look up the woman's number. Zoe couldn't complain about him making a phone call while she showered.

Afternoon sun poured through the schoolroom window as Zoe picked up a bottle of white glue. She wiped the sticky mess around it with a damp paper towel. Her students had made Christmas decorations, and she had a mess of glitter, glue and little bits of colored paper to clean up. She didn't mind. She needed time to think.

Her anger toward Grant had finally cooled about the time her first class of kindergartners had gone out to meet the midmorning school bus. She could not maintain fury when surrounded by five-year-olds excited about Christmas.

Breakfast had been a disaster. He had done everything possible to make her feel as welcome as a coyote at a roundup. Running the water while she'd been in the shower had been truly inspired. It was something almost as good as what *she* might have cooked up.

She bit her lip and swept some glitter off the table into the trashcan she carried. For as long as she could remember Grant had been the only person in her life to accept her unconditionally. When she'd become a vegetarian and her dad had gone through the roof, Grant had bought her *The Tofu Lover's Cookbook*. When her date had gotten sick the day of Senior Prom, Grant had taken her.

He had always been her knight in shining armor.

Remembering the hash browns that had about burned a hole in her tongue, she thought, *Some knight!* He'd gone from her hero to her sexual nemesis in the space of hours. Why was he so set on keeping their relationship platonic? He'd been every bit as involved in that kiss last night as she had.

And he wasn't exactly celibate. She didn't think he was a complete playboy. No one could afford to be in today's age. But he was experienced. Light-years ahead of her. If only he knew. She'd tried dating in college, and even gone so far as to go to bed with one of her dates. She'd been feeling like an anachronism, being a virgin at twenty, but it hadn't gone anywhere. She'd made a complete fool of herself, telling her boyfriend she just wasn't ready, getting dressed and going back to her dorm room.

He'd broken up with her a week later and she hadn't blamed him. She just could not imagine sharing her body so intimately with anyone but Grant, and if she didn't do something about it soon she was going to be the oldest living virgin in the United States. The more she thought about it, the more she was convinced that he would not have made such an all-fired effort to get rid of her this morning if last night hadn't affected him as strongly as it had her.

Scrubbing at a stubborn stain of dried glue, Zoe glared at the offending white blob. People had been saying she and Grant should get together for years. Saying they were a natural couple. Even their parents got on that particular bandwagon once in a while. Of course her dad disagreed. Said Zoe had no business marrying a rancher with her affinity for animals.

It appeared that Grant took her dad's view. He acted like dating her would be tantamount to breaking the law. His law. Zoe wadded up the used paper towel and tossed it in the garbage. Well, she didn't want to date him either. She just wanted to have sex with him. Maybe then she could start looking at other men as something besides biological creatures that took up space on her planet.

She finished tidying up the classroom and headed to her car. She needed to pick the cats up from Grant's. Maybe she should offer to cook him supper tonight. No way was she letting him cook, but they had to eat.

She grinned, planning a meal that would make the asparagus spears look chaste.

Walking into Grant's kitchen half an hour later, the first thing Zoe noticed was a bouquet of roses on the counter. Her smile intensified and her heart started slamming against her ribs. Taking a deep breath, she inhaled the heady scent of the crimson blooms. He had not apologized this morning, but flowers were even better.

She plucked the card from the arrangement. It said "Carlene" on the tiny white envelope.

Carlene? Who in the world was she, and *why was Grant buying her flowers?* Hearing footsteps, Zoe hurriedly replaced the envelope among the scarlet roses. The jerk. He treated *her* like a pariah and bought flowers for some other woman.

She whirled around to confront Grant when he came in. She stopped dead, staring at the apparition before her. "Grant?"

"What?"

It *was* Grant. The voice was the same. The incredible blue eyes. The nose. The masculine jaw shaved smooth. The mouth. That darned sensual mouth. That was Grant's body encased in tight black jeans and a T-shirt. Those were Grant's chest muscles rippling under the knit fabric stretched taut across his rib cage.

She'd seen him dressed for the office, and wearing similar suits or smart Armani sweaters for dates with his usual glamorous women. She'd seen him dressed to work the ranch. But never before had she seen him dressed so provocatively sexy. He might be worth millions and own the ranch he worked, but right now he looked like a cowboy going out on a date. A very sexy, dangerous cowboy.

She swallowed.

He leaned against the wall, his arms crossed over his chest, the muscles rippling in his forearms. His dark brows rose. "What's the matter, Zoe? You look like you've been eating my hash browns again."

"Who's Carlene?" she forced out between stiff lips.

"My date."

"Your *date*?" Was that husky voice hers?

"Yeah." He even sounded like one of his cowboys. She wondered if his Spanish great-grandfather had been equally chameleon-like. The man had certainly made the Double C a solid going concern, through hard work and business acumen a lot like Grant's.

"As in for tonight?"

Grant gave her a look that said he thought she'd been sniffing glue instead of wiping it up. "Yeah."

There went her plans for another sexy dinner. Looking around the kitchen, she noticed other things besides the roses. Grant had set out silverware and plates on the counter to be carried into the dining room. "You're having your date *here*?"

"She wants to cook me dinner."

Carlene probably planned on serving him asparagus and a whole lot more. The hussy. "Are you sure that's a good idea?"

"Why not?" The sound of a bird screeching reached her ears. Grant frowned. "Is there any way to keep that parrot quiet tonight? He's going to ruin the mood."

Too bad. She did her best to look apologetic while silently praising her parrot for his screeching tenor. "I'm sorry. He's just like that. Nothing I can do."

"I'll think of something."

She just bet he would. "I guess I'll pick up the cats and get out of your way."

"Great."

It was a good thing Zoe didn't have a glass of water handy. Grant would be the only contestant in a wet T-shirt contest otherwise. "Right. Well. I'll just get the cats."

She found Alexander and Princess and put them

in the cat carrier. Walking into the bedroom she had slept in the first night, she stopped to talk to Bud, the hamster. "Things are looking bleak, Bud. I've finally decided to stop pussyfooting around my feelings for Grant and he's got a date with another woman."

He ran on his little exercise wheel, ignoring her. Males.

Zoe wondered if Carlene liked rodents. She racked her brain, trying to remember if she had ever met the woman. An image of deep cleavage and incredibly tight, short skirts rose in Zoe's mind. The weekend bartender at the Dry Gulch. The woman went through men faster than Grant went through relationships—or at least that was what people said.

Zoe wanted to scream. She smiled instead, and loosened the door on top of Bud's cage.

Whistling a Christmas carol, Zoe picked up the cat carrier and left. She didn't bother saying goodbye to Grant. She could do without another dose of his sexy, tight T-shirt.

Grant put the finishing touches on the table. The roses looked good. Romantic. So did the rest of the dining room, thanks to his mother's penchant for French provincial décor. She'd been gone for more than two decades, but because Lottie had only been interested in changing a few rooms of the ranch house, her influence remained.

The front doorbell rang and he rushed to answer

it. When he opened the door, cold air and perfume assailed him. It wasn't an unpleasant scent, but it wasn't Zoe's either.

Which was the point, he reminded himself.

"Hi, Grant," Carlene said softly, smiling. Her dress wasn't nearly as revealing as the gear she wore to work in, but it accentuated her voluptuous curves all the same. "There's one more bag in the car if you'd like to get it."

"I'll get it. You go on in."

He moved back, but she still managed to brush his arm with her chest. He was surprised when she jumped and apologized. When he walked into the kitchen with the bags a minute later, he found her rummaging through the cupboards.

She smiled, her expression a cross between nervous and welcoming. "I was looking for a pot to boil the pasta."

"Over here." He pulled out the pot he had used to make dinner for Zoe the night before.

"Thanks."

"Sure."

She turned to the sink and started filling the pot with water. "Want to make the salad?"

"Okay."

She tossed him a bag of salad.

Zoe never bought premade salad. She said it was a drain on the environment's resources. And that was the last comparison he was going to make between his date and his best friend tonight. After rinsing the lettuce and tossing it in a bowl along with the pre-mixed dressing, Grant had to admit it sure was easier than cutting everything up.

"I'll have to make Zoe try this sometime. It's a snap." He grimaced, wishing he hadn't brought her up.

Carlene gave him an inquiring look. "Is she the schoolteacher? The one that dated Tyler?"

Grant frowned. "Yeah."

Carlene laughed. "I would never have picked those two for a couple. She treated Tyler nice, though. He was always going on about what a lady she is."

"That's Zoe."

"She even introduced him to his new girlfriend. Another teacher. I think Tyler's really in love."

The last thing Grant wanted to do was talk about Zoe, love and Tyler, the man in leather. "Want me to do anything else?"

"Sure, sugar," she said flirtatiously, her Texas accent drawing the words out. "Only it will have to wait until after dinner."

Maybe this whole date thing was not such a good idea after all. He wanted sex, but the knowledge that it wasn't going to be with Carlene hit him between the eyes with the force of a hammer. She was a lovely woman, but right now the only female who attracted him was Zoe.

So much for his great diversionary tactic.

"You can make dessert." She said it nervously, and he wondered why.

"Sure."

"I brought whipped cream, chocolate, and maraschino cherries."

"I don't have any ice cream."

Carlene winked at him, but her face looked like she'd just added a whole layer of blusher. "I'm sure we'll come up with something."

She moved forward almost awkwardly, her bee-stung lips parted for a kiss. Grant started backing away and she kept coming. The sound of an earsplitting screech came from down the hall.

Carlene jumped and let out a pretty good screech of her own. "What was that?"

"Zoe's bird."

"What is her bird doing here?"

Grant explained about Zoe getting evicted. He left out the part about Bud, not proud of the fact that he had been instrumental in getting his friend evicted from her apartment.

"That's a lot of pets for a single woman to have. No wonder she's having a hard time finding a new place. I wouldn't try to take care of so many, but I bet she never gets lonely," Carlene said wistfully.

Grant frowned, the comment about loneliness making him wonder for the first time if Zoe had so many pets for that very reason. "She just has a soft spot for animals."

"And then some."

"I better go check on the bird."

"All right."

As he walked down the hall toward the bedroom

with the parrot, he wondered what in the hell he was supposed to do about Carlene's whipped cream and cherries. She acted like a woman ready for a night of no-strings sex, but it didn't ring true. Maybe Carlene was the lonely one. Whatever her motives, he wasn't making dessert with her, tonight or any other night.

And, damn it, he should have realized that before he ever asked her out. He kept telling himself he wasn't a stupid man, but he certainly gave a good imitation of one sometimes.

The sound of screaming from the kitchen interrupted his thoughts. Grant rushed back in the room without checking on the bird.

Carlene stood on a kitchen chair, yelling loud enough to be heard in the next county. When she saw Grant she launched herself at him, literally flying through the air. *"Mouse. It was a mouse."* She grabbed his shirtfront, shaking him. "He ran over my foot. He was brown and white and…" She trailed off with shuddering breaths.

A brown and white mouse? *Bud.* Grant pushed Carlene into a chair. "I'll get you a glass of water."

"Water?" She jumped up and started screaming again. *"There."* She pointed at the corner. *"He's over there."*

Grant made a dash for Bud, but the hamster scurried under the cabinets. Grant turned around. Carlene was no longer screaming, but she was back on top of the chair.

"It's okay. It's just Zoe's pet hamster."

She made an obvious bid for composure. "Your friend keeps rodents for pets?"

"Well, actually it was my hamster, and she agreed to keep him for me." Grant got down on his knees and peered under the cabinet. "Do you mind helping me find him? He could get hurt, being out of his cage like this."

The look of horror that cast her features in stark relief could not be feigned. "I'd like to, I really would. I don't want him hurt, even if he is a…" She swallowed. "A rodent. But I can't. I'm sorry."

She sounded it too. She really was a nice woman, even if a little forward.

"It's all right. I'll find him on my own."

Grant heard her step down off the chair. "I think I'd better go."

Her turned toward Carlene, half of his attention still on the cupboard Bud had disappeared behind.

She was buttoning her coat. He jumped up. "Hey. I'll find the hamster. Relax."

She shook her head. "No, really… I don't think I was up to tonight anyway." Then she was out the door before he could answer.

What had she meant by that? *Damn.* Where was Bud?

CHAPTER SIX

"You lost Bud?"

How could he lose the hamster? Guilt settled in Zoe's stomach and made her defensive. "I cannot believe you let your date scream the place down and lost the hamster." She jumped out of bed, the phone still cradled to her ear. "I'm coming over."

It was not as if her idea to snuggle in bed watching old movies to keep her mind off Grant's date was working anyway. Images of Grant and Carlene had superimposed themselves over the people on the screen.

She arrived at the Double C to find all the lights in the house blazing. She knocked at the kitchen door, not wanting to give Bud a chance to escape when she opened it. Grant swung the door open almost immediately. His hair was disheveled. Had he been running his fingers through it in agitation, or had Carlene done it before leaving in a huff over the hamster?

Dislodging the torturous thought with effort, Zoe asked, "Have you found him yet?"

They *had* to find the little guy. Not only for Bud's sake, but also because she'd already promised one of her students he could have the hamster.

Grant ran his fingers through his hair and shook his head. "No. I found a space between one of the cabinets and the wall."

Zoe frowned. "You think he's in the wall?"

Grant nodded. "Yeah."

"I can't believe it." She groaned. "How are we going to get him out?"

Rubbing the back of his neck, Grant sighed. "I think we need to give it some time and some quiet. If I were a hamster, Carlene's screams would have made me go into hiding too."

Zoe fought to hide a smile. "I guess she doesn't like rodents, huh?"

"No. I don't think she likes me much anymore either."

Zoe could not lie and say she was sorry. She looked around the kitchen and took in the half-prepared dinner. "You didn't eat yet?"

He shook his head. "No." His stomach rumbled.

The poor guy was starving. Looking at the pasta draining in the strainer, and the half-prepared white sauce, Zoe figured she could finish dinner. She started pulling ingredients from the bags. "Run some hot water over the pasta to reheat it."

Grant nodded. He picked up a bowl of salad, the lettuce obviously wilted from sitting coated in dressing. "I guess this is a goner."

"Yeah." She peered into the bowl. "We'll have to have cooked vegetables."

"Okay. No asparagus, though. I'm, uh, not in the mood."

She turned her face to hide the grin his words provoked. "I saw a bag of California Blend in the freezer last night. Pull it out. We'll nuke it with a little butter and Parmesan."

She finished the white sauce, adding the canned salmon Carlene had left behind, while Grant reheated the pasta and cooked the vegetables. She made a mental note to drop off replacement ingredients with Carlene sometime the following week. Zoe hoped that would allay some of her current feelings of guilt. After all, she'd been responsible for ruining the date... and losing the hamster. She sighed and grabbed the last bag on the counter to empty its contents.

Suddenly Grant's hand shot in front of her and snatched the sack. "We don't need this stuff. It was for dessert."

Zoe made a grab for the brown paper. "Great. I deserve something sweet after cooking your dinner."

Grant did not release his hold on the bag. "Not this."

"Why not? Did Carlene buy some expensive dessert and you'll feel guilty eating it without her?"

He coughed. "Uh. No."

"Look, whatever it is, I'll replace it tomorrow. I'm in the mood for sugar." She yanked on the bag.

"No, Zoe." He yanked it back.

The paper tore. A spray can of whipped cream, a

squeeze bottle of chocolate sauce and a small jar of maraschino cherries tumbled onto the counter between them. "Mmm. Looks good. What kind of ice cream did she bring to go with this?"

Grant did not answer. Zoe looked at him. He would not meet her eyes. Puzzled, she looked from him to the toppings and then back at him again. "Come on, Grant. What kind did she bring? Sinful Pleasures or something?"

"Look, let's just get dinner on the table. I'm starving."

Fine. She'd see for herself. Moving across the kitchen, she still could not fathom what had him so embarrassed. She opened the freezer door and rooted around inside. She closed it, and then turned to face Grant. "There isn't any ice cream."

Grant frowned. "I know."

"Did you forget to buy it?"

"No."

"What good are ice cream toppings without ice cream?"

Maybe that was why Grant had acted so strangely about her opening the bag. She looked back over to the counter at the toppings. Sudden understanding stabbed at her with the pain of a branding iron. "You. Planned. To. Have. Carlene. For. Dessert."

How could he do this? She knew Grant wasn't chaste, but *this*? To her knowledge he wasn't into one-night stands, and this was his first date with Carlene. He hadn't even slept with his last girlfriend.

He'd be furious to find out that she knew, but women talked...just like men.

Zoe felt her throat clog with tears. She had to get out of there before she made an idiot of herself. She was definitely overreacting, but she couldn't seem to help it. She whipped around toward the door. "Leave a bowl of food out for Bud. He'll get hungry and come out."

She rushed into the mudroom and grabbed her coat. Jerking it on, she cursed her impulse to feed Grant. If she hadn't finished making dinner, she never would have known about his plans with Carlene and her heart would not be breaking in a million bitty pieces on the linoleum of the mudroom floor.

Just why her heart was involved at all was not something she wanted to dissect right now.

She did not make it three steps to the door. Grant spun her around, keeping a firm hold on her upper arms. "I did not plan anything. You know me better than that."

"I thought I did."

"You do, damn it."

She glared at him, her eyes blurred with tears she refused to shed. "Then what were you going to do with ice cream toppings? Eat them on top of crackers?"

"I was not going to do anything with them."

"You expect me to believe that?"

"It doesn't matter. Being my best friend does not give you the right to dictate how I handle my relationships."

The vise constricting her heart tightened until Zoe

thought she could not breathe. "It's already a relationship? I thought this was your first date."

He sighed. "That's not the point."

Zoe shoved away from him, breaking his hold on her arms. "You're right. The point is that I need to leave. Who knows? Maybe you can still salvage your evening with Carlene. At her place."

She spun around. Checking to make sure Bud was not waiting to make a break for outside, she yanked open the door and rushed out. She could not get away from Grant fast enough. He called her name, but she ignored it. She had already made an utter fool of herself. She wasn't going back for more.

She barely remembered her drive back to the Pattersons'. Her mind was filled with Grant's words. She fought against the truth, but finally had to accept it. Being his best friend did *not* give her the right to judge his actions or his relationships.

It didn't give her the right to try to seduce him either. Even if he *was* the only man she could seriously contemplate making love to.

She let herself into the house and then let the cats out of the bathroom. They followed her to the bedroom, obviously too sleepy to punish her for leaving them in the bathroom with their usual aloof behavior. She undressed. Climbing under the covers, she called the cats to her. Mercifully, they both came willingly and cuddled against her. She needed their warmth. She felt so cold inside. So lost.

Animals had always been safe. Safer than people.

For as long as Zoe could remember she had trusted her animal friends to give her the unconditional acceptance she craved and did not receive from the people around her. Everyone but Grant. It hurt, but she had to face facts. If she insisted on crossing the line into intimacy, she could very well lose the one person she could not bear to do without.

"I made a big mistake." She stroked Alexander's silky fur. He began to purr, the soft sound vibrating through Zoe's fingertips. "I went ballistic on Grant over his plans with his date tonight. And it wasn't any of my business."

So much for her idea to satisfy her lust for Grant and keep her heart out of it. Her reaction tonight proved her heart was involved on some level, though she refused to even contemplate the prospect that she might still be in love with Grant.

No. She'd been jealous, but it was a sexual jealousy. That was all. Not love. Never again. No way.

She shifted so she could pet both Princess and Alexander as she thought about her time over at Grant's.

He had a rule against kissing her.

He'd wanted to have Carlene for dessert.

How could Zoe compete with a woman who spray-painted herself into her clothes? Even if she could compete physically, did she want to? She'd thought she did, but if her behavior tonight was an indication of how she might respond when the physical relationship ended, she knew she couldn't risk it.

Not when it meant risking her friendship with Grant.

She'd really messed up, and she was scared to death she was going to lose her best friend. Tears that she hated to shed in front of others trickled down Zoe's face.

Grant loved her like a sister, and if she was smart he always would. If she tried to force him into a relationship he did not want, she would lose him. The cold that had begun to dissipate rushed back with arctic force. She would not lose the only person in her life who accepted her for who she was.

First thing tomorrow, she'd call Grant and apologize. Then she'd start looking more seriously for a place to live. He was the very best friend she had in the world, and the time had come for her to start acting like it.

Grant scraped the last of the uneaten dinner in the garbage. Why had he let Zoe leave believing he'd wanted to play dessert games with Carlene? The look of disappointment on her face had slammed into him like a drunk on Saturday night at the Dry Gulch.

One thing he had always taken for granted was Zoe's admiration. He would never forget the heady sensation of her adoration that first time he had met her and rescued her pet cow from being sold for beef. It had not been long before he had gotten addicted to that adoring gaze, and darned if he would not do just about anything to see that look in Zoe's eyes.

What demon had prompted him to tell Zoe his personal life was none of her business? All he'd had to tell her was that the whole dessert thing had been

Carlene's little surprise and he had not been interested. Instead, he had as much as told Zoe that he'd planned to follow through with it. Hell, he had even implied a relationship, when that was the last thing he wanted with Carlene—or any other woman for that matter.

He finished wiping the countertops and stove. The kitchen was back in order. If only the same were true for his life. He did not know what was going on with him and Zoe, but it was going to stop. He hated fighting with her.

He looked at the clock above the stove. It was only nine. Making a decision, he grabbed his jacket and car keys. He stopped briefly in the family room and selected a video. The entire evening did not have to be a waste.

A trip to the all-night donut shop in town and forty minutes later, he stood on the Pattersons' front porch steps. He rang the doorbell. The wind whipped against his hair and batted against his wool-lined denim jacket. She did not answer. Her truck was in the drive. He rang the bell again. No lights were visible from the front of the house. Maybe she was asleep.

He was about to turn around and leave, disappointment an almost palpable taste in his mouth, when the door opened. Zoe stared at him through the screen, making no attempt to unlatch the door.

He smiled at her. Lifting the orange and white bag in his hand, he said, "I'm here for a truce."

She pushed open the screen door and stepped

back. He looked down at her and felt like swearing. Her eyes were rimmed in red, and telltale moisture still clung to her cheeks.

She had been crying and it was his fault. He dropped the pastry bag on the hall table. "Oh, Zoe." He gripped her arms and pulled her against his chest, sliding his hands to her back. She remained stiff against him, but he was grateful that she did not attempt to pull away. "I'm sorry, angel. I'm so sorry."

Sobs erupted against his chest. "It's my fault. What you do with your women is none of my business."

Hearing that statement did not make him feel better. Pulling away from Zoe, he forced her to meet his eyes. "I was not going to have dessert with Carlene."

If anything, her tears fell faster. "It doesn't matter. It's none of my business. I'm just your friend. You don't owe me any explanations." The words came stuttering out between hiccupping sobs.

Just a friend? When had Zoe been relegated to *just a friend* in his life? She was the one person he trusted above all others. Not able to stand the sight of her tears, he pulled her back against him. "*Querida*, please stop crying."

"I'm trying."

She took several deep breaths. He rubbed her back, attempting to comfort her. "You're the best friend I've ever had. I don't trust anyone like I trust you."

"That makes it worse," she wailed. She broke away from him and backed up until she met the wall. Narrow, the hallway only afforded a few feet of distance between them. "You trusted me and I ruined your date."

Feeling like he did not know the script, he demanded, "What are you talking about?"

"I left Bud's cage door open."

What? "Why?"

"Because I was jealous of Carlene."

"I can't believe this."

She looked miserable. "I know. It was a despicable thing to do, and now Bud's lost. He could be anywhere, freezing his little paws off."

More likely in Grant's walls somewhere, eating his wiring. "We'll find Bud. That's not what I was talking about. I can't believe you were jealous of Carlene. She's just a date. You are my best friend."

Zoe's eyes locked on to his. "Am I?"

Furious that she could doubt their long-standing bond, he stalked over to her. He stopped when his boots met her bare toes. Moving his face inches from hers, he spoke, shooting his words out like bullets. "You might drive me right up a wall with your melodrama. You might piss me off royally when you refuse to let me drive you to town. None of that changes the fact that you are one of the most important people in my life."

"Thank you." She gave a half-smile and wiped at the tears on her cheeks with her hands. "I think."

"For the record, I am not interested in playing dessert games with Carlene."

Zoe's smile blossomed to a grin. She looked down at the bag on the table. "Donuts?"

He returned her smile. "Yeah. Your favorite—toasted coconut." He pulled a video case from his coat pocket and waved it in the air. "Movie."

"The Quiet Man?"

He nodded. "Uh-huh."

"You really aren't mad at me about Bud?"

He shook his head. "Uh-uh."

"Okay." Zoe turned around and headed toward the back of the house.

Grant grabbed the donuts and followed her. When she passed the entrance to the living room, he stopped. "Where are you going?"

"To the bedroom. I moved the VCR in there earlier."

"I'll move it back to the living room for you."

"Why bother?" She turned around to face him, her tearstained cheeks causing guilt to tug at him. "It's already set up. Why not just watch it in there?"

Because he did not want to torture himself. Not about to admit that to her, he shrugged. "Be more comfortable in the living room."

Shutters came down in her eyes. She nodded. "You're probably right. You set up the VCR while I put on some sweats."

He did not like the emotionless expression on her face, or the flat tenor to her voice. She was slipping away from him again, and that scared the hell out of him. "Forget it. We'll watch it in your room."

When she remained silent, he added, "If you fall asleep, I won't have so far to carry you."

She looked at him, serious as a heartbeat. "I won't fall asleep."

"I was just teasing."

Her smile looked forced. Damn, he had to get things back to normal with them. Taking long strides, he passed her by. Grabbing her wrist, he towed her behind him. "Come on, *niña*. You've got a date with the Duke."

He did not stop until he got to her bedroom. Doing his best to ignore the effect the sight of her rumpled sheets had on his libido, he tossed the donut bag on the bed. "You break out the donuts. I'll set up the video."

She laughed a Zoe laugh. A cascading breath of amusement, sweet with joy. His heart tripped at the sound and he thought the torture of watching a movie next to her tempting body would be worth that one giggle.

She dove onto the bed and whisked the covers over her bare thighs. He nearly let out a sigh of relief when the supple limbs disappeared beneath the quilt. She opened the bag and pulled out two napkins, placing the pastries on them. He set up the video and then joined her on the bed, grateful for the covers between him and Zoe's enticing legs.

She snuggled next to him and munched on her donut. They watched the opening credits roll in silence. As the movie started he heard her say quietly, "Thank you."

He turned his head, but could only see the top of her hair. "For what?"

"Being my friend. I promise not to do anything else to jeopardize our friendship."

Something about the way she said it tugged at him. "You could feed my new ropers to Maurice and it would not jeopardize it. It might jeopardize your life, but not our friendship."

"My demise would seriously hamper our relationship."

So would throwing her on her back and making love to her enticing body. He forced down his raging desire and remembered that fact as she shifted to a more comfortable position next to him. It was going to be a very long movie.

Two hours of torture later, Grant was still castigating himself for choosing a video they both knew so well. It had done nothing to distract him from Zoe's proximity. Her laughter at the final scene choked off mid-giggle as she yawned hugely, covering her mouth with her hand.

She turned to face him. "You'd better head home. I need to get some sleep if I'm going to look for a place to live tomorrow."

"Got any leads?"

"No. Not many people want to rent to a zookeeper."

"You are not a zookeeper."

She yawned again. "Thanks."

He stood up and then walked over to the VCR. Popping out the video, he asked, "Why don't you just buy a house?"

Zoe looked at him, and unfathomable sadness settled in her eyes. He wished he understood it. What was making her so unhappy? "I told you, a teacher's salary does not stretch to a heavy mortgage."

"You know I'd help you."

She just looked at him.

"Okay, what about your parents? They'd help out with the down payment and you know it."

"The same parents who aren't coming home to spend Christmas with me?"

He felt the pain he saw in her eyes. "Yes."

"No."

"Why not?"

"Look, even if I wanted to buy a house, this is the worst time of year to find one. Even if I did find one, it would not close before the Pattersons return. I need a place to live *now*."

He knew she was right. "You could stay at my place until your house closed."

Zoe's eyes narrowed. "We've been through this. I seem to remember you saying something about unprecedented damage to my reputation."

He grew uncomfortable under her pointed gaze. "I'm sure we could think of something."

"Something like an apartment complex that allows animals?"

He picked up the now empty pastry bag and wadded it up. He tossed it in the garbage and then turned to face her again. "I'll let you get your beauty rest, then."

She nodded, clearly ready to do just that.

He stopped at the door. "I could take you. I need to go into town tomorrow and apologize to Carlene anyway."

She pondered the question a lot longer than he'd expected. He wanted to demand what was taking her so long to decide if she wanted his company, but something held him back.

"I guess that would be okay. If you are sure you want to."

Stung by her lackluster attitude toward spending time with him, his response came out more sharply than he'd intended. "Don't sound so happy to have my company."

She smiled sleepily at him. "Go home. You're tired and cranky."

She was probably right. What else would explain his current bad mood? "I'm going. What time do you want me to pick you up?"

She looked at the clock on the VCR and then back at him. "Not too early."

"Fine. You going to come lock the door behind me?"

She groaned, but got out of bed. He wished he had not said anything. Her oversized sleepshirt draped off nipples that had hardened when she'd slipped out from the warm cocoon of blankets. He could not drag his eyes away from the sight of the hard nubs pressing against the stretchy fabric.

His hand itched to reach out and brush first one and then the other. Then he would cup the fullness around them and caress it until she moaned like she had on his couch and rubbed her delectable body against his. He would then slide his hands down to caress the smooth skin below the hemline of her shirt, letting his fingertips glide under to touch the fleshy curve of her behind. His breathing grew ragged and he felt his penis pressing against the buttons of his fly.

"Grant?"

He shifted his unfocused gaze to her face and tried to make out her expression through the passionate haze blurring his vision. "Huh?"

"Are you okay?"

The genuine concern in her voice snapped him into focus. What the hell was he thinking? He took a deep breath and let it out slowly. "Yeah. Just tired, I guess."

She cocked her head to one side and looked at him. "Are you sure?"

He kept his eyes firmly on her face. "Yeah."

He turned and headed for the front door. She followed him, her bare feet slapping against the ceramic tile of the hall.

They said goodnight at the door, and it took more self-discipline than getting out of bed at the crack of dawn to muck stalls not to kiss her soft lips before he turned to leave.

CHAPTER SEVEN

ZOE stumbled into the kitchen, only half awake. Staying up watching *The Quiet Man* with Grant might not have been the smartest thing to do last night.

She hated apartment-hunting. Grant was right. She needed to buy a house. It was ridiculous to hold onto the belief that buying a house was something you did after you were married and had started talking about having a family.

Even if she found homes for all her pets, like she had for Bud, she knew it wouldn't take long to get herself back into the same predicament. She had no desire to live alone, and didn't like being limited on the number and type of animals she kept.

She slumped in the kitchen chair. She had been saving for a trip to Europe since her first paycheck. Her dad would say that was impractical. Maybe it *was* time to earmark that money for something more lasting and practical.

Something like a place to live.

Even with her savings, she didn't have enough for

a decent down payment. But Grant had been right about something else too. Her parents *would* help her. If she asked. That was a bridge she'd have to cross later. She still needed to find a rental. It would take a miracle to find a house to buy, close on it and move in before the Pattersons returned.

She stood up, fumbled for the coffeepot and then filled it in the sink. Opening the canister of coffee she had brought with her, her nose perked at the vanilla nut aroma. Princess and Alexander rubbed against her legs.

She couldn't imagine life without her cats. "Morning, guys. Want some coffee? No? You don't know what you're missing." Zoe turned on the coffeepot. The sound of water filling the filter chamber lifted her spirits.

She opened a can of cat food and split it between Princess and Alexander's dishes. "How about breakfast?"

The cats walked regally to their dishes and sniffed delicately at the food before condescending to eat. Zoe smiled. "One of these days I'm going to give you some off-brand cat food and watch in glee when you eat it without being able to tell the difference."

Her pets ignored the empty threat.

She poured herself a cup of coffee, feeling decadent when she added flavored creamer. She took a sip, and savored the sweet concoction as its warmth slid over her tongue. Sighing with pleasure, she locked both hands around the steaming mug. Taking a few more sips, she gradually woke up.

Time to get a move on. She pulled the newspaper she had brought from town out of her book bag. Spreading it over the table, she searched for the rental ads. After circling as many likely possibilities as she could find, she started calling.

Twenty minutes later, she groaned in frustration as she crossed off the fifth ad in a row. No pets. *Someone* in this community must allow pets.

She needed a break. Time to shower and dress.

The hot spray felt heavenly against her body. She stood for several minutes, relaxing under the jets of water. She lathered her hair, enjoying the floral scent of her shampoo.

The sound of pounding penetrated her consciousness.

Someone was at the door. *Grant.*

Muttering an expletive that would have gotten her mouth washed out with soap as a child, she stepped out of the shower. She grabbed a bath towel and wrapped herself in it. Rushing to the door, she cursed Grant's lousy timing.

The doorbell rang, and Zoe frowned. "Hold on. I'll be there in a minute."

Why was he being so impatient? It had to be pretty obvious she had not gone anywhere. Her truck was still outside. Flinging open the door, she said, "Jeesh. You didn't need to pound the door down. I was in the sho…"

Her words trailed off when she realized that it was not Grant standing on the doorstep, but Tyler.

"Zoe, am I glad you are here. I need your help."

Apparently oblivious to her state of undress, he shouldered past her into the kitchen. "Jenny isn't speaking to me. You've got to fix it." He sat down heavily in one of the kitchen chairs and dropped his head into his hands. "I don't know what I'll do if she breaks up with me."

Zoe edged toward the hallway, tightening the towel around her. "I'll get dressed and then we'll talk."

His head came up, his gray eyes looking right through her. "You've got to help me, Zoe. Jenny's one of your friends and you introduced us."

And that made her responsible for the health of their relationship? Evidently to Tyler it did. She sighed. Seeing Tyler's tough-guy-in-leather persona dropped completely to reveal his vulnerability tugged at her heartstrings.

She edged one more step toward the hall. "I'll help you. Don't worry. Just let me get dressed."

Tyler nodded. "Is that coffee I smell? I could really use a cup. I didn't sleep at all last night."

"Sure, the mugs are in the cupboard to the left of the sink. Help yourself."

"Thanks." He stood up and took a step, then stopped in the middle of the kitchen. His big shoulders started to shake. "I really love her."

Zoe's heart melted. She stepped forward and tugged Tyler back into his chair. Patting his shoulder, she said, "I know. It's going to be all right. She cares about you too."

Tyler used his fists to wipe the tears from his scruffy cheeks. "You think so?"

Remembering Jenny's rapturous listing of Tyler's attributes in the teacher's lounge that week, Zoe smiled. "I know so."

"Thanks." He put his beefy arm around her and gave Zoe a rough hug. "You're a good friend to have, Zoe."

Using one hand to keep her towel firmly in place, Zoe put the other one around Tyler and hugged him back.

"What the hell is going on?"

Zoe jumped back from Tyler at the sound of Grant's angry voice. Unfortunately, Tyler still had a grip on her, and her towel stayed with him. She screeched.

Grant bellowed.

Tyler looked past Zoe's now naked body and said, "Hi, Jenny. What are you doing here?"

"I don't know. I came to talk to my friend. At least I thought she was my friend. I did *not* expect to find her naked with you in the kitchen."

Jenny spun around and ran out the door.

Tyler chased after Jenny, Zoe's towel still dangling from his hand.

Zoe stood rooted. Shock warred with embarrassment at her predicament. Grant yanked the floral print tablecloth off the table and wrapped it around her shoulders.

"Get dressed." He glared at her. "You can explain when you are decently covered."

Still shocked from the unbelievable string of

events in the kitchen, she did not register his words at first. She had returned to the bathroom, shut the door and dropped the tablecloth in a pile of purple pansies on the floor before she fully comprehended Grant's imperious demand.

She did not owe him an explanation. Grant was her friend, not her lover. Hadn't they established that yesterday?

Besides, it should have been obvious that she was not trying to seduce Tyler. The man was a basket case, and had taken off after Jenny without even a glimpse at Zoe's naked body. If the facts did not speak for themselves, there was not much she could add to them. Jenny was another matter entirely. Zoe would have to explain everything to her friend and hope Jenny was rational enough to believe her.

If only Tyler had let her get dressed when he'd first got there. But in his misery he had been oblivious to her scanty covering. *Men.*

Feeling annoyed at men in general and Grant in particular, Zoe stepped back into the shower. In her pique, she refused to rush herself. Grant could just wait for her, and for any explanations she might deign to give him.

Half an hour later, Zoe reentered the kitchen. This time she was fully clothed, in a pair of comfy cotton pants she had batiked the year before, a matching mock turtleneck and an oversized sweatshirt from her alma mater. Her tennis shoes squeaked as they hit puddles of water left from her dripping body earlier.

Grant sat at the kitchen table, a mug in his hand. The set of his shoulders and his thin lips let her know that he had not gotten over his initial reaction to finding her in the kitchen with Tyler. She frowned at him, letting *him* know she did not appreciate his attitude.

She walked by him and grabbed a paper towel from the counter. Going back to the puddles of water on the floor, she knelt down and wiped them dry. "You can stop glaring at me. Tyler and I were not in the middle of some hot and heavy loveplay when you got here."

Grant's chair scraped the linoleum as he pushed away from the table. "You could have fooled me. You were wearing nothing but a towel and Tyler when I walked in."

Zoe looked up to meet Grant's gaze. Mistake. His eyes were filled with fury and he loomed over her like an avenging angel. Trying to scoot back and gain some distance, she lost her balance and fell back onto her bottom with a plop. "Correction. I was wearing the towel and hugging Tyler. He needed comfort."

"If you comfort every guy who needs it with your naked body, I'm surprised your reputation isn't already shredded."

Putting her hands beside her and her feet under her, she pushed up from the floor. She landed two inches from Grant's chest. She met his eyes unflinchingly, giving him glare for glare. "That was a rotten thing to say."

She was so close she could see his nostrils dilate,

a sure sign that Grant was furious. Zoe prepared for a rip-roaring argument with him. Instead he wrapped his arms around her, settling one hand on the small of her back and the other behind her head. Yanking her forward, he lowered his head and stopped.

Zoe felt like a deer caught in her daddy's headlights. She knew this meant danger, but she was too shocked to move. "Grant, I don't think—"

His mouth cut off the rest of her words. His lips were warm and she could taste coffee on his tongue. The tongue he roughly plunged into her mouth, still open to finish her statement. It felt good. He tasted wonderful.

Using the hand on the small of her back, he pulled her body into alignment with his. Electric shocks sizzled along her front where her legs, pelvis and breasts made contact with the hard contours of Grant's body. Of their own volition her arms lifted, and she locked her hands behind his neck.

The bones in her legs turned to warm candle wax and would not hold her up. They didn't need to. His mouth was no more possessive than his hands. He held her against him like a vise.

In the back of Zoe's mind, she knew this would not last. Anger had prompted Grant to do something he had made it very clear he did not want to do. Kiss her. She already felt the pain of his withdrawal, although it had not happened yet.

Refusing to give in to it, she determined to enjoy the sensation of being in his arms while it lasted.

Relaxing against him, she gloried in the feel of his tongue branding her mouth, his hands holding her so strongly. She moved her lips under his, exulting in the groan that issued from him. He lowered his hand and cupped her bottom.

She could no more stop herself from rocking her pelvis against him than she could hold her breath under water indefinitely. She needed this. Too much.

He responded to her movements by backing her against the counter. He lowered his other hand to her bottom and lifted her until she sat on the very edge of the counter, her thighs open and Grant between them.

He didn't waste any time getting as close as he could get with only the layers of clothes separating them. He pressed his hardened shaft against the juncture of her thighs, and with only a small wiggle of her backside he was hitting her where it counted most.

She moaned at the feelings that rocketed through her at the contact. She wanted to be naked, with him buried deep inside her.

He squeezed her breast. She could not get enough air. Twisting her mouth from his, Zoe gulped in necessary oxygen. Grant moved his mouth to her ear and pressed wet, breathy kisses against it. Zoe felt herself spiraling out of control. She had never responded this way before, and if she didn't know better she would think she was about to climax.

He spoke into her ear. Whispering encouragement. "That's right, *querida*. Let go."

He thrust hard and fast against her. She ground herself against him.

"Yes." He yanked her shirt out of her pants. The first touch of his fingers against the naked, heated flesh of her stomach made her suck in her breath.

He moved his hand up under her shirt until he met her bra. Finding the front clasp, he undid it with a minimal amount of fumbling. She arched against his palm. When his thumb and forefinger closed over one nipple, she went rigid. He pulled and squeezed, moving his lips back to cover hers. His tongue plunged inside again. This time she met it with her own, thrusting her tongue against his in a dance as old as time.

The shudders took her by surprise. She yanked her head away from his and screamed. *"Grant—"*

"See, Jenny, I told you I didn't have anything going with Zoe. You think she would be making it with Grant on the kitchen counter if she was interested in me?"

A woman should *not* have to deal with this after her first ever orgasm in the kitchen. Between the look of abject horror on Grant's face and the glee on Tyler's, Zoe felt like punching someone. Jenny was giving her a look of wary hope, her freckled face streaked with tears and her red hair in a wild cloud around her head. Zoe decided that as a fellow woman and friend she could not disappoint her.

Grant pulled his hand out from under Zoe's shirt as if he'd just realized where it was. He would have stepped away, but Zoe hooked her arm around his neck and pulled. He was not going anywhere. "That's right."

Jenny swallowed. Even though she had not done anything wrong with Tyler, Zoe felt guilty when her friend scrubbed at her cheeks. "Then why were you naked and hugging my Tyler?"

Grant tried to pull away again, but Zoe held on. She whispered in his ear. "Work with me here. You owe it to me for the crack about sleeping around."

He stopped straining against her hold. Zoe let go of him and pushed until she had enough room to slip off the counter. Taking Grant by the hand, she led him to the table. "Sit."

He sat.

She patted his cheek and smiled. She turned back to Jenny and Tyler. "Do you two want some coffee?"

Tyler looked at Jenny for her answer. She shrugged. He said, "Yeah. That would be good."

"Fine. Sit down, and I'll explain how you found me hugging your Tyler wearing nothing but a towel."

Jenny frowned, but she sat down. Turning toward the coffeemaker, Zoe felt her still swollen nipples rub against the fabric of her shirt. Embarrassment swept through her. Changing her mind about pouring the coffee, she headed toward the hallway. "Grant, you get the coffee. I'll be right back."

Tyler asked, "Where is she going?"

"Don't be an idiot. What do you think we walked in on? I think she wants to put herself back together," Jenny replied.

"Oh."

Her cheeks hot enough to fry eggs, Zoe headed for the bathroom. She felt a little guilty about leaving Grant to face Jenny and Tyler alone, but not too guilty. He deserved *something* for that stupid look of horror on his face after the most beautiful experience of her life. Taking her to new sensual heights aside, Grant had clearly not changed his mind about his rule. He still didn't want to kiss her.

Well, this time he had done a whole lot more, and she was not sure she would ever get over it. Sighing, she looked in the mirror over the sink.

Her pupils were still dilated with passion and her mouth looked thoroughly kissed. Running cold water over a washcloth, Zoe let the liquid cool the heated skin on her hands and wrists. She bathed her face and smoothed the tendrils of hair that had escaped from her French braid. She refastened her bra and tucked her shirt back into her pants.

There was not much else she could do, unless she wanted to take another shower and change her clothes. She didn't. She wanted to get the discussion with Jenny over and start looking for apartments. Preferably without another all-out confrontation with Grant.

Coming back into the kitchen, she noticed that Grant and Jenny were both glaring at Tyler, and that Tyler looked like a man waiting for the executioner. Zoe's patience snapped.

"You can both wipe that look of nasty displeasure

right off your face. Tyler has not done anything wrong, and I'm in no mood to deal with assumptions."

Tyler turned a grateful smile on her and Jenny's soft brown eyes widened at her tone. Zoe nodded. "I mean it. You want the truth, or not?"

Jenny looked at Tyler, then at Zoe. "I want the truth."

"Me too."

Zoe ignored Grant. She sat down at the table and looked her fellow teacher square in the eye. "Fine. I was taking a shower this morning when I heard someone pounding on the door. I thought it was Grant, because he was supposed to come over and go apartment-hunting with me. You with me so far?"

Jenny nodded.

"Good." She took a deep breath. "As you know, it was not Grant. It was Tyler. And to be honest I don't think he even noticed I was wearing only a towel and still wet from the shower."

"I *told* you," Tyler said.

"He was really upset. I guess you two had a fight?" Jenny nodded.

"Well, he was beside himself at the thought of losing you, and he came over to beg me to talk to you."

"I couldn't stand to lose you, Jenny. I love you."

Hearing Tyler's declaration did nothing for Zoe's mood. She gave him an impatient stare and went on. "He hugged me when I promised to help him, and that's when you and Grant walked in."

Jenny's shoulders slumped. "I guess I owe you an apology."

Zoe shrugged. "Just talk it out with Tyler."

"I will." Jenny stood. "Come on, Tyler. We need to talk."

Tyler jumped up like a well-trained pup, which was pretty amusing considering how big he was. His look of eagerness resembled a pet as well. Jenny stopped at the door. "I am sorry I jumped to conclusions."

Zoe did not want to know. "I forgive you."

They left. She stood up, grabbed the coffee mugs and carried them to the sink. "You ready to go apartment-hunting?"

"Don't you think we should talk first?" Grant spoke from right behind her. She had not heard him move. How strange.

"About what?"

"A couple of things come to mind. The first being, why didn't you just go get dressed when Tyler got here?"

She lost it at the residual anger she heard in Grant's voice. "Because I *like* entertaining men wearing nothing but a towel. Why do you think?" She turned around and brushed past Grant. "Maybe you should go do your Carlene thing, and I'll search for apartments by myself."

"Forget it. We're going to discuss what happened here."

She spun around to face him. "I'm through discussing Tyler. Either you believe the worst of me or you trust me. It's your choice."

As she said the words, she realized that she owed Grant the same consideration with Carlene.

"I'm not talking about Tyler."

She sighed. The big confrontation. "Do we have to discuss the other? I already know you've got a rule against kissing me. I figure you've got one against what happened to me on the counter as well." She looked at him. "Can't we just leave it at that?"

Grant's frown speared her. "At what? At the place where we both realize that I should not be kissing you but I keep doing it?"

"Uh, I think we did more than kiss. Well, I did anyway."

He ran his fingers through his hair. "I know."

"I'm sorry you didn't. Is that what's bothering you?" Men could get really cranky when they were left hanging, or so she had been told.

The look of horror was back. *"No."*

"I'm losing my patience here. There isn't anything we can do about what happened. Like I said, I know you did not want to do it. For some reason neither of us understands you have kissed me twice in the last week although you are firmly against the idea."

He sat down in the chair and dropped his head in his hands. He looked so much like Tyler had earlier that Zoe laughed.

His head snapped up. "It's not funny, damn it."

She stifled her giggles. "I know."

He fisted his hands against his legs. "We've got to do something about this attraction between us."

He had already ruled out the most logical course of action—giving in to it. "Like what?"

"Maybe we shouldn't spend so much time together for now."

Fear clawed at her insides. Was he saying that he wanted to end their friendship? He couldn't be. He had promised last night that he would not give up on their relationship even if she fed his boots to the goat.

"Please clarify."

He smiled. It was strained, but nevertheless a smile. "Sometimes you sound like a college professor, not a kindergarten teacher."

So? She'd talk like a blithering idiot if he would just explain what he meant by not spending time together. "Do you mean like not going with me to look for apartments, or not spending Christmas together, or what?"

He frowned. "I promised to take you looking for a place to live and I will."

"Okay."

"As for Christmas—we've spent every Christmas together since I was eleven years old. I'm not about to stop now. Besides, I like being in the good graces of my folks."

Relief seeped into her in tiny increments. "What exactly are you saying, then?"

"I don't know." He shook his head. "No more time together on kitchen counters, I guess."

She had been the one on the counter, but who was keeping track? "That's doable." Tongue in cheek, she promised, "If it will make you feel better, I'll stay out of kitchens with you entirely."

"Maybe that would work."

At the look of serious relief on his face, she didn't mention they were in one now. Or that their first kiss had happened in the entertainment room. Why burst his bubble?

"Well, then, shall we go apartment-hunting?"

He nodded. "Get your coat. I'll drive."

He definitely made a better driver than navigator, so she did not argue. Gathering the paper with her listings circled, her coat and her purse, she followed Grant out to the truck.

"Shoot." She shoved her purse and the paper toward Grant. "Here. Put these in the truck, will ya?"

"Where are you going?"

"I forgot to put the cats in the bathroom."

"Oh. Speaking of animals. Bud came out this morning."

She had forgotten entirely about the missing hamster. "Great. That's a relief."

"Yeah. He didn't seem damaged by his sojourn into my walls."

Zoe just hoped the same was true for Grant's wiring.

She found the cats and shut them in the bathroom, and then rejoined Grant in the truck. "Let's go."

He put the truck in gear. "Where to first?"

She named an apartment complex near the Dry Gulch. Grant could get his apology to Carlene out of the way. Looking in the backseat, she saw the beautiful crimson roses Grant had bought Carlene. It hardly seemed fair that Grant would bring her, Zoe, to a shattering climax and then give flowers to another woman.

Life was certainly twisted sometimes.

Grant must have noticed her eyeing the flowers.

"I bought them for her yesterday."

"I know."

"I should have given them to her when she insisted on going home, but I was too worried about Bud to think of it."

"Yeah."

"Damn it, Zoe. They *are* her flowers. I've got to give them to her."

"I never said you shouldn't."

"Right. Well. So long as you understand."

CHAPTER EIGHT

GRANT fought to concentrate on the road.

Zoe's presence and his uncertain feelings toward her distracted him. It really bugged him the way Zoe could go from falling apart in his arms one minute to disinterested sidekick the next. She *understood* his rules. Didn't complain about them. Didn't she know that women were supposed to feel used and abused when men did the things he had done with her in the kitchen without committing to at least a casual relationship?

Zoe acted like the entire incident was nothing more than a small blip in their friendship. She wasn't even mad that he was giving flowers to Carlene. He should be giving flowers to *Zoe*. Dozens of them. A man did things like that after experiences like the one they had shared.

It took what was left of his self-discipline not to demand an explanation for her behavior.

A little self-interest was mixed in as well. If he asked her what was making her respond with such insouciance to their passionate encounter, then she might expect him to explain what had happened. He wished he knew. The sight of Zoe hugging Tyler wearing nothing but a scanty piece of terry cloth had sent Grant right over the edge.

Rather than soothe him, her explanation had only made him angrier. More jealous. The feel of Zoe losing control in his arms had been so incredible he had forgotten everything but her.

Until Tyler and Jenny had come back.

Unfortunately, by then it had been too late. Grant was never going to forget the way it had felt to hold Zoe shivering in his arms. He gripped the steering wheel tightly. *Never.*

Zoe's prolonged silence finally registered. He shot her a sidelong glance. "You okay?"

She met his eyes briefly, the brown depths of her gaze hiding her thoughts from him. "I'm fine."

He nodded, refocusing his attention to the road. Right. "You want to check out the apartment complex while I stop by and get things straight with Carlene?"

"That's what I planned."

Great. So why did he feel like such a heel?

He dropped her off in front of an apartment complex across the street from the Dry Gulch. He didn't like the proximity to the bar, but vowed not to argue with her about it. Not unless she actually ended up wanting to rent the place.

Zoe stepped out of the rig. "I'll come over to the Dry Gulch when I'm done here."

"Okay. See you in a bit."

* * *

Grant walked into the dim interior of the country and western bar. His eyes took several seconds to adjust to the lack of light after the bright glare of sun off the snow outside. Tim McGraw was singing a ballad with his wife, Faith Hill, over the speaker system. The romantic words made him think of Zoe, and how *un*romantic he had been with her.

A man was not supposed to be romantic with his best friend—not if he wanted to keep the friendship intact. But what about the woman he spent a mindblowing passionate encounter with? What about her? And what if they were one and the same? What was a man supposed to do then?

"Hey, Grant. Don't tell me those are for me?"

The sound of Carlene's soft Texas drawl interrupted his confused musings. She stood behind the bar, her smile covering more than the tight leather vest that passed as her top.

"I forgot to give them to you last night in all the hullabaloo over Bud."

She blushed. "That's so sweet. I felt like such an idiot, leaving and not helping you look for him."

"He came out on his own. Hamsters are small, but they're resilient." He set the flowers on the bar in front of her.

She leaned forward and sniffed them. "Mmmm. These smell wonderful. You're a real romantic, aren't you?"

Not if you asked Zoe. "I'm sorry about dinner."

"Me too. I really am." She leaned across the bar and

touched his cheek, the movement strangely hesitant. "Why don't we try it again? This time at my place."

Oh, hell. He moved a step back, breaking the contact of her fingertips with his face. "I...uh...I can't leave Zoe's pets without supervision right now." The lie came out sounding as ridiculous as it was.

Carlene looked down at the roses and then back at him, her expression thoughtful. "Maybe we can work something out."

"Maybe." Even as he said the noncommittal word, the image of Zoe's face as she climaxed filled his mind.

Their friendship had been irrevocably altered that morning, and pretending it hadn't wasn't going to change a thing. He did not want to be with any other woman, and it wasn't fair to Carlene, himself or Zoe to pretend otherwise. He opened his mouth to tell Carlene, but was interrupted by a man demanding another beer from the other end of the bar.

Carlene grimaced. "I'm sorry. I've got to go."

"No problem. Look, I—"

The customer banged loudly with his beer bottle on the bar and Carlene turned away without giving Grant an opportunity to finish his sentence. He'd have to call her later and let her know he wouldn't be dating anyone but Zoe from here on out.

He wasn't sure what Zoe would think of that. It hadn't been the most successful of endeavors when she'd been nineteen and he'd allowed himself to treat her like a woman instead of his best friend for a few mad weeks. The one time he'd let his passion get the better of him, she'd ended up looking like a wounded pup and running from him. He'd been very careful to keep his libidinous thoughts about her under lock and key since.

She hadn't looked shocked or dismayed in the kitchen, though. And why should she? She was a professional woman now, not an innocent teenager still in college. She'd come back to Sunshine Springs of her own volition. She had the career of her choice and she did not need to be protected from him any longer.

He didn't know why it had taken him so long to figure that out, but one thing was certain. His attempts to ignore the desire that was always one step away from bucking out of control like an unbroken horse had failed.

When he got outside, he scanned the street and parking lot of the Dry Gulch before noticing Zoe sitting in the truck cab.

He loped over to the navy blue rig and swung open the driver's door. "I thought you were going to meet me inside."

She tugged her knitted cap more firmly onto her head, tucking a stray strand of her pretty brown hair under it and behind her ear. "You were busy. I decided to wait here."

Why had she left the bar without saying anything? "I told you I had to apologize to Carlene."

Zoe pulled out the newspaper page with several red circles around ads, many of which had already been crossed out. "I think we should concentrate on older apartment complexes. They are more likely to allow pets. Let's go to the Courtyard. It's on the other side of town, near the county line."

Grant knew where Zoe was talking about, and just thinking about her living there was enough to side-track him from demanding a reason for her leaving the bar without saying anything. The apartments were in a small rundown complex near the one and only topless bar in the county. "No way."

She turned hostile brown eyes on him. "I've got to find a place to live, and most apartments won't take pets. The ones that will don't allow the number I have."

"You can't seriously consider living in the Courtyard."

"Right now, I'd consider just about anywhere."

"What about that place near the school?"

"No dogs."

He tossed out several more names and met with the same terse reply. *No.* He could understand her ir-ritation. "I'm not taking you to the Courtyard."

"Where I live is my decision." Her bravado melted and she sighed. "It will just be for a little while any-way. I'll start looking for a house come spring."

He wondered what had changed her mind about buying a house. He didn't ask. Instead, he said, "There has to be someplace better, even if it is only temporary."

She frowned, her pixyish face set in mulish lines.

"I don't want to waste the entire day looking at places that won't even consider me."

But that was exactly what they did. Over the next several hours they visited every apartment complex, room for rent and house for rent in the nearby county. No one wanted to rent to a woman who had a large dog, two cats, a hamster, a parrot and a goat.

Grant would not back down and take her to the Courtyard. They argued about it again when they ran out of alternatives.

"Zoe, living in a place like the Courtyard is not an option. I used my cellphone to call the Sheriff's office while you were talking to that couple about the duplex. They get calls to the Courtyard at least once a week."

She glared at him. "I'm not going to be causing any disturbances."

"Don't be stubborn." He knew he had hit rock-bottom with his arguments when he asked, "What would your parents think?"

Her silence spoke with more volume than any shouting match.

"Don't look like that. Just because they aren't coming home for Christmas doesn't mean they don't care about you." But he decided it was time he called her father and told the older man a few home truths—like that was exactly how Zoe saw their actions. He'd talked more intransigent men than Mr. Jensen into doing what he wanted, and he wanted Zoe's parents there for her at Christmas. "Your mom would flip if she knew you were even thinking about living there."

Zoe took the newspaper and folded it with exaggerated precision. She tucked it into the side pocket in the door of the truck, and then pulled her seatbelt across her small waist and buckled it. "Do you want to pick up dinner before you drop me off, or just take me home?"

She had always had a knack for changing the subject when she did not want to dwell on something. He sighed, and started the truck. "Dinner first. I'm starving."

He pulled out of the parking lot and headed toward Main Street and the few restaurants in Sunshine Springs.

She said, "Okay, but let's make it a drive-thru. I want to get home. I've got work to do, and the cats are probably sick to death of the bathroom."

He turned onto Main Street. "I have a better idea. Let's get pizza, pick up your cats and eat at my place. We can drive to the pageant together afterward, and let the cats roam free."

She looked out the window. "I was thinking about skipping the Nativity Play."

"I know you get nervous when your kids are on stage, but they're counting on you to be there."

Her almost child-size hands clenched in her lap. "You're right, but you don't have to go with me. I'm a grown-up. I don't need you along to hold my hand."

"Are you trying to get rid of me?" he asked jokingly.

"Yes."

He nearly ran one of the only two stoplights on Main. "Why?"

"I think you were right. We need to spend less time together. Tonight seems like the ideal place to start."

Fear washed over him like water from a mountain stream, leaving his heart cold in its wake. He'd decided to explore the possibilities of a relationship with her and she was pulling away. "I said the kitchen. We need to spend less time together in the kitchen."

Realizing how idiotic he sounded, he shut up. Damn. He'd known kissing Zoe would be a risk. He was losing her, and he wasn't even dating her yet. Had she already decided he wasn't worth compromising her lifestyle for?

His mother had made that decision when he was too young to understand but old enough to remember the pain. His ex-fiancée had followed the pattern his mom had set when she'd dumped him because he had opted to run the ranch rather than stay on the east coast. Even his stepmom, Lottie, was a prime example of the way women used marriage and love to tie men in knots and force them to change or be abandoned.

She'd given his dad an ultimatum: move to Portland and leave the ranch to be run by someone else, or lose her.

His dad had opted to keep his wife—unlike when Grant's mother had made a similar demand about returning to the east coast, where they had met on one of his frequent business trips. She hadn't liked life as a rancher's wife either. Living without the glittery nightlife she'd been used to had been too difficult an adjustment for her to make.

So she'd gone.

He pulled into a parking spot in front of the take-and-bake pizza place.

Zoe gave him a smile tinged with sadness. "That's not what you meant and we both know it."

It took him a minute to remember what they'd been talking about. When he did, he felt his insides tighten. "What I know is that I'm not about to stop spending time with you." He gritted his teeth, but could not stop the words from coming out. "I need you, Zoe."

She frowned. "You have Carlene. You don't need me."

"I don't have Carlene."

"You're seeing her. I heard you in the bar."

"You heard Carlene ask me to reschedule our date?" Could that be what this cold shoulder was all about?

"Yes."

"You didn't eavesdrop long enough, then."

She huffed. "I was not eavesdropping."

He grinned. "Right. Look, *niña,* if you had stuck around a few seconds longer you would have heard me resort to dishonest measures to *avoid* another date with Carlene."

Her soft brown eyes mirrored wary hope. "I would?"

"Yes. I told her that I couldn't leave your pets alone."

Zoe laughed with disbelief. "Didn't she think it was odd that you were in town now if that were true? Not to mention the fact that you have a ranch full of hands, even if quite a few are spending time with their families right now?"

He shrugged. "I don't know."

The laughter died. "You gave her roses."

"I explained that. I bought them yesterday. Before."

She measured him with a look. "Before what?"

"Before we made out on the counter."

Her face turned crimson. "We didn't technically make anything."

He raised his brows and she bit her lip in embarrassment. "We didn't?"

"Well, maybe *I* did…"

"Yeah, I'd say you did. And if you'll let me, I'm going to real soon, too."

"Are you saying what happened to me on the Pattersons' kitchen counter changed the dynamics of our relationship or your relationship with Carlene?"

"Both." Didn't she feel the same way? If she wanted to forget what had happened, he didn't know how he was going to oblige her. Not when all he wanted to do was repeat the experience.

"I see."

"What do you see?"

"You no longer have a rule against kissing me."

"I'd say it went a whole lot deeper than that."

"Maybe." She opened her door and slid out of the truck. Sticking her head back inside, she asked, "Aren't you coming?"

It wasn't going to work this time. She was not changing the subject. "Yeah, I'm coming." But not the way he wanted to be right then.

He got out of the truck and walked around to

where Zoe waited for him on the sidewalk in front of the take-out pizza place. "Well?"

She fiddled with something in her purse. "Well, what?"

He frowned, his chest tightening inexplicably. "Don't play games with me, Zoe. Did it change things for you too?"

She glanced behind him and smiled at someone. "Hello, Mrs. Givens."

Grant tensed at the sound of her former landlady's name. He had a few things he'd like to say to that old biddy, but right now he wanted an answer from Zoe more.

"Good afternoon, Zoe— Grant." Mrs. Givens stopped with every evidence of wanting to chat. "Finished with your Christmas shopping yet?"

He fixed his gaze on the older woman. "Zoe's been a little busy looking for a place to live. She hasn't had time to do her shopping."

Zoe gasped and Mrs. Givens frowned. "I'm sorry to hear that. It was a very difficult decision to encourage Zoe to find a new place for her and her pets to live. However, I assumed that since I hadn't been called for a reference she had decided to move in with you at the ranch."

"Surely you've spoken to Mrs. Patterson?" Zoe said. "She must have told you that they've very generously allowed me to stay at their house while I look for a new place." Grant thought her voice sounded strained.

Mrs. Givens' eyes widened. "I haven't spoken to my dear friend since the night you left. I cannot imagine that she has allowed you to move your pets into her home."

Grant answered for Zoe. "She didn't. The animals are staying at my ranch."

"If I had known you would be willing to give up your pets, my dear, I would never have encouraged you to leave."

Like hell. The old biddy was lying through her teeth to make herself look better, but Grant wasn't fooled. He gave her the frozen look he usually reserved for boardrooms and drunken ranch hands. "Letting the animals stay at the ranch was *my* idea. You didn't leave Zoe with a lot of options when you *kicked her out.*"

Mrs. Givens drew herself up. "I could not condone rodents living in my house, and I was not merely referring to the animals staying at your house." She faced Zoe. "I read the advertisement looking for homes for your pets in the weekly."

He felt his body go tense. "You advertised for homes for your animals?" Damn it, she shouldn't have had to do that.

Zoe shrugged. "No one was going to rent to me with so many pets."

Mrs. Givens nodded her agreement. "Well, I've got a few more things to pick up before the shops close as well. I'll see you tonight at the pageant."

"Not if I can help it," Grant muttered as she walked away.

Zoe grinned at him. "Behave. I know you think you have to protect me from the world, but I'm perfectly capable of handling my former landlady."

He didn't return her smile. He didn't want to discuss Mrs. Givens. He didn't even want to talk about her giving up her pets. But he'd have something to say about that later. He wanted an answer to his earlier question, and he wasn't going anywhere until he got one. "Answer my question."

"Let's talk about this later, Grant." She gave him the smile that usually disarmed him. "I don't want to discuss what happened at the Pattersons' on a public sidewalk."

"I want to talk about it now."

Zoe's smile disappeared. "Well, I don't." She turned and walked into the take-and-bake pizza place. She marched up to the counter. "A double pepperoni calzone, please." She faced him. "What do you want?"

"An answer."

Her expression took on a hunted quality, and all five feet, two inches of her stiffened with her usual brand of stubborn resolve. "Later. Right now you need to order."

"I'll share your calzone. You can never eat a whole one." Before she could argue, he turned to the cashier. "Add an order of bread sticks and a large salad, please."

The kid behind the cash register gave Grant and Zoe a bored smile. "That'll be about fifteen minutes."

Grant said, "Fine." It shouldn't take more than a minute or two for her to answer his question. It wasn't that tough. Either their experience at the Pattersons' had changed their relationship for her, or it hadn't. He couldn't believe after the way she'd come apart in his arms that it hadn't, but he needed to hear her tell him so.

He grabbed her arm to pull her to one of the chairs that lined the small store's walls. "Did it, or didn't it?"

She crossed her arms over her breasts, drawing his attention to the curves under her coat. "It's not that simple."

"Yeah. It is. It's either *yes* or *no*. Which is it?"

She gave a pained smile to an elderly woman sitting next to her husband in the waiting area. She turned her gaze back to Grant. "I'm not sure we should change our relationship. Being friends has worked for a long time."

"You don't respond to my kiss like a friend, Zoe. You respond like a lover." The best lover he had ever had.

Her eyes skittered to the interested faces of the other patrons in the restaurant and she blushed. "Please, Grant, let's talk about this later."

He wanted her to admit that things had changed. "Just say yes or no."

"Yes." She shot up from her chair. "Yes. They've changed. But you aren't exactly a poster boy for commitment. I don't want to end up another notch on your bedpost."

He reached for her, but she yanked away. "I'll wait outside."

CHAPTER NINE

"A NOTCH on my bedpost?" They were the first words Grant had spoken about their argument since returning to the truck with their dinner.

The drive to the Double C had been a silent one, with her thinking about the ramifications of Grant wanting her to acknowledge a change in their relationship. Evidently he'd been mulling over her comment about bedposts.

Zoe felt her face heat. "You know what I mean."

"No. I guess I don't." He pulled her from where she stood spooning salad onto plates into the space between his jean-clad legs as he leaned against the counter. "We haven't even been to bed together. I can't notch anything."

"Don't be so literal." She didn't know why she was arguing this particular line of debate. She didn't want a commitment from Grant; she wanted to get rid of this desire that stopped her from wanting other men and seeing them as potential mates.

"I'm not *afraid* of commitment. I've been engaged once."

She looked him straight in the eye. "So you're saying you are looking at the possibility of marriage to me?"

His gaze shifted and his expression turned troubled. "I don't know what the future holds, but I want to explore the possibilities between us."

Right. He wanted to go to bed with her. Somewhere between his horrified reaction to their encounter that morning and when they'd gone for dinner Grant's attitude toward having a physical relationship with her had changed. *He no longer had a rule against kissing her.* That did not mean he was looking at forever. *But she wasn't either*, she reminded herself.

She refused to acknowledge the emptiness inside her the thought provoked. Grant was offering her the thing she'd decided she wanted most—an opportunity to assuage the lust she felt for him. He wasn't offering love, but then neither was she. *She wasn't.*

"Okay."

"Okay, what?" He was looking at her with a distinct air of wariness.

"I'll go to bed with you."

He frowned. "Just like that?"

"Did you want me to play hard to get a while longer?"

His frown turned up a notch. "No. I'm just not sure what we're saying here."

"You're saying you want to go to bed with me, and I'm saying yes. It's pretty straightforward."

He didn't look convinced, but she didn't want to talk about it any longer. So she took the steps necessary to bring her body into frontal contact with his. She grabbed the back of his head and yanked. His mouth landed against hers with a gasp of surprised air. She took advantage and slipped her tongue inside to tease his. His response was everything she had hoped for.

He stopped trying to talk. She wasn't even sure he kept breathing. He planted his hands on her backside and lifted her until she hooked her legs around his waist, and then he kissed her back with a masculine passion that left her panting and her heart racing faster than the pace car at the Indianapolis 500.

She was enjoying their kiss so much that the annoying ring of the telephone did not immediately register. Grant peeling her from his body and pushing her gently away, however, did.

The phone shrilled once more, and with a look of apology Grant leaned past her to answer it. "I'm expecting a call from Mom and Dad," he explained as he lifted the receiver off the wall phone.

"Hello? Sure, just a minute." He handed the phone to her. "Your principal."

She cradled the phone against her ear. "Hello, John. What's up?"

"Hi, Zoe. I need to talk to you about something. Are you going to be at the Christmas Pageant tonight?"

"I'll be at the program, but can't we just talk about it now?" He had interrupted an incredible kiss, for heaven's sake. They might as well talk.

"I'd rather do this face-to-face, if you don't mind."

His serious demeanor was making her nervous. "What—am I fired or something?" She said it jokingly, but a small part of her was worried that it must be pretty serious for him to be unwilling to discuss it over the phone.

"Of course not." His immediate denial soothed her nerves. "We just have a small matter to work out. That's all."

"Is this about the bunny incident? I apologized to the other class, and I have been very careful to keep Pete in his cage since then."

"I hadn't heard about that. You'll have to enlighten me when we talk tonight."

Shoot—hadn't that police officer who'd pulled her over for a broken headlight told her never to volunteer information? That had been *after* he had asked her if she knew why she'd been pulled over and she had proceeded through a litany of ticketable offenses before he'd finally shut her up and told her to get a new headlight. Well, she was done offering information.

She'd wait to find out what was on John's mind tonight. "Fine. I'll see you there, then."

She hung up the phone and met Grant's gaze.

"What was that all about?" he asked.

She shrugged, her brows drawn together in thought. "I don't know. He wants to talk to me about something tonight at the program."

Grant pulled her back into the circle of his arms. "I take it he wasn't calling about the bunny incident?"

She smiled. "No."

All thought of bunnies and principals went out of her mind as Grant's lips fastened on hers again.

Zoe slid her gaze from the moonlight reflecting off the snow out the truck's window to Grant's profile. His handsome face took on a mysterious quality in the dim light. It was as if this man that she had known for most of her life had become a stranger. A sexy stranger.

She'd felt this way once before—the summer she'd been nineteen. She'd loved him then. Almost desperately. This time she just wanted his body—didn't she?

She'd given up on his heart after he'd hurt her so badly when she was nineteen, but the feelings roiling round inside her now felt like something more than lust. That scared her more than the conversation she'd had with her principal at the Christmas Pageant.

John had suggested she stop seeing so much of her best friend for a while, to let the gossip die down. Evidently rumors were circulating about her living with Grant...with the most intimate connotation of the words.

John had been more than a little worried about how the gossip would affect the reputation of the school, even after she had assured him she wasn't even living in *non*-connubial bliss with Grant. Part of her understood the school administration and board's attitude about the matter. Despite its influx of the rich and famous twice a year, Sunshine Springs

was so small a town that building the second stop-
light had been cause for a town dance and barbecue.

She'd seen a different way of life when she'd gone
away to college, but she'd never been able to completely dismiss the morals she'd been raised to
believe were right. Those morals did not include
moving in with a man without the benefit of marriage. She knew the majority of the townspeople held
similar ideas, particularly the parents of her five-
year-old students.

John had been right about that. But she wasn't living with Grant and she refused to be punished for
rumor rather than reality. She wasn't giving up her
relationship with Grant for anyone, and she'd told her
principal that very thing.

He hadn't been happy.

"You've been about as talkative as a sleeping
bull since you and John talked after the pageant."
Grant's words brought Zoe back from her reverie.
"What's going on?"

She smiled. "I'm sorry. I didn't mean to ignore
you. Really. I was thinking."

"I could tell. I want to know what you were thinking
about. Are you having second thoughts about us?"

The vulnerability in his voice surprised her. "I'm
not having second thoughts."

"Then what is it?"

"John had heard from some *reliable source* that I
was living with you. He wanted me to know that the
school administration, the school board and the par-

ents of my students would all take a very dim view of such an arrangement."

Grant's head whipped around to face her. "Did he threaten your job?"

Zoe sighed. "Not in so many words. And I don't know how far he would have pushed it either, because I told him immediately that I'm staying at the Pattersons' and looking for a place of my own."

"What else?" He knew her so well. Someone else would have assumed that had been the end of the discussion, but Grant could read her too well.

"He's as concerned about the rumor as the reality. He wants me to cut back the time I spend with you to allay gossip," she said.

"Like hell." The words exploded in the truck cab like a Christmas firecracker. "What did you say?" There was that vulnerability again.

She put her hand on his thigh, reveling in the hard muscle and the sense of intimacy of the action. "I told him that I refused to have my private life dictated by the gossips in Sunshine Springs."

"Did he accept that?"

She started to draw little shapes with her finger on Grant's leg. "He wasn't thrilled, but he had no choice."

Grant's breathing quickened. He put his hand over Zoe's to still it. "I'm going to drive us into a ditch if you keep that up." He squeezed her hand and went silent for about half a minute. "Maybe we should consider what John said. I don't like the idea of you being the brunt of gossip in town."

Frustration poured through Zoe. She hadn't stood up to her principal for Grant to go chicken-hearted on her. "Make up your darn mind. I'm tired of playing this tune. This morning you were so appalled by what happened in the kitchen that you wanted to curtail our friendship. Then you apparently chucked your whole rule about kissing me and your concerns about getting too close out the window."

She took a deep steadying breath. "You demanded that I acknowledge the change in our relationship, which I did. Now we're back to maybe we should not spend so much time together."

He pulled into the Pattersons' drive. He parked next to her truck, but didn't turn off the engine. "Let's talk about this tomorrow. It's been a long, emotional day for you, and you didn't get a lot of sleep last night."

She unbuckled her seatbelt and shoved her door open before jumping out. "Silly me—I thought the emotion was mutual today." She grabbed her purse off the seat and slammed the door.

She'd gotten the front door open before he caught up with her.

He spun her around to face him. He didn't say anything. He just slammed his mouth down on hers in an incinerating kiss. His lips were hard and demanding as they moved over hers, forcing a response even though she was still angry. She pressed her body against him in an instinctual move that felt pretty dang primitive.

He slipped his hands inside her coat, and it wasn't

until his fingers had closed over bare flesh under her sweater that she came to her senses. She struggled against him, dragging her mouth away from his. "Stop."

He kissed the side of her neck when she denied him her lips.

She pressed against his chest and shoved. "I mean it. Stop."

His breathing harsh, he did as she demanded.

She pulled from his arms. "I'm not going here again. I need some time to think. Apparently so do you."

He took a step back and dug his fingers through his dark hair. "Fine. You're right." He stepped toward his truck. "I'll call you tomorrow."

She nodded. She couldn't speak. Her throat was too tight. She watched him move toward the truck, her insides twisted in knots. He stopped when he reached the driver's side door.

"Zoe?"

"Yes?" The word came out as no more than a whisper, but he heard her.

"The emotion *was* mutual." Then he was gone.

Grant finished feeding the horses and headed back up to the house. He wanted to get in his truck and go to Zoe, but that wasn't an option. He'd called her this morning on the phone, figuring she'd had plenty of time to think about their relationship. She'd had all night. Evidently she hadn't spent it thinking about them. She'd had the gall to tell him that she had slept and slept well. He rubbed his tired eyes.

He hadn't. He'd spent the night tormented by images of Zoe on the countertop in the Pattersons' kitchen. Zoe coming apart in his arms. The hurt on her face when she'd thought he'd made a date with Carlene. The feel of Zoe's lips under his. He kept playing her reaction to his suggestion that they follow John's recommendation to protect her from gossip over in his mind. He couldn't get the look of wariness in her eyes when she'd told him they both needed time to think out of his mind.

Why had she been so upset last night? He'd only been trying to protect her. And why had she been so hesitant to admit the change in their relationship? He didn't like it that she needed time today to think about it either. Or that she'd refused to see him until she was ready.

She should be ready now.

To heck with it. She'd had all day. He was going over there and they were going to talk things out. Besides, he needed to tell her that Bud had been picked up by his new owner. Grant could have used the phone, but he'd rather tell her in person.

He wasn't going to say anything about the phone call he'd made not long after hanging up with her that morning, though. He'd called Mr. Jensen and read the older man the riot act. It was time the Jensens started treating Zoe like their valued daughter and not an afterthought. The older man was too stubborn to promise to change his plans, but Grant could tell he'd been shaken by the things Grant had said.

If the two didn't show up for Christmas he would be surprised, but he wasn't warning Zoe about the possibility on the off chance he was wrong. She would only be hurt more then.

He slammed into the house, leaving the back door open. He went to grab his truck keys from the hook by the door, but at the sound of tires crunching over the snow on his drive his hand froze midway. She'd come to her senses. He looked out the back window. Carlene's stylish compact came into view. It halted a few feet from his back door.

Oh, hell. He'd forgotten to call her and set things straight. After giving vent to his frustration with a few well-chosen words, he went outside to face the music.

"Hello, Carlene."

She turned on her high-heeled boot and gave him a strangely tentative smile. "Hi. I got off work early tonight, and instead of going home I thought I'd bring dinner. To make up for the other night, you know?"

"Look, there's something I need to tell you."

She shivered. "Can you tell me inside? It's freezing out here."

"Sure."

She started taking off her coat when they got inside, and innate courtesy had him reaching out to help her. The words he wanted to say stalled in his throat as he became aware of what Carlene was wearing under the coat.

Her boots stopped at her ankles and fishnet covered the rest of her bare legs. Her dress looked more like a shiny Spandex slip. The way she kept tugging on the hem was probably meant to draw his attention to her skimpily clad thighs. The top of the dress was skin-tight and off the shoulder. If she was wearing a bra, it had to be the size of a Band-Aid. Nothing else would fit under the snug fabric.

Her lips curved in a smile that looked a little ragged around the edges. What was going on?

"Like it?" she asked.

What the hell was he supposed to say to that? All he could think of was that if Zoe walked in now, he was a dead man. "Isn't that a little cold for this time of year?"

She sidled up to him and trailed her fingers down his shirtfront. "It's my working gear, but I'm counting on you to keep me warm."

He stepped back hastily, before she could get any more ideas. The thought had him jumpier than a colt in his first batch of snow. "I'll turn up the heat."

Her laughter trilled over his stressed nerves, sounding more forced than seductive. "I'm counting on it." She undid the top button on his flannel shirt with trembling fingers.

Grant stumbled backwards and escaped into the hall. Rejecting a woman's advances never got any easier. It went right against the strictures his dad had drilled into him about courtesy toward women since Grant had been old enough to notice the difference between the sexes.

He stood staring at the thermostat stupidly, forgetting what he had come into the hall to do—besides get away from Carlene. Taking several deep breaths, he reminded himself that he was a man and in control of the situation.

Yeah. Right.

When it came to women, men were rarely in control.

He walked back into the kitchen and stopped short at the darkness. Carlene had extinguished the lights and lit two candles on the counter. "What the…? I can't do dinner. I'm sorry. I was just about to leave when you showed up."

Her smile faltered and then came back, turned up a notch. "Maybe you could put off your errand for a little while?"

"We need to talk." He started backing up toward the light switch.

Her eyes flared with what looked like hurt at his rejection.

His shoulder hit the wall and he desperately searched for the light switch. His grateful fingers closed over it and he pushed upward. The kitchen flooded with light.

Carlene jumped, her eyes blinking at the bright fluorescent light. Under the bright light of the kitchen she looked tired…and sad.

He hated what he had to say next. "I should never have asked you out in the first place."

"Are you in a relationship?"

"Not exactly." Not until Zoe said he was. "But I want to be."

"Oh." Her expression was pained. "I'm sorry I

misread your signals. The roses…" She sighed.
"You know?"

"It's not your fault."

She nodded, obviously agreeing with him, and
turned to go. That was when the lights went out,
quickly followed by the high-pitched whine of the
fire alarm.

"Hell."

"What is that?" Carlene shouted.

"My fire alarm."

"There's a fire?"

"No," he shouted over the alarm. Remembering
how the light had gone off on its own, he yelled,
"There must be a short in the wires or something."

The hiss of escaping water put the cap on Grant's
endurance. "Get out of here!" he yelled.

Carlene was already headed for the door. It didn't
save her. The automatic sprinkler system went off and
both Carlene and Grant were drenched in seconds.
Grant headed for the phone on the counter. If he
didn't call the fire station immediately, he'd have a
whole lot more to worry about than a wet floor.

It took two tries to get the receiver, slippery with
water, to stay in his hands before he could dial the
number. Thankfully, he got through immediately,
and explained that his place was not on fire.

Leaving Carlene in the kitchen, where it was
warmer, if not drier than outside, since she was
soaked to the bone, Grant sloshed outside to find the
emergency shut-off switch. After only six tries, he got

it to turn off. He stepped back into the house, relieved that the high-pitched wailing had finally stopped.

The blessed silence was interrupted by the sound of another rig coming down his drive.

This time Grant's insides churned with dread rather than anticipation. It would be Zoe. He had no doubt. When her truck came into view he just stood there, like a man ready to face his executioner. Only he wasn't ready.

Zoe stopped the truck three feet from Carlene's car and got out. She glanced briefly at the car, and then at him. Her eyes widened when they took in his waterlogged state. "What happened?"

"Fire alarm."

Carlene chose that moment to make her appearance in the open doorway. Mascara ran down her face like an athlete's black line gone amok. Her hair was plastered like wet string against her skull, and she was glaring at him as if he had set off the alarm on purpose.

After the mess he'd made of things, he couldn't blame her.

A choked exclamation from Zoe had his attention careening away from the woman glaring at him. He turned to face Zoe.

"I didn't realize that you had company." Her even tone belied the stricken expression in her eyes. "I came by to tell you Tyler will be out to pick up the parrot sometime tomorrow. At least something good came from yesterday."

Was she trying to say that the change in their relationship *wasn't* good? He wouldn't accept that. "It's not what it looks like. I didn't know she was coming."

Zoe didn't say anything. She turned to leave and he chased after her, grabbing her arm. "I mean it, Zoe. I was planning on coming to see you when she showed up."

He turned back to Carlene and demanded, "Tell her."

Carlene swiped at her wet hair. "So she's the one, huh?"

Zoe tried to yank her arm away. "No."

He blew out a frustrated breath and wouldn't let go. "Yes."

Carlene's gaze met Zoe's. "He's telling the truth. I came out tonight on a whim. I felt bad about the way I left last time, and I didn't realize the two of you had become an item. If it will make you feel any better, he made it clear from the start he wasn't interested. I didn't mean to hurt anyone. I'm sorry."

Some of the tension drained from Zoe, but she still tugged against his restraining hold. He let go.

She turned and started walking toward her truck again. His insides froze. "Zoe?"

It came out like a plea and he didn't care.

"Call me when you aren't otherwise engaged," she tossed back over her shoulder when she reached the driver's door. Then she left.

Carlene sighed. "I didn't mean to cause problems between you two. If I'd known it was like that I wouldn't have come. I probably shouldn't have come anyway."

"We'll work it out." He hoped. "I'm sorry if I misled you with my actions."

She shrugged. "These things happen. But if I were you, I wouldn't make a habit of giving flowers, especially roses, to one woman when you want another one."

"I won't." But he had no idea if the one he wanted to give flowers to would accept them from him.

CHAPTER TEN

THE smell of bleach burned Zoe's nostrils as she finished scrubbing the bathtub and then rinsed it.

She peeled off the bright yellow rubber glove from her right hand and swiped at her forehead. "Whew."

The cats were hiding somewhere. They knew better than to get in her way when she was in a cleaning frenzy.

She'd already tried venting, but it hadn't helped. Forty-five minutes of girl-chat with Jenny had only served to fan the outrage Zoe had felt, driving up to Grant's home and finding him and Carlene in what could only be termed a compromising circumstance. Jenny had reminded her that Grant had caught Zoe and Tyler in a similar situation and it had been innocent.

It hadn't helped. It wasn't the same. There was too real a risk that Grant had wanted Carlene there, even if he hadn't invited her. After all, he'd invited her once before.

The pain in her chest was way too familiar. She'd felt exactly like this four years ago, when Grant had dropped her off at home in order to take that New York model on a romantic evening flight in his plane. She'd cried for two solid hours that night. She refused to cry this time.

The stinging in her eyes had everything to do with the bleach she was using to clean and nothing to do with overactive tear ducts. She took a deep breath and held it, trying to assuage the very physical ache in her chest. It shouldn't hurt this much. She wasn't in love with Grant like she had been when she was nineteen.

The air hissed from between her lips as she let it out and drew another quick breath. *She wasn't.* Only a total idiot would let herself love a man who had rejected her so completely once already and had given red roses to another woman. Sure, he'd tried to justify it, but the details hadn't done a thing to explain why he'd asked Carlene out in the first place.

Grant had said their relationship had changed for him, but he'd also grabbed at the first opportunity to back off. He'd been all too willing to follow her principal's advice and spend less time together. Not a week ago he'd had a rule against kissing her. Why?

And why did thinking about him and Carlene hurt so much? Zoe should be angry, not hurt. After all, it was supposed to be physical for her—a way to get over the desire for Grant that had plagued her since she was sixteen.

Her emotions were not supposed to be involved.

She yanked her glove back on and surveyed the

bathroom, looking for something else to clean. The small room sparkled more than it ever had when she'd cleaned it for her mom, when her family had lived in this house.

And she still felt the ache in her heart.

She had already vacuumed every inch of the Pattersons' home. Even the rooms she had left closed up. She had scrubbed down the counters in the kitchen, the floors, the windows and the mirrors. She pushed herself to do one more thing, to clean the last little nook, hoping that in doing so she would fall exhausted into bed tonight.

Then perhaps she would not lie awake for hours, tormenting herself with thoughts of Grant and Carlene.

Sighing, she peeled off her gloves and sat on the toilet seat. *Right.* She could work sixteen hours shoveling horse manure and she'd still go to bed and dream about Grant, with the dreams becoming nightmares mixed with memories from four years ago now Carlene had entered them.

The insistent chime of the doorbell penetrated her acidic thoughts. She considered not answering. Maybe whoever it was would go away. She knew it wasn't Tyler this time, because he'd been with Jenny when Zoe called. Which left Grant.

She'd told him to call her, not come by. She wasn't up to seeing him.

She tucked her feet up on the toilet seat and locked her arms around her knees, staring at the opening to the hall and willing him to leave. Loud pounding was interspersed with repeated peals from the door-bell. She tried covering her ears, but the sounds penetrated. She glared at the bucket of cleaning supplies, but they weren't going to help her—unless she planned to get rid of him with a squirt from the ammonia bottle.

She pushed herself up and went to answer the door.

Opening it a crack, she peered out.

She'd been right. It was Grant. "Open the door, Zoe. It's damn cold out here."

"I don't want to talk to you."

"That's too bad, because I'm not leaving." His tone had the implacability of a rock wall. "You might as well open up and let me in."

The thought of sending him away hurt more than the prospect of talking to him, so she obeyed, and then stood in shocked amazement at the sight before her. She could barely see Grant for all the flowers he held in his arms. He had at least three dozen roses in different shades, a bunch of colorful blooms made into a bouquet cradled in one arm and a potted mini-rosebush clutched in his free hand.

"Do you think I could come in?"

She stepped back and let him inside.

"Where do you want these?"

"Are they for me?" She wasn't taking anything for granted.

"Who else would they be for?" When she just stared at him, his mouth set in a firm line. "Don't answer that. Just tell me where to put them."

She led him into the kitchen. "I'll look for some containers."

She found a box of wide-mouth quart-size mason jars with Mrs. Pattersons' canning supplies. Zoe used them for the roses and the colorful bouquet. Grant went back outside and returned with several more bouquets and potted flowers. She put the mini-rosebush and other live plants on the counter next to the sink. When she was done, and Grant had made one more trip out to his truck, Mrs. Patterson's kitchen resembled a florist shop.

"What's this all about, Grant?"

His blue eyes speared her with their intensity. "It's about giving the right signals. I didn't want there to be any more confusion."

"You mean it's not an apology for me catching you entertaining Carlene dressed like a male fantasy come true?"

He frowned, running his tanned fingers through the thick blackness of his hair. "No. I didn't invite her over. I know you believe me about that."

His eyes dared her to disagree with him. She didn't. The fact she believed he hadn't invited Carlene over didn't make the memory of the other woman standing in his doorway wearing fishnet stockings any less painful.

His gaze speared her. "The only fantasy come true for me is you…dressed any way at all…but undressed would be even better."

Her heart jogged and her betrayer of a body jolted at his words. "Then why did you bring the flowers?"

"Like I said, I wanted to give the right signals."

"What do you mean by signals?"

"A man shouldn't give flowers to one woman when he wants another one. It sends mixed signals."

Zoe looked around the kitchen at the plethora of flowers surrounding her. Warmth spread throughout her insides, but she remained wary. "And does the amount of flowers indicate in any way how much you want a woman?"

His eyes glittered midnight-blue in the fluorescent light and he started toward her. "I don't know, but I bought out the floral department at the grocery store to be on the safe side. I would have bought out the florist too, but they were closed."

"So, what happened tonight?" She backed up a step when he would have touched her. "Why did Carlene come over if you didn't invite her?"

"Mixed signals."

The roses. "I see. I guess you won't be giving other women flowers for a while, huh?" At least as long as their affair lasted.

He took another step closer, crowding her. "Right."

"What set off your sprinkler system?" She avoided meeting his eyes and focused on the yellow roses in the mason jar on the counter opposite.

"I don't know."

But they could both guess. Bud. "I'm sorry. It's my fault, isn't it?"

He reached out and pressed his big hand to the side of her face, gently turning her head until their gazes met. His expression was as serious as a heart-beat. "It doesn't matter."

Her breathing reflex short-circuited and she had to concentrate on sucking air into her lungs. "Of course it matters. Bud probably ate your wiring, and I'm the one who let him out of his cage."

His thumb brushed down her chin and settled lightly against the pulse in her neck. "I don't care."

"But—"

"The only thing I care about is your promise to make love to me." He leaned down until their breath mingled.

She fought hard to concentrate on what they were saying. "I thought you wanted to back off for a while."

"I wanted to protect you. It's an instinct I have a hard time ignoring. But if it means losing you I'll ignore it—and anything else that could send you away from me."

"Even gorgeous models from New York?" She couldn't keep the residual pain from her voice. Her refresher course in that emotion was too recent.

His eyes narrowed while his mouth stopped a centimeter from her own. "What are you talking about?"

She tipped her head back, straining her neck to gain some distance. "It just seems to me that on the two occasions when you and I might have taken our friendship into the realm of the physical, you went for another woman instead."

"What do you mean by *might have*? Are you saying you don't want to make love to me? If you are, then think again. Things have gone too far for us to turn back to our old platonic relationship."

"That's what I thought when I was nineteen, but I was wrong then and maybe you're wrong now." She wanted to make love with Grant, but some irresistible compulsion was prompting her to rehash old memories and hurts.

"Four years ago neither one of us was ready for this."

"Well, you certainly weren't. It would have meant giving up the model."

Suddenly she found herself sitting on the counter, a plethora of flowers and plants surrounding her, the smell of damp soil and the fragrance of flowers in bloom teasing her senses while Grant made a place for himself between her spread legs. "I didn't *have* the model."

"Come on, Grant. You took her for a midnight ride in your plane. What else were you going to do when you brought her back to the ranch?"

"Take her home."

She let her expression speak her disbelief for her.

"Zoe, I took Madeleine up in the plane so I wouldn't take you to an empty line shack and finish what we'd started in the barn. I didn't want to have sex with her."

For four years Zoe had taunted herself with the image of Grant and the willowy blonde in a clinch, and now he was telling her he had not even slept with the woman.

"Then why did you reject me?"

Confusion clouded his eyes. "Reject you? I never rejected you. You're the one who ran from the barn wearing an expression that accused me of damn near attacking you."

"I never did!"

He just stared at her.

"Okay. So, I ran. I'd never experienced anything like that before. It scared me, and I wasn't ready to make love for the first time."

"That's what I said earlier."

"But I got ready."

His hands settled on her thighs. "What do you mean?"

"I wanted to make love with you that night you took Madeleine up in your plane, after dropping me off at home like a pesky younger sister."

"Well, you couldn't have wanted it very damn bad. You left for college two days later—a full month before you had to be back for classes. And you didn't come home for a long visit again until you moved back a year ago."

Old anger and hurt welled up inside. "What did you expect me to do? Stick around and watch you have an affair with the bimbo model after treating me like your girlfriend for several weeks?" She shoved against his chest. "Let me down."

He didn't move an inch. "No way. We're talking this out."

"What's the point? It happened years ago. It's over and done with."

"If it were over for you, you wouldn't have brought it up."

He was right, darn it. "Okay. Tell me again why you took Madeleine up in your plane if you didn't want her, and while you're at it try explaining why you had a rule against kissing me and why you asked Carlene out."

He wanted a conversation? He could do the talking as far as she was concerned.

He opened his mouth and then closed it, an arrested expression coming over his face. "I did it all for the same reason. To protect you and our friendship."

"Oh, right."

His grip on her thighs tightened, reminding her that talking wasn't the only thing on Grant's mind. "You weren't ready to make love when you were nineteen. You even admitted it. I knew if I didn't do something, I'd end up seducing you."

"And seducing me would have been bad?"

"Yes. You were nineteen. A teenager. Totally innocent. And if that weren't enough you had two years left of college and a career choice that could have taken you anywhere in the country after you graduated."

Well, she was twenty-three now, but she was still pretty innocent. She wasn't in college any longer, but her career could still take her away…if she wanted it to. She didn't want to leave Sunshine Springs, but apparently Grant didn't know that. "I came back to Sunshine Springs and you still had that stupid rule against kissing me."

He smiled wryly. "I was still stuck in that mode of protecting you from my evil desires. It's a tough instinct to fight once embedded in the male psyche, and I've been protecting your feelings one way or another for the better part of my life."

"And Carlene?"

"I'd done a pretty good job of forgetting how much I wanted you, but all of a sudden everything about you turned me on—and I knew if I didn't do something I was going to seduce you."

Everything about her turned him on? Her fingers trembled as she laid them over his hand on her thigh. "And seducing me would still be a bad thing?"

"I thought so—at first. But then I realized two things."

"What?"

"One, you aren't nineteen anymore."

"Four years of living will do that."

He leaned his forehead against hers. "Yeah."

"And the second thing?"

"I can't resist you."

"But you resisted Madeleine and Carlene?"

"Absolutely, and without any problem."

A sudden thought stopped her from closing the distance between their mouths. "What about Bud and the parrot?"

His laugh sounded something like a strangled groan. "I didn't get a chance to tell you, but Tyler has already come by for the bird and your student's dad picked up Bud this afternoon."

"That's good."

He nodded, but said nothing, his intensity surrounding her like a physical presence. She opened her mouth to say something else—she wasn't sure what—but his lips cut off anything she might have said. Passion exploded inside her like a launching space shuttle, fire and sound roaring through her with amazing force.

The second his tongue touched her lips she opened for him. He groaned his approval and pulled her body into his, holding her still for one slanting kiss after another as the urgency behind each one increased with every subtle shift of his lips.

He placed hot open-mouthed kisses against her chin and throat. "You smell like bleach."

She laughed, the sound coming out strangled. "I've been cleaning."

He tunneled his fingers in her hair and kissed her ear, tickling her with his tongue. It was a good thing she was sitting on the counter because her leg muscles had turned to water.

He tugged her hair out of the ponytail holder she'd used to keep it out of her face while she was tidying up. "I didn't know household cleaning products could be so erotic."

"Me neither."

He didn't reply. His mouth was too busy tantalizing her collarbone. She didn't mind. In fact, she threw her head back to give him better access. "I like that."

"You don't taste like bleach. You taste so damn sweet. Just like I fantasized."

"You fantasized about me?"

He licked the column of her neck and she shivered. "Yeah."

Remembering what he had said when he'd first got there, she asked, "Was I naked in these fantasies?"

"Yes. I never forgot the sight of you without your top that one time we went crazy together in the barn."

That was nice. She melted back into his embrace, eager for another of his searing kisses.

Talking about it was making Grant desperate to feel her naked flesh. Flowers weren't the only things he'd bought at the grocery store. He leaned forward and scooped her up in his arms.

She gasped. "What are you doing?"

"Taking you to bed." He leaned down to kiss her again. She averted her face, so he concentrated on her neck while making his way to her bedroom. He walked in and dropped her on the bed. He started stripping out of his clothes.

She began to unbutton her blouse, and he stopped moving just to watch her.

She stilled. "You're watching me."

"I want to see you. All of you." With a body as beautiful as hers, she should expect it—or had she always made love in the dark?

Her cheeks turned a very pretty shade of pink. "I want to see you too, but there's something I need to tell you."

"What?"

"You know how tonight seems so much like four years ago?"

Except for the fact that tonight he was going to have Zoe, and four years ago he had only dreamed about it. "Yes."

"Well, it's a lot more like it than you might expect."

"What do you mean?" If she didn't get to the point soon, he wasn't sure he'd have the patience to let her.

"I was prepared to give you my virginity that night, Grant."

He realized that was why she had been so hurt. "I wish I had known, *querida*. I would have handled things differently."

"That's the point. I need you to know now."

His breath stilled in his chest. "Are you saying you are still a virgin? None of the men you dated in college and since…?"

"No."

His knees threatened to buckle. She'd never had another man. She belonged to him. Completely.

"I…" He didn't know what to say. Emotion welled up, clogging his throat.

She finished unbuttoning her shirt. "Promise me something?"

"Anything." He was so overwhelmed with his desire to touch her that nothing else registered.

She peeled out of her shirt and his fingers literally trembled with the need to touch the sweet flesh she'd exposed. She stopped with her hands on the front clasp of her bra. "Promise that you won't regret this."

Regret it? He wanted her more than anyone or anything he had ever desired in his life. "The only thing I regret is how long you're taking to get out of your clothes."

He loved the way her breath hitched at his words. "No more talk about spending time apart?"

He frowned. How could she even suggest such a thing? They were about to make love. Her for the first time. And he liked that more than he should. "You know I only said that because I was worried about your reputation. I wanted to protect you."

She smiled. "We'll have to discuss that tendency of yours sometime, but not right now." She unclasped her bra.

He was out of his jeans in seconds.

He stopped his rush across the room when her wide brown eyes looked at his erection with a certain amount of trepidation. "It's going to be okay, baby. I'll be gentle."

She swallowed, and then shifted her gaze to his eyes. "I know. I trust you." She opened her arms to him.

He dived across the space that separated them, wanting to touch her, to taste the nipples that peaked at him like raspberries on top of two scoops of luscious, sweet, French vanilla ice cream.

She gasped when he landed on her with a thud. He smiled, feeling like a predator blessed with the sweetest prey ever sighted. "Sorry. Did I hurt you?"

"No." She sounded breathless, but not nervous, and for that he was very, very grateful.

He shifted his weight to his forearms and started kissing her again. She hadn't made it out of her jeans, and they rubbed against the bare skin of his thighs and his hardened male flesh, making him burn. He skimmed his hand down her shoulder, then over her chest, until he cupped the fullness of her breast against his palm. Its soft resiliency intoxicated him.

She groaned, and bucked against him with her hips.

He lifted his mouth from hers and looked down, drinking in the sight of his hand against her breast. "Zoe, *mi precioso,* you are so damn beautiful."

Zoe stilled beneath him and he looked up to her face. Crystalline tears trembled on her lashes.

He sucked in his breath. "You okay?" She didn't move. "What's the matter? What did I say?"

Maybe he was rushing things. She hadn't seemed nervous, but maybe she was.

"You think I'm beautiful?" Her smile did as much to warm him as her naked body beneath him. He bent his head and kissed each eyelid, brushing her tears with his lips.

"I have always thought you were beautiful."

"You never said so." Her voice trembled with emotion that Grant did not understand.

"That's not true. I've always told you I thought you were the prettiest girl in Sunshine Springs."

She sniffed. "But that was because you were my friend."

"It was because it was true. But it wasn't enough, was it?" He brushed his index finger over her pebbled nipple. "You're beautiful. Pretty doesn't cut it." He wanted to taste her. Moving down until he could take the sweet little bud in his mouth, he reveled in her silky skin. "You are so soft."

She groaned and bowed under him, pressing her breast against his lips. "Grant, I want you to touch me everywhere."

He was more than willing to oblige. He started by nibbling on the tender, creamy flesh surrounding the wet morsel he'd been suckling.

She nearly came off the bed. "Don't stop. Oh, please, don't stop."

He caressed her shoulders, her rib cage, and reached under her to squeeze her bottom. Her hands twisted in his hair, pulling his head tight against her breast, silently begging for more of the same.

"Oh, Grant, oh, Grant, oh, Grant."

Exultation filled him at the need he heard in her voice. He lifted his mouth and she protested. He smiled at her. "Don't worry. I'm not done yet, but you still have too many clothes on."

He levered himself off of her and immediately set about unbuttoning her jeans. He unzipped them and then put his hands on her waistband, ready to tug them off. She lifted her hips for him. She wiggled until he got the denim past her derriere. He stopped. He could not help it. The scrap of turquoise silk covering her most intimate place paralyzed him.

She looked at him with a question in her eyes.

He licked lips suddenly gone dry. "Do you realize what a privilege this is? How honored I feel that you chose me to be your first lover, *querida*?"

"That's nice—but could you get on with it?" She wasn't smiling, because he knew she wasn't trying to tease him. She meant it, and that did things to him. Her eyes were filled with heated desire. "I feel like I'm going to die waiting for you," she moaned.

He smiled and felt things inside him shift. Where he had been mindless with his desire to couple with her, he now had an overwhelming need to cherish her first. To show her how much he appreciated the gift of being able to touch her and be with her.

Of being her first lover.

CHAPTER ELEVEN

"Grant?"

He slid her pants an inch down her thighs. "Yes?"

"Um, are you going to take off my jeans, or what?"

He loved the sound of impatience in her voice, loved knowing he was doing this to her. "Oh, I'm going to take off your jeans, all right. Relax, Zoe. I want to cherish you."

She put her hands over his and pushed on her jeans. "Cherish me naked, okay?"

He laughed, the sound strangling in his throat. "I guess I can do that."

Moving back to the edge of the bed by her feet, he pulled her pants off and stood back to appreciate the sight of her in nothing but the little scrap of fabric covering her most feminine place. She was so beautiful and, at least for right now, she was his. Totally and completely.

He leaned forward and kissed her stomach, letting his tongue explore the indentation of her belly button, reveling in the way she writhed below him. She was so responsive and still a virgin. Somehow he knew, even if she didn't, that she had been waiting for him.

Kissing a trail over her smooth skin, he stopped when he reached the top of her panties. Taking them in his teeth and hooking his fingers on the waistband at either side, he pulled them off.

Slowly. Very, very slowly.

She groaned and squirmed, trying to get her legs free, but he kept her captive with the panties as he continued down the naked flesh of her legs centimeter by centimeter.

She shouted his name and he felt a sense of primitive male power surge through him. She wanted him. Damn, it felt good. He finally brought the scrap of silk over her ankles and then her feet. Standing up, he dropped them on the floor.

The sight of her naked body on the rumpled bedding once again paralyzed him. He had sublimated the feelings rushing through him for so long, it was almost impossible to believe he was here, in Zoe's old bedroom, with Zoe lying on the bed wearing nothing but a dusky red blush.

He'd had other women, but he could never remember feeling like this. This was more than physical. Hell, it was more than mere emotion. There was something spiritual about making love to this woman.

He met her eyes and smiled. "You're blushing."

Her lips twisted in a shy frown. "You're staring at me."

"I can't help it. You're so perfect." Didn't she realize that?

"I'm not perfect."

He gave her a considering look. "Yes, you are. Let me show you." He picked up her foot and started giving nibbling kisses to each tiny digit. "Your feet are so sexy that just the sight of this little toe—" he wiggled her pinky toe "—gets me so hot my jeans get uncomfortable."

She stared at him, her mouth opened slightly, her brown eyes dark with emotion.

He gave her instep an open-mouth kiss, letting his tongue tickle it before pulling back. "You've got a really erotic arch, *niña*. You could do feet commercials."

"Feet commercials?" Her voice broke in the middle of the word *commercials*.

"Uh-huh." His lips moved their way up her calves to the inside of her knee. Her breathing became ragged. So did his. He knew where he was going and, by the tensing of her thighs, he figured she did too.

"Grant?"

"Sweetheart, you've got legs that could stop traffic. I have never appreciated your particular style of dress as much as I do at this moment. If you wore short skirts, I wouldn't get any work done. I'd spend all my time staring at your sexy knees." He punctuated each word with a kiss on one of her legs.

"Sexy knees? I didn't know anyone had sexy knees."

He shrugged. "Like I said, you're perfect."

Then he zeroed in on his target, gently parting her swollen flesh with his tongue and licking the slick little bud at the apex of her femininity. Zoe's hips strained up off the bed and she screamed. He flicked her with his tongue while inserting a finger slowly into her hot, moist, very tight passage. He wanted this to be perfect for her.

He wanted her to remember this night as the most wonderful experience of her life.

"Grant!" His name sounded like both a demand and a plea.

He gave in to both and pulled her swollen button of love into his mouth, suckling it like he had her nipple earlier. Her scream reverberated through his body like an electric charge.

"Please, please, *please*..."

Did she even know what she was begging for? What he planned to give her? She bucked against him and he continued kissing her intimately, until he could taste her sweet honey flow and she shuddered with release against his mouth. She cried out again, a high-pitched scream that went on for several seconds. He didn't stop his ministrations and she thrashed against the bed, trying to dislodge him and press herself more firmly against him all at the same time.

She came again, this time sobbing his name, and then just sobbing. The swollen tissues of her sex contracted around his finger and he almost came, thinking what that was going to feel like when he was inside her.

He kept on until she begged him to stop, and her body went completely limp around him, convulsing sporadically when his tongue hit a particular spot of soft feminine flesh. He gentled her with the soothing touch of his fingers and soft kisses pressed against the sensitized flesh at the juncture of her thighs.

He stood up and donned a condom. She watched him put on the protection, her eyes slumberous with spent passion.

He smiled, but his heart felt tight. This act was so important. It had never been this way with another woman, but he felt as if taking Zoe would be permanent. It was more than being her first lover. It was knowing that she belonged to him on a fundamental level he couldn't begin to explain. She always had, but he'd been too stubborn to admit it.

A desire that did not die after four years of suppression was not born of lust. He shied away from identifying what had given it birth. It was enough to know that this was something special.

Zoe could not believe that her body was once again responding to the sight of Grant's arousal. The way he'd brought her to multiple orgasms with his mouth had totally exhausted her—or so she'd thought. Now she felt the stirrings of renewed need, as well as a deep longing to satisfy her lover every bit as thoroughly as he had satisfied her.

She didn't doubt she could do it, even if she'd never had a lover before. She'd read books—and not just erotic romance either. She'd read sex manuals when she'd been trying to find a way to want a man besides her best friend. But now that problem was solved. It was Grant standing so sexily above her, so obviously ready to join his body with her own.

How could she help but satisfy him? She longed to give him every bit of pleasure her body was capable of providing.

She smiled in welcome as Grant lowered himself over her, pressing the head of his erection against the sensitized flesh of her femininity. Her legs widened of their own accord to make a place for him.

"I want you."

"I'm glad, *querida*." His voice sounded strained.

She arched her hips against him and the head of his shaft slipped inside. He groaned and pressed into her, but she was tight and he was big. Bigger than she'd expected. She bit her lip and did a little shimmy with her hips, which allowed him another inch of access.

She tried to relax, but she felt so stretched. Yet the sensation of his invading manhood felt so right that she vacillated between wanting all of him and fearing that she couldn't take it. She could only say a prayer of thanks that she'd been riding horses since she was three. There was no fleshly barrier that had to be torn for him to gain entrance, no source of pain to mitigate the pleasure of their joining.

He rocked against her, pressing inexorably closer, and her swollen tissues gave all at once, allowing him to seat to the hilt. She moaned. The sensation of his hard shaft inside of her and the press of his pelvic

bone against her splintered her thoughts and tormented her senses.

"Oh, Grant."

"I know, Zoe. I know."

She didn't know if she could stand it if he moved,
but she wanted it. Oh, man, she wanted it. *"Grant."*

He seemed to read her mind, because he pulled
back and rocked forward in a withdraw-and-plunge
move that rasped every nerve-ending in her feminine
core. Pushing her legs together and settling his
outside, he forced his hardness against her clitoris
with every thrust. She felt the excitement building
again, even more shattering than when his mouth had
been on her.

She tried to move under him, and succeeded in small
pelvic thrusts that seemed to drive him wild. Grant's
movements became more forceful, until he was driving
into her like a jackhammer. Her body tightened like a
bow, pushing against his muscular length, forcing him
to fight her for the embrace. Which he did, with amazing success, pushing her closer and closer to a mindless
pleasure unlike anything she'd ever known.

"Zoe, baby, come! Come for me. Now!"

And she did, feeling him bucking with his own release as she felt all the wonder of the universe coa-
lesce in her mind and body for one timeless moment.

Afterward, she lay under him, completely undone.

Zoe woke to the delicious sensation of Grant's
warmth surrounding her. She snuggled closer, enjoy-

ing the feeling of rightness being in his arms engendered. He was sleeping soundly. Poor man. She had worn him out. She smiled with satisfaction. She had never felt this intimate with anyone before.

The only thing that marred her perfect happiness this morning was the realization that she and Grant had started an affair last night, not a forever. A small voice that would not be silenced taunted her with the idea that a future together was not such an impossible scenario. She wasn't supposed to want that. She'd meant this to be about sex.

But after what they had shared she could no longer deny that, far from being a clinical satiation of her sexual drive, last night had been the culmination of nearly a lifetime of loving. She was one hundred percent, head over heels in love with Grant. But she still wasn't sure she could trust him with her heart. He'd explained *The Night*. He'd even explained why he'd asked Carlene out, and both explanations had made sense.

If Grant didn't love her, if his desire for her was the physical thing she'd tried to convince herself hers had been, then it would make sense that he'd wanted to protect her from his "evil lust", as he'd put it. He wouldn't have wanted to hurt her by making love to her and eventually moving on, but she'd made it clear she was open to a physical relationship with him and, like he'd said, he hadn't been able to help himself any longer.

She didn't know what he felt about the future and,

like an ostrich with her head buried in the sand, did not want to ask. What if she were right and he only wanted a friendly passion between the two of them? She'd rather deal with a broken heart down the road than now. If she waited to find out, she could enjoy the time they shared now, and maybe, just maybe, that time would bring Grant to a realization that he was as deeply in love with her as she was with him.

Their giving into the attraction between them had happened so abruptly that she still felt like she was in the aftermath of a tailwind. She definitely wasn't prepared to force a "relationship discussion" with Grant.

She slid reluctantly from the bed. She would like nothing better than to stay in bed with him for the rest of the day, but they needed to get his house cleaned up before his parents arrived from Portland. She also wasn't sure she had the *savoir-faire* to handle a naked-between-the-sheets morning after. She tiptoed to the closet and pulled out jeans, T-shirt and an oversized flannel shirt she had pilfered from Grant's closet sometime last summer.

She took a quick shower, not wanting to use up all the hot water. Grant would have to shower, and they needed to get a move on.

She smiled when she thought of the Cortezes' arrival. Having them around for Christmas would help make up for her own parents' defection. She dried her hair and pulled it back in her typical French braid, leaving some wisps to frame her face. After making coffee, she padded back to the bedroom in bare feet, carrying a mug of the steaming brew for Grant.

He was sitting on the side of the bed when she walked in. He grabbed the sheet and yanked it across his lap. She smiled at his modesty, even though she was sure she would have done the same thing herself. "A little late for that, isn't it?"

The smile he gave her in return looked a little forced. "Maybe."

If he was already regretting giving in to his desire for her she was going to scream—and not with pleasure like she had last night.

"I'll leave you alone to shower." She set the coffee on the table next to the bed. "This will help you wake up."

"Thanks."

She couldn't resist. She leaned forward to kiss him lightly on the lips before leaving the room. He averted his face and she ended up kissing the stubble on his chin instead. Zoe's insides froze. Last night had been a mistake. She could see it in the wary way he watched her.

She straightened and moved away from him. "I left you plenty of hot water, but you might want to make your shower quick. The faster we get to your house, the sooner we'll have everything cleaned up and ready for your parents."

She turned around and started from the room, ignoring him when he called her name. No tears came. Nothing. Just frozen pain. The way she'd felt when her dad had told her he'd sold the ranch and her parents were moving to Arizona to retire. Ranchers did not retire. But men who had lost their only son and heir, who saw their daughter as a complete write-off, did.

Grant's grip on her arms was the first inkling she had that he had followed her out of the bedroom. He spun her around to face him, every glorious naked inch of him. "What is going on?" Fury laced his words.

She felt the pain building. "You tell me."

"This is not a game, Zoe. Last night you went wild in my arms, and now you're walking away from me like I'm a cow pie on your boot."

"You promised." She glared at him, fighting the urge to cry. "You don't even remember, do you? You were just so hot, you said whatever you had to say so I wouldn't stop."

The dull red on his cheeks confirmed her suspicion like nothing else could. She struggled for release. "Let me go."

"No. Explain what you mean by my promise."

"You promised you would not regret what we did last night."

"You think I regret it?"

She searched his face, her conviction wavering. "Are you trying to tell me you don't?"

"Hell, no." His thumbs started a slow circling on her upper arms and she had to concentrate hard to remember what they were arguing about.

"But you turned your head when I tried to kiss you."

He closed his eyes and she had the distinct impression he was counting to ten. "Why weren't you in bed with me when I woke up this morning?"

She felt her face grow warm. "We need to get over to your house to get the place cleaned up before your parents arrive."

"Actually, we don't. I called an electrician and a cleaning crew out last night before I left to come here. But what has that got to do with you leaving the bed without waking me?"

"I thought if I took a shower first, we could get back to your place all that much faster." That hadn't been the only reason, and it must have shown on her face because he looked skeptical.

"And?"

She swallowed. "And I've never woken up naked with a man before. I didn't know how it was done."

"I'm not just any man, Zoe. I'm your best friend, and now I'm also your lover."

She craned her neck to meet his blue-eyed gaze. It was better than staring at his totally tantalizing naked body. "It's the lover part that I find a little disconcerting."

He reached out and held her shoulders, his expression grim. "Are you regretting last night?"

"No."

He leaned down and kissed her. "Good."

"So we both don't regret it?"

He kissed her again, this time with a little more passion. "Right."

"So why didn't you kiss me earlier?"

It was his turn to look chagrined. "I was mad when I woke up alone, and I thought you might be looking for a way to tell me last night was a mistake."

She laughed, and felt warmth cascade through her. He really did not regret making love to her. "I was just trying to be conscientious about getting back to your place before your parents got there."

"And shy."

She grinned in acknowledgement of his astute observation. "And a little shy."

He smiled and released her. "I'm going to take a shower. Why don't you pack while I'm at it?"

"Why?" She let her gaze roam down his naked body and felt the air leave her lungs in one big whoosh. His entire body was taut and hard.

"We might as well take your stuff to the ranch this morning." He talked as if standing around conversing naked, and with an obvious erection, was nothing out of the ordinary for him.

Heck, it probably wasn't. "What do you mean?"

"There's no point in you staying here, honey."

She bit her lip. "I can't move in with you, Grant."

He smiled again, this time with a definite glint in his eye. "My parents will be there. That's sufficient chaperonage in anybody's books."

"I don't want to flaunt an affair in your parents' faces."

"Affair?" His eyes darkened dangerously and he moved toward her, resolve written in every feature of his face.

Evidently he had a problem with the word *affair*. Maybe the word sounded too cheap to him. "Relationship. Whatever. I don't want your mom and dad thinking badly of me."

He stopped, his bare body inches from her. He didn't seem the least bit embarrassed by the fact his rather impressive male flesh brushed her stomach. "They're not going to think badly of you."

"They will if they find out we're sleeping together, and they'll want to know when the wedding is."

They would also tell her parents, who would then do one of two things. Demand to know when the wedding was to take place as well, or express their disappointment in a daughter who would make love to a man without the benefit of marriage. Maybe even both.

She didn't want to deal with either scenario. She also didn't want Grant put under that kind of pressure. If he decided they had a future together, it would be because he couldn't imagine his life without her—not because his parents and hers had guilted him into it.

"And we aren't planning on a wedding, right?" His voice was laced with an indefinable emotion. It sounded almost as if he were angry, but he had no reason to be.

She touched his arm in a conciliatory gesture. "Right."

His expression was serious and a little frightening as he bent and hooked one arm under her knees while using the other to support her shoulders.

She was airborne before she could gather her wits enough to demand, "What do you think you're doing?"

"Giving in to my instincts."

That was it. That was all he said as he carried her into the bedroom. He didn't talk again. Not while he kissed her senseless as he stripped her clothes from her body; not while he aroused her in ways he hadn't even done the night before. He said nothing as he brought her to one shattering climax after another, but she said plenty. A lot of *pleases, Grants,* and even swearwords and demands she'd blush about later.

They didn't make it to his house for another three hours.

CHAPTER TWELVE

"EUDORA GIVENS evicted you this close to Christmas?" Roy Cortez's voice boomed with a condemnation that for some reason Zoe could not fathom rang a little false.

She watched him, trying to figure out why his eyes expressed something that looked like satisfaction while his mouth voiced censure. He and Lottie had arrived from Portland an hour after Grant and Zoe had made it back to the Double C, and Grant had just finished telling them about her eviction.

"I can't believe it."

Zoe smiled at Lottie's words. "Large dogs intimidate her, and she positively hates rodents. She freaked out when she found Bud in the bathroom."

"Bud?" Roy's angular face, so like his son's, creased in amusement. "You say he's a hamster?"

"That Grant gave you?" Lottie wasn't looking at Zoe.

Her entire attention and disapproving frown was settled on her stepson. An inch shorter than Zoe, the older woman's regard still managed to bring a sting of red up Grant's throat and into his cheeks.

"Yes." The word carried a wealth of guilt, which stung Zoe's own conscience.

"The hamster wouldn't have been such a big deal if I wasn't already four pets over my one pet quota."

"You wouldn't have any fool quota for your pets if you'd let Grant rent your old house to you." Roy shook his head as he shifted his tall frame on Grant's living room couch, moving infinitesimally closer to Lottie.

Zoe took a sip of the Christmas blend coffee Lottie had brought with her and insisted on making when they arrived. The subtle cinnamon flavor teased her tastebuds as she prepared to defend her decision not to rent her old home from Grant yet again. She wasn't taking charity from Grant and that was that. "I can't afford the rent a house like that would command."

Roy glared at her, his expression so like his son's Zoe couldn't help an internal smile. "Grant wouldn't have charged you more than you could afford. He'd have been happier if you would have taken the house as a gift, like he wanted you to in the first place."

Zoe grimaced, but held onto her temper. It wasn't Roy Cortez's fault he saw the world through the eyes of independent wealth. "Bottles of expensive perfume are gifts. Houses are not."

Grant frowned at his father. "Zoe didn't want the house."

Zoe stifled an urge to sigh. Grant was wrong. She *had* wanted the house, and the security it represented, but she'd had to prove she could make it on her own. If her own parents could cut her loose, she couldn't rely on the Cortezes to take care of her.

"That's right, Roy. Leave the poor girl alone. She's independent, and we wouldn't want you any other way," Lottie said as she smiled gently at Zoe.

Roy shrugged. "Stubborn too, but I still say Grant would have felt a whole lot better if Zoe'd taken the house. He felt pretty bad, advising Jensen to sell."

Zoe felt as if everything inside her had gone still. She turned to meet Grant's wary blue gaze. "You *told* my dad to sell the ranch?"

He'd never said. Neither had her dad. Not that *that* surprised her.

"Yes."

"Did you also advise him to sell it without telling me first? Without giving me a chance to talk to him about it?"

It was Grant's turn to grimace, his gorgeous blue eyes reflecting frustration. "No. I didn't tell him to make the sale without talking to you first. But what would you have said, *niña*? You couldn't run it."

Ignoring Roy's interested gaze, and Lottie's sympathetic one, Zoe demanded, "How do you know?"

Grant's expression said it all. He knew—just like her dad had known. "Come on, Zoe. You never wanted to be a rancher. You're a kindergarten teacher and you love it." He leaned forward in his chair, tension vibrating off him. "Can you honestly say you would be happier trying to run the ranch?"

Of course not. But that wasn't the point. "If my brother had lived, you can bet my dad wouldn't have sold off the land and house without talking it over with *him* first."

Grant sighed. "If your brother had lived, your dad wouldn't have sold the ranch at all. But—"

She broke in before he could go on. "But he didn't live and my dad was stuck with me. I flunked at being a rancher's daughter and he knew I'd fail at running the ranch as well."

Pain coalesced inside Zoe as so many unmet needs rang hollowly through her soul. She had needed her father's unconditional acceptance, but she'd never gotten it. She'd needed to know she counted for something in her family besides the "oops" baby that had grown into the incomprehensible child. Those needs had never been met, and now Grant was telling her he'd been a part of one the most painful experiences of her life—her parents' final rejection.

They had sold her childhood home, bought property in Arizona, and waited to tell her until everything was a done deal.

Grant trapped her gaze with his own. "When you were six, you took a cow you'd befriended out on the range to save it from the stock sale. When you were nine, you buried the branding irons in your mother's garden. When you were thirteen, you opened the gates on the cattle-holding pens that had been marked for beef. You became a vegetarian when you were sixteen and you refused to come home from college for Spring Break your freshman year because it co-incided with spring roundup."

She couldn't deny a single one of his charges.

He sighed, pain she did not understand reflecting in his eyes. "This isn't about failing. It's about wanting you to be happy—and your dad knew it wouldn't be running a ranch."

Grant stood up and moved toward her. He looked like he was going to touch her and she couldn't bear it. She jumped up. "I need to get back to the house. I've got presents that still need wrapping." And she desperately needed time to think—to come to terms with Grant's role in her dad's decision. "I'll leave the cats here for now, if you don't mind."

He put his hand out to grab her, but she evaded him and rushed from the room.

Grant wanted to shoot something, and his dad, sitting next to Lottie and looking so calm, made a likely target. "Why the hell did you have to tell her I advised Jensen to sell?"

"I didn't know it was a state secret."

Grant gritted his teeth. "It wasn't. It was something Zoe didn't need to know and clearly won't understand."

"Maybe you should try explaining it to her again, when she's had a chance to calm down." Lottie laid a hand on his dad's forearm. "And maybe *you* should learn to leave well enough alone."

His dad shook his head. "I've left well enough

alone long enough. It hasn't gotten me one step closer to being a grandfather. Jensen neither."

Lottie groaned. "I should have known. So, you think putting their friendship at risk is going to catapult them into each other's arms?"

"It's worth a try. Jensen selling his ranch and leaving his daughter homeless sure as hell didn't do the trick."

Grant experienced a glimmer of understanding at his dad's belligerent words, along with more than a glimmer of aggravation. "Are you saying Zoe's dad sold the ranch to me as a way to bring the two of us together?"

His own father shrugged. "I'm not saying anything. But it's what I would have done if it had been left up to me."

Aggravation grew to anger. "And causing a major disagreement between Zoe and me is *your* idea of matchmaking?"

"It's time you two stopped dancing around each other and figured out the reason I don't have any grandchildren is because my son is in love with his best friend and too blind to see it."

Grant controlled the urge to yell. "I'm not blind."

It was his dad's turn to look enlightened. "So you figured out you loved her, did you?"

"I don't know about love, but I care about her."

"Hell, what else would you call it, boy?"

Grant remained stubbornly mute.

"Are you seeing each other again?" Lottie asked.

"We never stopped seeing each other."

"You know what I mean. Are you dating?"

After last night there could only be one answer to that question. "Yes."

His dad frowned. "So, what's the problem?"

"Don't you mean problems?" Grant sighed. "Zoe hated being a rancher's daughter. Really hated it. She was miserable on the ranch. But I belong here. And when I'm not here, I live in a world that doesn't impress her much either. She's a small-town girl, but not a rancher, and I'm not sure where that leaves us. Added to that, you've got her so mad at me I'm not sure she'll ever speak to me again."

"Are you sleeping with her, son?"

Tension arced right up Grant's spine and landed behind his eyes as a pulsing headache. Zoe was going to kill him, but she'd have to get him out of jail first, after he'd strangled his dad. "That's none of your business."

"I agree." Lottie's voice held the firm authority Grant had learned to respect as a child, and he knew his father didn't dismiss it lightly either. "Whatever is happening between the two of them is just that—between the two of them. I think you and Mr. Jensen have done enough."

His dad opened his mouth to speak, but closed it again at one look from Lottie's usually gentle gray eyes, now gone hard as slate. She turned her attention to Grant.

"Have you asked yourself what the ranch would mean to you if you lost Zoe because of it?"

"You mean like my dad had to do when you demanded he choose between you and his life as a rancher? He wouldn't give up the land for my mother, but he did for you, and, yes…maybe I'm beginning to understand how he could have made that choice."

But it wasn't one Grant wanted to make.

His dad leveled a look of censure at him. "Lottie may have made me choose between the ranch and her, but she didn't do it because she couldn't stand living the life of a rancher's wife."

"Then why did she do it?" Grant asked.

"I did it because your father was running his health into the ground, trying to run both the Cortez ranch holdings and his business ventures in Portland. He had a heart attack a couple of months before I gave him my ultimatum. It was a mild one, but the doctor told him something had to give."

Grant felt sucker punched and glared at his dad. "Why didn't you tell me?"

"I didn't want you to feel pressured into coming home from the east coast. You had your plans, and I wasn't going to ruin them, but then Lottie left for Portland and told me I could follow or be divorced."

"I meant it too." Lottie's eyes filled with a militant gleam. "I wasn't going to stick around to watch your father work himself into an early grave. Nothing was worth his health—not the ranch, nothing."

Grant couldn't argue with that. Lottie was right. His dad's health was more important than his former lifestyle, and Zoe was more important to Grant than his current one.

Nothing was worth losing Zoe. Not the ranch, nothing. Hell, it had to be love…nothing else could feel this damn scary.

As she drove toward the Pattersons', Zoe's mind kept replaying her conversation with Grant and his parents.

Grant had advised her dad to sell, and she couldn't blame him. Not when she thought about it rationally. He had been right. She didn't want to be a cattle rancher, and selling the ranch had been the only alternative that made sense for her parents. What he and her parents didn't seem to understand was her need to have been part of the decision—to have been legitimized as an important part of her family.

But that had not been Grant's choice. She clutched the cold steering wheel tightly, missing the gloves she'd forgotten to put on…again. She shouldn't have run out of Grant's house without talking out Roy's revelation. She'd left Grant believing she blamed him for her dad's rejection, and she didn't. She didn't even blame her dad. Losing his only son had broken something inside him and she'd never been able to fix it.

And she had to give her dad some credit. She had been a difficult child for a rancher to raise. She smiled at the memories Grant had brought up. She'd been too attached to the animals, and she'd spent hours drawing and writing stories when she was supposed to be doing chores.

It wasn't Grant's fault her parents didn't see her as a contributing member of their family unit either. But frankly that old pain had been well and truly superceded by a new one. Grant's advice to her dad only confirmed the lack of any hope for a future between them. He wasn't going to marry a woman who'd failed so miserably at the whole ranching lifestyle.

He might not realize it, but she knew he had major baggage left over from the three most important women in his life abandoning him for his lifestyle. He wouldn't risk marriage to someone who couldn't love him more than she hated ranching.

Zoe had spent the last four years running from her love for Grant, but she wasn't going to run any longer. She loved that stubborn rancher-tycoon more than anyone or anything else on earth, and she believed he loved her. He couldn't have made love to her the way he had otherwise. It had been too reverent...too spiritual. It had not been simple lust.

She would live in a snakepit if it meant being his wife. Telling him she wanted to share his life on a working cattle ranch was nothing in comparison.

She smiled with grim purpose as she turned into the Pattersons' drive. She had plans. The Christmas wrapping would have to wait. Grant had invited her to spend the holidays at the ranch, and she intended to accept his invitation.

Grant stood under the pulsing hot water, steam billowing around him, and closed his eyes.

Zoe had come back. She'd shown up on his door-step not two hours after she'd left. She'd come in through the front door again. There was significance in that, but he didn't know what. She'd had all of her stuff too, not just a suitcase.

He'd wanted to yank her into his arms and kiss her until neither of them could breathe, but she'd made it clear she didn't want to flaunt the physical side of their relationship in front of his parents. He would heed her wishes, but as soon as the household had gone to sleep he was going to Zoe's room—even if it meant tiptoeing down a dark hallway.

He reached for the soap and touched a feminine hand instead. "Let me do that."

He spun around at the sound of the soft female voice and ran into a lot more female flesh. Naked female flesh. He opened his eyes and blinked. He rubbed them and blinked again. He still couldn't see anything. "Zoe?"

Soft, soapy hands started gliding over his torso. "Who else would accost you in the shower?"

"No one." He reached out to touch her, trying to see her tantalizing body in the inky blackness. "What happened to the lights?" His hand connected with resilient flesh and he cupped her breast, reveling in the feeling of her turgid nipple against his palm.

Her breath hitched and her hands started kneading his chest. "I turned them off. I wanted it to be just you and me. Nothing else. Not even the light."

She moved a step closer and their bodies contacted from chest to knee.

He shuddered, feeling his hardened flesh press against the slick wet skin of her stomach. *"Querida—"*

She cut him off with a kiss, her lips sliding against his wet ones with erotic purpose. And just like that he gave up trying to figure out why the room had gone dark, or why Zoe had come to him at the risk of being caught out by his parents. He didn't care.

He kissed her with reckless male passion and caressed her back, then brushed his hands over her bottom, pressing her closer into his male heat. The dark lent a touch of unreality to their lovemaking. Talk about male fantasy. He'd take Zoe's version any day of the week.

They were alone in a world of their own, where ranches and cattle sold for beef had no place. Where no one and nothing could separate them. Where the past had no power to hurt and the present was nothing more than two bodies pressed close together in a darkness no light was allowed to penetrate.

Brushing the wet and curling hair on his chest, she shifted her legs apart until she straddled one of his thighs. He gave an involuntary groan at the first contact between her feminine juncture and his hair-roughened thigh. She caught her breath, tearing her lips from his to suck in more humid air, and moved experimentally against him. Sensation shot through

him as he felt a wetness on his thigh that had nothing
to do with the hot water cascading over them.

"Grant." His name coming out of the darkness in
her voice, rough with passion, shivered along his
senses like a caress.

She moved again, and made a startled sound when
he lifted his leg and tightened his grip on her bottom,
pressing her sensitive flesh more firmly against his
thigh. "Do you like that, baby?"

"I…" Her voice trailed off as he moved his leg
again, and she shuddered, crying out with irresistible
feminine passion.

He had thought making love with her the first
time had been the most mind-altering experience he
could possibly have, but this wasn't just amazing—
this was soul-transforming.

"Give it to me, Zoe. I want it all." He punctuated
each word with a movement of his thigh, rejoicing
as the sensitive skin against his thigh swelled and
went silky smooth with wetness. "That's right, *niña.*"

"Please, Grant. You can have anything."

He stopped moving, his hands gripping her so
tightly part of his conscious mind warned him about
bruising her. "Anything?"

"Yes! Anything, Grant. Anything!" She tried to
move on him again, but he wouldn't let her.

Instead he kissed her, a soft warm caress that felt
like the sealing of something incredibly important.
"Can I have your love? Will you give that to me?"

He waited in an agony of need, knowing her answer was more important to him than the desire clamoring for satiation.

Her hands came out of the darkness to cup his face. "I love you, Grant. I always have. I always will."

His body went rigid, and in a convulsive move he crushed her to him, spreading her legs more widely until he'd speared her with his hard maleness, giving them both what they craved. "I love you, Zoe. I will love you forever."

He pressed her against the shower wall, warm and slick from the hot spray, and drove into her with almost frightening intensity. He needed to slow down, but he couldn't. Her avowal of love had torn away his control, leaving only a primitive need to confirm that love in the most elemental way possible.

She didn't seem to mind as she hooked her legs around his waist, opening herself up completely to him. He drove into her with a circling motion, pressing the swollen bud of her pleasure against his pelvic bone with every thrust.

"I want to go so deep you can't remember what it's like not to be joined with me."

She gripped his shoulders with fingers like talons. "Yes!"

He made love to her with his entire body, his hands busy holding and touching her, his lips all over her face and neck, his chest rubbing her hardened nipples until she was screaming with pleasure and convulsing around him with one pulsing contraction after another.

He shouted as his release came over him, feeling one with her in a way he'd only ever known when his body was joined with Zoe's. He held her tightly to him as their breathing returned to normal. She kept her legs tightly wound around his waist.

"Ninety years of this is not going to be enough."

"Ninety years?" she asked, her voice sounding uncertain.

He kissed her forehead and gently disentangled their limbs, before pulling her back into the shower and washing her body with reverent care and a thoroughness that led her to another shattering explosion of physical sensation. When he finally turned the water off and pulled her from the shower, she held onto him like she needed his support to stay upright, while he groped in the dark for a towel.

He dried her off, kissing her body between tender swipes with the towel. She returned the favor, and it was all he could do not to initiate another bout of loving in the steam-filled room. He went to turn on the light.

"No. Don't."

"Baby?"

"There's something I want to say."

"And you want to do it while it's dark?"

He heard a soft sigh. "Yes. I don't want distractions or interruptions. Only the words. I want you to hear the words and believe them. Will you do that, Grant? Will you believe my words in the darkness?"

She sounded on the verge of tears, and he couldn't help reaching out to touch her. He found her arm, and from there settled both hands on her shoulders. "Yes. I'll believe anything you tell me, whether it's dark or not."

Her hands settled against his chest like the fluttering wings of a sparrow. "I love you."

"I love you, too."

One of her hands left his chest, and then he felt her finger tracing his lips, silencing them. "Thank you." Her shoulders rose and fell as she took a deep breath. "I know you think I can't be happy on a working ranch."

He nodded. Her fingers were still pressing his lips closed.

"You're wrong."

He reached up and gently pulled her hand away from his mouth. "What are you trying to say?"

"Living with you, loving you, will make me happy. Living without you would be hell. Please don't make me do it."

He pulled her into a tight embrace. "Never. I want to marry you. I want you to have my babies. I'm not the one who started talking about affairs instead of a future after the most passionate night of love between two people known to man."

He reached over and flipped on the light. "Marry me, Zoe." He cupped her face with one hand while the other held her close to him. "I love you more than the ranch, more than my freedom, more than anything in my life. Marry me."

Her eyes filled with tears. "I love you. I love you so much. I'll live on the ranch with you. I'll have your babies, and I'll be as stoic as they come every year at the stock sale."

He smiled and shook his head, covering her lips with his thumb when she opened her mouth to answer. "I'd give up the ranch, if that was what it would take to make you happy as my wife, but I don't think I'll have to."

She nodded her head in agreement. "You don't have to."

How he loved this woman. She would do it. She would live a lifestyle she hated to be with him, and he knew deep down in his gut that she would never ask him to leave it for her sake. Zoe's love wasn't like that. She gave with both hands.

"We've got a couple of alternatives. We can venture into horse ranching. I've thought about raising Arabians before, but the cattle always required too much of my time."

Her brown eyes grew round and big. "Horses?" she whispered against his thumb.

"Yes. Or breeding cattle. They aren't sold for beef. What do you think?" He moved his thumb so she could answer.

The tears in her eyes spilled over, but her smile left no doubt in his mind that they were tears of joy. "I think loving you is the greatest gift I've ever had in my life."

"And loving you makes my life a gift." He crushed her mouth under his, knowing in his heart that even if he had to sell the ranch he would always be happy and complete as long as he had Zoe by his side.

CHAPTER THIRTEEN

ZOE sat in perfect stillness as she soaked in the feeling of rightness surrounding her. Her parents weren't here, but this was still the best Christmas she could ever remember.

The pastor had announced her and Grant's upcoming wedding at the Christmas morning service, and her principal had looked very relieved. She allowed a small smile to curve her lips.

"What's so funny, angel?"

Grant walked into the room with his dad, who carried the camcorder. Lottie was right behind them.

They'd already gorged on Christmas dinner, and now the time had come to open gifts. Next to church, this was Zoe's favorite part of the day. "I was just remembering the look of abject relief on my principal's face when the pastor announced our imminent wedding."

Grant grinned. "He doesn't have to worry about having another talk with you, huh?"

She smiled in return. "Uh-uh."

He moved to sit next to her on the sofa and put one arm around her shoulder, hugging her to his body. "Ready to open your presents?" he asked in a husky whisper against her ear.

She shivered in sensual response. "Do any of them come packaged in fancy Spanish dye-tooled boots, well-worn jeans and red flannel?" she asked, describing his current attire.

He kissed her temple. "Not yet, *querida*, but soon."

She affected disappointment, but secretly thrilled to the anticipation he was building for their wedding night. He'd refused to make love again until they were married. She hadn't argued—not after he'd pointed out that they'd forgotten precautions in the shower and that he'd prefer their children were conceived after the wedding and not before.

Just then the doorbell rang, and Lottie left the room to answer it. Zoe was wondering who would be calling on Christmas Day when a familiar deep voice boomed from the entry hall.

"It's colder than a witch's tit out there."

Zoe sat paralyzed as her parents walked into Grant's living room. "You came."

"'Course we came," her dad said. "It's Christmas, ain't it?"

"Yes." It was Christmas, and her parents had come. She smiled at them. "I'm so glad to see you."

Her mother smiled warmly back, but her father actually walked right up to her and pulled her from the loveseat for a hug. "Glad to see you too, Zoe."

Her dad held her so tightly she could barely breathe, and he whispered two words into her ear she'd never expected to hear. "I'm sorry."

The pain of a lifetime couldn't be eradicated with a hug, but a lot of healing could happen—and did. Her mom pulled her into an embrace before Zoe could respond, but she squeezed her dad's arm as she let go of him.

Zoe turned to Grant. "Did you know they were coming?"

He nodded, and something in his eyes told her that he'd had something to do with it. He'd told her about their dads' attempts at matchmaking. Learning her dad had sold the ranch to Grant expecting it to pave the way for them to marry had helped detract from the lingering pain at the way he'd handled it.

She smiled at Grant, letting her love shine through. She mouthed the words for him alone.

I love you.

He put his hand out and drew her to him. "I love you, too, angel."

She sighed, and snuggled against him.

They were married on New Year's Day.

The church stood bright and beautiful in the winter sunshine, acting as a beacon as Grant walked through the side entrance, anticipation zinging through his body. Today Zoe would become his wife. He listened to the cacophony of voices and figured the majority of Sunshine Springs had turned out on short notice to witness his and Zoe's wedding.

A hush fell over the assembly, and the minister motioned Grant to take his place at the front of the church. Grant looked out over the crowded pews and smiled at their guests. Jenny and Tyler sat next to each other, their hands entwined. Grant's parents occupied the first pew to his right. Zoe's parents sat in the corresponding pew across the aisle.

Remembering Zoe's emotional reaction to her parents showing up at Christmas brought a smile to his face. She had cried when they arrived. She had cried again when he'd given her an engagement ring. For a woman who rarely wept, she had been very misty-eyed lately. He wondered if she would cry when she spoke her vows.

The "Wedding March" started and Grant fixed his eyes on the back of the church. The guests stood, and then Zoe filled his vision. She wore her grandmother's wedding dress. It hadn't required any alterations, and the old-fashioned lace and veil suited Zoe to perfection. Grant's heart constricted at the sight, and he felt his hands twitching to touch her. She smiled at him and he knew that the radiant happiness he saw in her eyes was reflected in his own.

She reached his side and the minister instructed Grant to take her hand. He spoke his vows with assurance, gazing directly into her eyes. When he said, "I do," his voice sounded strong, as if he had been practicing all his life. He felt like he had.

A scream rent the air. Grant and Zoe both spun around to see what the commotion was about. Carlene stood on a pew at the back of the church, her peach-colored miniskirt visible above the heads of the couple in front of her.

"Rodents!"

Grant groaned. Zoe laughed, and a little boy, looking uncomfortable in his Sunday best, pushed his way into the center aisle. "That's no rodent. That's my hamster. He used be Miss Jensen's. He wanted to see the wedding too."

Surprised gasps and shrieks followed this announcement. Within seconds the entire church was a massive scene of pandemonium. Everywhere but the front two pews. Zoe's and Grant's parents remained in their seats.

"We're used to this sort of thing, pastor. We raised her." Zoe's father's words, spoken with resignation but some humor too, brought a smile to Grant's lips.

"The hamster?" the minister asked.

"No. Our daughter. Zoe."

Grant met Zoe's eyes, and they both burst into laughter. He turned back to the minister. "Go on."

The pastor rubbed his hand across his bald head. "You sure? Wouldn't it be better to wait until the rodent is found?"

Zoe shook her head. "That's not a rodent. It's Bud, and they'll find him eventually. Please go on."

Grant hoped they caught Bud before the hamster found his way into the church walls and its wiring.

The minister led Zoe in her vows. When it was her turn to speak, Zoe took a deep breath. Tears misted her eyes and Grant was pleased that he had been right. Her voice was husky and full of emotion when she made her promises.

Tyler shouted from behind Grant. *"I've got him."*

Grant looked back over his shoulder to see a small furry head peeking out from Tyler's fist. It seemed only right that Bud had witnessed their marriage. After all, he had been instrumental in bringing Grant to his senses where Zoe was concerned.

He turned back to his wife. *His wife.* Damn, that sounded good. From the look in her eyes, she felt the same way. They smiled and turned together to face the minister, who was muttering about most irregular events. The pandemonium in the church settled down, and the minister finished the ceremony and gave Grant permission to kiss Zoe.

Grant lowered his head and took Zoe's mouth in a kiss that sealed their future and their love.

One Night Before Marriage

ANNE OLIVER

Anne Oliver lives in Adelaide, South Australia, and has two adult children. When not teaching or writing, she loves nothing more than escaping into a book. She keeps a box of tissues handy – her favourite stories are intense, passionate, against-all-odds romances. Eight years ago she began creating her own characters in paranormal and time travel adventures, before turning to contemporary romance. Sharing her characters' journeys with readers all over the world is a privilege…and a dream come true.

Anne Oliver's next steamy Modern Heat™
Mistress: At What Price?
is available in February 2010

This one's for you, Mum!
Also, thanks to my great critique team and to editors Kimberley Young and Meg Lewis for their valuable insight and revision suggestions to the original manuscript.

CHAPTER ONE

THE scent of her grandmother's perfume was the first sign. The prickle at her nape was the second. While Gran's scent was benign and loving and familiar, the second sign sent a shiver down her spine.

Carissa Grace never ignored signs.

Anxious, she scanned the stream of cars outside Sydney's Cove Hotel. Her stepsister Melanie had insisted on picking her up since Carissa's gig at the piano bar had finished after midnight tonight. That had been twenty minutes ago.

Hurry up, Mel. Something's—

The screech of brakes sheared through the balmy night, an agony of metal on metal over the mellow sound of sax drifting from a nearby nightclub. As the dented Holden mounted the kerb, its headlights loomed like silver lasers before her, terrifyingly stark against the subtle orange glow of the city night.

For a stunned second Carissa couldn't move. She was one with the crowd as it held its collective breath, movement halted, time suspended, minds frozen.

An instant later the car was gone, leaving only the acrid smell of exhaust fumes and hot bitumen.

'Anyone hurt?' a male voice demanded in a deep timbre that rippled down Carissa's spine like an arpeggio. In the awed hush that followed, a man emerged from the knot of people huddled against the hotel's sparkling lobby windows.

Tall, broad-shouldered. Awesome. He looked as dangerous as the chaos around him, from the heavily shadowed jaw and unkempt brown hair that curled over his neck to the faded black jeans and T-shirt. Not the kind of man she'd have expected to get involved in anything but trouble. Every 'bad boy' fantasy Carissa had ever had vibrated into shocking—and inappropriate—awareness.

'Someone call an ambulance.' His order snapped with authority.

Then she saw the form sprawled on the concrete. In two strides he was there, crouching over the slumped figure, speaking low. It was an old woman, Carissa realised, the bag lady she'd seen scrounging through the bin only moments ago. Despite the heat, she was covered from neck to ankle in a filthy coat. Her limbs flailed as she struggled up.

With no hesitation the man scooped a hand beneath her head, holding her against his thigh, murmuring soothing noises against her ear.

Carissa pulled herself together and hurried to rescue the woman's over-stuffed garbage bag nearby. Ignoring the crowd, which was curious but unwilling to get involved, Carissa set the bag down and crouched beside them. 'Here you go.'

The woman shot her an accusing glare as she grabbed the plastic.

'Is she okay?' Carissa asked.

'I reckon so,' he said, taking the woman's dirt-smudged fingers in his own large hand. 'But I'll get her checked out to be sure.' Preoccupied with his patient, he didn't look at Carissa.

Mingled with the odour of unwashed woman, she detected the distinct smell of male. A purely feminine appreciation sharpened her senses. It had been a long time since she'd smelled earthy masculine sweat. Alasdair always smelled of fancy French cologne. Nor could she imagine her fiancé handling this situation with such calm confidence.

The man sat the woman upright and stroked her back through the coat. His forearm twisted, drawing Carissa's attention to the gleaming silver of an expensive watch on his wrist. A disconcerting tingle spread through her limbs as she watched the muscles bunch and flex beneath his tanned skin. 'Do you think you can—?' A car's horn drowned the rest of his words to the old woman.

Carissa glanced at the street. Her ride. She raised a hand to Melanie as she backed away. Clearly he had everything under control and didn't need her assistance.

'Sorry I'm late,' Mel said as Carissa climbed in. 'Emergency was a war zone tonight. What's going on?' She honked her horn again and pulled into the traffic.

'We've had something of our own war zone.' Carissa's heart was still pounding with the drama. 'It's all under control now.' Thanks to the hero of the day.

Her gaze remained glued to the man as he ushered the bag lady towards the Cove's gleaming entrance. She could see the powerful square shape of his shoulders and his black T-shirt taut over one thick bicep.

A wildly sexy, *dangerous* man. He looked as if he'd just stepped out of one of her forbidden erotic dreams. The ones she'd been having with disturbingly increasing regularity of late.

She let out a sigh. She'd not seen Alasdair in a year, which made any man with half the rugged sex appeal of that stranger dangerous.

Not that she hadn't been more than willing to wait while Alasdair finished his PhD in France. But the promised twelve weeks had stretched into twelve long months.

She took one last look at temptation before turning to the red rear lights of the cars in front. A girl could only wait so long before that temptation reached out to tickle her fancy.

She shook away the delicious little shiver at the thought of the stranger's long, thick fingers reaching out to tickle *her* fancy… And bit back a moan. It was sexual frustration, that was all.

In seven days Alasdair would be home, and her bed was already turned down in anticipation. There'd be no more of that waiting he'd told her was the 'right thing' to do. Her already sensitised body hummed at the thought. Everything would be fine when Alasdair came back.

'Alasdair's not coming back.'

With the single handwritten page in her fist, Carissa sat down on the back step beside Melanie. The numbness had worn off enough to trust herself to talk about it. Rationally. Calmly. Maybe.

Mel's eyes widened. 'Oh, Carrie.' She set her iced tea on the verandah and reached for Carissa's hand. 'I'm so sorry,' she said quietly. 'You two have been together, what, seven years? What happened?'

'He's met someone else. I should've expected it with him studying overseas and all those chic mademoiselle research assistants.' She closed her eyes. 'But I *didn't* expect him to tell me his new love's name is *Pierre*.'

'Oh. God.' Melanie let out a slow breath. 'I don't know what to say.' She twined their fingers together. 'Are you okay?'

'I will be.' Carissa squeezed their hands briefly, then stood. A restless energy she didn't know what to do with was coursing through her body. 'I trusted him; I waited for him. Even though I wasn't sure any more that he was the One, I waited, at least until I saw him again. I must be the world's most naïve fool.'

'No. It's not your fault he's a two-timing creep—in the worst way. You sure you're okay?'

'Fine.' Enclosing that energy into a tight fist, she crumpled the paper and squinted against the glare of the parched backyard. The hot summer wind kicked up, rattling the loose drainpipe she hadn't gotten around to fixing yet.

'It's been so long, I'm used to it. My life will go on as usual. I've got my own place, such as it is.' She frowned at the sagging porch trim. Her grandparents' old home needed major repairs. 'And a job.'

'You've still got me,' Mel said quietly.

'I know.' She met Mel's eyes with shared affection before turning away. 'Want to know a secret, Mel? I've still got my well-past-its-use-by-date virginity.'

'You mean you and Alasdair never...? Oh...'

Carissa paced up the verandah and back. 'Now I

know why Alasdair was so noble and self-sacrificing. Every time I came on to him he said I'd thank him for making me wait.'

'So...days before your twenty-sixth birthday, you're still a virgin?' Melanie blew out a breath. 'Wow.'

'At this rate, on my fifty-sixth birthday, I'll be taking out a full-page ad.'

The urge to lash out rose up like a black wave. She needed to channel the energy productively. Some serious piano-pounding. Something dark and passionate. Bach, she decided. The fly-screen door squeaked on rusty hinges as she swung it open.

Melanie followed. 'Do you really want your life to go on as usual? No man, no sex, no fun?'

Carissa's hand paused on the door. *Don't answer that.*

'You need a fling, Carrie, a one-night stand.'

The suggestion was outrageous. And at this point Carissa felt almost reckless enough to consider it. 'You know, Mel, I just might take your advice.' She tossed the balled paper in the bin on her way.

'Don't rush it, though,' Mel warned as if she'd gone cold on the idea already. 'You want your piano tuned, you don't call a plumber.'

'So what's wrong with a plumber if he's got the right equipment?' Carissa couldn't help smiling at Mel's frown. She slung an arm around the one person she could always count on to look out for her. 'I'll be careful.'

The usual Saturday evening crowd buzzed in the Cove Hotel's piano bar. Carissa's eyes roamed the faces while she played her selection of dreamy Chopin nocturnes. She noted the few regulars, but most were anonymous tourists with a couple of hours to kill before heading off to Sydney's nightclubs.

So much for finding a man. Working six evenings a week seriously impinged on one's social life. She hadn't had a social life in so long, she wasn't sure she was ready for centre stage in the dating scene just yet.

She saw him the moment he entered the room.

He filled the doorway, all six-feet-four-if-he-was-an-inch of him. Her fingers faltered as she drank in the rock-solid body crammed into faded denim and black T-shirt.

Her mouth watered. God help her, if she could choose, she wanted that body, naked and next to hers. It was the kind of body that made women forget all about sexual equality—there was absolutely nothing *equal* about it.

Her fingers automatically drifted into *Moonlight Sonata* as her eyes followed him to the bar. She watched him order a beer, then move to a table near the window where the last rays of sunset turned the water beyond to liquid fire and the white tablecloths crimson, and glittered on his fancy silver watch.

Oh. My. God. It was the guy she'd seen last night. Her pulse rate zipped straight off her personal Richter Scale. He'd shaved.

But he was still dangerous.

She shifted on her stool for a better view of yesterday's hero. The evening glow accentuated the angular contours of a tanned face on the wrong side of pretty-boy handsome and a strong, shadowed jaw. Mid-thirties, give or take. His teak-coloured hair, although shorter, was still somewhat dishevelled, as if he'd run his fingers through it, prompting images of lazy lust-filled afternoons on black silk sheets.

She should be so lucky.

But he had the most soulful eyes she'd ever seen. She reached for her mineral water, checked her watch and sighed. Two hours and ten minutes till she finished for the night—but he'd be gone by then.

Ben Jamieson flicked an eye over the pianist, then returned for a longer, in-depth perusal. And decided his evening had just taken a turn for the better. Why spend it alone dwelling on his own personal anguish when the distraction he needed was right here?

Rave would tell him to go for it—he could almost see his mate grin and raise a glass in salute to women everywhere. For tonight at least he could appreciate the soothing harbour view while he watched those clever—and ringless—fingers on the keys.

Kicking back, he took a large gulp of beer and studied her. The way those fingers tickled the ivories, he imagined they could do a pretty good job on a man.

So classical wasn't his thing. The classic lines of the pianist more than made up for it. That full-length slinky sapphire number she'd poured herself into begged to be taken off. Slowly, an inch at a time. You didn't hurry over a body like that.

Tall, he noted, but not too tall. Like a long, slim candle. He'd bet she'd burn with a cool blue flame, and damned if he didn't want to singe his fingers. And that hair—a loose twist of sunshine at the crown of her head, held by a sequinned clasp. There was something about upswept hair that made his fingers itch. That smooth, exposed nape, and all that silk tumbling into his hands.

It was shaping up to be an interesting evening after all.

* * *

As Carissa launched into another bracket of light classics she couldn't resist another peek. He didn't look the classical type. His music preferences didn't bother her. His head turned as if he'd felt her watching him, and their gazes collided over the raised lid of the baby grand. Instant heat flooded her body.

She dragged her eyes away, fumbled with the keys again and swore softly. She'd played the cocktail bar Friday and Saturday nights for two years and not missed a note. With her brain threatening meltdown, she reached for her sheet music and refused to look his way again.

Concentrate on the important issues, she reminded herself. Such as not losing this gig and how she was going to pay the land-tax bill. Her Monday to Thursday job at the suburban café paid half what she made here. Even the extra money a lodger would bring in would only skim the top of the pile, and if she didn't get someone pronto she'd have to advertise beyond the staff cafeteria; something she didn't want to do. Always risky for a woman living alone.

She'd always been able to put distractions aside when she played. Not tonight. Tonight she couldn't raise the shield that shut out the rest of the world. She was all too aware of the clink of glass and ice and money, conversation, the light outside as it changed from dusk to dark.

And him.

At ten-thirty Carissa closed the piano, shuffled her music into a neat pile and slipped it into its folder.

'Can I buy you a drink?' The deep liquid voice with its hint of gravel made her jump.

The scent of aftershave and beer hit her as she turned,

her habit of a cool smile and polite refusal already on her lips, but the words died in her throat.

Something like panic leapt up and grabbed her by the throat, then worked down to her stomach, squeezing the air out of her lungs on its way. 'Sorry, management doesn't permit employees to socialise with guests.'

Refusing—was she nuts? Taking a deep breath, the new, unattached Carissa smiled. 'Leastways, not in the hotel.'

He grinned. 'A walk, then, and a drink by the waterfront. The name's Ben Jamieson.' One corner of his mouth lifted crookedly, revealing the most kissable dimple in his right cheek. Up close she saw that his eyes were bright jungle-green and sparking with interest.

She clutched her folder to her chest to hide the sudden tremble in her hands. 'I've a train and a bus to catch, and I don't like to leave it too late.'

'I'll pay your cab fare home.'

'Oh...I...'

'Walk with me. It's a pleasant evening and we'll only go as far as you want.'

Those erotic images popped into her head again, but if he'd intended it as a double entendre he was astute enough to show no sign.

She smiled as she pushed in the piano stool. 'It's the best offer I've had all night.' The best in years, in fact, and the mind-set was still taking some adjustment.

'Why don't you start by telling me your name?'

'Carissa.' She kept her eyes on his, aware of his body heat, his fresh soap smell, his masculinity. *Dangerous,* she warned herself. 'Just Carissa.'

He smiled again, and everything inside her melted a

few more degrees. 'So, Just Carissa, do you have a bag or something?'

'In the staff locker room. I'll change and meet—'

'No.' His eyes didn't leave hers, but their green fire scorched all the way to her toes. 'Do me a favour—don't.'

She cleared her throat. 'Okay… But I need my bag.'

He accompanied her past the press of bodies at the bar, and across the foyer, checked his messages—ah, he was a residential guest—while she headed for the locker room.

Her brain was a whirl; her insides were doing a quick shuffle. To waltz off with a complete stranger—she'd never done anything so impulsive or so reckless.

'Why don't we combine the two and walk to the station?' she suggested as they walked out into Sydney's tropical summer evening.

Streetlights attracted bugs, which hummed in a seething ball around the globes. A languid breeze drifted off the water.

He glanced at her. 'Why? Is someone expecting you?'

If she was going to back out, now was the time. But he was on a first name basis with the concierge, had a room there, and people had seen them leave together. 'There's no one.'

'I don't like the idea of a woman catching a train alone at this time of night. Then a bus, for heaven's sake. Do you always travel by public transport?'

'Since I sold the car.'

His hand touched the small of her back as he ushered her to a table at an open-air café. Just a brush of fingertips on the silk of her dress, but the thrill curled her toes inside her four-inch stilettos.

'What would you like?'

You. 'Mineral water over ice, thank you.' She sagged onto the plastic chair he pulled out for her and slipped her bag onto the ground beside her feet. She didn't need anything stronger to have that dizzy, tipsy rush.

He paid at the counter, handed her a glass and lowered himself into the chair opposite with a bottle of beer. 'Here's looking at you.'

The way he said that had shivers chasing over her skin. To distract him from her nipples that suddenly puckered painfully into tight little buds against her dress she asked, 'You like music?' He didn't reply and a shadow crossed his eyes. She watched his fist tighten infinitesimally around the neck of his bottle. 'Okay, you don't like classical and you're too polite to say so.'

'Doesn't matter what it is when it's played with heart and soul by a woman whose...what colour would you say your eyes are?'

She blinked, glass poised halfway to her lips. 'Blue.'

'Blue.' He rubbed a hand over his jaw, a distinctively masculine sound, as he watched her. 'I'd say ultramarine. Deep and mysterious. Which begs a question: what do you do when you're not at the keyboard, Just Carissa?'

'Waitressing and piano take up six days a week. I don't have time for much else.'

It amazed her that she could sit here and make reasonable conversation with this man when all she could think of was what he'd look like with every inch of golden skin bared for her pleasure, every working part primed to— *Stop right there.* She mentally slapped herself and asked, 'What about you?'

He glanced at the water, avoiding her gaze. 'I have a few business interests.'

She eyed him over her glass. 'When you're not being a hero.'

'I beg your pardon?'

'Last night. I was outside the Cove, I saw you.'

He took a deep gulp of beer. The shadows were back in his eyes. 'I'm no hero.'

'Wrong. I was there. You risked yourself for others, stopped to help an old lady most people would avoid.'

'No big deal. And it was hardly a risk; the car was gone. Those stupid kids…' He shook his head. 'We'll all end up in the sewer one day.'

'You're not an optimist, then. You don't believe good outweighs bad? That everything happens for a reason?'

He seemed to remember something sad because his mouth thinned even more, and he smiled without humour. 'I'm more of a realist. Realists are rarely disappointed.'

He had a point there. A realist would have expected Alasdair to walk. Good-looking guys, whatever their gender preference, didn't hang around for long. 'What about your family?' *Is there a fiancée waiting to be jilted somewhere?*

'I grew up in Melbourne. Never married, never tempted. Lived in the outback, came to the city a few years ago.'

'Your parents?'

'Mum's in Melbourne. My father's dead.'

End of story. Chewing her lip, Carissa watched him toss back the contents of his bottle. His father's death must have hit him hard and he didn't want to talk about it. 'Are you staying at the Cove long?'

'Not sure yet.'

She saw the residual tension in his hand as he set

the empty bottle on the table with a clunk. The man had problems. Did she want to get involved? But she remembered last night. He was one of the good guys. Besides, she wasn't getting *involved* involved.

'Come on,' he said, slowly reverting to the flirtatious man she'd started out with. 'It'll be cooler by the water.'

They left the glare of lights and wandered to where the air was shadowed and filled with the scent of sea and summer. Carissa took off her shoes and lifted her face to the faint breeze. 'I've worked at the Cove for two years and never walked here.'

'A night for firsts.'

She almost smiled. He didn't know the half of it.

He stopped and looked down at her. 'Do you know what I was thinking about while I was watching you play?'

'What?' The word spilled out on a husky, almost breathless exhalation.

He lowered his mouth till it was a sigh away from hers. 'This.' He skimmed her lips with his own, a tantalising hint. 'Touching you. Tasting you.'

Oh, yes, she thought, her mouth tingling with the promise. *Me too.*

He tangled calloused fingers with hers, watching her. Still watching her, he deliberately pressed his body against hers. One body part in particular. One very thick, very hard, very insistent body part.

She didn't step back. He was big, he was male, and, unlike her ex-fiancé, he wanted her. He lowered his lips again, and, dropping her shoes, she leaned into him, her bag skimming her hip as she wound her arms around his neck.

Her mind shut down. Her senses went into overdrive. The flavour of his mouth, beer and something salty, the textures of tongue and teeth as he deepened the kiss, his roughened fingertips skimming her arms.

After the first flutter of nerves she relaxed and acquainted herself with the new and exciting sensation of male arousal against her belly. So far, so good, but how would it feel horizontally? With no clothes on?

She wanted to know how it felt to have a man's weight on her, to have him pumping all that heat and strength inside her. She wanted to know whether fantasy lived up to reality. And she wanted *this* man to be the one to show her.

She'd never have to see him again. If she didn't ask more personal questions, didn't get to know him, she could walk away, no emotional ties, the way men did. Her birthday present to herself. She hadn't taken anything for herself in a long time. And Melanie would definitely approve.

He pulled back, hands on her elbows, his eyes dark with lusty impatience. 'What do you want to do about this?'

A ball of heat lodged in her gut, her knees went weak, her pulse hammered. Keeping her eyes on his, she reached up, trailed unsteady hands down the unfamiliar contours of his neck.

Sex with a stranger. Through his T-shirt she rubbed over his tight little nipples with her thumbs before moving over the plane of chest and stomach to the fabric's hem. She crept her fingers underneath and found hot, hard flesh. Then she hooked her hands in the waistband of his jeans. And tugged.

His stomach muscles tensed against her knuckles.

His breath jerked in. He'd think her easy and experienced. She stifled an almost hysterical laugh.

'Carissa, I can put you in a cab now, or we can continue this in my room. The decision's yours.' Restless hips shifted against her fingers. 'But make it quick.'

Something hot and dangerous shot through her body like a flame-tipped arrow. She only had to say, and she could be in his room. In his bed.

In the Cove Hotel.

She let out a frustrated breath. 'Employees aren't permitted in guests' rooms.'

'Is that a "no" or a problem?'

'A…problem?' She shrugged. 'Rules are rules.'

His eyes crinkled at the corners as he watched her. He smiled that crooked smile as he took her hands from his jeans, rubbed a thumb over her knuckles. 'So we'll break a few rules.'

CHAPTER TWO

THEY separated before they reached the door and met again at the elevator. Shocked, Carissa watched as Ben keyed his card. 'The penthouse?'

'I like space and a room with a view.'

Seconds later the elevator doors whooshed open. She stepped into the room and stared. Low lighting didn't dim the view of Sydney's coat-hanger bridge, the Opera House like luminous swans on the harbour. The room was black on white. Silver glinted, marble shone. The whole scene screamed money. 'Wow.'

He moved to the full-length glass door, slid it open. Sheer curtains billowed in on the sultry breeze. 'One of the best views in the world,' he said.

She hadn't come for the view. She hadn't even come for romance.

She'd come for sex.

And the man of the moment lounged against the balcony with wind in his hair, an intriguing blend of casual and remote as he stared over the water. Her first lover, a man she didn't know.

The jolt of realisation must have shown on her face

because when he finally looked at her, the expression warmed. 'Relax and come here.'

She swallowed and stayed where she was. 'I want you to know, I'm not in the habit— I mean…this isn't…' Now she was babbling and way out of her depth.

'I like you pink and flustered. An interesting contrast to that cool, classical beauty at the piano.'

Shifting into defence mode, she lifted her chin. 'I am not flustered.' But she did relax when she saw the glint of humour in his eyes as he came towards her.

'Okay, then…' He trailed fingers of fire up the side of her neck and into her hair under her clasp at the back of her head. 'Sophisticated *naïveté.*'

A buzzer dinged. Her eyes whipped to the elevator door.

'Hey.' He squeezed her nape. 'I told you to relax. Admire the view a moment.'

She turned away and waited out the brief exchange and the sound of the doors sliding shut before turning back.

'Happy Valentine's Day. Red roses for a blue lady.' He held out the dozen perfect long-stemmed buds.

Oh, my. Something inside her sparkled, like a snowflake under the first rays of spring sunshine. No one had ever given her flowers. 'They're beautiful, thank you.' She buried her nose in their rich velvety fragrance. 'But Valentine's Day was yesterday.'

'Somewhere in the world it still is.'

'How did you manage these? It's after midnight.'

'The gift shop's always open for the right people.'

What did he mean by that? Who *was* Ben Jamieson? Someone important? Obviously someone with money to burn.

Still, something about being here with him, surrounded by the fragrance of summer roses, made her
want to weep. She'd never think of Valentine's Day
again without remembering Ben Jamieson. He'd
reached deep inside her and found something she'd been
determined to keep buried. Need. A need for more than
simple lust.

But with that need came vulnerability. *Don't get
emotionally involved. You're walking away tonight;
you'll never see him again.* 'You shouldn't have,' she
said, caressing a bud.

'Why not?' He tipped her chin up. 'You in that blue
dress makes me wish I could whisk you away to the top
of the Sydney Tower. Just us and the stars.'

Clasping her hand, he led her to the balcony where
said tower shone like a golden lollipop. Lights shimmered on black water. Somewhere below music drifted,
the breeze sighed.

This wasn't supposed to happen. With gentle persua-
sion he was changing something simple into something
romantic and complicated.

He took the roses, laid them on the smoked-glass
table and cupped her face before lowering his lips.

Again his mouth was firm yet soft, and moved over hers
in a slow, sensuous kiss that had her mind blotting out all
thoughts but the mindless pleasure of it. His hands moved
to her shoulders, kneading away the growing tension.

Her world was suddenly intense, alive and filled with
colour and movement. She heard the muted noise of
traffic and a distant ferry's horn as he pulled her closer.
The sensation of falling, spinning, had her clutching at
his chest, sleek muscle over bone.

'Come with me.' Twining their fingers together, he walked her through an arch to the adjoining room.

The bedroom was as impressive as the rest of the suite. A single black-shaded lamp threw out a muted, seductive glow in one corner. The king-size bed had been turned down for the night and her heart leapt at its intimate invitation.

Skilled fingers slipped inside the back of her dress and down. The zipper slid open with a whisper, the hooks of her bra loosened. Smoothing his hands over her shoulders, he skimmed down her arms until her dress and bra fell to the floor and she stood only in high-cut sapphire panties, lace-topped thigh-high blue stockings and spiky-heeled shoes.

His eyes darkened and he stepped back. 'Leave them on,' he said as her fingers moved to her thighs. 'I want to look.'

Goosebumps chased over her body; her nipples puckered and throbbed. The whole thing was surreal; she felt like a model in a men's magazine.

He blew out a long breath, arms crossed over his chest. 'You're a living fantasy. Now take off the panties— slowly. Very slowly.'

With an excitement she'd never felt, she hooked her fingers in the skinny blue straps and slid them down her thighs. She could see the sweat beading his brow as he shifted his stance, drawing her attention away from his face to the straining and impressive bulge in his jeans. Oh, God.

He gestured to the discarded undies. 'Put them on the bed.'

Why? Then she felt his eyes consume her body as she bent down to obey his request and knew the answer.

'Now release your hair. With both hands.'

Her breasts lifted with the movement, swollen and heavy. She let out an uneven breath as she tossed the clasp on the floor and separated the thick strands. He'd barely touched her and she was glowing.

'Anticipation's half the fun,' he murmured. But he sure didn't smile as if he was having fun. A muscle in his jaw clenched; his mouth hardened.

Her cheeks were on fire, and, yes, anticipation—every pulse point hammered with it. She focused on his gaze and told him with her eyes.

But he didn't reach for her. With a swift tug, he rid himself of his T-shirt, tossed it on the floor beside her dress. His eyes burned. 'Touch me.'

She swallowed over a healthy dose of nerves. Clothed, no problem, but alone with a semi-naked man and knowing he was going to get a lot more naked any minute... What if he wanted her to do...something she didn't know how to do?

Get a grip, he's only asked you to touch him. So far. Tentative, she touched the dark hair sprinkled over that massive chest, felt the texture against the warm, hard skin beneath. She trailed her fingers lower, following the line of hair to his navel and below, where his jeans rode low on his hips...

Taking her hand, he pressed it against his thick, throbbing erection and squeezed. Heat burned through his jeans; his body jerked. Very soon, that heat, that hardness was going to be inside her. The last thing she needed was a pregnancy. She gazed up into his eyes again. 'You do have protection. Don't you?'

'It's okay, Carissa. I won't let anything happen to you. Trust me.' Then with a growl he tumbled her backwards onto the bed. One shoe fell to the floor. A flick of his wrist and his jeans snapped open. He pushed them off his hips, down his legs with his boxers and a hard, hairy thigh nudged between her legs.

The contrasts were stunning. His heat, the angles and planes of his masculine body, the coolness of the crisp cotton sheet, the sultry air against her dewy skin.

Soft light played over bronzed flesh and hard-packed muscle and his, oh…his restless hands as they slid across her belly and up over her breasts. He sifted his fingers through her hair with a murmur of masculine appreciation.

Lowering his head, he closed his mouth over one nipple, then the other. She felt the tug all the way to the soles of her curled feet. She arched her back on a moan as sensation layered over sensation.

The stockings were last to go. He took his slow sweet time, his fingers brushing aside the nylon, laying a sensuous trail of kisses behind until there wasn't a square inch of skin that wasn't tingling. Except where she wanted him most.

At last, when she didn't think she could stand it any longer, he parted her thighs with his hand and slid a finger over moist flesh that had never been touched. She went weak, moaned again. She'd never dreamed it could feel this…*good.*

He was familiar with things about her woman's body she'd never known. Exactly the right place to touch. When to stroke, slide, dip or plunge. How absolutely arousing a slow, smooth hand could be. Their world became her only world.

'Ben…' She couldn't help the breathy little sounds coming from her throat, couldn't help arching blindly towards the source of that pleasure. But there was more; something just out of reach. Something her body instinctively sought. 'Ben, I want…I need…'

'I know.' The hot glide of his clever fingers over slick and swollen flesh increased. Darts shot through her body, lights exploded behind her eyes. Her body spasmed as her climax ripped through her, sending her to another dimension.

He was still there when she floated back to earth. Time drifted like the tide, the air hung heavy, languid, scented with desire.

Then he rolled away, reached for something on the night stand. She heard the rip of foil and closed her eyes as his weight settled over her. She felt his heart thundering against her breast, his breath hot against her ear, and prepared to be swept away.

But when the blunt tip of his sex nudged her, rosy dreams and soft sighs vanished, and reality intruded like a harsh white light. The magnitude of what she was doing hit her.

Too late. With one deep thrust that stole the air from her lungs, he pushed inside her, then went utterly still. And bit out a short four-letter word.

She tensed at the quick sharp pain and held her breath, trying not to panic. She felt impaled, his hardness invasive and foreign. Only his rapid and heavy breathing broke the silence.

'Why didn't you tell me?'

'You didn't ask.' She could barely speak, so focused was she on her own body and what was happening to her. Already the pain was subsiding, already she wanted more. Until an added vulnerability cooled her enthusiasm. Perhaps he didn't like virgins; perhaps the reason he was speaking in that harsh tone was because he was disappointed. 'Does it matter?'

'Too bloody right.' He carefully withdrew a little, propped himself on his elbows over her and dropped a sweat-damp forehead on hers. 'There are rules…'

'We…I…broke a rule coming here. You said—'

'*My* rules. There's a difference.' He traced a finger over her cheek, her lips. There was a myriad emotions in his eyes. 'Why now…why me?'

'Because I want it, because you're here. Please…' She grasped his hand, took it to her breast. 'Tonight you've made me feel beautiful and so alive.'

An infinitely more wary look crossed his face. 'Don't make this into something it's not, Carissa. I'm not that man of your dreams, nor am I a settling-down kind of guy. This is all there is.'

She swallowed and forced herself to remember how it was. 'This is all I want. I'm not looking for permanence. That makes us ideal partners for this evening.' She twined her arms around his neck and experimentally moved her hips.

His jaw tightened, his arms quivering with the strain of holding his weight off her. 'Look, Carissa, I don't want to hurt you…'

'Don't give me that sexist rubbish about it being different for a woman.' She raked her nails over his back and the hard curve of his buttocks, making him shudder.

'Well, then. You'll want something worth remembering.' His eyes darkened. '*That* I can give you.'

He was true to his word.

Hungry for his taste, his body and completion, she took what he gave greedily, storing the sensations and emotions for later. Dark, heavy heat engulfed her, molten fire flowing through her veins, spreading over her skin. Her body relaxed as she became familiar with him moving over and within her. She'd never forget this one time with him. He was everything she'd dreamed of and then some.

Strength. His body was hard and smooth against hers, tempered with a gentleness she hadn't expected.

Patience. Another surprise, his willingness to linger over small things—a touch, a kiss, a murmur.

Tenderness. It flowed from his touch like soft summer rain.

And when the ache built again and became unbearable, he knew, and let her fly.

After, he lay silent and still, holding her against him, but somehow removed. As if he'd distanced himself.

How it should be, she told herself. He'd be moving on and she'd go back to her two jobs, her falling-down house and her debts.

But rather than the satisfaction she'd expected, she felt…empty. And cheated somehow, as if she'd opened the door to another world and had it slammed in her face. And she still had to find a way out of his arms, out of this hotel and home—without being seen by management.

She hadn't meant to fall asleep. That was her first coherent thought when she woke to the unfamiliar weight of a hand on her abdomen. As she surfaced the night flooded back in a tide of exquisite sensations and images. For a fuzzy moment she drifted with them, aware of a vague tenderness in her lower body and a sense of togetherness she'd never experienced.

Then she blinked as her brain caught up. A grey-pearl sky heralded approaching dawn. A jolt of panic swept through her. Her reputation and job were at stake here. She fought the impulse to leap off the bed. Slow was the wisest course; the last thing she wanted to do was wake him.

She couldn't resist a last look. She'd never seen a naked man for real. Her moist, tender flesh throbbed at the sight of the thick jut of his sex, which seemed to augment as she watched. Her gaze shot to his face, but he was relaxed, long lashes resting on his cheeks.

Heart racing, she turned away. *Get out while you still can.* Easing her body out from under his arm was no mean feat, but he was dead to the world, his breathing calm and even.

Her stockings lay at the foot of the bed. She grabbed her bra and dress from the floor, hesitated before stuffing bra and stockings in her bag. She wriggled into the dress, jerked the zip up, then twisted her hair into its clasp while she searched for shoes.

Her panties were nowhere in sight, buried somewhere among the rumpled sheets or under that heavy, slumbering body. She had no intention of risking him waking, and counted the loss of a pair of knickers a minor one under the circumstances.

Then she noticed his wallet on the night stand. Money. Thank you, God. She hunted up pen and paper in her bag, wrote an IOU, promising him she'd reimburse him at the desk tomorrow, then slipped a bill into her purse. Couldn't be helped—he'd offered, and she absolutely, positively couldn't catch a train wearing nothing but an evening dress at six o'clock in the morning.

She looked longingly at the roses, but she couldn't take them. *Goodbye, Ben Jamieson.* She refused to look at him again as she stole from his room and out of his life.

Through barely raised eyelashes Ben watched her stumble quietly around his room. He'd lain awake the whole night afraid he'd succumb to his usual nightmare and scare her. And embarrass himself.

There was enough light to showcase the slender curves, the glint of gold at her ears and her shadowed secret places as she bent to find her clothes. She straightened, hesitated, giving him a close-up of those tempting globes of flesh with their dark puckered nipples.

Then she turned her back to him and slithered naked into her long blue tube, an innocent striptease in rewind. His blood heated, his already hardened sex turned painful and he had an irresistible urge to lay his lips on that moon-pale patch of skin above the swell of her bottom. Then she yanked the zip up and the moment was lost. Probably just as well.

He wondered if she intended catching her train at this hour, in that state of dress, and what he was going to do about it. He was relieved when he saw her write something on a scrap of paper, then slide a single furtive bill from his wallet. She could have robbed him blind. The fact that she didn't only confirmed what he already knew. Carissa was an honest if naïve young woman.

Her movements ruffled the air so that her scent

wafted to his nose. Not an expensive perfume, but a scent that made him think of a spring morning—cool, fresh, unspoiled. Maybe she was too embarrassed to face him—she'd obviously never done the morning-after routine. It beat the hell out of him why a woman would opt for a stranger for her first sexual experience.

He watched her leave his room and head for the elevator, then stretched, punched up the pillow and shoved his hands behind his head. The trouble with virgins—one intimate encounter and they started looking at engagement rings. Carissa was different.

He heard the elevator doors open, close, and felt more alone than he'd felt before he'd met her. As if she'd taken part of him. Which was plain stupid. No woman took anything from Ben Jamieson.

Throwing off the sheet, he padded to the window to catch a glimpse of her. There. He watched her hail a cab, climb in and drive away. His fists clenched on the window ledge. Damn her for making him feel…needy. He didn't want to get involved. Not with her, not with anyone. And not now, when his life was going down the toilet.

Moving to his bed, he reached into his jeans pocket and pulled out the slender gold chain he'd slipped off her wrist. Antique, by the looks. Insurance, he told himself, pocketing it once more. He could see her again if he wanted, if he chose to. He knew where she was on a Friday and Saturday night. Simple.

Or he could keep it even simpler. *Just Carissa,* an intimate stranger who'd shared his bed for a night. Some soft curves in the bumpy road that was his life right now.

She didn't know he had her bracelet. And her panties, he noted, spotting the scrap of blue silk on the bed amongst the tumbled sheets. Ah well, he'd have them gift wrapped and handed in to her at the front desk. But he'd see she got the bracelet back personally.

A girl with her classical background wouldn't know anything about a band like XLRock, he decided, hunting up a room-service menu. Rave's band had needed financial backing to get started and Ben had been happy to put down the money.

Fourteen years ago in a tiny pub on the edge of the Nullabor Plain, Ben had taken the fifteen-year-old runaway pickpocket under his wing and taught him to play guitar. The kid had become a runaway star.

Ben stared sightlessly at the ceiling. All he saw was Rave. A couple of weeks ago he'd stepped in with his own guitar to help out when one of the band members had quit on the eve of the open-air concert, Desert Rock. But Ben hadn't been able to resist the lure of Broken Hill's Musicians' Club on the way home.

The memory taunted him. His stomach tied itself into those familiar knots and he decided he wasn't hungry after all. Grimly he grabbed his jeans from the floor where he'd shucked them last night and headed for the shower.

Adjusting the temperature to just above cold, he let the water pelt him and shivered as he soaped up. He could still see the frustration in Rave's eyes. But he'd grown accustomed to the tantrums. 'Jess won't mind one extra night, Rave. Phone her and blame me. Here, take the Porsche for a spin.' He'd handed him the car keys himself.

It was the last time he'd seen him.

Ben wrenched off the taps, pressed his fingers to his

eyelids. He hadn't expected Rave to be irresponsible enough to get plastered before he got behind the wheel. He should have seen it. He'd tried to escape the visions that plagued him—waking, sleeping—but the guilt stuck like barbed wire.

And the nightmares kept coming.

For one brief evening, Carissa had made him forget.

When he re-entered the main room, the *Sydney Morning Herald* had been slipped beneath the door by some faceless night porter. Without glancing at the headlines he tossed it into the bin. He was so tired of the smell of impersonal hotel rooms. Sick of the sight of staff with their plastic smiles, the clatter of service trolleys.

He turned to the spectacular view of high-rises against a gold sky. Just once he wanted to look out a window and see an untidy cottage garden or a stand of stringy eucalypts, a wooden letterbox with the paint peeling off. How many years had it been since he'd slept in a house? A home? Too damn many.

He needed a place where no one who knew him could find him. Space where he could think for a few days before the gut-wrenching prospect of facing up to Jess.

Even if he had to pay a couple of months' rent for a few days, the room on Sydney's coast advertised in the staff cafeteria might just be the temporary hideaway he was looking for.

CHAPTER THREE

Sliding his sunglasses down his nose, Ben studied the house from his hire car, checked the ad again. 'Want a quiet retreat away from city noise?' it read. 'Spacious old family home. Own bed/sitting/bathroom, share kitchen. Meals cooked if preferred.'

The house itself was a gracious old bungalow but someone had let it go. The midday sun glared off a khaki lawn and a row of straggling rose bushes. Faded paintwork was peeling along the verandah and around the windows. The roof sagged and one of the wooden steps leading to the front door was missing.

Mozart—at least he thought it was—drifted through an open window as he unfolded himself and climbed out of the car. He pushed open the gate, caught the scents of coffee and fresh-baked cake as he walked up the path.

He knocked and a voice sounded from somewhere inside. The door opened and a young woman with a long flow of black hair and grey eyes looked out. Her skimpy olive crop-top revealed smooth tanned skin. Black Lycra shorts clung to shapely legs. She was, in a word, a knockout.

'Good morning, my name's Ben Jamieson. I've come about the room.'

She stared at him a moment, then her mouth curved into a wide grin. 'Hey, Carrie, your piano tuner's here,' she called in an amused voice to someone down the passage.

'No,' he began, 'there's some misunderstanding, the room—'

'Ben Jamieson.' Her eyes narrowed. 'Wait up. *The* Ben Jamieson?' She grinned. 'I'm Melanie Sawyer, Carrie's stepsister.' She offered her hand, her grip firm. 'I just called round on my way home from the hospital—I'm a nurse.'

'I didn't ring for a piano tuner, and the kitchen sink…' A woman joined Melanie, her voice trailing off when she saw him.

His blue lady transformed.

Biting back the first word that sprang to his lips, he exhaled sharply, rocked back on his heels.

'Carrie, there you are,' Melanie said. 'This is Ben Jamieson. He's come about the room. Ben, this is—'

'Carissa.'

He compared the two females, both gazes fixed on him. Melanie might dazzle the eye, but Carissa shone with an inner spark that set her apart.

Right now her hair was an out-of-control waterfall of gold. A buttercup-yellow vest-top clung to braless breasts. Mile-long legs gleamed beneath short denim cut-offs and she had two dark stains on her knees and a glob of something black on her cheek. Her feet were bare.

She didn't look pleased to see him.

Her cheeks flushed but those blue eyes turned a dangerous shade of cool. 'What are you doing here?'

'I was in the staff cafeteria…' He held out the ad.

Her eyes narrowed. 'How did you manage that?'

'Friends in high places?' He should just get the hell away, but he couldn't seem to move his feet.

Melanie frowned. 'You know each other?'

'I don't…' Carissa threw him a suspicious look, then turned to her sister. 'How do *you* know him?'

Melanie shook her head at Ben. 'The queen of pop, Carrie is not. Ben's a songwriter.' Her brow creased. 'You were there when…oh, God.' Her sentence hung in an awkward silence broken only by the chattering of birds and Mozart pouring from the stereo inside. 'Rave Elliot, XLRock,' she finished in a low voice.

Carissa's eyes widened and thawed to lukewarm. 'That horrific accident. I read about it.' She leaned a shoulder against the door. Not flushed now but pale as milk. 'I had no idea you… I'm sorry. For your loss.'

The pain struck hard. 'Rave and I were like brothers.'

For a few hours this woman had taken his mind off his grief. Not just with her body, but with charm and optimism. Could she be good for him a little longer? If they laid the ground rules from the start…

He took a fortifying breath. His best decisions were often ones he didn't think about too deeply. 'I'd like to look at the room.'

But Carissa frowned. 'Why? Why would you choose a cheap rented room over a penthouse suite?'

A fair question. 'I need a private place for a while. If you're worried about the short stay, I'm happy to pay you six months' rent up front.'

The frown remained.

Melanie flashed him a reassuring smile. 'Excuse us

a moment. Wait right here,' she said, tugging Carissa inside and pushing the door to.

He paced a couple of steps away and considered the wisdom of his offer. Carissa obviously didn't want him here and he—

'Ben?'

He turned at the sound of Melanie's voice.

Carissa stood beside her, flicking one hand against her thigh and looking aggrieved. He saw her throat bob as she swallowed, then she nodded. 'Okay, you can take a look.'

'So, how did you two meet?' Ben heard Melanie ask.

Carissa swallowed again. 'The piano bar. We had a drink…'

Knowing eyes met his, deep ocean-blue, and he had a mental flashback of that long, slender body laid out and arching beneath him. 'Which reminds me.' He dug into his pocket. 'I have something of yours.'

'Oh, no…don't…I…' She did a quick embarrassed shuffle.

He took his time, watching the way her eyes darkened, heated, pleaded, then chilled. 'You must've dropped this.'

'Oh…my— Thank God.' Pink and flustered again now, she made no move to take the gold chain he held in front of her eyes.

He cocked a brow. 'You sound surprised. Have you lost something else?'

Her eyes skittered to Mel, then away, and she seemed to fight a little war within herself before the glare was back, the chin up. Ignoring his last question, she opened her hand, palm out. 'It was my grandmother's. I only discovered I wasn't wearing it this morning.'

His fingers grazed hers as he poured it into her hand. He lingered over them a second before she snatched them away.

'The room's this way, Mr Jamieson,' she said, all business as she turned and headed down the passage. 'The upkeep of the room is the tenant's responsibility. There's no room service here.'

'Carrie,' Melanie scolded, bringing up the rear. She cast an apologetic glance at Ben. 'She's not been herself all morning. I don't know what's gotten into her.'

He almost smiled. Was this the same woman who'd melted—burned—in his arms last night? That fragrance, her cool blue water scent that had enveloped him like a misty morning, was tantalising him again, reminding him of the passion he'd woken in her. Only him. The thought persisted a little longer than he'd have liked.

It was an airy house with only the basics, and echoes of a time when it had looked different. They passed a couple of empty rooms, then entered a spacious area that must have been used for entertaining. A piano filled the space by a huge bay window. Sheet music was scattered over the lid; some lay in a cardboard box. A tatty sofa, a couple of sagging chairs and a coffee-table were the only furniture.

He wished she'd stop, wished Melanie would get lost so he and Carissa could talk, but she strode on, long legs flashing beneath those skimpy shorts.

'Careful,' she warned at the kitchen door. 'Sink's blocked.'

Which explained the black knees. They trod carefully over the slippery floor. 'You called the plumber?'

Melanie let out a hoot, which earned her a black look from Carissa.

'I'll take a look—' he began.

Carissa waved him off. 'Got it covered.' A phone rang. 'Can you answer that, Mel, please, and tell whoever I'll call back?' She pushed at a door. 'These are the rooms. Not up to your usual standard, I'm sure, so—'

'I'll take it,' he said, without bothering to look. He preferred watching the conflicting emotions play over her face. 'Hold still,' he murmured, flicking the drop from her cheek with his thumb. 'A spot of drain dew. Gunk,' he clarified when she just stared at him.

She touched her cheek. 'This is *not* happening.'

He cocked a brow. 'Think of it as a coincidence.'

'I believe in signs, not coincidences, Mr Jamieson.'

'A sign, then.' Of what, he wasn't sure. Stretching a lazy arm across the doorframe, he foiled her getaway. 'What's with the Mr Jamieson? We've seen each other naked. Shouldn't we be informal?' He watched her colour flare and gentled his voice. 'We need to talk, Carissa.'

'If you're referring to last night, there's nothing to talk about. Anything else is purely business, *Mr* Jamieson.' Her voice was crisp and edgy. She started to push past, then stopped, obviously unwilling to touch him.

He saved her the trouble, curling his fingers loosely around her arm. The faintest tremor ran through her. 'I think there is. I'm making you uncomfortable. If we're going to be living together we need—'

'I haven't decided yet whether or not to take you on. And *if* I do, we will *not* be living together.'

'Okay,' he conceded. '*If* you decide I'm the right man

for the job, we're inevitably going to be in each other's space. I don't want you uncomfortable in your own home.'

He was all too aware of the smooth skin beneath his palm. He was trying to reassure, but it was too tempting to remember her flesh sliding against his. Damn, but he wanted that feeling again.

'I'm a good bet, Carissa. You don't want someone you know nothing about coming into your house.'

'And I know you?' she said wryly. She chewed her lips a moment. 'Okay, we'll give it a go, but I'm not making any long-term deals.'

'I'm not looking for long term.' He cruised his hand up that slender neck, felt the rapid pulse, the shallow breathing. His gaze dropped to that full mouth and he watched it tremble before it firmed. Proud and defensive. He liked that in a woman. 'Carissa…'

'A one-night stand, that's all,' she whispered, her eyes pleading with his.

Ironic that he'd echoed those same sentiments until it was second nature to him. 'Seems fate has other ideas.'

'No.' She swung away, stubbing her toes on a chair in her haste. 'Ouch!' Her face turned waxy pale.

'Ouch,' he echoed with feeling.

Clutching her foot, she staggered to the nearest available surface, a sofa with a bright hand-quilted throw-over. 'Fudge, fudge, fudge!'

Ready to render first aid whether she needed it or not, he crossed the room and knelt in front of her. 'Let's take a look.'

'It's fine. Great. No, really.'

Her foot jerked, but he grasped her heel before she could pull away. It was smudged with dirt, the toenails painted silver. One nail was broken and bleeding. He whipped out a handkerchief and wiped away the blood, but his thumb slid back and forth over her cool, smooth instep of its own volition.

The urge to slide his hand on up that firm calf muscle, and higher, beat through his blood. His body hardened. Living under her roof might be more difficult than he'd anticipated. He looked up at her. Her teeth were worrying her lip again, a provocative sight if he ever saw one. He could press his advantage, or act like a gentleman, which he wasn't.

But he let her go. 'Okay, Cinderella, I think you'll live.' Shoving his handkerchief in his pocket, he walked to the window, willing his inconvenient erection to subside.

This bed-cum-sitting room was better furnished than what he'd seen of the rest of the house, with a view overlooking the rear grounds, *grounds* being the operative word.

Filmy white curtains moved in the breeze, another handmade quilt in maroon and cream covered a single bed. The rug on the floor was new, the pine floor freshly lacquered. He could still smell polish, disinfectant and sunshine on the fabrics.

'There's no air-conditioning, but you've a fan,' she said, still hugging her foot. 'Bathroom's through there.'

He took the opportunity while inspecting the sixties-style green and black room to moisten a dainty embroidered towel. 'This is a beautiful old house,' he said, offering her the cloth.

'I think so. Thanks, but I'm okay.' She folded it neatly and put it on the table in front of her. 'It was my grandparents' home. I've had to let things go a little. Upkeep on a place like this costs an arm and a leg, but I don't want to sell. It's all I have left of my family.'

'That's tough,' he said, and meant it. He knew all too well about losing the people you loved.

'I do just fine on my own.' The unconscious lift of her chin told him she had to work hard at it. It was obvious she needed money.

She glanced at her watch. 'I have to go out for a while. There's cake and coffee in the kitchen. Don't use the sink. You're free to use the kitchen, but the rest of the house is private, just as I'll respect your privacy. That way we can keep out of each other's hair.'

'Okay.' He nodded, but keeping his hands out of that tangle of gold was going to be a serious exercise in restraint.

She pushed up. 'I'll be back in time to cook tea, if you want to settle in.' She slid open a drawer, took out a set of keys and put them on the table. 'Back and front doors. And you can park that bomb you call a car in the garage; it's empty for now.'

'Hey, that's a fine car. Paintwork's a bit dodgy but the engine's reliable—so they tell me. We'll have to take a drive some time, see if they're up to their word.'

She didn't reply to that, but knotted her fingers at her waist. 'Rent's payable up front, two weeks in advance.' She paused, and twin spurts of colour sprang to her cheekbones. 'And, please, knock off the money I borrowed this morning. I intended to drop it off at the hotel.'

'No,' he said quietly, drawing out his wallet. He counted the notes and held them out. 'It's yours.'

'Okay. Thanks…um, Ben.' She took them, carefully avoiding contact with his hand.

He was tempted to cuff her wrist and test the beat of her pulse, but thought better of it. Business was business.

As she closed the door behind her he pulled out his keys. He'd head back to the city and grab his gear. Then maybe he'd take a stroll to the beach, a few minutes' walk away from here, and make some short-term plans.

Plans that might or might not include Carissa Grace.

As expected, Melanie leapt off the couch with a 'Wow!' the moment Carissa entered the living room.

'Yeah. Wow,' Carissa mimicked less enthusiastically as she snatched up a fabric band from the piano and dragged her hair through it. 'Who was on the phone?' she asked as casually as she could manage.

'Didn't say. I told him you were out, said he'd ring back. So, come on, Carrie, you were going to knock back his offer, for goodness' sake. You wouldn't say no to the extra income from a gorgeously handsome guy. What's going on with you two?'

Her stomach jittered. 'Nothing's "going on".'

'Don't give me that. I saw the way he looked at you. Hot.'

'I didn't notice.' She glared at Melanie, but she could still feel that flash of heat on her skin. 'Wipe that smirk off your face.' It was making her nervous. She could feel her face flaming, so she began collecting the scattered sections of yesterday's newspaper.

'The piano tuner?' Melanie murmured.

'Stop it, Mel.'

'Okay, but look at the points in his favour. He's a hunk, you have to agree.' She held up her fingers as she checked them off. 'He's available, he must be loaded, he's here—'

'That's just it,' Carissa interrupted. 'He's *here*. If I wanted a one-night stand, would I choose my lodger? Someone I see day in, day out?' And felt hot all over again.

'I don't know—would you?'

Carissa looked up to see Mel's eyebrows arched and a speculative gleam in her eyes. 'And five, he's interested. You want someone to tickle your ar…peggio—he's a songwriter and musician. What better credentials?'

'I don't know why I'm still talking to you, but stay for tea, Mel. Help me out here.'

Mel shook her head, setting her long hair swinging. 'You don't need any help from me, sis. And Adam and I made plans to go bowling tonight.'

'Bring your sexy and *available* flatmate too. The more the merrier.' And safer.

'Not tonight. You're on your own with this one.'

'Traitor,' Carissa muttered, tossing the paper on the coffee-table and throwing herself onto the couch.

Melanie grinned, picked up her bag and swung it over her shoulder. 'You'll thank me later. Gotta go.' But she paused at the door. 'You're not still thinking about Alasdair, are you? If you want to talk, I'm always free, or if you want to kick something, Adam's available.'

Carissa couldn't help smiling back. 'I'll tell Adam you offered him. And, no, I'm not thinking of Alasdair.'

When Melanie had gone, Carissa slapped on her floppy old hat and stepped out into the zap of a white summer's afternoon. The heat seared her exposed skin and baked the ground to biscuit, burning the soles of her worn sandals.

She welcomed the distraction. First up he'd walked into her piano bar. What were the odds of that same man walking into her home? Her life? She lifted the sprigs of lavender and rosemary she'd picked from her miniature herb patch, inhaling their calming scent as she walked.

She wanted alone. She liked alone. The desperate need for money was the only motivation for letting some of the spare rooms, not any desire for company. Now she had someone she neither needed nor wanted in her space.

Well, he wouldn't follow her here. A row of tired casuarinas shaded the tiny graveyard behind the old church. The gate registered her arrival with a mournful screech of rusted metal. She walked straight to her grandmother's grave.

'Hi, Gran.' She arranged the herbs in the earthenware pot, then sat, tossing her hat to the ground beside her. Her father and Mel's mother's grave lay a couple of rows away. Her own mother had been out of Carissa's life longer than she could remember.

She'd been visiting her grandmother's grave for fourteen years. It was Gran she talked to when she wanted to get something off her chest. No one interrupted here. She made important decisions under these trees. Solved problems, answered questions.

The peace of the hot afternoon lay over her like a languid blanket. Closing her eyes, she tuned her senses to her surroundings. The kiss of warm air on her skin, the scent of herbs and casuarina needles, the drone of a plane.

She opened her eyes and traced the grooves of her grandmother's name. 'Gran, I've done something I'm

not sure you'd approve of. I met a man.' She found her
heart thudding louder and rubbed the heel of her hand
over it. 'You know the type—tall, dark and deliciously
dangerous. We had a drink and I gave him my virginity.
I'd known him an hour.'

She clasped her hands around her knees, conscious
of her breathing, a little faster than usual, skin newly
sensitised, the tingling in her breasts as the memories
flowed back, clear and fluid.

'And you know what else? I'm not ashamed of it.
Even knowing there'll never be anything between us. He
didn't seduce me. I went in with my eyes wide open. *I*
used *him,* knowing I'd never see him again. How's that
for women's rights? Except now…now he's living
under my roof.' She heard the tremble in her own voice
and stood up.

'The moment I saw him standing at my door it was
all I could do not to lay my lips on his and take.' She
shoved her hands in the pockets of her shorts and
frowned at the ground. 'But that's not going to happen,
I made it quite clear. I think.'

A car whizzed by, a blur of sound. The air stirred,
thick and heavy with summer scents.

'How am I going to face him over the kitchen table
knowing what we've done?' Her head suddenly filled
with Ben's face, his eyes on hers as he drove into her.
Her body writhing beneath his, her shameless moans…

She shook it away, clenched her fists. 'Alasdair's got
someone else.' Her lip curled. '*Pierre.* I thought I'd feel
hurt but I feel used and angry. I was counting on his
financial support. He'd promised to fix up the house. It
was going to be my turn to study at the conservatorium.'

She blew out a breath. 'I've realised I'm more upset at the loss of his income than the man himself. We had a good partnership. Now I realise that's all it was.

'So I had no choice but to rent those rooms. It was supposed to be temporary, but now it's vital. I'll keep your house, Gran, if it's the last thing I do.

'And Ben Jamieson's going to help me pay for it.

'He likes rock, for heaven's sake. We're worlds apart.' She bent, picked up her hat, then kissed her fingers and touched the headstone. And sighed as a smile curved her mouth. 'But I haven't felt so alive in for ever.'

CHAPTER FOUR

BEN spent a quiet half hour unloading his gear. It felt good tripping up the rickety front steps, hearing the squeak of the porch screen door. If Carissa had no objections he might put his energy to productive use and fix the place up a bit, bring the garden back to life.

As he set his laptop and paperwork on the tiny desk in his room he noticed the homey touches. The dish of pot-pourri, a handmade candle that smelled of vanilla, the embroidered pillowslip and tissue-box cover.

Twenty-four hours ago he'd never met Carissa Grace; now he was living in her house. He stared at the ad still on the table. What twist of fate had led him to that notice-board yesterday? Was this one of those mystical signs Carissa believed in? He sure as eggs didn't believe in that mumbo jumbo.

So why did he have this odd niggly feeling in his gut?

To distract himself, he wandered to the kitchen, found a vase for the roses he'd brought from the hotel, put them on the table. Next he picked up the tools Carissa had left and inspected the sink. So she was a plumber too. He wasn't, but he was prepared to give it a try.

Half an hour, a bruised elbow and a few curses later he had the drain flowing freely—he hoped. He let himself out the back door and hunted up a hose on top of a pile of cracked pots in an old garden shed. She obviously didn't find time for gardening, which was a crying shame. The garden could be quite spectacular with a little time and effort.

He'd never had a backyard of his own. The simple pleasure of pottering around in your own garden, watching it grow, was not something he'd ever given much thought to. He connected the hose and soon had the water playing over what he imagined had once been lawn. He wasn't sure it could be revived, but he'd give it his best shot.

The activity reminded him of his mother. Her garden had been her pride and joy. His gut tightened at the memory. Even then she'd been lost. At sixteen he'd been too focused on himself to look at what was going on around him—he'd just known he wanted out of there.

He'd come back four years later and been shocked at what he'd discovered his drunken father had been doing. But she'd refused to go to the women's shelter he'd arranged, refused to return with him to the outback pub he'd been working in at the time. Still, the guilt that he'd had to leave her with the bastard remained like a wound that never healed.

'What are you doing?' The steel in Carissa's voice had a red-hot edge to it.

He turned to see her marching across the yard towards him, hat in hand, eyes blazing. 'Giving the lawn a helping hand,' he said. 'Looks like it needs it.'

'And who appointed you gardener?'

He couldn't resist. He adjusted the nozzle to a fine spray and grinned. 'You look a little hot and bothered. Let's cool you off.'

'Don't—' She gasped as the fine mist enveloped her.

Her hat sailed into the dust. Water sparkled on her shoulders, in her hair. She didn't look cooled off at all. He wondered that the water didn't turn to steam, she looked so darn angry.

'Turn it off. Now.'

When he just stood watching in fascination, she renewed her march, this time towards the tap. He moved to intercept her.

Her fingers closed over his as she struggled for the hose, drenching them. 'Stop it!'

Mud spattered their feet. The smell of wet earth rose around them as her breasts rubbed against his chest. She pulled back, her T-shirt plastered to her body, her pebbled nipples jutting up at him.

'Now look what you've done,' she muttered, swiping her face.

Oh, yeah. He was looking.

Then for just a moment laughter bubbled up, bright and sunny and uninhibited. 'This'll cost you, Mr Jamieson.'

The hose slipped to the ground, spraying water over their feet. 'Tack it onto the rent.'

'I was thinking along the line of no showers for a week. Teach you a lesson in water conservation.'

'Then I'd be forced to share yours.'

Her eyes shot laser-bright blue sparks as he hauled her up against him. He felt the exasperation sing through her arm as she pushed at his chest, relished it as he tugged her back against him. It had been a while since he'd enjoyed a tussle with a woman, even if he'd have preferred somewhere more horizontal.

'What's the problem, Miz Grace, afraid of a little water?' Silky legs rubbed against his and he shifted to take advantage. Something about this woman called to him. Her vitality, her innocence? It was more than physical, although his physical needs took precedence at this moment.

Everywhere her body touched him came alive. He knew she felt his erection when she tensed and went very still. That knowledge and the taut, unspoken silence hummed in his ears, beat through his blood. He lowered his mouth until it was an intimate suggestion away from hers. 'Or are you afraid of something else?'

Her eyes snapped shut. 'I'm *afraid* the water's wasting. I'm *afraid* when the water bill comes I won't be able to pay. So now you know, turn off the tap.'

It cost her to admit that, and he eased back. 'Is that why you let the garden go?' he asked softly.

Diamond drops clung to her lashes, her pretty mouth was a thin line. 'You think I like a baked yard?' She shook her head, scattering droplets.

'I apologise.' Reluctantly he disentangled his body from hers and stepped away to shut off the tap. He wanted to help, but knew her pride wouldn't allow her to accept cash. He'd have to find another way.

He didn't expect her to be right behind him picking up her hat when he turned. His foot slipped as he tried to compensate and they slid to the ground in a slow-motion pinwheel of thrashing limbs and hot skin. He heard her strangled cry, felt the cool sensation of damp earth rise up to meet them as he frantically twisted his body to take the brunt of the fall.

He ended up on his back, Carissa's legs around his waist, her breasts fragrant pillows against his nose.

Her moan—or was it his?—sounded through his muffled senses as his hands reached up and clamped on firm buttocks. She squirmed, one nipple brushing his face, his mouth. He acted on instinct, turning his cheek and closing his lips around the hard little bud beneath the cotton.

With a startled yelp she pushed up instantly, giving him a tantalising close-up of wet T-shirt. Wet, *transparent* T-shirt with a puckered circle where his mouth had been.

He tipped his head back. Stunned wide and aware eyes met his. Fingers of lust seared his veins and clutched his groin. Wordlessly he slid his hands to her hips and dragged her body lower so that she sat poised over him. Pain or pleasure? He wasn't sure, didn't care.

Her hands splayed over his chest. 'No,' she breathed, a throaty sound that echoed through his head and over his body, but her fingers bunched and twisted into his vest-top, her knuckles dragged over his nipples. God.

He loosened his grip briefly to give her the opportunity of escape. She remained frozen in place, the only movement the rise and fall of her breasts as he flexed his fingers against her again.

He traced the long, smooth muscles at the front of her thighs, let his thumbs curve inwards and upwards to the hem of her shorts, until he found the lacy edge of her panties.

Her quick indrawn gasp turned his body to fire. Her focus blurred, her lips parted as he slid his thumbs beneath the lace to find her hot and wet. Guilt stabbed through him when he remembered how he'd taken her innocence last night.

He drew in a harsh controlled breath. 'Are you sore?' he murmured, hearing the sandpaper rasp of his own voice as he explored deeper, hearing her moan as he rubbed his thumb over the engorged knot of flesh.

'No…oh.' Colour flared up her neck and into her cheeks. 'This isn't working,' she muttered thickly.

He cocked a disbelieving brow, tugged on the crotch of her panties and slid the knuckles of one hand back and forth over her delicious heat. 'It's not?'

She moaned, her head dropping forward so that her hair brushed his shoulders. 'You…offered to…cool me off.'

'This is more fun.' Absolutely, definitely… Except… He inhaled her incredible female scent as he absorbed the wet heat against his fingers and tried like hell to ignore the insistent pounding of his own need to roll on top of her and plunge inside.

No condoms.

He touched her again, once, and she came apart, her body arching, then melting down onto him with a satisfied moan. An experience he wasn't going to get any time soon.

Then her gaze locked on his. The dreamy focus sharpened as his body jerked against her. *Hell.* In one not-so-smooth motion he rolled her off him and sat up.

'You don't wa…?'

Oh, yeah, he did. Right now he wanted it more than his next breath, but he didn't do unprotected sex. No woman was going to trap him with an unwanted pregnancy.

A shower—he needed that shower. Cold. Alone.

Now. 'That's enough for one day,' he muttered through his teeth. 'You're new at this. Bound to be a bit tender.'

To distract himself from the soft, puzzled look in her eyes and the erotic scent of her sex on his fingers, he reached out beside him and picked up her hat.

'Looks like we both need that shower,' he said, looking at their damp, dirt-stained clothes. *Not* looking at her breasts and crotch. 'Then we could eat out, get some take-away. My shout.'

We. Without his being aware of even saying it, his heart tightened and something inside him needed.

Suddenly the scenario seemed way too domestic. If he wasn't careful, that need to be a part of someone's life, to share their day, could spring to life again as easily as the brown grass beneath his feet.

He needn't have worried. Averting her eyes, she swiped at her knees with tense, jerky movements, but he saw the telling blush that stained her cheeks.

'It's my night off,' she said, her voice husky. 'I'm going to the movies with a girlfriend.'

A lie, he knew. 'Hey,' he said quietly, and stood up. He lifted her chin with a finger and looked into those wide blue eyes still shiny with the afterglow of sex. 'It's okay. You don't have to leave your house on my account. I've got some work to take care of in my room. I'll grab myself a snack later.'

He shook the dust off her hat, set it on her head, then turned and walked to the house. But he felt her eyes on him all the way to the back door.

'You were seen exiting the employee entrance at dawn in a less than seemly state, Ms Grace. The Cove Hotel will not tolerate such shameful behaviour from its employees.'

The scents of the summer evening filled the air. Carissa hardly noticed as she clutched the phone in front of the open kitchen window. Angry humiliation stung her eyes. Once. She'd made one tiny indiscretion. Okay, not so tiny. 'I'm sorry, Mr Christos.' For the sake of her job, she swallowed her pride and said, 'I let the Cove down. It won't happen again.'

'No, it will not. I want to see you in my office tomorrow morning at 9:00 a.m.'

'I'll be there.'

She stabbed the disconnect button and slammed the phone down, then banged her forehead against the kitchen cupboard. 'Jerk!' How many more surprises could she take today?

'Your boss?'

She whirled at the deep voice to see Ben at the door, hair still damp from his shower, one hand on the door-frame.

A hand that had only a few hours ago wreaked devastation on her body with one expert glide between her spread legs. Good Lord. Heat spurted into her cheeks; her heart hammered in her chest. But now he was witnessing a different kind of devastation. 'How long have you been there?'

'Long enough to get the drift.'

'I see.' And obviously, so did he. Humiliated, embarrassed and determined to ignore him, she marched to the pantry and pulled out ingredients. She dumped flour and salt into a bowl, then added a generous squirt of blue food colouring and stirred till her arm ached. Anything to avoid looking at him.

He pushed away from the door. 'If that's supper, I'll pass.'

'Thought you were going to fix your own.'

'Thought you were going to the movies.'

Oh. 'My friend cancelled.' She wiped her brow with the back of her hand. 'It's play dough.'

'Kid stuff play dough?'

'For the kids at the hospital. Mel often helps out in the children's cancer ward.' She put the bowl in the microwave, set the timer. Watched the turntable. Ben sat—obviously he'd finished whatever work he had—and made himself comfortable.

When the timer dinged, she scooped the hot dough into a ball, then carried it to the table and set it beside the fragrant bouquet Ben had put there. 'I haven't thanked you for bringing the roses back. So thank you. I love them.' Even if they were a reminder of an evening best forgotten. Hell, a reminder of a whole twenty-four hours.

'You're welcome.'

'Try this.' She broke off a piece of dough for Ben, then sank her fingers in and began to knead. 'I love the texture, and when it's warm… Someone reported me.'

Ben rolled his dough between his palms. 'I'll make a call—'

'No. Definitely not.' She almost snorted. As if he could do anything. No way was she letting him get involved in her problems.

'So we'll take a drive,' he said. 'Blow away some of the day's stresses. Give me five minutes.'

Tempting. It was a genuine offer of support and she sure needed a change of scenery. 'You said you had work.'

'It's not going anywhere.' He leaned over, lifted her chin with a finger and their eyes met. 'For the record, whatever last night was, it wasn't a mistake.' Something in his gaze shifted, darkened, as the full-frontal memories of hot and heavy and wet rose between them.

She squeezed the dough till it oozed between her fingers. 'I'm fine. It's going to be fine.' After all, optimism was supposed to be her strong point.

He set his ball of dough on the table beside her hand. 'Of course it will.'

Yeah. He would think that. The complete confidence of a man who had everything. A man who didn't understand what it was like to go without—anything.

'One condition,' she said, not looking at him. 'No sex.'

She felt the air stir as he stepped away. 'Whatever you say.'

They drove with the windows down as fast as the car could safely go until Sydney's lights were only a glow on the horizon.

'You have a destination in mind?' Melbourne, perhaps?

'I'll know when we get there.'

He tuned into a rock station playing nineties party hits. 'Guess it's not your thing, huh?' he said after a few moments.

'Just because I play classical doesn't mean I don't like other music.'

'Guitar?' he asked.

'I love guitar. Spanish, classical...'

Ben nodded. 'Classical guitar's the only "classical" I know much about.'

'And now a hit from XLRock's latest album…' The DJ's voice faded and the guitar riff slid out of the tinny speakers.

Without warning, Ben punched the radio off. Only the sounds of wind and engine filled the silence. He stared ahead, his clenched jaw reflecting the sombre green dashboard lighting. He could have been carved from stone.

'I'm sorry,' Carissa said, wishing she knew how to ease his hurt.

Ignoring her miserable attempt, he pulled over near a flat, almost treeless expanse of land. 'Let's walk,' he said tautly.

Away from the city's glare, the sky was brilliant indigo and full of stars. A full moon rode above low hills on the horizon. Cricket song and buzzing insects filled the air. The calming sounds and soothing sights went some way to easing the awkward tension.

'Know your stars?' he asked, finally. Some of the strain had gone from his voice.

'I know the Southern Cross.' She looked up at the familiar kite shape. 'And there's the Saucepan.'

He nodded. 'The constellation of Orion. And that bright one's Sirius. See the big red one? That's Betelgeuse. Have you ever seen the outback night sky?'

'I've never been more than a couple hundred kilometres from Sydney.'

'You should see it some day.' His eyes glittered with the reflected starlight as he gazed up. 'All that black emptiness. Makes you feel small and insignificant. Like we don't count for much in the big picture.'

'Or it fills you with wonder, knowing there must be a purpose behind it all.'

He looked at her, a half smile on his lips. 'Spoken like a true optimist.' He found a spot where the grass was flat, sat down and patted the space beside him. 'What do you want to do about your gig at the Cove?'

She blew out a disgusted breath. 'What *can* I do? I'm at old Georgie Christos's mercy.'

'I'm responsible. Let me—'

'No way. No way.' She shook her head. 'I stand on my own two feet. *I'm* responsible for me. I made a choice. I'll live with the consequences.' Whatever they might be. And it wasn't only her job she was thinking of.

'I don't want to work in a place where loyalty counts for nothing. If I lose it I'll live with it.' But she thought of the overdue bills on her desk and wondered if she was being stupid knocking back Ben's offer. 'I've still got my Monday to Thursday waitressing at the Three Steps. I'll ask them if they've got any Friday and Saturday shifts.'

'Waiting tables? You're wasted.' He angled towards her. 'I want to see you again at the piano in that blue number you wore last night.' His eyes barely flicked down, then met hers again. 'Better still, at the piano *not* in that blue number.

'Sorry, out of line,' he said immediately, pressing a finger to her lips, presumably to silence any complaints. She didn't have any. She did have an insane urge to take that finger into her mouth and wrap her tongue around it. To taste him again, to have a part of him inside her.

Oh, no. *No, no, no.* She couldn't let it happen again. And they'd made that sensible no-sex rule.

But she couldn't move. In the light of the rising moon

his face was silver and shadows, his eyes still focused on hers. Then she felt the warm glide of his hand over her collar-bone, beneath the tiny strap on her shoulder. Her stomach tightened, her nipples hardened and that newly discovered sweet, deep pull tugged at her lower body.

'Don't. Please,' she begged, her throat dry, her voice suddenly hoarse. 'You promised.'

He didn't remove his hand. 'It's a guy, right? A guy lets you down, a one-night stand—classic rebound.'

She hesitated, then nodded. 'You must think I'm a fool.'

'No.' He tightened his grip on her shoulder and rubbed his thumb over her skin. 'He didn't deserve you, Carissa. And neither did I.'

'Let's get something straight here. I didn't offer myself to you like some sort of sacrifice. Don't you get it? I used you to—'

'Scratch an itch?' His lips curved in the dimness. 'We all do that at some time or other. But pick a man, any man? That's downright dangerous and *that's* foolish.'

'Not just any man.'

She saw a muscle tick in his jaw. 'I'm not the kind of man a woman like you needs.'

'I don't believe that. You were gentle and caring… And what do you mean *a woman like me?*'

'I'm not just talking physical needs here, Carissa. Emotional needs. Stability, commitment. The long haul. That's what a woman like you is looking for. And I'm not the man for that job.'

'Who says I'm looking for commitment? I just got over one disaster. I'm not looking to get myself another. I also think you underestimate yourself, Ben. Find the right woman and—'

'I'm not husband material, period. No woman should shackle herself to someone who killed a man.'

Oh, my God. Something shivered down her spine as an image of the dark, dangerous stranger she'd seen two evenings ago flashed before her eyes. But it wasn't fear. That man *couldn't* kill, she knew that. 'What happened?'

'I handed Rave the keys to my car. He was like a brother to me, and I killed him as sure as putting a bullet in his head.'

Carissa released the breath that had backed up in her throat. The grief she heard in his voice, the pain she saw in the grim twist of his lips, tore at her heart. But the news had reported excessive alcohol and speed had caused the accident. 'No. He made a choice.'

Ben rubbed his knuckles over his chin. 'A choice that was a direct consequence of *my* actions. If he'd had his way we'd have been halfway home by morning. I put my own needs above his, something a father or older brother would never do, and that's what I was to him.'

Even in the dimness Carissa could see the demons that haunted him, the shadowed eyes, the cool wash of moonlight over the tense line of his jaw.

'Tell me,' she prompted, sensing he'd not talked about it with anyone and was only now finding the nerve.

He looked up at the sky but he wasn't seeing it. He was back in Broken Hill. 'Rave wasn't in his room when I rang later that night. His mobile phone was off—a bad sign—he wanted Jess to be able to contact him at all times. I borrowed a car. Someone had seen him so I knew the direction he'd taken. Ten minutes later I saw the flames, smelled petrol, burning…' Silence filled the growing chasm between them. 'He hadn't been wearing the seat belt. I found him twenty metres farther on.'

Suddenly Carissa felt cold. She didn't want to hear any more.

'I tried to remember CPR. I wanted to bring him back...' His stone-edged voice cracked. 'His eyes were...'

'Ben. Don't blame yourself.' She shifted nearer, but, sensing he wouldn't welcome physical contact, she didn't touch him.

But she wanted to. Her natural instinct to offer the comfort of touch welled inside her. He looked so lost and vulnerable. His eyes were too bright, too shiny in the moon-glow when he looked out across the paddocks.

'It shows you the sort of friend I am, the sort of man I am.'

The sort that couldn't commit to someone, particularly someone like Carissa, he was trying to say, even though she'd already told him she wasn't ready for that at this point in her life. 'It's okay,' she said. 'I get the message loud and clear. I'm not looking for anything from you except the rent money.' But, oh, my...if she had the nerve...a wild, no-strings-attached affair... The very idea sent a wave of heat crashing through her body.

One corner of his mouth tipped up momentarily. As if he'd read her thoughts. Her totally inappropriate, ill-timed thoughts. 'Whatever you say.'

Oh, he wasn't helping. 'Any time you want to... *talk*...' She trailed off, noticing his focus had already turned inwards again.

'I'll be away for the next few days. Some business I've got to take care of in Melbourne. I'm not sure when I'll be back.'

A woman. She didn't know how she knew, but she did. Perhaps it was the subtle softening in his voice, the almost sad, faraway look in his eyes.

She pushed up and stood hugging her arms against the cool evening air. 'Your life's your own. You don't have to report in to me.'

But an uncomfortable new sensation burned within her. She couldn't get past it. The thought of that hot skin and hard muscle, his clever hands on some other woman, ignited something inside her that she'd never experienced. After all, Alasdair had never looked at other women.

Jealousy, plain and not-so-simple.

Something she'd better get used to fast.

CHAPTER FIVE

ON MONDAY morning Carissa was too preoccupied to worry about her sexy lodger. She faced the unpleasant prospect of having George Christos throw her indiscretions in her face. Worse, much worse, there was no doubt in her mind she'd also be cleaning out her locker and collecting her final pay. Old Georgie was infamous for firing employees over the smallest infractions.

Ben had left before she'd risen and she hadn't seen him. She'd breathed a sigh of relief and told herself the less she saw of him, the better off she'd be.

She spotted George Christos by a potted palm on her way to his office and executed a quick ninety-degree turn. Damn. The last thing she wanted was a scene in the lobby.

'Ms Grace.' He puffed up to her. 'I tried to ring you at home but you'd already left.'

Squaring her shoulders, she turned. 'I thought we had a meeting—' she checked her watch '—in ten minutes.'

He mopped his brow with a stiff red handkerchief. 'I don't think that will be necessary. I've…ah…reconsidered.' He seemed to stumble on the word and his Adam's apple bobbed against his precisely knotted matching red tie. 'We all make mistakes and the Cove needs your expertise.' A pause. 'So we'll see you as usual on Friday evening?' He smiled, but it didn't quite reach his eyes.

She blinked in shocked amazement. 'You don't want to discuss it?'

He hesitated as if choosing his words, then said, 'I don't think that will be necessary. I'm sure it won't happen again.'

'Thank you, Mr Christos,' she said stiffly. Imagining yanking that tie and telling him right where to stick his job. Satisfying but out of the question.

Turning, she stalked away, heels tapping over the marble-tiled floor and, in defiance, exiting through the guest entrance rather than the employees' side door.

With an unanticipated free hour to kill, she headed for the Centrepoint shopping mall instead of the station. She stopped at a music shop, her attention drawn to the sign 'XLRock.' A trio of young males in leather and studs leered down at her from a poster on the wall. God. It was like looking inside someone's nightmare.

Beneath the poster she saw a book about the band. She flicked through the pages. Near the back was a small photograph of a long-haired Ben. She might have missed it but for the eyes—deep forest-green, soulful eyes.

But the sleeveless black leather vest over that bare chest... It threw her off course, making her shudder, yet shiver with a perverse thrill at the same time. She'd touched that chest, with her fingers, with her lips. Those nipples had brushed hers. And she was intimately acquainted with what hid beneath those tight leather pants. Whew. Her cheeks heated as she glanced furtively about her to make sure she was alone.

Dragging her gaze from the picture, she focused on the article. 'Ben Jamieson, financial backer for XLRock, is himself a passionate classical guitarist and composer... He's also written several tracks for XLRock, a departure from his usual style...'

Her breath caught in her lungs as amazement filled her. Classical guitarist and composer. Ben wasn't the man he wanted her to think he was. There was another side to Ben Jamieson that, for whatever reason, he'd not wanted to share with Carissa. Apparently he'd been a father-figure to Rave Elliot for the past fourteen years. And he said he didn't do long-term commitment. She shook her head at the contradiction.

Fifteen minutes later, Carissa stepped out into Sydney's bustle and the smells of pasta and pastries and exhaust fumes. Oppressive heat fought with blasts of cool from air-conditioned stores as she wended her way through the crowds to the station. But her mind was preoccupied with Ben. She'd read a list of his musical achievements, even recognised a couple of pieces he'd composed.

She stopped at the local supermarket on the way home. With no car she had to shop daily. When she arrived back at the house she found a package on the front step, which she balanced on top of the groceries as she pushed inside.

She dumped the groceries in the kitchen, then took the mystery parcel to her bedroom. She read the attached card first. 'An early birthday present. Enjoy. Love, Mel.'

Inside pink tissue paper Carissa found a skimpy, sexy,

see-through white nightgown. She ran her fingers over the cool, smooth silk and lace. Just what was Mel thinking?

The answer was obvious and she couldn't resist turning to the mirror. As she shook the gown out a small packet fell to the floor. She didn't recognise what it was until she read the label: 'Lubricated for her comfort. Extra large.'

Oh... She felt the hot surge of remembered passion, saw the flush spring to her cheeks, and spun away from the incriminating reflection. With a stifled whimper, she snatched up the dangerous packet and stuffed it in the bottom of her underwear drawer.

She should never have told Mel about the virgin bit. But it was sweet of her to think of the gown. She re-wrapped it in its tissue and slid it into the drawer with the condoms, out of harm's—and temptation's—way and hurried into the kitchen.

Did condoms have a use-by date? Carissa wondered as she stacked away the groceries. She shook her head at her own no-sex rule. It was a darn shame she wouldn't be seeing one of those condoms on display any time soon.

Ben stuffed the plush teddy he'd bought at the airport under his arm and walked up the path to the gracious apartment in one of Melbourne's trendy suburbs. If there was a time he'd wanted to be anywhere but the place he was standing right now, he couldn't remember it.

The woman who opened the door had flyaway brown hair tucked behind her ears. A sheer Indian-style dress skimmed ankles that jingled with tiny silver bells. The chubby baby on her hip ogled Ben open-mouthed, then tucked his head beneath his mother's chin. 'Ben.' Her face blanched as she backed up, grey eyes wide and sad. And angry.

He had to force his voice to work. 'Hello, Jess. Hey, Timmy.' He touched the boy's cheek, which was smeared with some sort of goo.

Her mouth compressed. 'I told you I'd let you know when I was ready to see you.'

'I couldn't stay away any longer, Jess.'

She blew a sharp breath through her nose. 'I guess you'd better come in, then.'

She turned and walked down an airy passage, feet padding on the parquetry floor. The aroma of fried food and stewed apples mingled with aged wood and polish as they neared the back of the house, and he stepped into a family area cluttered with toys. Dishes were stacked in the sink.

'I wasn't expecting company,' she said, removing a pile of folded nappies from an armchair to the table with one hand. She put Timmy in a playpen in the middle of the room.

'Here you go, champ.' Ben knelt down and set the teddy in front of the boy. Timmy watched him through Rave's black eyes and pain etched itself across the dark corners of Ben's heart. The kid would never remember his father.

'I'm not company, Jess.' He straightened and turned to her. 'Rave and I were family. *We're* family.'

'Is that so?' Her voice was chipped ice. 'Where were you, Ben, when my husband died? Was it gambling or a woman this time?'

Clenching his jaw, he took a step towards her, laid a hand on her shoulder. He would not allow her to think the worst of Ben Jamieson. That he reserved for himself. 'Jess, I'm sorry.' She remained unyielding as he folded himself around her, but he felt the tremors ripple through her too-thin body. 'Let go, I'm here. Please…'

'To ease your conscience, Ben?'

She pulled away. He closed his eyes briefly. He deserved that, and more.

Wet, racking sobs filled the silence. Timmy, sensing something was wrong, began to whimper. Jess pulled a tissue from her pocket, blew her nose, then picked up a training cup and gave it to her son. 'It's okay, baby, Mummy's okay.'

Ben watched her, light streaming blue and gold over her body through the old stained glass in the upper kitchen window, and thought how Rave would have loved to have seen her there.

Finally she looked at him. 'Tell me what happened. Don't pretty it up with what you think I want to hear. The truth, Ben.'

'Jess… It won't bring him back.'

'He was angry with you—I know because he rang me.'

'He wanted to come home. To you.'

'No, Ben, he wanted his own way. We both know how he was.'

Often egocentric, inclined to sulk. And on this gig he'd been more moody than usual. 'He was sober when I gave him the keys.'

'Of course he was. I know you wouldn't let him drink and drive.' She hugged her arms, knuckles white as she dug her fingers into her flesh. 'But you left him to do whatever it was you had to do—'

Guilt stabbed through Ben but he said, 'He was a

grown man, Jess. He didn't need a babysitter. But you're right. I shouldn't've left him alone that night.'

'We'd had an argument the morning you left,' Jess said. 'A loud, ugly one. I never got the chance to say sorry.' Her soft grey eyes filled. Shaking her head, she crossed the floor and curled herself against his chest. 'It's not your fault, Ben. I know I've acted like it was, but that's grief. It's easier to blame someone else. I could have gone with him. I could've made the effort, paid someone to help with Timmy. But even if I'd been there he'd have done it his way. It always had to be his way.'

He held her close, noticing that unfamiliar baby smell on her clothes. 'I'd like to stay a couple of days, Jess, if you've got the room.'

'Of course I have the room—several spare rooms. We bought this house with four kids in mind.' She looked up and met his eyes, then touched his cheek. 'There'll always be a place here for you, Ben.'

'Thanks, Jess. Anything you need, anything at all, let me know.'

She had everything except what she wanted most. Once he'd almost envied what Rave and Jess had together. Now he was just plain grateful he'd never gotten involved with anyone.

Late in the afternoon Ben watched Carissa pedal down the drive and off to work. He'd thought by staying an extra few days in Melbourne to see Jess and his mother he'd have gotten over this need to see her. Nope. He couldn't take his eyes off the cute way her buttocks curved over that too-small seat.

He turned from the kitchen window and shook his

head at the cold meat and salad she'd left. He was capable of feeding himself, but would she listen?

So he would put his evening to good use and see what needed doing outside since she couldn't afford to pay anyone. Feeling uncharacteristically domestic, he squirted a generous amount of lemon detergent and began rinsing the dishes she'd left in the sink. Mum always said that the dishes...

His hands stilled mid-swish. After he'd said goodbye to Jess he'd spent the better part of two days with his mother reminiscing about happier times. The same as he'd done last month, and the month before that.

Nothing changed.

He finished the dishes quickly. It would be more productive to put his mind to something he could make a difference to.

He was already outside when he heard the front door slam. He resented the way his heart shifted gears and his mood lifted at the thought of seeing her again so soon. But it didn't stop him retracing his steps.

He searched the house until he remembered he'd left the door open to catch the breeze. He stood in the family room and watched sunbeams dance over the piano's polished lid, and scraped at his jaw. His fingers itched but he shook his head. Leave the music to Carissa.

Then he remembered he wasn't supposed to be in here unless invited. As he turned to leave he saw the solitary birthday card. It was from Melanie and she'd written the date: twenty-seventh February. Today. He tapped it against his lips, then set it back. Apart from

Melanie he hadn't seen anyone else round here who gave a damn.

He returned to his room to make a supper reservation for two.

Carissa slid the last drinks onto the table, searched in her apron for change. 'Thank you, sir.'

Nearly ten o'clock. The zipper on her only black skirt had broken and the safety pin was digging into her hip. Her feet ached and she still had to cycle home. Uphill, and the air was probably still warm and sticky outside.

The aroma of char-grilled meat and hot fat hung in the air. She thought of the scented bubble bath she was going to treat herself to, and, what the heck, she might even crack open that mini bottle of champagne left over from Christmas. She didn't care in which order she did them, so long as the water was hot, the bubbly cold. If she had to spend her birthday alone, at least she could do it in style.

'Carissa, go home.' Rosie, a plump, redheaded waitress pointed to the car park as Carissa pushed through the swing door to the kitchen. 'I'll finish here; you look beat.'

'Thanks, I think I will.'

She changed into shorts and left by the rear door to collect her bike. The air steamed with the scent of hot tar and vegetation. One dim light slicked a faint sheen over the few cars left.

Perspiration slid down her neck as she strapped her pack to her bike, then unlocked the chain. She didn't see the flicker of movement or hear the furtive scuff of feet until it was too late.

A man slid out of the shadows to her left and a rough hand clamped over her mouth. 'I've got a knife.' His voice scraped over her like rusty nails. To prove it, something sharp prodded her ribs. Her stomach spasmed in terror. The odour of beer and stale sweat almost suffocated her.

'See that car?' She tried to nod, but her head was held fast. 'You're going to move, nice and slow.'

A strangled noise bubbled up her throat. Panic spurted through her veins; her mind whirled. Her fingers tightened on the bike chain she still by some miracle held in her hand. She swung it behind her head, felt it connect, heard the whip and thud as it hit its target.

The sudden loosening of his hold and his strangled curse had her tottering backwards for a second before she swung around, primed to scream. Then she saw Ben. And screamed anyway.

'Are you all right?' She felt the energy of his anger beneath the quietly spoken words.

When her head nodded like a puppet, he leaned over the mugger's sprawled body. 'Ring the cops.'

The rear door slammed open and Brad, one of the cooks, ran out. 'Hey! Rosie, someone, ring the cops!' He came at a dead run, a hot fry-pan dripping grease in his hand.

'Carissa, oh, my God!' Rosie was down the steps and all over Carissa in a shot.

'I'm okay, it's okay.' But she heard the edge of hysteria in her voice. 'I…I have to ring the police.'

'Someone else'll do it,' Rosie said, leading her back to the restaurant. 'The guys can keep watch out here. Come inside and sit down.'

Carissa sank gratefully onto a chair while Rosie rushed off. She couldn't seem to draw air into her lungs.

'It's okay, sweetheart. Breathe slowly.' Ben's voice in her ear, calling her sweetheart, his arms around her.

Relaxing instantly, she felt her pulse returning to something approaching normal. Then he was on his haunches, holding her against him, his freshly showered scent so sweet and safe against her nose as he smoothed her hair.

'Cops'll want a statement,' he said. 'You up to it?'

She nodded and looked at him for the first time. His voice might have been controlled, but his eyes were dark with concern, his mouth a tight, thin line.

'Can you walk?'

'Yes.'

'We'll go outside where it's less crowded.'

'What are you doing here?'

'Coming to see you.' He hustled her out to the front of the restaurant as the sounds of sirens drew closer.

'Why?'

'Later.' He set her on the chair at one of the little wrought-iron tables, then started back inside. 'I'll get Rosie for you.'

A breeze cooled her sweaty skin. Her legs were smeared with grime and she really, really wanted a shower to wash away the lingering sensation of the scum's body on hers.

Twenty minutes passed before the excitement died down. Rosie sat with her while she talked to the police, then she caught sight of Ben's car as it exited the car park and pulled up in front.

'He's your lodger?' Rosie said as he stepped out and rounded the hood.

'Yeah.' Grimly gorgeous in what had been a white T-shirt, and freshly pressed khaki trousers, he looked as if he'd been on his way to a night on the town.

'Had him long?'

'Couple of weeks.' Carissa couldn't help the weak laugh. 'You make him sound like some kind of condition.'

'Hey, in the interests of medical science, I'd suffer him gladly.' He stood by the car, hands in his pockets. 'I think he's waiting for you.'

Carissa's heart bumped at the idea. She smoothed clammy hands over the front of her thighs and rose. 'Thanks, Rosie.'

Ben stepped forward as Carissa approached. 'I'm taking you home.'

'My bike…'

'We'll get it tomorrow.' He opened the passenger door.

As she hauled her aching backside onto the seat she was greeted with the smell of old vinyl and roses. Ben reached behind her to the back seat, then laid a bunch of yellow roses on her lap. 'Happy birthday.'

'Oh…' She met his eyes and fought a sudden fierce desire to cry.

'You leave this lot behind and I'll develop serious feelings of inadequacy.'

'Thank you. How did you know it was my birthday?' But he'd already shut her door.

'I'm driving you to work from now on,' he told her as he slid inside, swung a U-turn and headed home.

The no-negotiation statement startled her. 'No.'

'What do you mean, no? You were attacked, for God's sake, anything could have happened—why did you put your bicycle in such an exposed place?'

'I'll put it somewhere else. It wouldn't have made a difference if I'd driven or cycled, the risk's the same.'

'Not if I'm there. Listen up, Carissa, while I'm here I'll be driving you and I don't intend discussing it.'

'Fine.' She crossed her arms. 'Let's not discuss it.'

'Fine.' He shoved the gear stick through its paces.

She looked away, out the window. 'I can take care of myself.' But, oh, it felt nice to have someone watching out for her. She'd been independent for so long, she'd forgotten there was any other way. But it would only make it harder when he left.

'Thought you said you weren't going to discuss it.'

'Discuss what?' she said, and drew the scent of roses to her nose.

Two minutes later Ben pulled into the drive. He could barely contain his fury. The image of that low-life with his hands on Carissa burned into his brain. Every time he thought about what might have happened if he'd been a few seconds later…

'If you hadn't turned up you wouldn't even have known,' she murmured.

'Is it women in general or just you?' He slammed his hands on the nearest available surface—the steering wheel.

'Meaning?'

'Do you always have to have the last word?'

'It's hard not to when you live alone.'

'You don't live alone. For now.' He pushed out of the car as the pale moon slid behind a shifting cloud. The sounds of night drifted through the air, the distant rumble of waves breaking on the beach, a nightjar's hoot.

He rounded the hood, but Carissa was already marching towards the steps, back stiff, shoulders squared. He followed a few steps behind. She'd cope with whatever life tossed her way, including him, he knew. But that cowardly bastard tonight had put a serious dent in her self-assurance.

In the kitchen he leaned against the sink as he watched her take a vase from the cupboard, fill it with water and arrange her roses. She was making an effort to appear unfazed, but he knew better. Her face was china-white and fragile, her fingers not quite steady, her eyes dark, and right now avoiding his.

He hesitated a beat, then laid a hand on her shoulder. He felt her flinch, but she didn't shake him off. 'Go take a shower or a soak in the tub. You'll feel better for it. I'll still be here when you're done. I'll brew coffee.'

He felt her loosen beneath his fingers. 'Okay. Thanks. And thanks again for the flowers.'

Then she turned and looked at him and something unfamiliar settled in his chest. Because he didn't know what to do with the feeling he shrugged, stepped away. 'Hey, what are friends for?'

She left him standing there with the sensation that he'd somehow been sucked out of his depth.

He brewed the promised coffee, then took a wander around the house. Someone with Carissa's talent shouldn't be working in a dump like that. And if he hadn't been there, if he hadn't known it was her birthday... But he had, and he had to be content with that.

Thirty minutes later she entered the kitchen wrapped

in an amethyst silk robe, her hair damp and piled on top of her head and smelling like flowers.

She rubbed at her arms. 'Thanks for your support tonight.'

'No worries. Just glad I was there.' He pushed up and moved to the coffee-maker. 'Feeling better?'

She rolled her shoulders, an unconscious movement, then stopped when she saw him watching. 'I'm fine.'

She didn't have a clue what a sight she made, tall and slim, like a lone fresh-picked iris.

She got to him. As he continued to watch her, deep down where he'd buried his vulnerability, he felt something stir. And he didn't like it, didn't want it.

Didn't need it.

They'd shared one night and she'd made it clear that was all she wanted. All he wanted. He wasn't looking for permanence; she wasn't his type.

But... He reached for her arm; his hand closed around firm flesh beneath smooth silk. Her breath jerked and he saw her swallow. There were marks on her neck, he noted grimly. 'It's okay,' he murmured. He wanted to reassure her, not frighten her. He wanted to make her forget the past couple of hours and just *be* with her.

'I told you I'm—'

'Fine. I know. Relax a minute.' He eased her onto a kitchen stool, then moved behind her and let his hands rest on her shoulders. When she didn't pull away, he slid his fingers beneath the edge of the silk. Slowly and gently dragged it out of the way, exposing her spine and the delicate lines of her collar-bones.

He slid his thumbs up either side of her spine and was rewarded with a sigh. Her skin was creamy smooth and fragrant, but the muscles beneath remained knotted and tense. He kneaded for several minutes in a silence broken only by the breeze whispering through the window and the night sounds beyond.

'Heard you playing Gershwin this morning,' he said, keeping his voice casual. '"Summertime," if I remember correctly.'

'One of my favourites. Did you grow up with music?'

'My father only allowed classical music in the house.' His hands tightened and he had to make a conscious effort not to press too hard.

'And your mother?'

'Had no say in it.'

'Your dad's the reason you don't like classical.'

He was the reason for a lot of bad things. How had the conversation circled to the unpleasant topic of his father?

'But you learnt guitar,' she prompted.

'When I was ten a mate's mum taught me in exchange for doing odd jobs around her garden. I used to practise with her old guitar in the shed when Dad was at work.' He no longer trusted his hands not to betray the dark emotions the memories had dragged up and dropped them to his sides. 'That'll do for now.'

'Thanks.' Rising, she shrugged back into her robe. 'You're a kind man, Ben Jamieson.'

Against his better judgement he let his eyes drop to her mouth, full, untinted and, right now, irresistibly tempting.

'Maybe you'll change your mind about that judgement,' he murmured, and, leaning in, he laid his lips on hers.

The instant jolt of heat, of lust, was expected; the tenderness he felt for her was not. The scent from her bath, subtle, cool and alluring, surrounded him until he thought he might drown in it. He thought he heard music, soft, haunting piano, but it was probably the night breeze stirring the wooden wind chimes outside.

He wanted to slide his hands lower, over that silk, feel her heat beneath the cool, but kept them stubbornly on her shoulders. She needed a friend tonight, nothing more.

With an effort he pulled back. He caught the dreamy light in her eyes before she masked it with something resembling indifference, although he sensed she was far from unaffected.

'You were on your way out tonight and I ruined your plans.' Her voice was husky as she brushed at the dirt-smeared T-shirt. 'That makes you a kind man.'

The touch of her fingers reminded him of how they'd felt on his bare skin. The thought of her touching him again in other places… He turned away to hide the hard evidence. 'It was nothing important.' She was better off not knowing. They were both better off. 'Good night.'

He headed for his room before she could reply.

CHAPTER SIX

CARISSA shot up in bed, heart pounding. Something had woken her. She heard it again, a shuffling outside her window. Her saliva dried in her throat. What if the low-life who'd tried to attack her the other night knew where she lived and had come to collect? She shook her head. Of course not; the police had him now.

Throwing back the sheet, she crept to the window. In the streetlight's dim glow a man was hunched on the verandah, head buried in his hands.

Ben. She watched his big frame heave and her throat constricted. What demons haunted him? Whatever they were, he kept it to himself. He needed a friend; he had no one right now. Except her.

Yet he'd shown her a tenderness she'd not expected. Nor would he knowingly display a hint of the open grief she was witnessing now. He slammed a fist against his thigh and her hand crept to her throat. She couldn't go to him—his pride would suffer if he knew she'd caught him at such an unguarded moment. But she wanted to.

Oh, hell. The timing was all wrong. She didn't want a relationship right now. She'd never know if it was the 'classic' rebound he told her it was. It could never be more than sexual attraction between them. He was wealthy, worldly and she was totally out of his league. The spark was there but that was all it was. All she'd let it be.

But there was something she could do. She could help him feel valued and useful, things she knew were lacking in his life right now. So she could let him help her—up to a point.

'Damn!' Carissa glared at the inch of murky dishwater in the sink. So not what she needed after a long day. She dragged the toolbox from its shelf and dumped it on the floor with a clatter.

'Problem?' Ben poked his head around the door. She hadn't seen him all day but he looked gorgeous and thoroughly beddable.

'I was getting a glass of water and the bloody sink's blocked again,' she muttered, sorting through the tools, trying not to think about Ben and bed at the same time.

When she looked around again, he was in the middle of the kitchen wearing only a pair of white hip-hugging briefs scrunched at one side as if he'd pulled them on in a hurry. And Lycra, for heaven's sake—didn't he realise it outlined every shadow, every masculine bump? Made every female cell in her body jump to attention?

She raised her eyes to his. He was watching her watching him. Of course he knew.

Dismissing the view with a silent snarl, she opened the cupboard door below the sink. Then she remembered she was going to give him the odd jobs to keep him occupied. 'Would you mind, Ben? I'm—' she spotted her hand and body lotion '—just going to give myself a hand massage.'

A smoky heat flickered in his eyes at the erotic image she'd unwittingly conjured as he leaned one tanned arm on the sink. *Much too close.* So close she could smell the warm, sleepy scent of his body.

She took a hasty step back. 'You just need to unscrew that U-shaped bit and—'

'I know.' All masculine know-how, he picked up the wrench, dropped to his haunches and inspected the plumbing while Carissa stood back in her nightshirt and played the role of helpless female.

He muttered something to himself about plumbers, then turned, lay down on his back and wiggled himself into position under the pipe. The sight of that bronzed skin and finely honed torso taking up all the space on her kitchen floor snapped through her blood. The overhead light sheened the hard planes of muscle in his calves and thighs and…

And she needed to look somewhere else. Needed to *be* somewhere else—

She heard the sound of metal chiming on metal followed by, 'Grab the buck—' then the splash of water and a disgusted, 'Never mind.'

'Are you okay?' She dropped to her knees, then all fours when the only response was a muttered oath.

'Just wet.' He wriggled back out. Water glistened on the smooth line of his brow, in the grooves that bracketed his mouth. Her eyes followed a single drop as it slid over the faint stubble on his jaw into the hollow at his shoulder and onto the floor. Then their gazes caught, and in that sultry beat of heat she saw the water, the two of them, opportunity…

Déjà vu.

Heat pumped through her veins and ribbon-danced in her belly. She scrambled up, swiped up the tea-towel and thrust it at him. 'I'll leave you to it. Let me know when you're done,' she said, grabbing the bottle of lotion, backing away and escaping into the living room.

Good Lord. Collapsing onto the couch, she blew out a breath, squeezed her eyes shut. It didn't help. All she could see was Ben's semi-naked body as she made her escape. His semi-naked *aroused* body. Oh, she hadn't missed that not-so-tiny detail.

She unscrewed her bottle, poured lotion onto her hand and set the bottle back down with a firm 'chink.' The cream's smooth texture as she massaged her skin only fuelled her sensory overload. If she'd really wanted to escape she'd have gone to her bedroom. A traitor to herself. On the other hand she felt duty-bound to stick around until he finished, thank him politely and say good night.

She suddenly became aware that the clanging had stopped and heard his shower running. Now she had no choice but to wait and think about that big body slippery with water. Five minutes later he appeared at the doorway. His chest and its sprinkling of dark hair gleamed with damp under the old chandelier. Not that she was looking at his chest. Or the silky black boxer shorts he'd changed into.

'All fixed. For now.' Smelling of soap and clean man, he sat down beside her and squirted a dollop of her hand lotion onto his palms.

'Thanks.' She didn't know what else to say. It was nearly midnight, the job was done and she'd thanked him—she should go to bed. Instead, she rubbed in more cream. More heat.

The moment stretched on and on, thick with the scent of sweet ripe peaches and Ben. And temptation. Her body was already anticipating his touch. Her pulse was playing a fast "Minute Waltz" and a line of sweat prickled her spine. But she knew nothing would happen unless she wanted it to, unless she gave permission. She had that small control at least.

'Give me your hand.' His husky gravel voice scraped away any thought she'd had of being in control. In his eyes she saw a mutual acknowledgement they both understood. Lust, she assured herself. Nothing more.

She watched his hard, blunt fingers envelop her slim fair ones. His thumb drew a lazy circle in the centre of her palm, a slow, slippery massage that sent hot-cold shivers up her arm and through her veins. He raised their joined hands to eye-level, sliding his fingers against hers, liquid silk to liquid silk.

His eyes turned molten and sparked with green fire as she joined in the dance, sliding her slick fingers over his wrist, feeling the pulse that beat thick and strong and steady.

He pressed their joined hands to his lips. 'My room or yours? Or does the no-sex rule still stand?'

She felt his warm breath on her skin, the fullness of his lower lip against her thumb as he spoke. And totally melted. Why should she fight it? One night with Ben Jamieson wasn't enough. Why not take what he was obviously offering? What she wanted.

'No rules. My room.' She stood, amazed at the smooth way she'd said it when the word seemed to come from somewhere outside her body.

But he didn't release her hand. 'Are you sure?'

'It's only sex, right?'

She thought he looked momentarily taken aback, his eyes a mix of desire and bemusement. 'Is that what you want?'

He was almost at eye-level, lip-level. She leaned closer, touched her burning mouth to his. The spark smouldered, caught, sizzled. More sparks as he took a leisurely journey over her lips, then a long slow burn as his tongue slid inside and tangled with hers.

It was electric, carnal. Physical.

His breath hissed out. 'I need—'

'I have what you need,' she said against his mouth.

'I know you do, sweetheart, but I still need—'

'I have a whole box,' she said, tugging their joined hands, and watched surprise and arousal sharpen his eyes.

When they reached her room, she opened her drawer and placed the box on the quilt.

His eyes slid from the box to her. 'You're full of surprises tonight,' he said in that gravelly voice from the opposite side of the bed.

'It was a gift. From a responsible friend,' she added when he didn't reply. He just kept looking at her with hot eyes, as if visualising her without the nightshirt. Carissa reached for the hem of her nightshirt, drew it over her head and tossed it down. Cool air and hot eyes kissed her nipples. 'Your turn,' she said.

She kept her eyes on his as he pushed down his shorts, but she couldn't resist a downward glance. Flames licked at her belly. Oh, sweet heaven—and it would be. She swallowed. There was just so much of him. She hadn't seen him like this the last time. Big and bold and beautiful. And naked.

Drawing in a steadying breath, she shimmied out of her panties.

Cellophane crinkled as he slid the wrapper off and opened the box. 'Extra large,' she said, her eyes sliding over the fierce jut of his erection again. Was that sultry female voice hers?

A corner of his mouth kicked up. 'I noticed. You want to do the honours?' She shook her head once. 'I don't know how.' Unlike his other lovers, she thought. Another strike against her. But he didn't seem disappointed. Far from it. He smiled his crooked smile, that wicked smile that had no doubt seduced more than its fair share of the female population, and said, 'I'll teach you.'

He scooted around to her side of the bed, grasped her hand and clamped it around him. She felt the leashed power and stroked up, then down, testing, exploring, revelling in her discovery.

'Easy, sweetheart,' he muttered on a breathy exhalation. 'Here…' His hand closed over hers as he helped her roll the smooth latex down his hot, hard length. 'Simple.' The rasp in his voice stroked over her senses like serrated velvet.

She sighed out a trembling laugh. 'Yeah.' Not so simple was the rush of emotion that accompanied this intimacy, this developing bond, the need to be with him in this way.

Drawing back the covers, she lay down. The night beyond the open window was still and redolent with summer. The only sound she heard was her breathing as she struggled to draw oxygen into her lungs.

For a long time Ben didn't move. His dark, passion-filled

eyes devoured her body. 'I've been dreaming about you like this. But the real thing is so much more. You're perfect. Almost too beautiful to touch.'

Impossibly turned on by his gaze and his admission that he'd dreamed of her—naked—she managed a smile. 'That would be a big disappointment.'

'For both of us,' he said and stretched out beside her.

The caress of his mouth on hers was a sweet prelude to more. He stroked her body as if he touched the most fragile china—her ear, throat, breasts, navel. Too gentle, too reverent to be pure lust.

Something like panic swamped her. She couldn't risk her heart to a man who'd be out of her life in weeks. Someone who was used to experienced lovers. She reached out and turned off the bedside lamp to avoid his eyes, to hide hers. The streetlight cast a silver light over them and Ben slid his hard, hair-roughened body over hers.

She knew that come morning she'd be alone with only his scent to mingle with hers on the linen. That was okay. That was right. But for now… Shifting so that his silky tip slid along her moisture-drenched flesh, she arched her hips.

Then he was inside her, the cool sheets a stunning contrast to his heat, the scents of peaches and male filling her nose, the soft sibilance of skin on skin.

Only sex, she chanted to herself as she rode the dizzying spiral towards climax. *Lust.* But the tiny voice sounded far, far away and unconvincing.

This wasn't lust. This was something way more dangerous.

* * *

Carissa adjusted the air-con so it blew on her face as they slid out of the drive in Ben's shiny new black Porsche. And it wasn't doing her any favours. When he left, she'd be back where she'd started: on her push bike. But, oh, the seats were butter-soft, and it smelled so rich and extravagant.

'Don't you have anything better to do than take me grocery shopping?' she said. 'Like a drive in the countryside to put this new toy through its paces?'

'We'll get round to it.'

She didn't argue, but the way he linked them into the future did strange things to her already-queasy stomach.

'You said I could cook tonight,' he continued. 'I want to select the ingredients myself.'

'You cooked last night.' And the night before that. It was becoming a habit. She told herself it was therapeutic for him, but what about her? Enough was enough. The man was insinuating his way into her life. Heck, he was charging his way in like a lifeguard into surf at Bondi Beach.

'As a matter of fact, I do have something to do this morning,' he said. 'I'm going to pick up those supplies I ordered for the porch steps.'

'I told you it's not your problem.' He'd already sanded some of the woodwork, but she'd not told him what colour trim she wanted because she knew he'd go right out and buy it. He'd fixed the leak on the roof and planed the kitchen door so it shut properly.

'Honestly… Couldn't you go compose a few songs?'

'No.' She felt a mental door slam in her face at the mention of his songwriting.

'Okay, there's a skydiving school not far away.'

The tension cleared a little and he cast her an *almost* grin. 'Only if you promise to come with me.'

'Jump out of a plane? Just the thought's enough to turn my stomach…' The queasiness rolled up and over, then passed, but left her feeling clammy and weak. *Not now, please.* She simply could not afford to take time off.

By the time they reached the supermarket she was almost feeling herself again. Because it seemed too much like a couple thing to let him push the trolley, she strode ahead and took one first, then set a brisk pace, pulling items off shelves in a race to stay one aisle ahead of him.

'Slow down, you'll have a heart attack,' Ben murmured, offloading a selection of red peppers, mushrooms and beans. He looked closer. 'Come to think of it, you look a little off colour again today. Not sleeping well?'

He could ask that question? 'I slept fine,' she lied, and turned away from his probing eyes. 'Don't look at me like that. I've made a doctor's appointment for tomorrow afternoon, so drop it.' Distracted, she vacillated between China Pekoe and Earl Grey tea, then popped English Breakfast in the trolley. 'I need…jam setter,' she improvised.

'You make jam?'

'Not without jam setter, I don't.'

'I didn't know you were that domesticated. I thought those skills died in the sixties.'

'There's a lot you don't know about me, Ben Jamieson.'

For a moment his eyes challenged hers. Then he hooked his thumbs in the front of his jeans. 'What is it and where do I find it?'

She smiled at him. 'I'm not sure. Go look for me?' She watched his gorgeous jeans-clad backside as he strode off on his quest. Then she shook her head. What was she thinking? She couldn't afford to let her mind stray to forbidden territory.

But did he have to be so…nice? So attractive? So…everything. He'd be off in a few weeks. Maybe even days. Who knew? No point in getting used to having him around. Would he return to his music? Would he stay in Australia or head overseas? A man like him was always on the move, never settling in one place—he'd told her as much that first night. She wanted a home and family one day.

'Seek and ye shall find.'

She blinked as Ben tossed the requested packet into the trolley. 'Huh? Oh. Right.' Distracted, she pushed the trolley towards the checkout. Pulling out her purse, she laid cash on the counter before Ben could flip out one of his flashy platinum credit cards.

As the mall's glass doors slid open letting in a blast of hot air she almost gagged. Her knees turned wobbly; the sour taste of vomit climbed up her throat. She did *not* want Ben witnessing this. It would pass.

Gritting her teeth, she said, 'I want to browse the mall a while. I'll walk home when I'm through.' Abandoning Ben and the trolley, she walked casually until she lost herself in the crowd, then fled to the ladies' room.

'According to the date of your last period, you're seven weeks pregnant, Carissa. Which explains why you haven't been feeling well.'

Dr Beaton had been the family doctor for years, had treated her childhood illnesses and now…now he was telling her she was pregnant.

'But that's impossible. I can't be…' He slid his

bifocals down his nose. 'Not *seven* weeks. I mean…
we only did it once…that night…he used a condom.'
Her cheeks felt like fire and she could barely get the
words past her throat. Of course she knew sometimes
it only took once. And did that make her any less
pregnant?

'Condoms have a higher failure rate than people
often believe.'

She sagged against the chair. 'Are you sure?'

'Carissa.' His voice softened. 'Perhaps you'd feel
more comfortable discussing your options with my colleague. I'm referring all my obstetrics patients on now;
I'm getting too old.' He smiled at her over his glasses,
then scribbled something on a pad, tore it off and handed
it to her. 'Dr Elise Sharman's a gynaecologist and ob-
stetrician. If you like I'll ask Jodie to arrange for an appointment for you.'

'Thank you.' Her entire body felt numb. With those
few words her life had just been turned upside down.

'Do you have an ongoing relationship with the baby's
father?' She shook her head. 'Is there anyone you can
talk to? Melanie…? I can arrange for a social worker…'

His words seemed to be coming from a distance. As
if in a dream she nodded as she listened to his advice
about health care, heard him tell her Jodie would ring
her when she'd made the appointment with Dr Sharman.

Nothing seemed real. She stepped from the cool
surgery and out into the heavy afternoon heat. The
oyster-coloured sky was thickening. A car spewed hot
exhaust as it pulled away from the kerb, its fumes
smoking on the still air. A couple of kids yelled as they
sped by on skateboards, nearly knocking her down. It

occurred to her as absurd that in a few years' time it could be her child hurtling down the footpath.

Hers and Ben Jamieson's.

Where would he be by then?

She'd promised to call when she'd finished at the surgery but she wasn't ready to face him. Not yet. Not until she'd thought through all possible scenarios and decided what to do. And for that she needed Gran.

Half an hour later, she sat in the cemetery under the old casuarinas. 'Gran, I've got myself into what you'd have called "the family way".' She unscrewed the bottle of water she'd purchased at a deli along the way, took a mouthful, then dribbled a few cool drops from the bottle between her breasts.

Her hand skimmed her flat stomach, and wonder struck her. Family. She'd never be alone again. No matter how often she'd told herself that was how she'd wanted it, the knowledge that a new life was growing inside her, a part of her, filled her with awe and a sense of connection.

'A one-night stand, Gran.' She lifted her face as the first drops of rain pinged the ground. The damp, dusty scent mingled with the heat. 'A man doesn't get himself into this predicament. So much for equality of the sexes, huh?'

She reached out to the headstone and closed her eyes. 'If you were here, what would you have said to me now?'

The words came to her on a tide of love. She'd never questioned where they came from, nor did she doubt their wisdom. She simply knew, and accepted.

Everything happens for a reason.

'If only I knew what that reason was. He doesn't

want commitment.' Her gaze slid to the old trees that had stood since long before her grandmother had been laid to rest, their roots firmly in the ground. Not Ben's. 'He doesn't even want to stay in one place. Darn sure he doesn't want a child.'

Sweat and rain ran in rivulets down her face, her T-shirt clung to her back in the saunalike air. 'He's filthy rich and I'm scraping the bottom of my bank account. What if he thinks I want his money, that I trapped him into this? If he stays much longer he's going to see my pregnancy whether I tell him or not. I don't think he's the type to walk away from responsibility. He'd feel obligated. Obligation would turn to resentment.'

She thought of the lingering glances she'd become increasingly aware of, the way her heart leapt when she caught him watching, the way he turned away when she did.

'When he leaves it's going to hurt.' And he would leave—she'd make sure of it, for her own sanity, and his. 'He doesn't need me, or our baby. Ben Jamieson needs something in his life, but it's not us.'

In a defensive move she suddenly became aware of, she crossed her arms in front of her. She would protect herself and the child inside her with everything she had, that much she knew. She could take another lodger, take on some piano students in her home—if she still had a home.

Her thoughts circled back to Ben. How could she *not* tell him? A man had a right to know. What he did with the information was up to him. But not yet. When she had everything in place, she'd contact him, wherever he might be by then.

CHAPTER SEVEN

BEN eased the cumbersome plank into place and reached for the pack of nails. At least now Carissa could reach her front door without fear of falling through the steps.

He stopped a moment, caught in the past. The smell of fresh-sawed wood and Mum's roast lamb, the sound of hammering as he and his father worked together to put in kitchen shelving.

It should have been a team effort, father and son. His father had grudgingly agreed to let him help, and Ben was bursting with eight-year-old pride.

But the shelving was too heavy for a kid's scrawny arms to hold and somehow the end slipped out of his hands. The young Ben had let the team down. Again. He backed away from the red-hot anger in his father's eyes.

'Damn boy'll never be good at anything,' he muttered.

The child's self-worth took another dive.

'Get lost, kid. That's what you do best, isn't it? You hit a problem, you're gone.'

The past is past. Ben pulled out nails, hammered, pulled nails, hammered. Those hands his father the cop had scorned had learned how to lift a man's wallet in defiance, had learned how to make a guitar sing, bring pleasure to a woman.

He'd died before Ben could show him he wasn't the failure his father had told him he was. 'Wherever you are, Dad, this one's for you.' He drove the last nail in, threw the hammer down.

But there was a grain of truth in his father's words. He thought of Rave. Ben had let that team down too. He'd tossed in his songwriting, packed away his guitar. *Hit a problem and you're gone.*

Enough. Pushing the memories away, he moved back to look at the finished steps, vaguely annoyed that he'd have to put off the staining until the weather looked more promising. Then he gazed up at the roof trim, sanded and ready to paint. What would it be like to belong somewhere? To belong to someone, to share their life?

Carissa. What would it be like to come home to her every night? *Get that thought right out of your idiot head.*

It started to rain. He glanced at his watch. Carissa should have finished at the doctor's by now. Perhaps he should go over and check, but she wouldn't thank him for tracking her movements. They didn't keep tabs on each other. She'd ask for a lift if she needed one.

He collected the tools, then headed round the back to store them away. Inside he found himself drawn to the living room once more. The stained ivory keys reflected the sombre light from the window.

Perhaps he could play again after all. Not guitar, but piano. Carissa's piano. Touching the keys she touched, making the music she made. He raised the lid, picked out a few keys, noting the slightly out-of-tune E flat.

The click and scrape at the front door warned him Carissa was home. He watched her come in. She didn't see him immediately and slumped back against the door and closed her eyes. Rain dewed her skin and hair and an aura of fragility surrounded her.

He knew better, but he wanted to reach out, run his hands over those drooping shoulders, draw her close and protect her from whatever was bothering her. Unease slid through him. Had the doctor given her bad news?

Because he knew she hated looking to others for support, particularly him, he stayed where he was. 'Why didn't you ring, Miz Independence?' His voice was gruffer than he'd intended.

Her eyes flew open and she pushed away from the door as if she were on springs. 'What are you doing in here?'

'Piano needs tuning.'

'I know. You startled me. I'm not used to people lurking around the house.'

'Sorry. What did the doc say?' he asked, following her to the kitchen. He watched her open the fridge, pull out a carton of juice.

Ignoring his question, she lifted it in his direction. 'Want one?'

'Thanks.'

She poured two glasses, put his on the table and drank hers at the bench. Not once did she glance his way.

He waited for a reply and was deciding she'd gone conveniently deaf when she said, 'I need to take more calcium.'

'Okay.' He reached for his glass. 'Now tell me what's really bothering you.'

'I don't want to talk about it.'

He noted an underlying edge to her tone, and knew when a woman made up her mind not to talk about something it was pointless to pursue it. Still, he had to ask, 'You sure?'

Her shoulders stiffened, but still she didn't face him. 'If you really want to know, you're bothering me. Now, if you're through, I'm going to cool off in the shower before I get tea ready.'

Temper simmered but he tamped it down. 'I don't want you fixing my meals, Carissa. You've got six hours on your feet coming up.'

'It's called a job. It's what most of us do.' She finished her juice, rinsed her glass and upturned it on the sink. 'I'm going to take that shower.'

He waited till she'd left, then took two eggs from the fridge to make himself an omelette. Damned if she was going to cook for him. The frying-pan clanged as he dumped it on the stove. Damned if he was going to feel responsible for whatever her problem was.

The sound of the shower had his stomach clenching, and it had nothing to do with her state of mind and everything to do with her current state of undress. Heat rushed through his loins at the image that gentle splashing invoked. Her fingers slick with soap sliding over creamy flesh, dusky nipples puckering under the spray, rivulets of water running down her back between the tempting curves of her buttocks.

But she'd looked pale beneath that delicate summer tan. Tense. Vulnerable.

He slammed a hand onto the bench. And damned if he was going to let her get to him.

* * *

Some hours later, Ben set the platter of paté and cheese on the table. He lit the scented candle he'd found and stuck in a bottle, then turned off the overhead light.

'You shouldn't have.' Carissa's tone gave no hint of how she felt about his midnight supper. A lingering scent of fried onions clung to her work clothes.

He dropped the lighter on the table. 'Probably not.'

'Ben?' Clear and direct eyes met his. 'About this afternoon; I'm sorry if I was rude. Correction—I *was* rude, and I apologise.'

He smiled, relieved to have the air a little clearer between them. 'And I shouldn't have pushed. Relax, you're tired. Have a bite to eat and I'll let you get to bed.'

'Ben, we need to talk.' She sat down, resting her forearms on the table.

Her hair was still tied back, loose tendrils floating at her temples. He wanted to undo the tortoiseshell clasp and watch that pale gold silk tumble down and soften her face.

'Not tonight,' he murmured, and watched the way her eyes reflected the candlelight. 'Let's just sit here a moment and unwind.' He spread paté on a cracker and held it out. 'Try this. It's from the gourmet shop on the corner.'

'Thank you.' She took it from his fingers, avoiding contact, took a tiny nibble and set it down.

Was he imagining it or was she more than tired? She'd been uncommunicative on the short drive from work. He knew he shouldn't, but he wanted to know what was going on in that complex head of hers.

Hadn't he told himself he didn't want to get involved? But he'd never quite decided. A surprise, since he'd always known his own mind. Carissa had the ability to throw him off-track. 'Try the cheese if you're calcium-deficient. New Zealand gouda.'

But she shook her head. 'I've got something I need to say and I have to say it tonight.' She seemed to take a fortifying breath and placed both palms on the table. 'I have to renege on our rental agreement.'

Something in her tone told him whatever the reason was, she wasn't going to let him in on it, but he set his plate aside, his appetite killed. 'Mind telling me why?'

He saw the flicker in her eyes, the way her gaze didn't meet his when she said, 'I'm used to doing things for myself, on my own. Now I turn around and you're there—rescuing me, chauffeuring me, cooking, renovating my house.' She waved a hand. 'I don't want to depend on anyone. You're not here forever, and the longer you stay, the more I'll take for granted. It'll make it harder in the long term.'

'That's rubbish, Carissa. It's more than that and we both know it. You gave up your solitary existence when you took in a lodger.'

'You're more than—'

Her quick indrawn breath told him she'd said more than she'd intended.

'Yeah,' he said softly. Shifting closer, he cupped her jaw. 'Your lover. Your only lover.'

He didn't miss the flash of emotion in her eyes, her tiny shudder under his hand as the air charged with the heat of that encounter. The attraction was still there— on both sides—simmering beneath the impassive expression she'd reverted to. 'Forget the rental agreement,' he murmured, and leaned in.

She sat utterly still as he skimmed his lips over hers.

A breeze drifted through the room as if someone had sighed, setting the candle's flame wavering and bringing its jasmine scent closer.

His hand slid lower, and he felt the pulse in her neck leap beneath his fingers. Taking his time, he probed deeper, running his tongue over her lips until she opened for him, till he felt her jaw soften, her resistance melt.

He could change her mind about the rental agreement. He couldn't seem to come up with one solid reason why he should, except that for the first time in a long time he was content here in her home.

One slim-fingered hand rose over his forearm and crept up his chest. He felt the slight tremble in her touch and shifted nearer. He remembered the night he'd made more than her hand tremble. Her whole body had vibrated beneath his.

He wanted that feeling again. Now, now when he knew her better, he wanted something more than a sweaty bout between the sheets. The twinge of conscience that he'd taken that innocence without thought, without the care it had deserved, even if she had begged for it, had him gentling his movements.

He focused his senses on the moment. On the soft, sweet-tasting skin beneath his lips as he mated his tongue to hers, her unique feminine scent, the candlelight that flickered over her closed eyelids.

He'd never been a man given to romance, but Carissa seemed to draw it from him. The beginnings of a song hummed through his head, something slow and dreamy and he hoped he could remember it later and commit it to paper.

But he felt her stiffen, saw regret in her eyes as she pulled back. 'I shouldn't have let it get so complicated,' she whispered.

He touched her cheek. 'It doesn't have to be complicated. I don't mind helping out. I need something to focus on right now. You're doing *me* a favour.' She shook her head, and the tensed muscles he hadn't noticed tightened in his gut.

'No,' she said. 'I want to be alone and I can't be with you here. You…you're in my face, Ben.'

In her face. And right now that face was a mask. He didn't buy it. Not for a second.

He had no choice.

He stared at her for a long moment, wondering why it hurt so much for a man who didn't want to get involved. Then he pushed up. 'I guess that's my cue to exit.'

'I only meant…' She chewed on her lip, and to his surprise her eyes filled with moisture. She blinked it away. 'Another month's probably okay.'

Anger warred with impatience. Anger that he felt the tug of regret at leaving and impatience to be gone. 'I don't think so. I'll be out before noon tomorrow.'

'You will keep in contact, won't you? I…' She twisted her fingers together, as if she actually *cared* that she was kicking him out.

Was that the action of a logical person? 'You're one confused woman, you know that?'

'I want to know you're okay. Is that a crime?'

He saw her desperation and wanted, inexplicably, to reach for her, so he stepped back, putting the table between them, a barrier for his emotions. 'You want to worry about someone, worry about yourself.'

She flinched as if he'd slapped her. Her lips still glistened from their kiss, her hair was coming adrift from its clasp, and her eyes…something about the way she looked at him… He had the naked sensation that she was seeing all the way to his soul.

But she'd given him his marching orders. Whatever her troubles, they no longer concerned him—she'd made that plain enough.

'Oh, I almost forgot…' He pulled out the list of piano bars and clubs he'd made contact with over the past couple of weeks, set it on the table. 'If you want to give up waitressing you might want to check these out.'

Through his open bedroom window Ben squinted against the morning glare as he watched Carissa pedal her way down the drive, her backpack slung across her shoulders, her perky breasts jiggling under a faded green vest-top.

The jolt to his heart at the sight left him shaken. It should have been lust. Instead, a simple longing he hadn't known existed until he'd come here tugged at him. He clenched his jaw. The sooner he left, the better.

She disappeared from view as she turned onto the road. Anger crept through the sweetness. This was exactly what he'd wanted to avoid. From now on, no emotional ties.

He pulled on jeans, headed to the kitchen. Carissa's absence made it easier to grab that last coffee. While he waited for the kettle to boil, he saw her note saying she'd gone grocery shopping. Not easy without a car, but he shrugged. Not his problem.

The soapy scent from Carissa's shower hung on the

air. This woman was a puzzle that warmed him from the inside out. It would be a long time before he got her out of his system. So it made sense to leave before she returned. No last goodbyes. A clean break.

He loaded his car, then checked that the supplies for the renovations he'd started were stored away, took a last look at the new steps, watered the herb garden. He was stalling, and it annoyed him.

When he returned to the house the phone was ringing. He'd decided not to answer it when he remembered Carissa hadn't been looking well again this morning. Perhaps she needed help with the groceries after all. He picked up. 'Good morning.'

'Good morning.' A brisk, businesslike voice answered. 'Is Carissa available?'

'She's not here at present. Can I take a message?' He glanced around for pen and paper.

'This is Della from Dr Sharman's surgery. We've scheduled Carissa's appointment for two o'clock this Thursday. If you could pass the message on, please?'

'Hang on, what's the name again?'

'Dr Elise Sharman.'

He couldn't find any paper, so he scribbled the time and date on the wall. 'I'll be sure to let her know,' he muttered, then disconnected.

Something wasn't right. It had to be a specialist's appointment. He grabbed the phone book and flipped pages till he found it: Dr Elise Sharman. Gynaecology and Obstetrics.

The breath exploded from his lungs. He felt as if a bass guitar had ploughed into his gut. Because his knees were shot he sank to the floor, let his head fall back against the wall. Pregnant. Sweet heaven. She'd kicked him out because she was having a baby.

His baby.

It was one of those moments when everything suddenly seemed intense yet surreal, like the finale at a rock concert when the audience was whipped to a frenzy. The way his heart tripped—different somehow—the cool wall at his back, the threadbare mustard carpet, the odd feeling that he'd stepped into someone else's life.

And finally, a sense of betrayal. She'd not told him. Had she ever intended to? Did she think he valued his freedom above responsibility?

The man with no roots, no place to call home, accountable to no one but himself. Wasn't that what he did best? Hadn't he proved that over and over? To his mum and himself and others? To Carissa?

Pushing up, he dragged a hand over the back of his neck and scowled at the bare room. Not a bar in sight when you needed one. The kitchen didn't offer much more, but he found a Diet Pepsi at the back of the fridge behind the milk, popped the top, then sat at the table to wait.

Carissa took the long way home. She dreaded the final goodbye and was momentarily tempted to take the coward's way out and cycle to Mel's for the rest of the day until she was sure the coast was clear. But she wasn't going to back away from this, no matter how she felt. And she didn't feel good, in more ways than one.

The sun had lost summer's sting but the heat still had enough punch to suck away her already depleted energy. Her pack of supplies weighed hot and heavy on her back and the smell of someone's oily cooking wafted across the road.

A sudden nausea churned in her stomach and climbed up her throat. Her lips felt like chalk as she pressed them together and fought it down. She needed to get home before she disgraced herself on the side of the road.

Her heart did a fast staccato when she saw the Porsche. A crisp breeze with the faint tang of salt teased her hair and cooled the sweat as she parked her bike at the side of the house and let herself inside.

She came to an abrupt and startled halt at the kitchen door. She'd expected Ben to be in his room, not sitting at her kitchen table. With bloodshot eyes, tousled hair and a Pepsi can in his hand. His face could have been carved from granite. A blind woman stood as much chance of reading his expression.

She wanted nothing more than to crawl onto her bed and close her eyes, but sleep wasn't an option until he'd gone. She lowered her pack to the floor. 'Hi.'

Ben didn't move, but his eyes shifted from her face and travelled down her body, coming to rest on her belly. Her traitorous stomach muscles clenched and she had to fight to keep her hands loose at her sides.

He *couldn't* know. But her pulse drummed dangerously, the kitchen spun and she slid loosely into the chair opposite him before she fell.

'You weren't going to tell me, were you?' Ben drained the can, set it on the table with a firm 'clunk.' Cool green eyes glinted as he leaned back.

She dragged air into her lungs, opened her mouth to speak, closed it again. Panic was beating its way out of her chest. He knew. Somehow he knew.

'You were just going to let me walk. In fact you made it your business to see that I did.'

She tried to clear her throat but it was as dry as the Nullabor.

'*Miz* Independence.' The way he said it made it sound like one of the seven deadly sins. In a carefully controlled movement, he closed a fist around the empty can, squeezed till it crumpled like paper. 'Do you figure this is only about you?'

'I—'

He cut her off with a slash of his hand. 'It's about us. Us and *our baby.*'

Because her hands were shaking, she clasped them together beneath the table and wished herself a thousand miles away, preferably on a bed. 'I intended to tell you. Later. I needed time to think, to get used to the idea first. To decide what to do.'

'And what did *you* decide?'

'I will have the baby, if that's what you're asking. Beyond that...I...' Any further thoughts lay crushed beneath the force of that gaze of stone. But his eyes— she had to force herself to meet them—swirled with a jumble of emotions.

They watched one another for seconds that stretched into eternity. She heard the steady drip-drip of the leaky tap, the hum of the refrigerator, the rapid thump of her heart.

'I've had a couple of hours to think too,' he said at last. 'I'll tell you what we're going to do. We're getting married.'

'Married?' The word, the very idea sent a spasm of nerves twisting up her spine. 'I don't think so.' She pushed up from the table and moved to the sink to splash water on her cheeks before she faced him.

If it was possible, his face had hardened further, and there was a steely determination in his eyes tempered with something like understanding. A sense of connection rocked her. She wanted to drop onto those hard thighs, bury her face against that chest and let herself lean. Instead she said, 'I don't need you making decisions for me. I can get along just fine on my own.'

'You're not on your own anymore.'

He was right; she knew already. She had a child to consider. For once she had to put independence and pride aside for the sake of the baby. How could she provide for another when she could barely get by herself?

'We'll get married as soon as we can get the paperwork done,' he said.

'I'm not ready for marriage.'

His brow lifted. 'Hadn't you been planning just that when we met?' His eyes narrowed. 'Do you still have feelings for the guy?'

'No.' How could she when she suddenly knew with absolute certainty she was in love with the man in front of her? *In love.* She'd thought she knew that emotion, but it had never felt like this, an ache that filled her body to overflowing.

And it broke her heart.

'This…it's so…calculated,' she said, her voice hoarse. 'Like a business transaction.'

'If it doesn't work out we can always get a divorce.'

That he could talk so casually of marriage and divorce in the same breath made her want to cry. 'That's not the kind of life I want, for me or my baby.'

'*Our* baby.' His expression softened with those words, but he still had that steel in his eyes. 'I don't want you to do this alone, Carissa. You don't have the funds or the support.'

He was right, but she didn't want to think about it this minute, *couldn't* think about it. 'I can't talk to you now. Mel's coming over after she gets off duty, then I've got to go to work. I'd appreciate it if you could give Mel and me some time alone so I can explain all this.'

'No waiting tables until after the baby's born. No more waiting tables, period. My wife—'

'Now listen up, Mr Fame and Fortune, this is my life we're talking about, and I didn't agree to enter a life of submission. And if you think I'll give up work on your say-so, think again. If the doctor says its okay, I'm working.'

He watched her a moment, nodded slowly. 'Fair enough. For now. From your answer I take it that you agreed to my proposal.'

'Of marriage? Is that what it was? As marriage proposals go, I'd say there's lots of room for improvement.'

Stupidly, impossibly hurt by his offhand manner and the way he was laying down conditions, she made for the door and sanctuary of her room. But as she brushed past him his hand shot out, curled around her arm.

'Carissa, wait.' The heat of his palm burned into her skin. His eyes were clear and green and she was stunned to see the depth of honesty and openness. 'We don't have a lot between us now, but what we do have is good. I've never asked a woman to marry me, and I don't expect to do it again.'

The dull, sweet ache sharpened as the implication penetrated. 'What would you expect from our marriage?'

'You'll give me an anchor, something to hold on to. I understand you well enough to know you'll meet me halfway and you'll be faithful. In return I'll give you wealth and security—and think about it—even if you don't want my money, you'll be able to keep this house, and give the child what it deserves. And no one and nothing will come before the two of you. That I can promise you.'

What about love? she wanted to ask. But all those things he'd offered counted for a heck of a lot. She nodded slowly, meeting his eyes. 'Okay. But I want something in writing.'

Something to protect herself when things fell apart. *Stop right there.* Where was her optimism when she needed it most? Why should she fail any more than anybody else who took vows they intended to keep? He was the realist, and he was prepared to give it a go.

But unlike him, she was laying her heart at his feet, leaving herself wide open to having it broken. If only he knew. Well, he wasn't going to find out that little piece of information.

He let her go. 'Fine. We'll draft something together. By the way, we have an appointment with Dr Sharman on Thursday at 2:00 p.m. I assume you know where that is?'

So that was it. The damn phone. *Everything happens for a reason.* 'We? No, I don't—'

'Don't even try leaving me out of it. I'm coming and that's a fact.'

His expression was not at all loverlike as they eyed each other in the silence that followed. No shared happiness over the news that they were going to be parents. No celebratory dinner for two planned or excited phone calls to relatives.

She hugged her arms. 'Is this really what you want?'

'I could ask you the same question. I guess we'll find out together. I'll leave you to work out the details you want for the ceremony. I'm not bothered how we do it.'

He wasn't bothered? He'd told her he wasn't a for ever guy. Did he intend to stay on here in one place, to stay faithful, as he obviously thought she would? She was afraid to ask. She was better off not knowing.

She was taking the biggest risk of her life. And so, she thought, was he. She wondered who stood to lose the most from this deal.

CHAPTER EIGHT

'MEL.' Carissa hugged her stepsister at the door, clung for a moment, breathing in the strawberry scent of her hair before stepping back to let her in. 'Thanks for coming over at short notice.'

'You sounded different on the phone,' Mel said, studying Carissa's face. 'Something's happened. Let me guess.' A teasing smile lit her eyes. 'Mr Music's asked you to marry him and he's going to whisk you away to a life of luxury.'

Carissa turned away, gave herself a few seconds before facing her again. 'It wasn't so much a question as a statement of intent.'

'What was?' Melanie settled on the sofa and clasped her fingers around one raised knee.

Because her legs were shaky, Carissa opted for the piano stool. 'Ben's…' she lifted a shoulder '…proposal.'

Mel shifted from casual to full alert and leaned forward. 'Proposal,' she said slowly. 'As in marriage?' If it hadn't been so serious it would have been comical. 'You and Ben? Oh, Carrie, I'm sorry. I stole your thunder. I was joking. I wanted to get a rise out of you.'

'Believe me, it's no joke.'

'I had no idea.' With a whoop, she jumped up, lunged across the room and hugged her.

Carissa remained sitting and struggled against the urge to cry. She wished she could have been happy. Instead she was afraid and unsure and still numb with shock.

'So why the long face?' Mel pulled back and her grey eyes turned serious. 'You look like he asked you to cut off your piano-playing fingers. You accepted?'

'I told you it wasn't a question.'

'No one can force you, Carrie. First off, do you love him?'

Admitting what her heart had known for some time was a big, new and scary step. She swiped her eyes and nodded.

'So what's the problem? And why the tears, for heaven's sake? Hey, if he didn't ask the way you wanted, maybe it's because he doesn't know how.'

'Or maybe it's because he doesn't want to marry me at all.'

'Then why would he ask, silly? I've seen the way he looks at you. And I don't think a man like Ben would do anything he doesn't want to.'

If only Carissa could be sure that was true. 'I'm pregnant.' Suddenly she couldn't sit still. She paced to the window. A flock of galahs had descended on the gum tree, their raucous cries shattering the stunned stillness.

'You were supposed to use the condoms,' Mel said behind her.

'Take it from me, they're not fail-safe.'

'Just a moment...' Mel's hands came to rest on

Carissa's shoulders and she turned her around until they stood eye to narrowed eye. 'You've only known him, what, since mid-February? Just how pregnant are you?'

'Seven weeks. Dr Beaton gave me the good news yesterday. A one-night stand, Mel. Remember, you thought it was a good idea at the time.'

'Sure, with protection. I didn't think you'd actually go through with it on a whim. Not you, not steady-as-she-goes, think-everything-over-twice, predictable Carissa.'

'Not exactly a whim. I thought it over for at least an hour.'

Mel blew out an incredulous breath. 'An hour.'

'I saw and used an opportunity. And it felt right. But I trapped him, Mel. He doesn't want this baby.'

'Did he tell you that?'

'No.'

In fact she'd given him the perfect opportunity to simply disappear. He could have taken off after that phone call he'd intercepted and never looked back. But he hadn't. Didn't that tell her something about the man?

'There you are, then,' Mel said, and squeezed Carissa's shoulders.

'He comes with baggage. He's mourning his friend, blames himself. He won't discuss his family. He's involved in some sort of business but doesn't talk about it. He's obviously wealthy—what if he's involved in something illegal?'

'Do you really think that?'

Carissa sighed, knowing deep down Ben was a man of integrity. 'He's still a mystery man.'

'Look, sis, it may not be the love affair of the millennium, but if he's willing to take responsibility and make a go of it, even if only for the baby's sake, I'd say you're one lucky girl.' Mel turned to the kitchen. 'Where is this knight of yours and soon-to-be brother-in-law?'

'I wanted to talk to you alone.'

Carissa remained by the window. Ben's Porsche was still in the garage. Presumably he'd walked to the beach. She wondered how he was feeling, what he was thinking. Was he as devastated as she? He hadn't looked it; he'd looked determined and in control.

'When are you going to do it?'

'A week.' She set her jaw. 'No fuss, just you and Adam, and if Ben wants anyone special… There's his mum, of course…' Her heart squeezed in sympathy when she remembered his loss. 'Oh, Mel…his friend.'

'Then small and simple's the way to go.'

'We'll have it here. In this room.'

'Here?' Mel's frown said it all, but she raised a smile when she saw Carissa was serious. 'That could work…with some time and money. A lot of money. Maybe Ben could—'

'No. Definitely not. No way. It's take me as I am, cracks-in-the-wall and all. Ben's prepared to be a father for my baby—'

'He *is* the father, Carrie.'

The sharp, sweet pain of acknowledgement stabbed at Carissa's heart. 'I can't ask for more than that.'

'Honey, it's your *wedding*. And it's his wedding, too.'

'It's not a wedding. It's an exchange of words.'

Mel raised her palms. 'Whatever you say.'

Ben hadn't shown one iota of interest in the details, so it was as Mel said—whatever Carissa wanted. She thought of the wedding magazines she pored over, the gown she'd designed, the little church her grandmother had been married in, then put them out of her mind.

'Maybe he'll turn up in those hip-hugging, ball-breaking leather pants the band wears,' Mel said, eyes twinkling.

'Oh, God.' That poster. 'I don't know him at all—what am I getting myself into?'

'Calm down, I'm teasing. Underneath he's just a regular guy—a rich and *gorgeous* regular guy.'

The mention of *underneath* had Carissa's mind flashing back to that night. To the huge, hard masculine part of him that had gotten her into this predicament. Its dark and sensual beauty as he slid it inside her, his hot skin rubbing her nipples… She shivered. *Underneath,* he was no ordinary guy.

But he was marrying her for the baby's sake. Nothing more. And was that enough? Would it ever be enough?

As a distraction, she moved to the piano and belted out the first stirring bars of 'Phantom of the Opera.' For all their sakes, she hoped she wasn't making the biggest mistake of her life.

Ben returned from his jog on the beach to find Carissa in a frenzy of domestic activity. She was slicing fruit salad, something spicy simmered on the stove. She had an hour before she had to go to work.

'I hope you're eating some of that before you go.'

She squeezed passion-fruit pulp and lemon juice into the bowl. 'No, I'll grab a snack later.'

'I told you not to cook for me.' He frowned, suddenly aware of her paler complexion, the smudges beneath her eyes. 'Snacks aren't enough in your condition.' *Leave it be,* he warned himself. Grabbing a chair, he turned it around and straddled it. 'You talked to Melanie?'

'Yes.'

'And?'

Carissa squeezed detergent into the sink, turned on the taps full blast and began washing dishes. 'She's looking forward to getting to know her new brother-in-law.'

He felt a weight lift. At least Melanie was on his side, but Carissa had her back to him and he had no idea how to read her. 'What have you decided about the ceremony?'

'I thought we could have it in the living room. I've already asked Mel and Adam. I know a marriage celebrant if she's available at such short notice.' The sound of pots clunking in water filled the brief silence. 'Who do you want to ask?'

'No one.' Jess wouldn't want the reminder.

'What about your mum?'

He hesitated. 'There's something I haven't told you about Mum. She's in a home. Hasn't spoken in ten years.'

Carissa turned, her eyes full of sympathy. 'Oh. I'm sorry.'

The old ache that struck whenever he thought of his mother squeezed his heart. Instinctively he rubbed the heel of his hand over his chest. 'So am I.' She'd have been ecstatic watching him marry a class act like Carissa.

'Carissa, if we're having it here, I'd like to…' Melanie would be easier to approach and he could do a bit of manoeuvring. 'Do something for me. Wear blue, something long and slim.'

She muttered something as she pulled the plug. Water drained with an ominous glugging sound.

'I'm paying for the dress, so no talk about not being

able to afford it. If we're getting married, we share, and that means sharing expenses, as crass as the mention of money might sound to you. And I'm calling a plumber.'

He saw her shoulders droop and something uneasy worked through him. Was she thinking of another wedding she'd planned? Did she have a chaste white gown stashed away with her unfulfilled dreams? 'Wear whatever you want,' he said more gruffly than he should have.

'I haven't given my wardrobe a thought. I've more important things on my mind. But thank you.' She wiped her hands on a cloth. 'You do own a suit, I assume? I know it's only a small gathering, but...'

'I won't let you down, Carissa.' He realised then how much he wanted to believe it.

He'd give it his best shot; for his child, for Carissa, and for the memory of the boy trying to win a father's love that had never existed in the first place.

After he'd dropped Carissa at work, he rang Melanie, got her address and headed over.

'Hi, Ben. Come on in. I'm glad you called. I'm busy plotting and need your opinion. By the way, welcome to the family, such as it is.' Melanie pecked his cheek, then showed him into the living room where she'd spread paint chips and cloth swatches over every available surface.

'Redecorating?'

'Yes, but not here, this is for Carissa.'

He nodded, pleased he'd trusted his instincts with Melanie. 'Just what I want to discuss. I'd like to do something with the living room before the wedding but I don't want Carissa getting stressed out over it.'

'Of course not.'

He stuck his hands in his pockets. 'We'll have to get her out of the house for a few days.'

'I'll insist she stay here. A girl's last days of freedom should be with family. She'll go for it—I'll make sure. Trust me. I'll ask Adam to help you.'

'I want to hire a painter, if you could choose the furnishings—you know her taste. Then there's the catering and…'

Melanie picked up a pad and pen and smiled. 'Okay, sit down and let's make a list.'

Clutching a bouquet of white roses, Carissa stepped from the limo Ben had organised to collect her, Mel and Adam. 'I don't know if I can go through with this.' She smoothed a clammy hand down the ice-blue silk sheath and wished she felt as cool, calm and collected as Mel looked in her fuschia-trimmed emerald dress.

'You'll be fine when you see Ben,' Mel assured her. 'You'll both be fine. Adam told me Ben's as uptight as you are.'

Ben. She was marrying Ben. Her stomach heaved, and for a moment the house shimmered before her eyes. She clutched her belly. *Don't do this to me, little one. Your father wouldn't understand.*

A cool breeze kissed her cheeks and the nausea passed. The day was a perfect blue. Someone whistled and honked their horn as a car whizzed by.

Nerves were doing a fast rumba in her belly and she fingered one of the rosebuds Mel had twisted into her upswept hair. 'I feel ridiculous, all dressed up going into my own living room.'

'Pretend it's a chapel.' Mel laid a hand on Carissa's elbow. 'Give Adam a minute to open the door.'

She grasped Mel's arm. 'Adam's got a video camera.'

'You want a memento of the day, don't you?'

The first strains of a harp rippled through the air, something *olde worlde* and infinitely beautiful. Carissa could smell gardenias and fresh paint. 'There's one of those wedding horseshoe things over the door.' Her pulse shot up and she caught Mel's eyes twinkling. 'I knew I shouldn't have left Ben here alone. What's he done?'

'Planned you a wedding day you'll always remember.'

Tears of emotion threatened to engulf her. 'You were in on this, weren't you?'

But Mel brushed that off. 'It's time. And for God's sake—and Ben's—smile.'

Carissa had to make a conscious effort to relax her lips, and had just gotten that under control when she halted at the door and looked into what had once been her living room. She turned to Mel, but the traitor only smiled and moved past her.

The walls were a warm cream shot with buttercup, the carpet had been ripped up and the floorboards gleamed like warm honey. An oriental rug in rich gold lay in the centre of the room. A harpist played beside the piano. Carissa counted four urns of flowers. White and gold helium balloons with gold strings hovered on the ceiling.

Through a mist, her eyes locked with Ben's. He stood beside the piano in a white shirt, formal grey suit and tie, with a white rose in his lapel, fulfilling all the fantasies she'd ever had about her wedding day. She swallowed the lump in her throat and had to take two deep breaths before she trusted herself to move. She only hoped she wouldn't throw up on the new rug.

His gaze didn't leave her. Oddly, it gave her strength as she crossed the room. She felt as if she were walking in a dream. Finally she stood in front of him. He smelled of peppermints and some spicy new cologne.

'Hi there, Blue Lady,' he whispered. 'Ready?'

She lifted her chin, drowning in the unexpected depth of softness in his eyes. 'I'm ready if you are.'

His mouth, which had remained solemn, curved. 'Then let's get married.'

She put her trembling hand into his outstretched one and the tension melted away in the warmth of his touch.

They moved together, past the harpist, past Mel and Adam, to the celebrant.

'Good morning.' She smiled at them, then began to read from the notes Carissa and Ben had prepared.

'We are here today to witness and share in a marriage ceremony. Marriage is the establishment of a home where through tolerance, patience, courage and understanding two people can develop a strong and lasting relationship with each other and any children they may have. Carissa's and Ben's choice is responsible, free and independent.'

Carissa tried to concentrate on the words, but all she was aware of was the rock-solid comfort of the hand holding hers, the scent of the flowers mingling with Ben's cologne, the quiet cascade of harp strings.

'Marriage according to law in Australia is the union of a man and a woman to the exclusion of all others, voluntarily entered into for life…'

The words pulled her back to the present. This was for real. For life. *If it doesn't work out we can get a divorce.*

Then they were repeating the vows that would bind them. The celebrant asked for the rings. Ben slipped not only the simple gold band she'd chosen, but a second, studded with diamonds and deep sapphires, onto her finger. 'Carissa Mary, I give you these rings as a symbol of the vows we've made this day.'

Then it was her turn. As she slid the Celtic-designed band on his finger and looked into those deep green eyes she wondered fleetingly how long he'd wear it, then the celebrant was pronouncing them husband and wife.

Ben held her face between his hands as if he held the most fragile china. 'Hello, Mrs Jamieson.'

'Mr Jamieson.' *I love you.* How long before she could find the courage to say the words aloud?

How long before she heard them back?

The moment hung like a jewel on a chain of gold. She absorbed the scent of flowers and Ben, the cascade of watery music, his fingertips against her skin.

His lips touched hers, firm but gentle. She heard Mel's sigh, Adam clearing his throat, before Ben stepped back, his smile reflected in his gaze. Bronze highlights glinted in his newly trimmed deep brown hair.

Melanie was the first to break the moment. She moved in to kiss Carissa, then Ben. 'Congratulations.'

'The man's a lucky guy,' Adam said, dropping a light kiss on Carissa's cheek.

The celebrant stayed for the first glass of bubbly. Carissa toasted with soda water. The harpist entertained them with light classical while they ate a luncheon of prawn and avocado cocktails and chicken and salad, courtesy of the Three Steps. Mel had baked a white chocolate cake.

Carissa couldn't believe where the time had gone when the harpist packed and left and Mel, too, announced she and Adam were leaving.

'But it's only two o'clock.' A fist of nerves gripped her. It would be just the two of them, alone. Which was ridiculous when apart from the past few days they'd shared the same house for weeks.

Mel's eyes danced. 'You'll find what Ben has planned much more exciting,' she promised, and gave her a quick hug. Carissa wanted to hold on, but Mel tugged out of her grasp and almost danced to the door. 'And don't worry about the cleaning-up. I'll be over later.'

'Later?'

'Have a wonderful time. Let's go, Adam.'

Adam and Ben exchanged grins as they shook hands.

'She's bossy, that one,' Carissa told Adam as he leaned in for a kiss.

'I know. Take care.'

'Bossy? Who, me?' Melanie gave him a playful shove and they were out the door in ten seconds flat.

Carissa watched them get into the taxi and drive away. 'That was a little like being hit by a whirlwind,' she murmured.

'That's because we have a plane to catch.'

'A plane?' she said on a rising note of panic. 'I don't even own a suitcase. I can't possibly…'

'Before you say anything, just listen.' Ben's hands rested lightly on her shoulders as he turned her. 'We need some time away in a neutral environment. I've spoken to your boss. Rosie and the crew will work your shifts for a few days. Melanie'll be keeping an eye on the place and she's packed you a bag. The taxi'll be here in half an hour, so you've got time to slip into something more comfortable for travelling.'

'Where are we going?'

'You'll see when we get there.'

'I only hope I won't spoil it for you. Morning sickness. Don't believe the label, it hits at all hours.'

'Then this'll be good for you. You can sleep all day if you want. No one'll disturb you.'

Did he include himself in that promise? She wondered for the hundredth time whether he intended consummating their marriage. He hadn't attempted to touch her since he'd learned of her pregnancy, as if she were a changed person somehow. And sex with commitment—that was something else again.

Before she could ponder that he stepped back. 'But first, I want a good look at you in that gown.' His gaze warmed as surely as if he'd stroked a hand over her body. She felt…desired, cherished, though she knew it was only the power of the day, the euphoria she felt for the moment.

He'd married her, but he didn't love her.

But he'd made it so, so special. 'Thank you. For everything. I had no idea, even when Mel insisted I stay over.'

'I'm glad you enjoyed it.'

It was easy to take that step forward, to rest her hands against his chest. He'd removed his suit jacket and the scent and heat of his skin warmed her palms through the crisp cotton shirt. Her rings glittered in the light.

He bent and met her lips, brushed them, once, twice, before moving lightly to nip at her throat. 'I have to tell you, I have this thing for women with slender exposed necks.' Her head fell back as his hands slid into her hair and his lips moved like slow honey over her neck. 'Drives me crazy.'

Oh, my... 'Did you mention a taxi?' she managed to murmur.

'Yeah. And now I've messed your hair.' He tried to finger-comb it back without much success. 'And after you had it salon-done.'

'Hey, I did it myself. Mel helped me.'

'I left you money. Wasn't it enough?'

'I didn't use it. I'm not used to spending on a whim.'

He frowned. 'Well, get used to it. You married rich, Mrs Jamieson.'

She shook her hair and tugged at pins, annoyed that he'd brought the subject up. 'I didn't marry you for money.'

His eyes darkened. 'No. I guess you didn't.' He stepped back and stuck his hands in his pockets. 'Better go get ready.'

She nodded, backing away, aware she'd hurt him somehow and unsure how to fix it.

She'd never given a honeymoon a thought, but now, as she slipped out of the silk gown and into light trousers and sweater, she almost felt a sense of relief. No awkward wondering whether he'd sleep in his room or come to her bed. What would happen, would happen. Or not.

After a quick briefing with Joe, the pilot, Ben settled down beside Carissa for the flight to Mackay. From there they'd catch a helicopter to the island.

As the tiny sleek jet lifted into the air he watched her nerves turn to awe. Late-afternoon sun slanted through a gap in the thickening cloud and glinted off the wing, and as they banked it caught her hair, now in a braid over one shoulder, setting it ablaze in a rope of gold.

Her knuckles whitened on the arm rest as the plane hit minor turbulence rising through the clouds. 'Nothing to see for a while,' he reassured her. 'Relax and try to get some rest.'

Then it was all smooth sailing and clouds. Her eyes closed and soon her head lolled back. He popped the top on a beer and settled back to enjoy the brief hiatus.

She was his wife, soon to be the mother of his child, yet they were strangers. Married strangers. Their lives travelled different paths. Even for starry-eyed couples in love, it was a gamble.

He looked at his sleeping wife and something soft yet fierce tugged at him. Everything had already changed. For once in his life he'd hit the jackpot with Carissa and a wise gambler knew when the stakes were too high to risk.

CHAPTER NINE

THE tropical evening was alive with insect noise when they arrived at the Black Opal Resort, Emerald Island, on the Great Barrier Reef. Ben led Carissa along a path lined with palms and kerosene torches. Island music drifted on the air.

She gazed up at the glittering entrance. 'Wow.'

Her wide-eyed wonder made him smile. He turned his smile to the woman in the floral uniform waiting to welcome them in the lobby, then bent forward to kiss her cheek. 'Hi, Tahlia, good to see you again.'

'Ben, congratulations! I was so excited when I heard the news.'

Carissa's eyes were glazed over with fatigue as Ben smoothed a reassuring hand down her back. 'Tahlia, I'd like you to meet Carissa. My wife.'

'Mrs Jamieson.' Tahlia turned that familiar smile on Carissa. 'Congratulations, and welcome. If I can be of service for anything at all, let me know.'

'Thank you. I'm sure everything'll be wonderful.'

'You're in the Orchid Garden villa, as requested,' she informed Ben. 'Simon'll bring your bags.'

'Thanks, Tahlia. We'll make our own way.'

'So you're a regular guest here,' Carissa said as they strolled from the four-storey building towards the villas nestled among palms and lush gardens. 'I can see why. It's gorgeous.'

She slowed near a row of scarlet hibiscus, but he tugged her along the path. 'Come on, you're so tired you can barely walk straight. We'll explore tomorrow.'

'I think I'm sleepwalking and I'm having this wonderful dream.'

She was swaying as he decoded the door then led her inside to a wicker couch. 'Here, sit a moment.'

The ubiquitous bowl of tropical fruits and bottle of sparkling white and two glasses sat on a glass table. 'Mangoes, yum.' She picked one up and sniffed. 'Sorry, no wine for me.'

'I'll order something. Soda water okay?'

At her nod he rang Room Service, then moved through the suite, opening windows and drapes. The sounds and scents of the tropics drifted in on the heavy air. A fountain trickled by their private patio lit by a green lantern. Beyond, the languorous sounds of a sheltered sea calmed the soul. He turned on an overhead fan to set a lazy draught.

'I prefer the outdoors, but if you'd rather the air-con, I can…' He trailed off when he realised she wasn't listening. Something stirred in him as he watched her sleep, one hand under her cheek on the arm of the couch. Something big, something awesome, something downright scary.

He'd never felt it before, this cocktail of sexual desire and heartbreaking tenderness, and it brought a God-awful lump to his throat. Left him shaken, left his brain incapable of rational thought.

Their bags arrived with the water, sparing him the task of dwelling on his emotions. When the bellboy had gone, he crouched down in front of Carissa. Her slow breathing warmed his face. She was wearing some exotic perfume he'd never smelled on her before today, something mysterious and evocative. It reminded him of blooms that flowered only by the light of the moon.

He slipped his arms beneath her and she slid bonelessly against him. Switching the lights off, he moved through the quiet rooms and laid her on the bed. Moonlight poured through the window, gilding her features. He slipped off her shoes and wondered about removing her outer garments or whether she'd wake and think he was making a move on her.

So he left her and took a quick shower. A cold, quick shower. For tonight at least, to spare her the sight of his over-eager masculinity, he pulled on a pair of boxers rather then his usual habit of sleeping naked.

It wouldn't have made a difference; she was still asleep when he returned. Easing onto the bed beside her, he took a deep breath and wondered how many nights he'd lie like this in the darkness—wanting her, waiting for her to want him.

Her gut-wrenching groan had him fumbling for the lamp.

She pushed up, a hand over her mouth. Her face was chalk-white. 'Bathroom,' she whimpered, and rolled off the bed.

'Here.' He shot up, ready to help, but, ignoring him, she stumbled across the room, slammed the door in his face.

He hurried to grab a soda and glass, then knocked at the door. 'You okay?'

'What do you think?' Anger and impatience in that raw-throated voice.

'I've got some—'

'Go away. Go far, far away.'

He backed up. 'Okay.'

Feeling helpless and—dammit—responsible, he put the drink on the bedside table and moved to the patio and let the breeze touch his body. Probably the only touching he was likely to get any time soon.

How long did she have to put up with this sickness? He had no idea. He heard the toilet flush, the sound of running water, then the door opened.

He stood still, hesitant to approach her. 'You look like death on a warming dish.'

'Thank you. A bride loves to hear compliments like that on her wedding night. I feel much better now.' She waved a hand towards the door. 'Is that a private bathroom or do we have to share with the entire island? That spa's a lake, and the jungle of potted palms…' Colour was seeping back into her cheeks. She picked up her glass. 'Thanks.'

She eyed him with a trace of humour. 'One of us is over-dressed here.' She unzipped her bag, rummaged through it and pulled out something white and lacy, then disappeared into the bathroom again.

He turned out the light, slid between the sheets and waited. His blood pounded through his groin with a need that bordered on pain.

That need doubled when she opened the door and made her way towards the bed. In the dimness he could see her body outlined against the shimmering silk. Its pale sheen highlighted the shadows beneath her breasts, the darker nipples. He swallowed over a dry throat, his eyes moving lower to the triangle of hair.

All too well he could imagine lifting that barely there hem and pushing it up and up over her thighs… Sliding a finger into that warm moisture, dropping to his knees and tasting it on his tongue… A groan rumbled in his chest. He was rock-hard and ready to roll.

He closed his eyes. Then he mentally recited the national anthem. Backwards. Told himself she needed rest. He didn't move when the bed dipped a little as she slowly slid in beside him.

'Ben?' Barely a whisper.

She was close enough for the heat of her luscious body to torture him, but not so close that they touched. In the dark he almost smiled at the irony. She was trying not to wake *him*.

He lay for a long time listening to the night sounds and his own body's galloping thump, willing his erection to subside. Not a chance.

Something moved in the garden outside, a lizard, maybe. He heard the muted sound of music from the open-air cabaret and the slap of water on sand beyond their villa, Carissa's slow breathing.

Finally, as he drifted on the edge of sleep, he thought he heard a voice whisper, 'Thank you, Ben.'

His lips curved in the grey tropical night. *My pleasure, Carissa Mary.*

Carissa rolled over and out of bed and stumbled straight to the bathroom. What a way to spend a honeymoon. She moistened a cloth and wiped her mouth. Still, you weren't supposed to *be* pregnant on your honeymoon.

She stood up and stretched, revelling in the sun filtering through the skylight and onto the indoor garden. Amazing how you could feel so lousy one moment, so good the next.

Ben was asleep, sprawled on one side when she returned. His left hand dangled over the bed, wedding ring still attached. The sheet covered him just where it began to get interesting, below the arrow of dark hair beneath his navel.

His broad bare chest rose and fell with each breath. So tempting to reach out and run her fingers through the spattering of dark hair. To lave her tongue over the flat, pebbly nipple, take it between her teeth and tug.

She couldn't drag her gaze away. The stress lines that often furrowed his face had smoothed out. He looked younger. And innocent. She felt an unfamiliar and overwhelming tenderness, a warm tide that left her weak and wanting.

Then he rolled onto his back with a stertorous sigh and the sheet slipped low. Very low.

Oh…mmm. He was stretched out on the bed like a feast and her mouth watered. Even semi-aroused he was big. The blood raced through her body, its sultry heat causing drops of perspiration to form on her brow, between her breasts. As if by the power of lustful thoughts his erection grew, shooting sparks along her arteries.

This man was her husband. As his wife, all that masculinity belonged to her and her alone. Possessiveness wasn't something she was familiar with either, but it was there, lodged firmly inside her. Something she'd have to overcome sooner or later.

He'd leave eventually. Why would he want an

inexperienced woman like herself when he probably had a lover in every Australian state? A classical pianist when he wrote music for a rock band? Better to get used to the idea of loss.

His eyes snapped open, rather suddenly, for someone who'd supposedly been asleep. 'Good morning.' He stretched, unashamedly naked, stomach muscles rippling, the thick jut of his sex angling her way as he drew up a knee and put his hands behind his head.

'Good morning.' She walked to the patio to drink in a less unsettling picture. Through the lush green outside, sunlight danced on white sand and turquoise sea. The atmosphere breathed sounds and fragrances. Life, vitality. 'Such a beautiful view.'

'Not bad from here either.'

Licks of heat slid over her skin. In the full light of day and her sheer nightgown she was barely decent. 'I'll order up breakfast. What would you like?' As she spoke she moved to her bag and pulled out the slinky white robe Mel had packed to cover herself.

'Anything. Everything. Leave it off. I like looking at you. You remind me of a fairy-tale princess with the morning light on your shoulders and your hair tumbled.'

But he wasn't looking at her shoulders or her hair. A nervous laugh threatened. Instead she said, 'You've a way with words. You're a musician. Put them to music.' She put the robe down and refolded her travelling clothes to busy her hands.

'My songwriting days are over.' He punched his pillow, frowned up at the ceiling.

It distressed her to hear his sadness. 'You'll write new songs, better ones.'

'I'm dried up.'

She heard the resignation in his voice and wanted, suddenly, to shake him out of that hole he'd dug himself into. 'So get out the hose. You're good at that.'

'I'm hungry,' he said, dismissing her suggestion with a hand on his stomach. 'Why don't you order up that breakfast you suggested?'

She glared at him. 'You've not heard the last of this.' But she picked up the phone. 'Yes, good morning. This is the Orchard Garden villa.'

Twenty minutes later they were tucking into fresh fruit, croissants and coffee. She felt like a film star surrounded by luxury.

'What do you want to do today?' Ben slid a brochure across the table. 'We can take a glass-bottom boat and view the coral, scuba dive or take a walk through the rainforest.'

No suggestion of spending it in bed. Carissa rolled her shoulders, feeling the sunlight sparking off greenery by their patio while she filled her lungs with sea air and told herself she was *not* disappointed. 'I'll let the expert decide.'

'Okay. I suggest we take one of their famous gourmet hampers over to one of the little islands by dinghy. We can unwind with a massage after and enjoy our own private spa before dinner.'

'You've already done those things here, haven't you?' With some other woman, some other lover. An ache settled near her heart, but she took a slice of melon, bit into its sweetness.

'Not with my wife.' He set his knife down and met her eyes. 'The night you walked into my life I was a different man.'

She shook her head. 'Not true, Ben. You never intended to see me again. I certainly didn't intend seeing *you* again.'

'Maybe it started out that way. Do you remember what you wore that night?'

'My one and only. My blue gown.'

'What else?'

'Nothing. Oh…' She felt the tell-tale blush creep into her cheeks.

'A skimpy blue triangle that had me fantasising over you for the next few weeks. Something I'm still doing.' His voice was bland, hiding whatever feelings he had regarding their yet-to-be-consummated marriage, but his eyes turned molten, holding hers for several long heartbeats.

'Ben…'

'It wasn't just about sex.' He opened a croissant and spread it with jam. 'You got to me.'

His words sent a thrill through her, but she knew it cost him to admit it. 'Me too,' she said softly. 'The night before we got together, out the front of the hotel you were so in control, all anger and impatience. I imagined how…satisfying it would be to turn all that masculine energy to my advantage.'

He picked up his coffee-cup and kicked back in his chair, assessing her with deceptively lazy interest. 'Did your thoughts run to how you might achieve your goal, by any chance?'

'I may have been a virgin, but I have a rich imagination.'

That awful word again, the one that reminded her of her inexperience in the bedroom, that told her she wasn't Ben's ideal woman. Her upbeat mood deflated.

'Ben, if you ever…' Because she didn't want to look at him, she poured a second coffee that she didn't want. 'Our marriage is a partnership, a coming together to raise a child, so if you do ever want to… I'll understand, but I'd rather not know. But I would ask you to keep it discreet. I don't want to be an object of ridicule or pity.'

A gentle breeze with the scent of salt and green blew off the sea, cooling her suddenly heated face.

'Carissa.' He leaned forward, captured her hands clenched together on the table. 'Sweetheart…'

'No. Don't say something you'll regret later.' She pulled away and went to rummage in her bag. 'I'm going to take a swim in that pool I saw last night before I get too fat to wear a swimsuit. Meet you there when you're ready.'

She collected what she needed and retreated to the safety of the bathroom to change. With a sigh she lowered herself to the edge of the tub. She'd just given her husband of less than a day permission to go with other women.

He'd not made any attempt to touch her since they'd arrived. Which left her to assume he didn't want her anymore. She lifted a shoulder. So he'd told her he'd fantasised about her. He talked the talk, but did he walk the walk?

She slipped out of her nightie and took a critical inventory of her naked body. Tall, lean, breasts a little undersized, but getting bigger. A wife in name only. Because it hurt and frustrated her, she turned away and wriggled into a sleek black swimsuit, then covered herself with one of the resort's colourful orchid-print beach robes.

Would he ever want her again?

* * *

Ben stood on the umbrella-decked patio overlooking the pool where he could see Carissa sliding sunscreen over that long, sleek body. He frowned, his fingers crumpling the hotel's entertainment guide. It should be his hands doing the honours.

He watched as she slipped a strap off her shoulder, innocently provocative, and rubbed in slow, languid movements. She rose, sun gleaming on her skin, as graceful as her maiden name as she sauntered to the edge of the pool and dived in, her streamlined body a blur of black and tan beneath rippling blue water.

'Ben?' The sound of Tahlia's voice didn't distract him from the tempting scene a few metres away.

'What?' he growled.

'What are you doing here by yourself and scowling?'

He shifted, uncomfortable, clenched and unclenched his left hand, noticing the unfamiliar weight of his wedding ring. 'To be honest, I'm not sure.'

'Now there's a change.' She smiled, but concern clouded her eyes. 'Ben, is there anything I can do for you?'

'Can you reserve two masseurs at 5:00 p.m., please, and let's see, an arrangement of orchids delivered to our villa this afternoon. And that tear-drop sapphire necklace in the lobby boutique—I'd like it put in the resort's safe for now.'

She scribbled on her clipboard. 'I'll get right on it. Are you sure everything is okay? I'm asking as a friend.'

'Fine, Tahlia.' He forced a smile. 'I just got married, didn't I? Everything's peachy.'

'Your wife will be glad to hear it.'

'Will she?' he wondered aloud, and couldn't stop his

gaze returning to the scene outside. Glistening with water, she'd left the pool and was stretched face-down on a towel.

He felt Tahlia come up beside him, smelled her crisp, fresh scent. 'We've known each other too long, Ben.' Her fingers pressed into his forearm. 'If you want to talk, you know where I am.'

'Thanks.' He covered her hand with one of his, but he didn't take his eyes off the woman by the pool.

Time to find out just how glad she was to see him.

He ordered two mineral waters over ice, then walked slowly to the table beside Carissa, still stretched out, long eyelashes resting on her cheeks. When the water arrived he dipped a finger in one, then crouched down beside her and drew a line of cold moisture down her back.

She shuddered, gasped and rolled over. 'Oh, hi.' Her wary expression softened and he relaxed into a few seconds of sheer pleasure at seeing one of her rare, carefree smiles before the wariness returned.

'Hi.' He bent to drop a kiss on one sun-warmed shoulder, handed her the glass. 'I've come to take my wife on a picnic. Meet me in the lobby in half an hour?'

'Okay.'

He watched her long, lithe limbs as she rose. Every curve was perfection. She smelled of suntan oil and hot female flesh. His groin tightened. His hands itched. He wanted that body against his, under his. Now. It took effort but he remained where he was, having to content himself with the view.

So he wasn't prepared when long fingers dipped into the glass, and before he could duck she'd dropped a lump of ice inside his shirt. 'Hey!'

She drained her glass, picked up her towel and suntan

lotion. 'Half an hour,' she tossed over her shoulder as she walked away.

He was gratified to see she still had a sense of humour. Grinning, he went to collect a picnic hamper.

Carissa was waiting in the lobby when she saw Ben and Tahlia approach together. Her fingers tightened on the brim of the sun hat on her lap. She watched him touch Tahlia's arm in an easy way, then head back the way he'd come. Something hot and unwelcome stabbed through her.

The well-groomed brunette smiled and sat down on the sofa beside Carissa, placed her clipboard on her lap. 'Good morning, Mrs Jamieson.'

'Good morning. And, please, the name's Carissa.' She tried to relax, but couldn't stop herself wondering how well Ben and Tahlia knew each other. That hot feeling intensified and she willed the steamy images away.

'Ben forgot the camera. He asked me to keep you company a few moments.'

Carissa sensed a reserve in the voice behind the smile, but she smiled back. 'It must be great working here.'

'It is. So how did you two meet?'

Just the question Carissa had been itching to ask her. 'At work. I played piano for a hotel in Sydney.'

'The Cove.'

'How did you know?'

Tahlia's brows rose in what Carissa could only interpret as surprise. 'Everyone who knows Ben…' She trailed off, thumbs working over her clipboard.

'We only met a couple of months ago,' Carissa said, and instantly felt the woman sizing her up.

'Then you'll already know he's got a heart as big as the outback,' Tahlia said. 'He took a chance on a girl he knew next to nothing about and arranged this job when I was down to my last dollar. There's nothing I wouldn't do for him.'

Carissa never doubted it. She smiled tightly. 'It's reassuring to know he inspires that kind of loyalty.'

'Believe it.' Tahlia met her eyes squarely for a moment before switching smoothly into business mode. 'I hope you're going to take advantage of all our facilities while you're here.'

'I'm going to try. It's a magnificent place, though, heaven knows, it must be costing Ben a small fortune.' She stopped, appalled at her gauche words.

Tahlia's hostess smile turned genuine, if enigmatic. 'Let him worry about that. Ah, here he comes now.' She rose, her clipboard in hand. 'Enjoy your stay, Carissa.' She turned and grinned at Ben, wagging an admonishing finger at him. 'Talk to your wife.'

What the blazes was that all about? Carissa wondered, her stomach tying itself into knots again. Ben and Ms Efficient with the trim body and neat hair had something going. She ran her fingers through her own damp, flyaway strands. Something Ben hadn't seen fit to clue her in on. She hadn't figured it out yet, but she would. Oh, yes, she would.

CHAPTER TEN

As BEN had promised, the little island beach was deserted, the sand white, the sea a clear aquamarine. Palm trees leaned over the beach, offering shade for their picnic. Carissa sat on the rug Ben had spread out and absorbed the tranquil beauty. The ribbons of sunlight rippling on the water, the emerald colour of the islands in the distance, the sea-scented warm breeze that played with her hair and slid over her body.

Ben opened the hamper and pulled out a sunny hibiscus, slid it behind her ear. 'You look like you belong to the islands.' He trailed his fingertips over her cheek, along her collar-bone beneath her tropical-print shirt. 'You want to move up here someday?'

She thought of Mel, her grandmother's house and the memories there. 'I love my home. I'd hate to leave it.'

'Then you'll never have to, Carissa. I promise you.'

She looked out to sea. But what of Ben? She couldn't allow herself—allow him—to get close, because unlike the way she'd been with Alasdair, she'd shatter when Ben left. Pieces of her heart were already breaking at the thought.

He poured a wine for himself, soda water for her, then raised his glass. 'To happy memories.'

She tapped her glass to his. 'Happy memories.' But she could barely swallow over the lump in her throat. Was that all she'd have one day?

Searching in the basket, Ben pulled out a carefully wrapped parcel tied with silver ribbon. 'This isn't standard issue,' he said, passing it to Carissa.

She passed it back. 'The card's for you.'

'Now I wonder how it got here? You got connections in the kitchen?' His eyes sparked with something Carissa imagined she might have seen in the face of the young boy Ben, and felt a tinge of regret that she wasn't responsible for putting the package there.

She remained silent, waiting while he took pleasure in the simple task of unwrapping it.

'A Christmas star?' She frowned. 'It's only April.'

'When you wish upon a star…' Ben held it up by its thread, spun it. It twinkled in the sunlight. 'It's from Tahlia. Actually, she's returning it. I gave it to her one Christmas.'

Tahlia. Again. That treacherous feeling stole through Carissa and this time she couldn't ignore it, or what it was. Jealousy. Ugly and foreign.

Alasdair had never inspired such feelings and she hated it, didn't know how to deal with it. She tossed back her soda water, planted her glass firmly on the rug and started to push up, with no idea what she intended to do.

'Whoa, there.' Ben grasped her hand. The spark remained in his eyes but his grin sobered. 'My blue lady's green.'

'What do you mean, green?' She tried to tug her hand away, with no luck.

'You know very well what I mean. And I like it.'

She shook her head and glared at the horizon. 'I sure as heck don't.'

'Sit down, Carissa.'

She did, because she knew he'd not let her go until he was good and ready.

'First off, there's nothing romantic between Tahlia and me.' Still keeping a grip, he stroked the inside of her wrist. Her pulse quickened. 'She's got a man in her life. Philip Conrad's the resort manager, and they're very happy.'

Carissa felt the heat rush to her face, suddenly ashamed of her behaviour. Pregnancy was making her feel vulnerable. 'You must be close, though. She knew you stayed at the Cove in Sydney.'

He turned away to gaze at the sea a moment. 'I haven't seen her in over a year, but she knows…because I own it.'

'You *own* the Cove Hotel. Own it.' Incredulous, she stared at him, then blew out a slow breath. 'I've worked there two years and you own it?'

His eyes twinkled back at her. 'Technically, I'm your employer. But only for the past few months. I signed the papers just before I left for the Desert Rock concert.'

'Why didn't you tell me?'

'You never asked.' His expression turned serious. 'You obviously weren't interested in what I did and I decided it was for the best. The less involved we were, the better for both of us.'

'But we are involved. We're married.' The words sounded foreign on her tongue. 'And I did ask you…in a roundabout sort of way. You never gave me a straight answer.'

'Could be because you asked in a roundabout way.'

He leaned closer, stroking her hand again. 'I was going to tell you today. And while we're at it, the Black Opal Resort's mine too.'

'You own *luxury* hotels. No wonder Tahlia gave me a look. I was worried you were spending so much money—in your own hotel.'

He grinned. 'She'll be relieved you're concerned. And I didn't always travel first class. When my first employer died he left me a run-down pub west of Ceduna on the Nullabor Plain. It's taken fourteen years of bloody hard work to get where I am.'

Realisation hit. 'You rang Mr Christos. No wonder old Georgie was falling all over himself that morning. "Reconsidered", my foot.' She narrowed her eyes at him. 'I should be mad at you. You went behind my back and rang him after I expressly told you not to.'

Ben shook his head. 'I couldn't let you lose that job, sweetheart.'

Prepared to forgive, she said, 'Okay, I guess he was only following instructions. Stupid instructions, by the way. But he's still a jerk.'

'He's a dedicated employee,' he said, but chuckled nonetheless.

'Which came first, hotels or music?'

'I played after the pub closed for the night. There's not much to do at night in the middle of nowhere. I used to take my guitar into the desert and compose under the stars. When Rave hit the big time I wrote stuff for the band.'

At the mention of his friend his eyes clouded, the smile on his lips died. He opened the backpack he'd brought and pulled out a self-timing camera. 'I want something to remember our time here,' he said abruptly.

Sliding her sunglasses off, she watched him from the rug, the glints in his hair, the way the muscles in his forearms moved as he set the camera on a nearby rock and adjusted it.

'Coming ready or not.' In three quick strides he reached her, hugged her shoulders and they both smiled for posterity. 'Again.' And he was up, resetting the timer. 'Now.' Once more he fell on the rug beside her, scooting her body close.

After the camera whirred and clicked, he turned to look at her. She didn't want him to see the naked raw emotion she knew he'd see in her gaze and reached for her sunglasses.

'No.' He reached up and took her hat off. 'I want to see your eyes. Such a beautiful colour,' he murmured. 'They change with the surroundings. Right now they're as clear as the water and brimming with doubts.' His gaze dropped to her mouth, making it feel full and tingly. 'Kiss me. You've never initiated contact. It's always me making the moves.'

He leaned closer, till his face filled her vision, till his mouth was a soft sigh away from hers. Why should she deny him or herself the pleasure of a simple kiss? *Let go and live in the moment.*

She leaned in…and let go.

The world beyond them receded. The rustling palms, the waves lapping the shore faded to a blur of sound as her senses focused on him. Only him. His lips on hers, his breath on her cheek, the scent of tanning lotion and sun-warmed male skin. Heat drizzled through her body like liquid sunshine.

One hard palm reached behind her head, long fingers

slid into her hair to massage the base of her skull and she almost groaned with pleasure. He'd always been gentle, but today she felt something deeper, hotter, simmering beneath the surface.

Her hands rose to cup his smooth, bare shoulders, fingertips absorbing the different textures as they drifted down over the hard planes of his chest, only to creep up again to caress the rough velvet jaw.

His free hand slid beneath her loose shirt and the thin swimsuit strap and his fingertips, callused from years of strumming guitar strings, had her melting with desire. Just the thought of those fingers skimming lower to tease her nipples, which hardened with anticipation, almost drove her over the edge.

Her mouth opened beneath his. Something urgent called to her, something primitive and frightening in its intensity. She could almost believe he felt something stronger, deeper than lust as his tongue danced over hers. Mindlessly her arms tightened around his neck, letting her breasts graze his chest through the layers of fabric.

When he pulled back a little to look at her, she almost whimpered with the loss.

'I want you.' His voice was low, rough with need. 'Naked and under me.'

The image of them tumbling over that king-size bed, skin to skin, male to female, sent a thrill racing through her body. Her gaze dropped to his firm abdomen with its sprinkling of dark hair, the flexing bulge beneath his shorts, and her pulse stepped up another notch. She wanted it too, but she wanted the sexual act *and* the man.

Dizzy with churning emotions, she weighed his

words against the standards by which she'd lived her life. Wanting, lust was easily satisfied. It wasn't enough. She wanted—demanded—more of a life partner, the man she loved. She needed to be *needed*. For herself, not only for her body. She needed to be loved.

A man like Ben wouldn't understand. Heck, at this moment with her whole body craving completion, *she* didn't understand. She shook her head as she leaned away from him. 'Not here, not this way.'

'We can be back in our room in thirty minutes tops.'

'No. That's not what I mean.' She shook her head. 'There has to be more…' How could she explain that she needed something that went beyond a piece of paper that made it legal?

'Other than the fact that I'm your husband, and that kissing you feels damn good?' His voice was impatient, his breathing laboured and uneven.

'Yes.'

'Real life isn't a fairy tale. This is as real as it gets. You and me.' He splayed a warm, wide-palmed hand firmly over her belly. 'And our child.'

To cool the emotional intensity sizzling between them, she shifted so his hand fell away, and concentrated on the thin line of blue on the horizon.

He swore softly, harshly. With jerky movements he opened the beach umbrella, adjusting it so it shaded Carissa, then muttered, 'I need to cool off.'

He strode away, until he was waist-deep in the sea, then glanced over his shoulder. His bronzed body glistened in the sun. Frustration and something deeper burned like fire in his eyes.

She ached to call him back. To beg him to make love

to her here on the sand beneath the blue sky with only the wind and palms to witness her capitulation. Then he turned seaward, dived beneath the surface.

Probably just as well. One day he'd walk away for good.

On their last day Ben blocked out an hour to go over the books. It was only a formality; he trusted Philip and Tahlia, but he wasn't likely to get a chance to come this way again for a while.

He shot off a few e-mails and sat back to watch the sky. Tropical thunderheads were building like ice-cream cones, purple and apricot. A perfect evening for lying in bed with a lover and listening to the rain.

For the past ten days he and Carissa had lazed on white beaches, hiked through rainforest, sipped drinks by the pool.

But the nights… He leaned back in his chair with a sigh of frustration. Soft and warm and wasted. Carissa had made it clear their marriage was for the sole purpose of raising their baby. She'd practically handed him a carte blanche to take any woman he wanted.

Not good for his ego. Probably his fault; he'd handled the whole proposal bit badly. He scrubbed a hand across his jaw, reminded himself he needed to shave. He didn't want another woman; he wanted Carissa. He wanted his wife.

Tomorrow they'd be home, and the real business of married life would set in. Carissa looked fragile right now, but he knew she wasn't. There was a strength in her, both physical and emotional. She'd handle it.

The first drum roll of thunder rumbled across the sky.

Tonight. Tonight he'd end this self-imposed celibacy, barring Carissa's bouts of nausea, of course. She wasn't exactly falling all over him, but he guessed she was entitled to be temperamental. Still, it wouldn't hurt to throw in a candlelit dinner and soft music.

He shut down the computer, picked up the phone and prepared to call Room Service. It wasn't his area of expertise, but he could be romantic when the occasion called for it.

A cold meal of lobster, salads and fruit—so it wouldn't matter when they ate—lay beneath silver covers on a snowy tablecloth. Four scented candles waited to be lit. Fresh frangipani floated in a crystal dish.

With everything organised, Ben kicked off his shoes, flicked on the TV and fell back onto the bed. He'd sent Carissa off for aromatherapy and a full body treatment with orders to the beautician to keep her there a while and make sure she relaxed.

Rain-scented air stirred beneath the slow turn of the overhead fan. The steady plop of water on the banana palm fronds by the patio soothed. He lowered the volume on the TV till it was a whitewash of sound, closed his eyes and drifted…

Blackness engulfed him, dragging him down to a bottomless pit. He was dreaming again and he couldn't wake. He struggled, knowing it was futile. The screeching sound of metal, the crackle of fire, choking smoke that seared his lungs, stung his eyes.

He tried to claw his way out, but his legs were lead pipes. He tried to call, but his throat was dry, filled with the taste of bile and the stench of burnt flesh. He could hear the roll of thunder and his own heart pounding its way out of his chest.

'Ben, Ben, wake up.' The voice of an angel, disembodied and calm. Hands, cool hands touching his flesh, dragging him up, pulling him out.

'Ben, what is it?'

He dragged in a gasp as if it were his last. A sweep of damp air chilled his sweat-slicked skin. It was still raining; the sweet smell of the rainforest wafted through the open patio doors.

He opened his eyes. The lamp in the corner had been switched on, the TV turned off. Carissa's face swam before him, eyes wide, dark with fear. *God, don't let her see me like this.* He turned his face into the pillow. 'Go away, Carissa.' Right now he wanted her more than life.

'I'm not going anywhere. Are you sick? I can't help you if you don't tell me.'

How could he tell her the horrors he dreamed? How sometimes life didn't offer second chances, how the world you thought you knew and the people you loved could vanish like lightning. 'I'm not sick. Leave me alone. You're not part of this. I won't let you be a part of this.'

'I'm your wife. I'm part of it whether you like it or not. If you're not ill, you were having one hell of a nightmare.'

Hell. 'Yeah.' She didn't know how close to the truth she was.

She turned his face until his vision was filled with her. Light fingers traced his brow, his cheek. Fresh from her beauty session, she smelled like heaven's garden, a place he had no business in. She didn't belong here with him.

'Ben, let me help.'

Her quiet words, the concern in those lovely eyes

unmanned him. She unbelted her silky robe; it parted to reveal a glimpse of glowing skin. The swell of her breasts rose and fell with her breathing.

His stomach tightened at the implication. 'I don't need help.'

'You're not seeing you from where I'm standing.'

'You're not the only one who wants to be alone, Carissa.'

'Your response to that was to tell me I'm stubborn. And you were right.' Shucking the robe, she slipped onto the bed beside him. 'You try to shut me out and I'll just keep right on coming back.' She reached out with cool hands, cupped his tensed jaw in her palm.

He dragged her close until every gorgeous curve pressed against him. She went still but her eyes remained clear and steady on his. But his hands weren't steady as they moved over the cool, smooth skin of her hip. He could feel her heart thundering against his, matching his own erratic rhythm.

Blind need pumped through him. To touch and be touched, to be a part of life, and to be close to someone. Not just someone. Carissa. Not any willing body. Her body.

Her legs tangled with his as her arms slid around his neck. Then his mouth was on hers, hard and hungry, and he was lost in her. *Make me forget.*

Darkness, desperation, desire. He was aware of the sensations battering him, couldn't fight them as she drew his tongue against hers, traced circles on his nape with her fingertips. 'Need me,' she whispered. 'Need me now.' She arched and ground her belly against him, leaving him in no doubt about what she wanted.

Somehow he managed to shove down his boxers,

then rolled on top of her. Her flesh was tight, hot, wet as he pushed himself inside. He heard her sharp indrawn breath, perhaps in shock, perhaps in pleasure, but she tightened her arms around his neck and he heard his own groan in response.

The faint but seductive sound of the sax and clarinet in the dining room mingled with the rhythmic patter of rain as he drove into her heat. He couldn't think, couldn't breathe, only knew that this was where he wanted to be. She made him feel whole, healed.

He kissed her neck and her body blossomed to life beneath him. The taste of her skin was like the sweetest tropical fruit, her scent as heady as the frangipani on the table.

All he could think was how much he wanted her, how much he needed her. She was his wife, the mother of his child, something he'd not realised he'd wanted. Until now.

Carissa gasped as his hot steel length plunged inside her with an urgency she'd never experienced. This was deep, dark and dangerous. Unleashed power tipping them both over the edge.

His mouth burned and branded, his hands raced over her breasts, cupping, moulding, squeezing, until she ached with the sweet torment. He was hot, strong, demanding, and her blood heated, her pulse raced in response. Knowing the child they'd made lay safely within her made her feel strong and all female; that it nestled between them now, something shared, drew her to him in a way she'd never imagined.

Weeks of wanting were forgotten. *Only wanting?* No, she thought dimly as she splayed her fingers over his back and felt the strong ripple of muscle, the thin film of sweat, this was so much more.

And then she couldn't think at all. He was like the sea, restless, relentless. Sensation after sensation rolled through her, endless waves of pleasure swamped her. But beneath that power his torment brewed.

'Take me with you.' She uttered the words against his shoulder, tumbled with him through the shadows, raced with him as he fought his demons.

Instinct had her matching his movements. Desperation had her clinging, sobbing. She arched with her body's shattering release, felt him come with a ferocity that both thrilled and shocked her.

She lay limp for a few moments, hearing the rain, feeling her blood pump, the sweat-dampened skin cool, Ben's weight on her body, his breath against her neck.

Too soon, he rolled off her and away with a harsh sound that spoke volumes.

She stared at the back of his head, the long, naked and muscular length of him. The sudden loss of that intimate contact chilled her; his terse sigh panicked her.

Every tingling nerve ending rebelled, every heavy thump of her heart was a reminder of what they'd shared. She couldn't ignore it, wouldn't. But obviously he didn't feel the same way. And why would he? An inexperienced woman wouldn't be enough for a man like Ben, used to females swooning at his feet, working their way into his bed.

Before she made a complete fool of herself she reached for her robe on the floor, dragged it on and sat on the edge of the bed. Damn him for making her doubt herself. There'd never been an obstacle she couldn't overcome until Ben Jamieson had charged his way into her life. Until she'd fallen in love with an impossible dream.

In the muted light she saw, for the first time, the intimate table, the flowers and candles. Anger drained away, replaced by heartache and misery.

She didn't even feel him slide across the bed until his hands closed gently over her shoulders. She jerked at the contact, but his hold tightened.

'Carissa. I'm sorry if I hurt you. You caught me at a bad moment. You were trying to help and I came at you like some uncivilised brute.' The sincerity of his apology glimmered in his eyes.

She didn't want apologies. She wanted something he couldn't give her. Rather than let him see the pain in her eyes, she focused them on the floor.

'Carissa, what happened tonight…'

'Was a healthy bout of sex,' she finished for him.

He turned her till she was facing him, tilted her chin. His eyes locked on hers, dark and deep and intense. 'Oh, sweetheart, it was so much more than that.'

A thrill raced through her at his words. Perhaps there *was* something there besides an apology. If so, she'd do whatever it took. 'I know you'll try to use your nightmares to stay away. It won't work. You have them often, don't you?'

'Have I disturbed you?'

'I've heard you on the porch, seen you pace the yard at night. I can't help you if you shut me out.'

'You don't know what you're getting yourself into,' he murmured into her hair, then tugged her down so they lay side by side facing each other.

'You let me worry about that.' She replayed his words

in her head: *Sweetheart, it was so much more than that.*
Her heart couldn't find its natural rhythm. It might be
one small step in their relationship, but for the first time
real hope hovered in her heart.

CHAPTER ELEVEN

CARISSA decided the best part about going away was coming home. But now 'home' came with a new set of complications. It wasn't only hers now, but a family home with this man she was still learning about, and, in a few months' time, a baby.

For the past few days she'd been living a dream. *Welcome back to reality.* The salty tang of Sydney's beaches, the call of wattle birds. The wait on the porch while someone other than her unlocked the door.

She was nervous—nervous about entering her own house, for heaven's sake. She stood beside him catching the smell of fresh paint as it wafted out the door, two almost-strangers not knowing how to play the moment.

'Wait here,' he said. She watched him walk down the hall, set her suitcase inside her room. Those nerves fluttered again—where did he intend putting his gear?

He motioned her forward. 'There've been a few changes. I hope you'll approve.'

As she approached his eyes remained on hers and she could've sworn he wasn't as confident as he'd like her to think. She stopped at the doorway and her breath caught in her throat.

The tired cream paint and faded wallpaper were gone. The walls radiated cool white. A dressing table and white wicker easy chair had replaced the scarred, garage-sale dresser and kitchen chair. On the window sill a jug of daisies nodded in the breeze. A large rug in muted blues partially covered polished floorboards.

Then there was the Bed, a white wrought-iron production with a sapphire spread that flowed to for ever. 'Oh…'

'Mel helped,' he said, seeing Carissa stumped for words. 'She knows what you like, so I thought…'

'It's gorgeous.'

'I wanted you to be comfortable while you're pregnant.' He moved to the bed, pressed the mattress and nodded. 'Firm but not too firm.'

And big enough to get lost in. She could imagine Ben stretched out between the sheets. She wouldn't get lost if he was there to hold her.

Was she still living the dream? All the way home she'd relived last night's passion. How he'd clung to her as if she were a lifeline, their frantic coupling in the dead of night. *Oh, sweetheart, it was so much more than that.* Did this makeover and beautiful bed mean he intended to sleep with her now that the honeymoon was over?

'You must be tired. You barely got three hours' sleep last night.' His voice turned a trifle husky on the last two words, and her pulse picked up, but before she could think about, let alone voice an improper suggestion, he said, 'Why don't you stretch out and take a nap?'

You. Meaning alone—not precisely what she'd had in mind. So much for improper suggestions. Ben himself showed no sign of sleep deprivation, just the stubble and a slightly tousled look. Didn't mean she couldn't entice him to join her…

Except, she'd never seduced a man. Correction: until last night she'd never seduced a man. Her blood heated at the memory. Had that aggressive woman who'd refused food for another bout between the sheets really been her?

Now, in her own surroundings, in stark daylight, those old insecurities pressed in on her. He was used to experienced women; last night he'd needed someone, an entirely different scenario. Today he was back in control.

'I will.' Her heart beating hard, she focused her eyes on his and moved towards him. 'In a little while.'

He slid his arms around her waist and pressed a kiss to her temple. His heat seeped through her clothes, his masculine soap smell filled her nose. His hands on her lower back were soothing. But impersonal. He wasn't the desperate lover who'd taken her on that wild ride to heaven in the small hours of this morning.

That lover would have dispensed with clothes at the front door. He'd have had her up against the wall, spread-eagled before him while he did wicked things to her with his hands and tongue and teeth. And that hard wedge of masculine flesh she could feel poking into her belly despite his cool outward control would have been—

The sound of the front door opening had her jerking guiltily out of his arms. Her skin was tingling and the heat in her cheeks had spread through her body and throbbed dangerously between her thighs. She couldn't look at Ben.

'Hello?' Mel's voice drifted down the passage.

'In here, Mel.' With unsteady fingers Carissa adjusted her blouse, then laughed, still visualising the scene her stepsister *hadn't* walked in on.

'What?' she heard Ben say, but she was already halfway down the hall.

'Hi.' Mel hugged her, then grinned when she saw Ben leaning against the bedroom door, those wicked, *innocent* hands now in his pockets. 'Whoops, I guess I interrupted something.'

'No. I was being coaxed into a nap,' Carissa began, then realised how Mel would interpret that.

'Sounds like fun.' Mel's grin widened. 'I didn't expect you back for another hour. I wanted to drop a few things off before I go to work.' She picked up the grocery bag she'd brought. 'I'll put this in the kitchen and leave you lovebirds to get on with your…nap.'

Ben took the groceries from Mel. 'Carissa wanted to come home a couple of hours earlier. I'll let you two catch up while I take the car for a spin.'

Mel sighed as he disappeared into the kitchen. 'Cute backside.'

'So you've said, more than once.'

'Cute everything. Who'd have thought Ben Jamieson'd be such a marshmallow?'

'Who'd have thought.'

'Is that a hint of possessiveness I hear in your voice? Don't worry, for all his charm, he's not my type. Come on. Into the living room. I want the latest.'

'Thanks for all you've done here.' Carissa indicated the renovated room. 'I can see your hand in this. And the bedroom's gorgeous.'

'And if I'd stayed away you'd have christened the bed by now.'

Carissa wasn't so sure. At the sound of the Porsche purring down the drive, Mel pulled Carissa onto the couch. 'So tell me all about it. Well—not *all*. Skip the scenery and get to the juicy parts.'

'Mel,' Carissa scolded in a strangled voice. 'A honeymoon's private.'

'Okay. I guess I'll settle for the scenery.'

'The resort's something out of this world.'

'And how did you two get on? Apart from the s-e-x, I mean.'

'Okay, mostly.'

'Mostly?'

Carissa thought of the brooding side of Ben, the hurting that haunted him. 'Sometimes he's hard to reach. I want to get him interested in music again. He seems determined to shut that part of his life away.'

'Well, that segues perfectly into the other item I wanted to talk to you about. You're looking at the hospital's newly elected president of the Rainbow Road.'

'For the kids with cancer?'

Mel nodded. 'I'm organising a fun afternoon in June. Music, magicians, that kind of thing. I'd like you to play for them.'

'Sure.'

'We'll set up in the common room, there's a piano there, and if you can bring your guitar—it's more intimate with kids—nursery rhymes for the littlies and something more upbeat for the older ones.'

And just what Ben needed, Carissa thought. 'I'll bring Ben, it'll be good for him. Put us both down.'

'You don't want to check with him first?'

'No, he'll be there, but don't tell him yet. When he sees those kids he won't be able to say no.'

Carissa popped the honey biscuits she was making for the kids' afternoon into the oven, then wandered to the window to watch the resident gardener at work.

Scarlet and gold leaves littered the lawn, the trees were all but bare, but today he was installing a sprinkler system. Perhaps it was an odd activity to herald winter, but he seemed to find pleasure and solace in her garden. And it *was* a garden now—he had a surprisingly green thumb and she was more than happy to pass on the responsibility.

He squatted, his old T-shirt riding up his spine, jeans low at his back, revealing a patch of bare, tanned skin and a nice handful of backside.

She smiled, remembering how tight and warm it had felt beneath her hands in bed this morning. An almost-perfect lover. Her smile faded a little. In her books 'lover' implied 'love'. But Ben had never promised her love. The word had been absent from their marriage vows, nor had he ever spoken that word to her.

But they had an open and honest relationship—even if this afternoon's concert was a secret she hadn't told him about. During the day both were busy with work, but the nights… She sighed. She couldn't have wished for a more caring and gentle man.

And watching him wasn't getting the weekend chores done. It was getting harder holding down two jobs and making a home. She knew she could have chucked in waitressing any time and taken on an extra piano gig, but she had something to prove to herself.

It was a matter of pride and independence that she could stand on her own feet, even if those feet ached most of the time. If Ben left she needed to know she could.

She'd give waitressing one more month. By then she'd be five months along. Time then to hang up her apron and concentrate on herself and her baby.

She'd given strict orders that the room she'd earmarked for the nursery was off limits. She wanted the pleasure of doing the whole job herself, right down to painting the walls and hanging the curtains, although Ben hadn't agreed to letting her do anything requiring a ladder.

The little froth and bubble ripple fluttered deep inside her. She pressed a hand to her abdomen, held her breath. Again. The baby was moving. That tiny fragile life was saying, *I'm not ready to face the world yet, but I'm here.* Tears welled up and over. The rush of love, for her child, for the man who'd put it there, swamped her, leaving her shaken with its depth. And she wanted to share it.

Ben inserted the last dripper into the tubing he'd laid and stood back to view his achievements. A chill wind cooled the sweat on his brow as he turned on the tap and adjusted the water flow. Crazy time of year to put in a sprinkler system, he decided, but why not? Carissa seemed so anxious for him to do it now, while the ground was soft.

After the hard years of building a business reputation he could be proud of and the even crazier world of music, the peace and comfort here was a kind of therapy. Besides, he wanted the place finished before the baby came.

The thought that he might not be here come summer to see the garden in its full glory intruded into his mind like a rose thorn. No. He glared at the garden he'd resurrected. He'd be here. Damned if he wouldn't. But his father's words hammered at him. *The only thing you're good at is running away.*

And wasn't that the ultimate irony? Good old Dad had faced his problems by putting a bullet through his head with his cop's firearm. In the end he'd done his wife a favour. She no longer had to put up with the abuse he'd thrown at her for as long as Ben could remember.

It had destroyed her.

Ben wrenched the tap off and strode to the shed for the rake. He had a chance at something worthwhile here. This was his family now and he was staying. Anger and determination continued to push through him as he began to rake the leaves into piles.

The back screen door squeaked open, slammed shut. He looked up and saw Carissa on the top step and his dark mood lifted. She had a strange expression on her face, as if she was focusing inward. Pregnancy had rounded and softened her curves, but it hadn't diminished her sexuality, or his desire. The sky was dark, threatening rain, yet her cheeks glowed with the look of spring.

Their eyes met. The wind chased over the yard, scattering the leaves he'd raked and pressing his red plaid flannel shirt she wore against her body. Something deep and unfamiliar plunged through him. He felt as if he'd been tossed high, then dumped by a tidal wave. His pulse scrambled as he fought the feeling; his body tensed as his loins grew heavy. He couldn't move. Like some kind of idiot he could only stand and stare as if he'd never seen a pregnant woman before. *His* pregnant woman, carrying *his* baby.

'Ben?'

He jerked out of his thrall. 'What? Is something wrong?' The words came out harsh, clipped, as he fought the whip of panic.

'No. Everything's fine,' she assured him as she drew close. Her face was radiant, beautiful. 'The baby moved.'

Again that strange sensation rolled over him. 'Are you sure?'

'I'm sure. Here.' She hesitated, then reached out, took his hand, placed it on her belly.

Apart from lovemaking, he'd avoided conscious touching as her stomach swelled. It was one way to keep an emotional distance, not to let himself give in to the growing need he had to be with her, to be near her.

So he was as surprised as she when his hand moved under hers. 'Jeez…' His throat was thick, choked. He was touching his child. He splayed his fingers wider over the hardness and met her gaze.

She was smiling back at him, a deep, tender smile he'd never seen before. It made him weak at the knees.

He frowned. 'I don't feel anything.'

'Perhaps it's too early for anyone else to feel yet.'

'Yeah.' But his hand remained, wanting that connection a little longer.

Keeping his eyes on hers, he found himself inching up the flannel. He saw her quick intake of breath, and his own quickened in response. His fingers connected with warm, bare flesh. She was round and ripe, and all woman.

His other hand rose to cup the small mound between his palms. He dropped to his knees to see what he was touching. Her hands smelled of honey and spice as she threaded her fingers though his hair, reminding him of his childhood when his mother had baked.

It hit him like a bolt of lightning, as powerful as it was terrifying. He needed her and this baby more than he needed to breathe. This baby bound them together for ever. They'd always be a part of each other's lives.

Reeling, he dropped his hands. His whole body was on fire. The need to feel that baby against his own naked belly was like a molten storm in his veins. 'Come to bed.'

She shook her head, but she was smiling. 'We're going to be late to the hospital. The Rainbow Road's kids' concert, remember?'

He shoved a frustrated hand through his hair and ordered his body to cool off. 'Yeah.' Carissa wouldn't let those kids down. He was learning that his wife always put others' needs before her own. In this case those kids won hands down over his healthy libido. 'Guess I'll go take a shower.' A very cold shower.

But tonight… Tonight he was going to keep her hot, naked and close.

Ben parked the Porsche in the hospital's underground car park.

'Can you get my guitar?' Carissa asked as she climbed out.

He glanced behind him at the back seat. 'I didn't see you put that in. When did you learn guitar?'

'At school. I'm no pro but I get by.' Her fingers were restless, tapping a staccato on the music folder she was hugging to her chest. If he wasn't mistaken, she appeared edgy. Or was it excitement? She seemed high on energy. Surely she wasn't a nervous performer.

They walked to the elevator, her shoes making a quick tapping sound on the concrete. Inside the lift, she pressed the third-floor button, then leaned against the wall, watching the floor numbers light up.

As the elevator dinged and the doors whooshed open she turned to him, eyes dancing with anticipation. 'Ben…never mind.' Pushing away from the wall before he could ask her what she meant, she stepped out.

The banner strung across the double doors to the common room told him all he needed to know.

'The Rainbow Road welcomes Ben Jamieson, song-writer and guitarist.'

Something like a fist slammed into his gut and crawled up his throat. His hands, suddenly ice-cold, tightened on Carissa's guitar case. 'What the…?' His gaze cut to her and he knew he'd been set up. Set up by the one person who should have understood.

'Ben…' That sparkling excitement in her eyes died, replaced by uncertainty. She took a step towards him, one hand outstretched, must have thought better of it and stopped. 'I thought—'

But he cut her off with a slash of his hand. Anger was preferable to the icy fear that chilled his blood, the cold sweat breaking out on his body. '*You* thought? You thought wrong.'

The spectre of his nightmare, of Rave's dead eyes, rose up before him. He hid his shudder by doing a sharp about-turn and paced away.

All you're good at is running away.

'They're expecting you. I'm counting on you.' Her softly spoken words cut through his defences. He turned, every muscle in his body screaming to get the hell out before she saw what a coward he was. The rosy bloom in her cheeks had vanished. Beneath the jeans and loose blue shirt with its rainbow embroidery she was trembling. But she lifted her chin. 'I wanted you to pick up music again.'

'So you went behind my back and expect me to perform like your trick dog? I told you I wasn't ready.'

'You never will be if you don't start. If you can't do this one thing for me, do it for the kids. Do it for yourself.'

The doors opened and a stick-thin boy of about seven came out in hospital pyjamas. His skin was a waxy shade of pale.

'Hi, Miss Grace.'

Carissa cast a meaningful but sad glance at Ben before she smiled. 'Hello, Zac, how's it going?' She turned back to Ben. 'Your guitar's in the common room. I found it in your studio and had Mel bring it. I'm going in now. She'll wonder where we are.' She pushed through the doors, leaving her delicate scent to mingle with the antiseptic smell in the austere linoleum-covered corridor. And one sick boy.

Zac's eyes widened. 'Hey, you're Ben Jamieson! I listen to your music. XLRock's totally cool.'

Ben forced a smile. 'Thank you, but I don't… Why aren't you inside with the others?'

'Clowns are for kids. I was waiting for Ben Jamieson.'

'Well, you found him.'

'Can you teach me to play like you?' He nodded towards Carissa's guitar he'd forgotten he was clutching.

On the other side of the doors he could hear a clown's squeaky horn and kids laughing.

'Let's see your fingers.' He took Zac's hands, felt their fragility and something squeezed in his chest, but he said, 'Yep, they'll do the job. Come here.' Then he sat down on a nearby hospital bench, drew out the guitar and began tuning it.

'You'll have to teach me quick because I'm not well.' Zac's plain statement of fact, spoken without emotion, made Ben want to weep. His fingers tightened on the guitar. It was time to start living again.

'Mr Jamieson?' Zac tugged on his arm.

'Call me Ben,' he told him, slinging the strap over the boy's shoulders. He guided Zac's fingers to the strings. 'Let's see how we go here.'

Carissa silently thanked Zac for his timely interruption as she pushed through the doors. Fortunately the doors were at the back of the audience. It gave her a moment to pull herself together.

She'd made a big mistake not telling him. Huge. Music was a trigger for all those bad memories, the guilt, the nightmares. Why hadn't she realised that? A rising nausea wrenched at her stomach, clutched her by the throat, making it almost impossible to breathe.

His issues went so much deeper than she'd thought. Anyone with half a brain who saw him suffer in the dead of night would see it. Sweating, calling out in his sleep, twisting the covers off until he stole silently from their bed to sleep alone on the couch, or wander the yard.

She fought the cold sweat that broke out on her body and leaned against the doors, dragging in air. She'd allowed him to walk that yard alone, to sleep alone on the couch, to deal with his pain. Alone. *Stupid, stupid, stupid.* Hadn't she promised support and understanding when she'd made her marriage vows? Ben had upheld his end of the bargain.

The clown finished his act with a flurry of gold dust, which he showered over the kids. Then Mel saw her and she was out of time.

Plastering a smile on her face, she pushed forward, giving light-hearted high fives to the kids as she went. But she felt as if she were walking through quicksand.

'Where's Ben?' Mel whispered.

'In the corridor with Zac.' Swallowing over her dust-dry throat, she whispered, 'It's just me for now.' She turned and waved at her audience. 'Hi, everyone. Ready for some music?' She sat down at the piano and launched into a bracket of children's favourites while Mel handed out percussion instruments for them to tap along.

The round of applause signalled the next act.

Ben.

The baby chose that moment to kick, a heart-rending reminder of this morning when he'd kissed her naked belly, his expression of wonder and something deeper… Her chest grew impossibly tight, so tight she bit her lip against the pain.

Melanie lifted her shoulders in question.

'Where's Ben Jamieson?' someone asked.

Carissa took a steadying breath and prepared to stand, to disappoint a bunch of kids. And herself. 'Mr Jamieson is…' She looked helplessly towards the door.

Ben stood just inside with an adoring Zac beside him. Her heart stood still as his eyes locked with hers. She wanted to think it was forgiveness she saw in the dark intensity of their depths, an acknowledgement that in her own misguided way she'd tried to help. But in that split second across a room alive with noise and kids and balloons she couldn't be sure.

He nodded, a barely discernable movement. 'Right here.'

Her vision blurred with unshed tears. 'Let's give him a Rainbow Road welcome.'

Carissa knew nothing about Ben Jamieson the songwriter, the entertainer. This wasn't the same man who shared her bed and left the toothpaste uncapped on her vanity.

This man kept his young audience entertained with songs they could join in; he let Zac and a few other children try out his guitar. He had a natural rapport with kids. He flirted with the female nurses—he also had a natural rapport with women.

At the close of his performance he asked Carissa to join him with her guitar. He hugged her to his side and told the kids she was his wife. As if he was proud of her. As if he loved her. No one would have suspected those angry and heart-wrenching moments on the other side of the door.

But as soon as the performance finished, he took off. When she and Mel had finished tidying up, Mel dropped her home. Then she found the note on the bed. 'If you need anything, leave a message on my mobile.'

'I need *you*, Ben. Only you.' Sinking onto the bed, Carissa hugged his pillow, breathing in his scent and wishing with all the love in her heart that it could've ended differently. Because she had a feeling it was never going to be the same between them ever again.

CHAPTER TWELVE

BEN punched down on the accelerator as a rainstorm rolled in over Sydney harbour. He wanted the speed, the feel of power beneath his hands, the sound of the engine's purr. He had a measure of control over his car even if he didn't have it over his wife or his feelings.

The wipers thwacked over the windscreen, light bounced off the wet, windswept road as the evening closed in. He turned on the demister and lowered the window as the glass fogged, letting in exhaust fumes and the hiss of tyres on water, and worked his way through traffic and out of the city.

Carissa would be home by now. The thought sent a jolt of guilt through him. He didn't want to hurt her. But today she'd seen more than he'd been willing to show her. His hands tightened on the wheel. Worse, she'd held up a mirror so he'd had no choice but to take a good look at himself and he hadn't liked what he'd seen.

Which made him think about what he'd seen in Carissa today. She'd had faith in him; she'd believed in him. And earlier he'd held his unborn child between his hands. So she was stubborn; she also had strength and was fair to boot. She was also sexy as hell, and a goddess in bed.

He felt the familiar quick, deep clutch at his groin. The one he always felt when he thought of Carissa naked and glorious, her hair silky against his body, her lips soft and full on his skin.

It wasn't just the sex. He'd had more than his share of faceless women with perfect, athletic and silicone bodies, quick, hot, frantic couplings that left his body satisfied and his soul empty.

With Carissa it was so much more. The thought, quite frankly, terrified him. Shaking it away, he straightened, rolled his shoulders and concentrated on the road. He had some long hours' driving ahead.

Before he saw Carissa again he had to tell someone he should have told a long time ago.

The Arches Rest Home was a turn-of-the-century bluestone structure in Melbourne's leafy eastern suburbs. Care cost an arm and a leg, but the place was immaculate. A sea of lawn flowed gently to a perimeter of oaks, the last brown leaves fluttering in the watery morning sun.

Security demanded he check in at the front desk before heading to his mother's room. Light from a huge arched window limned the high-backed armchair where his mother spent her days. Soft chamber music drifted from the CD player he'd had installed for her.

'How's she been?' he asked the nurse who'd accompanied him.

'The same. She's comfortable.' She moved to the window, flicked the curtain wider. 'You've a visitor, Mrs Jamieson.'

Ben rounded the chair. 'Hello, Mum.' He kissed her cheek, smelled the subtle fragrance of the expensive soap he'd left her last time. She looked the same as she had last month. Lost.

She had a pretty face, but her eyes, so like his own, were vacant. Her short hair was carefully combed, her loose green dress clean and ironed.

'Can I get you something to drink, Mr Jamieson?' the nurse asked at the doorway.

'Thanks, no.'

'I'll be at the desk if you need me.'

'How've you been, Mum? You're as beautiful as ever.' He stroked her hand, willing her to come back, if only for a moment, so he could tell her what was in his heart. His jaw tightened. This was almost worse than death. You could grieve over a death and move on.

He increased his pressure on her hand. 'Mum, I've got some news. You're going to be a grandmother. Did you hear me, Mum? A grandma. Carissa—that's my wife's name—I haven't told you that either, have I? She's a wonderful pianist. You'd love her music…

'Next time I'll bring Carissa and let you hear for yourself. Would you like that? Beautiful music—Beethoven and stuff. She's strong and smart and caring.' *And I don't deserve her.*

Somewhere down the hall a vacuum cleaner hummed, dishes rattled. Another day like the last. An endless string of days his mother wasn't aware of. Her life was slipping away, wasted, and it damn near broke his heart. Now that she could live the life she deserved, had earned, and she couldn't even feed herself.

'Mum…' He broke off. He found he couldn't say

what was in his heart after all, because he couldn't acknowledge it aloud, not even to himself.

He *cared* for Carissa, dammit, and knew she cared for him. They had a good relationship barring a few wrinkles which could be ironed out. They fitted well together. In some things they were miles apart, totally in sync in others. He wanted her, in bed and out. If he needed her, she needed him back. Partners, a duo act.

'Mum…' he began again. 'We have a chance to be a family. I want you to be a part of that family too. I want to see you bounce our kid on your knee and sing those crazy kid rhymes you used to sing to me.'

He barely noticed the way his voice had softened, the way his hand tightened over hers. He was too aware of the pain that gripped his heart. 'A family, Mum. The way we used to be before it all went wrong. Wake up, Mum, and you can come live with us—there's plenty of room.' His voice broke. *'Come back.'*

She continued to stare beyond the window at something only she could see.

'Mr Jamieson? Are you okay?'

He felt the nurse's hand on his shoulder and realised his eyes were watering. 'Been driving for hours,' he muttered. He pulled himself up off his knees, pressed a last kiss to his mother's cheek. 'I'll be back.'

He'd reached the door when he heard the words that stopped him in his tracks.

'She's in your heart.'

Pulse thundering in his ears, he turned slowly. Retraced his steps. His mother's eyes were still vacant, her hand resting on her lap as he'd left it. But he'd heard her voice. A voice he hadn't heard in ten years.

* * *

Carissa lifted the kitchen curtain and told herself it was for the last time. Outside was dark and still, a few stars twinkled between the clouds. She shivered and snuggled deeper into Ben's flannel shirt, breathing in his scent. She'd rolled up the sleeves, but the fabric stretched across her middle.

Ben hadn't answered her message to let her know where he was and if he was all right. There was nothing she could do but wait. The guilt and helplessness were a gnawing pain eating away at her soul. Her fingers twisted in the curtain's fabric. Obviously he wasn't coming home tonight.

The past thirty hours had been pure torture. She didn't know if he'd had an accident, where he was or who he was with, or if he was ever coming back. If he'd been here she'd have reached out to him, told him how sorry she was and asked him to make love with her. No, begged, if that was what it took.

As she paced she tried to bring his face to mind, but all she could see was his white-lipped anger when he'd told her he wasn't ready.

And still he'd performed. Because she'd asked him to. And only she would have seen the emotion behind that clever mask when he'd picked up his guitar and strummed that first chord.

On a sob of frustration, she slammed her palm on the table, then marched to her bedroom. There was nothing left to do but go to bed and try to sleep. Pacing the floor and worrying wasn't doing her or the baby any good and she had to work tomorrow afternoon.

A hot shower would ease the tension. She shivered as she stripped down and tied up her hair, then sighed as she slid under its soothing spray. As she reached for the shower gel she felt a draught of air, saw the blur of movement through the fogged glass.

For what seemed like an eternity everything inside her froze. Hardly daring to move, she closed her fingers over the long-handled back scrub, then, with her heart tripping double time, reached towards the glass door, her feeble weapon raised.

Before she could get her stiff fingers to work, the door slid open with a smooth slide of metal on metal.

'You want me to help you with that?' The familiar smoky voice slid through her muddled senses.

'Oh… Ben.' She sobbed out his name as relief poured through her.

He stood on the fluffy white bath mat while steam gushed out and water spattered his jeans and sneakers. He hadn't shaved, his eyes were bloodshot and shadowed with fatigue.

It was the most beautiful sight she'd ever seen.

'Oh, yes. Please…'

He took the brush from her limp hand and turned her around, then stepped in behind her.

Her whole body went weak. She felt as if she were dissolving like jelly in the rain. Mingling with the spray, the scent of leather upholstery and male sweat surrounded her like a warm mist. His breath was a hot pool of air on her nape.

He slid the brush from neck to buttocks in one slow pass. Every bristle was an exquisite pinprick of pleasure as he slid it over her shoulder, along her collar-bone. *More.*

The brush dropped to the floor with a clatter as he

turned her to face him. His T-shirt was plastered to his skin, his nipples dark against the fabric.

'You came back.' She heard the slightly hysterical edge to her voice as she raised her eyes to his.

Desire met desire, his nostrils flared, but his mouth remained grim, his jaw rock-hard and unforgiving. Like the ridge she felt against her swollen belly as he shifted his squelching runners in the tiny cubicle.

'Did you think I wouldn't?' Without taking his eyes off hers he toed off his sodden shoes, peeled off his socks. Dragged the shirt over his head and tossed it down. It hit the floor with a wet slap. A loud, impatient, needy sound.

'I tried *not* to think.' Her hands were on his flesh. His stomach was hard, lean, ridged with muscle. Water cascaded over his chest, catching on the masculine hair and running in rivulets into his waistband.

His eyes darkened and the bulge below his waist jerked against her, but his hands remained at his sides. 'Then you don't know me, Carissa. You don't know me at all.'

Carissa willed away the sting and concentrated on the difficult job of working the top button of his sodden jeans. 'I want to know you, Ben.' Her hands trembled as she tried to tug denim and briefs down over his hips as one.

His hands moved as if to push her away, but she looked into his passion-filled eyes and shook her head. 'All of you.'

Finally she managed to shove the offending garments down far enough so that her hands closed over his hard, silky length.

He jerked, his elbow colliding with the tap. 'Hell, Carissa…'

'Let me. We've got plenty of time. It's two showers for the price of one.'

She watched his face contort as if in pain as she dropped to her knees and he realised her intention.

'Carissa…' he warned, his voice hoarse.

'Shut up, Ben.' The soft skin at the top of his thighs begged for her lips, but she resisted for the moment to take in his mile-long, hairy legs as she shoved his jeans the rest of the way to the floor.

She batted his hands away when he would have pulled her up. While the water ran over their bodies, she kissed her way up one leg, lingered over the smooth skin of his groin.

She cupped the heavy weight of his testicles, squeezing gently, massaging the base of his thick arousal with her thumbs. On a groan he jerked beneath her fingers and fisted his hands in her hair. Encouraged, she lowered her head, swirled her tongue over the tip.

'Enough,' he rasped. He tugged her up his body, the slippery slide of flesh against flesh.

Steam rose around them, enclosing them in a cocoon of intimacy, shutting the world and its problems out. He reached for the shower gel, poured a generous dollop onto a palm and rubbed them slowly together.

The first touch of his hands on her breasts had the blood pulsing beneath her skin, her nipples contracting until they were tight little points of desire.

Weak with wanting, she leaned against the tiles for support. Her head fell back, exposing her throat for his hungry mouth. She felt boneless, as if she just might slide down the wall into a puddle of pure bliss.

While he lapped at her neck, his hands glided lower,

over her swollen belly in slow, slippery circles, then lower still, till he found the place that ached for his touch.

'I want you.' His voice was harsh and filled with need. Joy flooded her as he slid one finger inside her, sending her pulse sky-rocketing. 'Tell me you want me.'

'I want you, Ben Jamieson. I've never wanted anything or anyone more than I want you.'

His body was hot, the tiles cool and smooth as he pressed his body against hers, drawing her hands over her head. Intense eyes, shifting from jade to midnight, watched her as his mood darkened, deepened. 'You're mine,' he said, and pushed inside her.

She met his gaze. 'That makes *you* mine.'

Her words seemed to have an instant effect on him. His grip tightened, and something raw and primitive crossed his expression. She'd never seen that look before and it drew a similar response from her, like some sort of mating call, both thrilling and terrifying. She felt bound, owned.

She matched him stroke for stroke as she yielded to him, sagging against the wall, only prevented from falling by his grasp on her wrists. She arched as he drove her up, up and over, then he spilled inside her with a sigh that seemed to come from the depths of his soul.

For a moment Ben buried his face against her neck and held her, knowing she'd slide away. Her full breasts and hard belly pressed against him. A fierce protectiveness welled up. He wanted to stay close like this a little longer, but lack of sleep was taking its toll. Dammit. Reluctantly he let her hands go, and she rolled her shoulders, rubbed her wrists.

He took over that task himself. 'Did I hurt you?'

'No.' She pressed a kiss to his chin. 'But if I don't get out of here I'm going to turn into a prune.'

She'd lightened the moment deliberately, he guessed, but he felt a twinge of disappointment. The powerful emotions wrung from the past few moments deserved more. He had to work to match her tone. 'I'm very partial to prunes.'

He nibbled at her neck, breathing in the fragrance of her flushed skin. Shut off the water. Then he handed her a towel and patted himself dry.

She reached past him for the hairdryer. 'Will you wait for me?' She sounded casual, but her eyes were vulnerable.

'I'll be waiting.' He strolled naked into the bedroom, turned back the cover and slid between the cold, crisp sheets.

He was exhausted, but all he could think about was her fierce declaration. *That makes you mine.* Warmth glowed through his body. On the first day of their marriage she'd all but given him a carte blanche to take any woman he wanted. She didn't know how badly he wanted it to work between them.

He hadn't looked at another woman since the first night he'd seen her. He hadn't known then that pleasure could be so inextricably bound up with pain, that need could be so sharp that it pierced the soul and left you weak...

He stirred to reluctant wakefulness as Carissa shifted beside him, her legs twining with his. God, what time was it? He glanced at the clock. 6:00 a.m.

Grey light softened the darkness, enough to see the dim oval of her face. And her wide eyes watching him. He reached out to touch the soft curve of her jaw, traced the slim column of her throat. 'Sorry.'

'You fell asleep the moment you hit the bed.' Her tone was faintly accusatory.

'I drove to Melbourne. To see my mother. Guess the shower did me in.'

Her eyes glittered with awareness, but she remained silent a moment as if weighing the truth of his words. 'So how was she?' she said at last.

'The same. No...' He hesitated. 'She said something—at least I thought she did. I spoke to the doctor about it and he looked her over, did a couple of tests. There's no change. He said that happens sometimes. It doesn't mean she's getting better.'

Carissa propped her head on a hand, eyes warm and understanding. 'What did she say?'

He shook his head. 'I didn't catch it,' he lied. He couldn't tell her, not yet, but someday...

She leaned over and took his hand, pressed it to her porcelain-smooth cheek. 'I'm so sorry for that. Are you going to take me to visit sometime? I want to meet this incredible woman who raised such a wonderful son.'

The way she looked at him—tender, warm, compassionate... He swore the sky brightened a little faster at that moment, bringing the rose of dawn to her cheeks. 'We'll go soon,' he promised.

Stress and overwork and finally grief had led to his mother's current state. He wasn't going to let it happen to Carissa. Starting now. 'I know you want your independence but there'll be no more working at the Three Steps.'

To his surprise she didn't bristle at his no-negotiation. In fact she smiled. 'I made a deal with myself, that if you came back I'd give up work and make a home for us.' She hesitated. 'If that's what you want.'

'I want.' The glow inside him grew and spread until it pulsed like fire, and his hand moved to her breast where he could feel her heart, matching the rhythm of his own. 'I wasn't prepared for the hospital gig and I just plain lost it. Nothing else has changed.'

'And I should've asked you first.'

'Maybe it's best you didn't.' He leaned up on his elbow, wanting to forget the last few days. 'We'll shop for nursery furniture today. I saw this great wooden rocking-horse…it's not too early, is it?'

He saw her lips curve in the semi-darkness. 'It'll be a while before we get to the rocking-horse stage. But that doesn't matter. Let's go get a rocking-horse.' She snuggled into him and closed her eyes. 'After lunch.'

He scooted her closer, pressed a kiss to her brow. Life meant something again. He was standing on the cusp of something so huge, so powerful it threatened to overwhelm him. She gave him hope when he'd forgotten what hope was. His mother was no longer able to, but Carissa reminded him how it felt to have someone care enough to worry when you didn't come home.

Somehow this woman had brought healing and closure to the darkest months in his life, and for the first time since Rave's death, he truly felt he'd make it.

Carissa stood in the centre of the room they'd chosen for the nursery and turned a slow circle. She hugged the framed picture of a white unicorn they'd bought yesterday while the hand-painted rocking-horse waited for its young rider in the corner.

A protective sheet covered the most adorable cradle she'd ever seen and a cute teddy night-light sat on the chest of drawers. She'd unearthed her grandmother's rocking-chair from the store room, stripped and lacquered it till its original wood gleamed.

Ben had gone to the Cove for a staff meeting and to meet with an architect about some renovations. Then he was going by the hospital to give Zac another guitar lesson.

She smiled to herself as happiness sparkled through her. At last he'd begun to heal. To look beyond his immediate surroundings and take those first steps towards a new life. If she could be patient a little longer, her dreams of a home filled with love and laughter and a husband who returned that love might not be out of reach. There'd be more kids, a dog with floppy ears and big feet, a cat or two.

Propping the print against the wall, she dragged the ladder across the scarred wooden floorboards, then grabbed the hammer and picture hook.

Then she remembered. Ben had absolutely forbidden her to climb the ladder. He'd insisted on painting the upper half of the walls himself. He'd also promised to hang the print last night because she couldn't wait to see how it looked, but they'd gotten seriously sidetracked on the new Persian rug. Then he'd promised faithfully to hang it before he left this morning, but he'd forgotten—they'd gotten sidetracked again.

Well, she was pregnant, not disabled. She hauled her considerable five-months-and-counting mass carefully to the first rung, the second. She hammered the hook home, climbed down just as carefully and picked up the print, then made her way up again. She hooked the wire, leaned back a little to check the alignment. Perfect.

She didn't have time to reach for support when her

foot slipped. Just a split second of terror before she was tumbling backwards. Then time seemed to slow, an eternity as her hands flailed wildly, grabbing at air, and a scream choked her throat.

She braced for the inevitable contact. The ladder creaked and wobbled, the hammer she'd left hanging at the top connected with her elbow in a knuckle of pain as it fell, hitting the floor with a deafening clatter.

For a stunned, terrifying moment she lay flat on her back, gulping air and finding none. Black stars crowded in on her, spiralling, dragging her towards darkness. 'No!' She was alone, she couldn't give in to the overwhelming need to close her eyes.

Gingerly she moved each limb and found them all in working order. She breathed more easily and drew in a deep, slow lungful of cold air. It smelled of paint and dust from the floor. No broken ribs, then.

Her hands curved over her belly. 'Okay,' she breathed. 'It's okay. *We're* okay. Daddy's going to hit the roof when he hears about this.' So she wouldn't tell him; she'd say Mel came by and hung the picture.

She rolled onto her side, waited a moment, then pushed up to a sitting position, wavering while the dark spots intensified, then faded. Her elbow throbbed where the hammer had hit, and now her lower back felt as if it was on fire.

She gave herself a moment before grasping the ladder and pulling herself up. Her legs felt like spaghetti but she managed to make it into the living room. A soothing cup of warm tea...

The sudden cramp clenched like a cruel fist at the base of her spine and had her gripping the door jamb.

'Oh, God.' Sweat broke out on her brow, chilling instantly in the cool air. Terror flooded through her in a black tidal wave, but she struggled to rise above it.

Sagging against the door, she cradled her baby. 'Just a twinge,' she told herself through clenched teeth.

The pain subsided as if it hadn't happened, leaving her limp and drained. She wanted to pretend it wasn't real, it wasn't happening, a nightmare—she'd wake up and Ben would hold her and tell her everything was all right.

'Ben.' Tears sprang to her eyes. 'Come home, we need you.' But he'd still be in his meeting and wasn't due back for at least two hours. She couldn't let him disappoint Zac. The boy had been over the moon when Ben had bought him his own guitar.

Another stab of pain shot up her back, lightning-hot, radiating outward, searing muscle and bone, until she gasped and doubled over. When it passed she lifted her head and saw the framed honeymoon photo on the piano.

Their marriage was built around this baby. Her dreams, her man, her life, depended on this baby.

Keeping close to the wall for support, she moved to the phone, punched in 000. Her heart cried and tears overflowed, streaking her cheeks with moisture. 'I need an ambulance right away.'

She didn't remember much about the quick trip to the hospital beyond the wail of the siren, the concerned face of the ambulance officer as he worked on her and her own numbing fear. She recited Mel's phone number to him, but in her distress she couldn't remember Ben's.

Then she was being rushed down a corridor. She was aware of fluorescent lights on the ceiling, the squeak of rubber soled shoes on linoleum, the smell of antiseptic mingling with cooked cabbage.

The pain was like a living thing, clenching her belly, tearing at her insides with unrelenting claws, ripping the tiny life within her away.

Then everything went dark.

CHAPTER THIRTEEN

'THE alfresco dining area will encourage more people off the street.' Ben and John Amos, the architect, studied the renovation plans. 'We'll—'

'Excuse me, Ben, phone call for you.' Rochelle, the perky office assistant, stood at the door. 'She says it's urgent.'

Ben straightened, annoyed at the interruption. It wasn't Carissa—Rochelle would have said. 'Did they leave a name?'

'Melanie Sawyer.'

A flicker of alarm ran through him as he reached for the phone. 'Hi, Mel. What's up?'

'Ben, it's Carrie. The ambulance just brought her in. I just came on duty and—'

'What's wrong?' His voice was suddenly hoarse, his knees weak, and someone was turning a screwdriver in his belly.

'Carrie's not doing so well…the baby—'

But he was already grabbing his jacket with his free hand. 'I'm on my way.'

Adrenaline pumped through his veins as he plunged

though the hotel's ornate double doors. Sweat slicked his skin even as a chill wind swept the pavement and snuck under his shirt, sending his tie flapping over his shoulder.

To save time he hailed a cab, then cursed Sydney's traffic from the back seat as they crawled along streets crowded with cars and lunch-hour shoppers. He drummed his fingers on his knees, then clenched them around his tie before tugging it off and stuffing it in his jacket.

What the hell had happened? He'd not stopped long enough to get details. Carissa had been fine this morning, eager to sew the nursery curtains ready for him to hang.

The baby. His stomach knotted with fear and a frustrating helplessness. She was only five months pregnant—not enough time— He snapped off that train of thought and glued his eyes to the road, as if he could will the traffic to disappear.

Before the cab drew to a halt he threw a fistful of notes on the seat, muttered a terse, 'Thanks,' and was out and racing for the hospital doors. Sterile air-conditioning greeted him as he raced for the desk. 'Mrs Jamieson,' he demanded. 'Where is she?'

The receptionist looked up, frustratingly cool and businesslike. 'Are you a relative?'

'I'm her *husband*.' He raked his hair. 'Where is she?'

She consulted a board. 'She's on the third floor. Ask at the nurses' station.'

He didn't wait for the elevator.

Melanie was wringing her hands when he arrived out of breath from his dash up three flights of stairs.

'Ben.' The way she looked at him, the sadness in her eyes, her hand closing over his…

His heart dropped like a stone. Dear God, he'd never

known such fear. He didn't want to hear the words. The world he'd built over the last few months was about to crash around his ears and he didn't know how he was going to build it again. 'Carissa, is she…?' His voice, choked and harsh, threatened to break.

'She's still in Surgery. Ben, the baby…' Her eyes filled. 'I'm so sorry.'

Black agony twisted inside him. He beat back the pain and said, 'When can I see her?'

'I'll go check for you.'

He paced, hands shoved in his trouser pockets.

She returned a moment later. 'She's in Recovery. She'll be in room 34A when they bring her down.' She gestured and they walked down the corridor together. 'You might want to go home, grab a few things for her.'

'I'm not going anywhere until I've seen her.'

'Okay, you can wait in her room, or there's a common room with a TV, but it might be a while.'

'As long as it takes,' he said grimly. 'How did it happen?'

'You'll have to ask Carrie. She was in too much distress to talk.'

They reached the room. Melanie poured him a glass of water from a pitcher and put it on the bedside table. He shrugged off his jacket, rolled up his sleeves and sat down on the hard plastic visitor's chair.

He felt as if he were sinking into a dark abyss. *Ben, the baby moved.* The image of that day was crystal-clear. He'd known that day, known his heart was hers, but he'd been too afraid, too stubborn to acknowledge it. Now maybe it was too late.

This was to be his personal hell for what had

happened in Broken Hill. His hell seemed to be watching those he cared about suffer. But Carissa? She wasn't guilty of a crime. Her big mistake was shackling herself to someone like Ben Jamieson. He had a knack for hurting everyone he cared for most. She'd be better off without him.

Melanie laid a hand on his shoulder. The gentle empathy in her touch tore another piece of his heart. 'Ben, I have to go. I don't get off till tonight. I'd stay but Emergency is short-staffed. Will you be okay?'

'Sure.'

Like hell. The moment Melanie left he was up and pacing again. His child was gone and his wife—God only knew what was happening to her. Every time a gurney came into sight his heart stopped. Every time he demanded to know what was going on he got the same evasive answer. *She's still in Recovery.*

When they wheeled her in several black coffees later, Ben was practically climbing the walls. No amount of cajoling, demanding, pleading had gotten his wife here earlier.

The first glimpse of her face, as white as the sheet, the bruised colour beneath her closed eyes, had his gut twisting into knots. 'How is she?' he asked the accompanying nurse. He hovered over Carissa while the orderlies transferred her to the bed.

'She's going to be fine.'

His heart squeezed tight as a fist in his chest. He reached for her hand, twined her limp fingers in his, willing her to open those lovely blue eyes and see him so he could talk to her, tell her she had to get well because he needed her.

'She'll sleep for a while,' the nurse said, checking

Carissa's pulse. 'She might like some of her own things around her when she wakes up. Why don't you go home, pick up a pretty nightdress and some cosmetics?'

'She might like her husband here when she wakes up,' he replied tautly without taking his eyes off her. Then again...

He pressed the heel of his free hand to his brow. Would she want him now the baby no longer existed? The question shivered through him like ice-water, leaving him chilled to the bone. It wasn't a question he was ready to tackle right now.

He squeezed her hand gently, untangled her fingers from his, then lay her hand on the sheet and whispered so only she could hear. 'Carissa? I'll be back very soon.'

Carissa didn't want to wake up. She wanted to stay in that dark place where there was no pain, no loss, no heartache. Nothing. But someone seemed determined to bring her back. The layers of mind fog lifted, revealing a grey world where life no longer held any meaning.

Sterile smells of hospital sheets, disinfectant and anti-septic. Impersonal sounds—the clank of metal trolleys, the hum of air-conditioning. A stranger's hands, prodding, pressing, saying her name. She sank back to the dark.

After several attempts—over how long? She didn't know—she reluctantly opened her eyes. She noted without interest that she'd been moved to a private room.

'Hello, Carissa.' The nurse taking her blood pressure smiled, finished her task, jotted notes on her chart. 'Try to drink.' She held a glass of water with a bent straw to Carissa's lips.

Her mouth was dry and tasted like chaff, the water cool and soothing. 'Thank you.'

'Use this if you need anything,' the nurse said, pressing a buzzer into her hand.

Carissa heard the woman's footsteps recede and stared up at the cold fluorescent light. Nothing could soothe the despair that surrounded her like the dark clouds beyond the window. Every part of her body ached and the chill of the winter evening outside seemed to settle in her bones.

No one had told her, but she knew she was no longer pregnant. She clenched a hand over the place where only hours ago she'd felt it kicking. Now all she felt were contractions—angry fists of pain deep inside where her womb had betrayed her.

She remembered her ultrasound. *Look, Ben, its little heart's beating like it's run a marathon already.*

Her heart shattered. She'd never looked on her child's face, would never touch that satin-soft baby skin or hold it to her breast, would never hear its first cry or exclaim over its first smile.

She felt empty, numb and alone. She wanted the only other person who understood, who'd share her misery. Ben.

Where was he? Why hadn't he come? She watched the clouds darken and lights wink on in nearby buildings as night closed in. Their marriage was built on a mutual agreement to care for their child. That foundation was gone.

And it changed everything.

She didn't want to go back to her life without Ben. A life without love was only half a life. Even if the person you loved didn't return that love in full measure, it was better than nothing at all. While he stayed, there was hope. She knew him well enough to know he wouldn't up and leave her until she recovered.

Or would he? If he knew what she'd done, would he turn his back on everything they'd made together? She closed her eyes. He'd been so adamant about not climbing the ladder. She'd promised. But she'd had to do it her way.

He'd trusted her to carry his baby and she'd failed him, failed herself. The bright after-pains clenching her belly were nothing compared to the emotional agony tearing at her heart.

Leave the ladder climbing to me. Had she listened? Had she waited? A cold she'd never felt before crept into her bones, and she hunched deeper into the unyielding hospital mattress with its clammy rubber under-sheet.

No, she'd had to hang that picture herself. Now she'd have to live with the consequences for the rest of her life. Not only her. Why did she think it was only about her?

She fought the drugging effects of the medication. The need to talk to Ben was stronger than her urge to simply close her eyes and drift away.

With nothing to hold him, he could be gone in a matter of weeks—or days—because when he learned what she'd done he'd leave. How could she live in that house without it reminding her of him? The king-size bed where they'd made love and plans, the horseshoe he'd nailed over the door on their wedding day, the chip in the kitchen bench-top when he'd dropped the hammer.

She'd tell him the truth. If there was to be nothing between them, at least there'd be honesty.

That now familiar warm sensation stroked her like a

velvet glove, and she knew he was there before she looked. Propping up the doorway, big and sexy and male, just as he had the first time she'd seen him at the piano bar.

But this was different. They were different. Bitter-sweet pain clenched in her chest. She knew his strengths, his fears, his past, his body, just as he knew hers. It might have been enough to build a life on, a family.

'Ben...' She lifted her hand, watching, waiting for him to do something—anything. His hair was spiked with rain, his T-shirt rumpled as if he'd thrown on the first one he'd come across.

For a few seconds that stretched to eternity their gazes remained locked and a shared well of pain seemed to open up between them.

'You're awake.' His voice sounded tired and rusty as if he hadn't used it in a long time. Then he moved towards her as if the world dragged at his feet. 'I wanted to be here when you woke.' He shoved a hand through his wet hair. 'Dammit, I should've been here.'

'You're here now, that's all that matters.'

He put her overnight bag on the bed. 'Some comforts from home.' He stood, awkward and uncertain, as if he'd run at the least opportunity.

'Thanks.'

'Carissa, I...oh, God, Carissa.'

Metal creaked as he sat down heavily on the bed. Then he was clutching her shoulders, burying his head against her neck. He smelled of rain and sweat and an underlying hint of the cologne he'd used this morning.

This morning—a world away, another lifetime away. *Need any help in that shower? I'll pick up a pizza on my way home.*

His big body heaved and she knew he was crying inside. A man like Ben didn't wear his emotions for the world to see, not even for his wife. Her own tears, which she'd kept dammed, fell like a silent river for both of them.

His eyes were over-bright but dry when he lifted his head and smoothed her hair gently from her face. 'How are you doing? Sorry, stupid question.'

'I've been better.' She knuckled a damp cheek.

'Let me.' He cradled her face in his palms as if she might break and smoothed his thumbs over her cheek-bones. 'You're a strong woman. You'll get through this.'

'I'm sorry, Ben, so sorry.'

'Hey,' he said softly. 'It's not your fault.'

Guilt and misery stirred a deadly cocktail with the drugs in her stomach. Her head felt like a melon, too heavy to hold up.

'Here.' He unzipped the bag and pulled out a parcel.

'A CD player. And Chopin.' She shook her head, forced a smile. 'Only you would think of that.' Only you.

'And a nightshirt. Let me help you put it on.'

He untied the hospital gown, eased it down over her shoulders. His eyes narrowed and his lips compressed when he saw the swollen purple bruise on her elbow. 'What's this?' And shoved the sheet down to her waist. A similar discoloration bloomed beneath her left breast. 'What the hell happened?'

She wanted to pull the sheet over the evidence, but the damage was done. 'I…slipped. Next thing I knew I was flat on my back.'

'Slipped? On what?' He touched her cheek. The infinite gentleness made her want to cry all over again. 'Carissa. Are you in pain? Shall I call a nurse?'

She shook her head. 'No.'

He clasped her hands in his. 'What did you slip on?'

'Slipped *off,*' she began. The need to sleep was dragging her down but she owed him the truth first. Feeling vulnerable, she tugged the sheet back up over her breasts. 'It was more like slipped off. The ladder.'

'The ladder.' Oh, his face. In that single moment she saw disbelief turn to shock. His hands slid from hers. 'You went up the ladder.' His voice was dangerously soft.

The silence rose like a living thing, broken only by the faint hum of the air-conditioning and the patter of rain on the window. A wall dropped between them. An impenetrable barrier she didn't know how to broach.

'I was only two steps up…' she said into the silence. 'I wanted to hang the picture… The hammer caught my elbow on the way down.'

She forced her heavy-lidded eyes to meet his. Grief and dark emotions she couldn't read swirled in those deep green eyes. Another tear spilled over to sting her cheek. This time he didn't attempt to wipe it away. Didn't try to touch her at all. Everything—her own grief, the guilt, the love, twisted inside her.

'Well,' he said at last. 'That'll teach you.'

She heard it all in those few words, the cold, hard finality of a door slamming shut. Her world was spinning apart and she couldn't catch the pieces fast enough.

'Put this on.' He eased her nightshirt over her head, helped slip her arms through the sleeves, but his hands might have been those of any nurse or care-giver.

He was pulling away, physically and emotionally. She wanted to wrap her arms around his neck and never let him go. 'Ben…' His name seemed to be all she was capable of. The residual anaesthetic was a dark mist enveloping her. She couldn't fight it anymore.

'You need to rest,' she heard him say as her eyelids drooped shut. But she felt callused fingers cup her jaw. 'Keep that chin up, Carissa, and you'll be okay.'

Ben breathed a sigh of relief when those eyelashes drifted closed. He waited a few moments to make sure she was asleep before pressing his lips gently to her forehead, her eyelids and finally to linger on that beautiful cushion-soft mouth before dragging himself up.

If he'd had to look at those grief-stricken baby blues a moment longer he'd have lost it right there in front of her. His control was hanging by a hair, his throat was a desert, and there was a fire in his chest that was consuming his heart, beat by agonising beat.

Their baby was dead.

He wanted to wrap his arms around her and never let her go. But now, for Carissa's sake, for her future, he had to be strong, to pull back and play the role of carer and friend. That was what she'd want. Not a lover, not a husband. Intimate sexual contact would remind her of what they'd made and lost.

So he did what Ben Jamieson did best. He walked away.

The night was wet with a blustery wind. He welcomed the cold slap of it against his face, the sting of rain against his shirt as he left the hospital grounds and hit the footpath. He had no idea where he'd left his jacket.

A few pedestrians hurried past huddled under umbrellas, tyres swished, the occasional horn blasted as the caterpillar of cars crawled homeward.

He'd never been big on promises—careless words,

easily forgotten—but he did believe in his promise to Carissa.

Nothing would come before her and the baby.

He'd let her down. If she'd forgotten her promise not to climb the ladder, he blamed his own failed promise to hang the picture. She wanted everything done yesterday, was used to doing it herself—she was like him in that way. Yet he'd left the bloody ladder in the nursery instead of putting it on the verandah out of temptation, and harm's way.

If only he'd taken that moment to hang the print before he left.

If only. His gut twisted. She wouldn't want him now. Hell, she hadn't wanted to marry him in the first place. As soon as she recovered he'd step away and walk out of her life for ever.

Over the next few weeks Carissa recuperated at home. No one could have asked for a more dedicated carer than Ben. She only had to twitch and he was there.

At odd times she'd catch herself at the closed nursery door. *Can't you see it, Ben? The light'll sparkle on the sun-catcher and I'll watch rainbows on the ceiling while I sit in the rocking chair and feed her... The cradle should go here, where we can see him from the door...*

The nursery door remained closed. Though he didn't talk about it, she knew Ben was hurting as deeply as she. In the early hours she'd wake to find the bed empty and hear him pacing the verandah.

But something good came out of those midnight sessions, even if it would ultimately take him away from her. He began playing again. His music was different now—soulful, haunting, nothing she'd ever heard before. He was composing. Once when she'd slipped out to the shed where he played at night, presumably so as not to disturb her, he'd told her to go back to bed.

Shutting her out.

Then she began to notice that more and more, he was spending the days holed up in his old room that they'd converted into an office-studio, or working at the Cove. He came to bed after she was asleep and rose before she woke. The only time they seemed to come together was for the evening meal.

It was cold outside, but Carissa welcomed the refreshing feel against her cheeks a few weeks later. 'Look, Gran, your daffodils are coming up.'

New life, new beginnings.

'You're right, Gran,' she murmured. She'd never been disappointed in the thoughts she liked to think came from the other side. It was time to tuck her love for that tiny life away in a corner of her heart and look to the future.

And she was going to give it her best shot. She was going to seduce her husband with a romantic dinner, candlelight and soft music.

Ben shrugged deeper into his jacket as he stood on Sydney's Harbour Bridge watching the ferries glide across the water. The Opera House rose like white swans over a blue lake. Traffic whizzed by with the unrelenting roar of rubber on concrete.

He'd left the architect's plans he'd told Carissa he had to work on unopened on his desk. He hadn't needed to go in to the office, just as he shouldn't be here. He should be cosied up in a warm bed with his wife, not standing alone freezing to death in a hurricane wind.

He blew on his clenched fists as he imagined how he might otherwise have spent the morning. Breakfast in bed; hot coffee and hotter woman.

It was torture lying next to her and not touching her. He ached to take her in his arms and kiss away the pain he saw in her eyes, to lose himself inside her and forget what had gone before. And not only the miscarriage. He wanted to forget they'd married because she was pregnant.

In a perfect world she'd have married him because she couldn't live without him. But this wasn't a perfect world and it was obvious she could manage just fine on her own, thank you.

He loved her independence, her strength in tough times, the way she could turn a bad situation into something better. She'd turned his life around. He loved her optimism.

He loved her.

His heart constricted with a sweet pain he'd never felt for anyone before and his fingers tightened on the cold railing. Yep, time for a reality check. He was hopelessly, helplessly in love with his wife.

And a realist knew that didn't mean happy ever after; more likely it spelled disaster. Unless he did something about it.

Turning into the teeth of the wind, he checked his watch as he began the long walk back to his office. He had a late afternoon meeting. Then he was going to take her out to dinner at the fanciest restaurant he could find at short notice. *Then* he was going to tell her.

* * *

Carissa spent the afternoon pampering her body with a bubble bath. She washed her hair and left it down so it flowed around her shoulders. Knowing Ben's preference for blue, she chose a turquoise sweater of the softest cashmere—nice to touch—over black trousers, and applied just enough make-up to bring colour to her cheeks and highlight her eyes.

By six o'clock she was ready. She'd gone for the formal dining area and covered the scarred mahogany table with her best lace cloth. Jasmine rice and chicken korma curry with coconut and coriander perfumed the air. She'd made green salad and pappadams. A bottle of wine chilled in the fridge and two fat candles waited to be lit. The music was a compromise—a compilation of slow pop favourites.

At six-thirty, Ben rang. 'Hi, listen, I'm sorry, but I'm running late. I had a meeting which ran overtime.'

Her smile at hearing his voice faded a little, but she tried for a bright tone. 'Okay, when shall I expect you?'

'I'll be an hour or so. Don't cook, I'll grab something on the way home.'

'Oh, I…' Her eyes swept the intimate table setting as she moved to the kitchen, phone in hand, and switched off the oven. But she swallowed her disappointment, the feeling she'd been let down. 'See you later, then,' she said, and disconnected.

She should have told him, but all wasn't lost. First she dialled for a cab, then she rummaged in the store room and found the old picnic basket. If Mohammed wouldn't come to the mountain…

She'd give him a surprise he wouldn't forget.

CHAPTER FOURTEEN

'SURPRISE!'

Ben was already on his way out of his office, a hot date with his wife on his mind, when he heard the familiar voice in the corridor. He banked his frustration and turned to grin at the woman with a pushchair in tow.

'Jess. What are you doing in Sydney?' With no alternative, he pushed his door wider. 'Come on in.'

'I needed a break. We both needed a break with the weather we've been having in Melbourne.' She moved in for a hug, smelling of milk and crackers. 'The plane just got in. I would've left a message, but since we're staying at the Cove, I thought I'd come up and catch you if you were here.'

'And Timmy. How's it going, champ?' The sight of the kid brought a lump to his throat, but he shoved the emotion away and gave the little guy a friendly punch on the shoulder. Timmy grinned back.

'He's walking, Lord help me. I couldn't wait for the day, now I've changed my mind.'

'They grow so quick.'

'Yeah.' Her wistful sigh echoed his own sentiments.

'How are you, Jess?'

'I'm fine. Better. It gets easier with time. So…' She plunked herself in the nearest chair. 'What have you been doing with yourself since I saw you?'

'Getting married.' He hoisted one buttock on the edge of his desk.

She stared at him. 'You? Married? When?'

'Back in April. I'm sorry I didn't let you know. It was kind of sudden.'

'I can't believe it. Love 'em and leave 'em, eh?' She grinned. 'When do I get to meet this woman who snapped up Australia's most eligible man? What's her name?'

'Carissa. How about tomorrow night? Come for tea. I'd ask you tonight, but I want to prepare her. She just lost a baby.'

Her smile faded. 'Oh, God, and here I am with Timmy. I'm sorry, Ben, I know you always loved kids.'

'It happened a little sooner than I expected.' Like ten years sooner. 'Jess…can I unload on you?' He glanced around. 'Not here. Let's grab a coffee somewhere.'

Her brows lifted. 'Trouble in paradise already?'

He hesitated. 'Could be.'

'Just answer this. Does she make your skin itch?'

His lips curved at the thought. 'Like a fever.'

'Does your heart leap when you catch sight of her unexpectedly?'

'Every damn time.'

'Would you walk through fire for her?'

'If there was a point.' He picked up a paper clip from the desk and proceeded to pull it apart. 'I…it's just that we got married bec—'

But Jess raised a palm. 'Doesn't matter. Is she the last

thing on your mind when you go to sleep, the first thing you think of when you wake up?'

'Yes,' he snapped, tossing the mangled clip onto the desk as the frustration and denial he'd held inside for so long unleashed itself. 'I love her, Jess. I love her so much and it's tearing me apart.'

He watched her eyes soften as women's eyes always did at the mention of the word. He'd never understood it, until now.

She shook her head. 'You haven't told her, have you?'

He blew out a long, calming breath. 'No.'

She rose and took his face in her hands. 'Oh, Ben, for God's sake. *Tell* her. A woman loves to hear it. Every day. As often as possible. No one understands better than me you never know when you might not get another chance.'

When Timmy began to squirm and fuss, she released the pushchair's harness and pulled him onto her hip. 'Why don't we go grab that coffee? You can tell me all about it.'

As the cab slowed a short distance from the Cove Carissa prepared to take her basket of goodies, including a candle, up to Ben's office. Her heart fluttered with a mixture of anticipation and panic. All she'd left behind was her filmy white nightgown, and with any luck she wouldn't be needing it.

A couple were heading out of the hotel lobby for a stroll, a toddler hoisted on the man's shoulders, but even as she watched her hand froze on the basket.

Ben.

She felt the blood drain from her face. It couldn't be... She shrank back as they walked right past the cab—she could have reached out and touched him.

The woman was tall and slim and wearing a bohemian-type flowing dress, a felt hat perched on her head. As she linked her arm in his he smiled at something she said, showing off that cocky grin Carissa hadn't seen in too long.

She didn't realise the cabbie had come to a stop. 'Here we are, lady. The Cove Hotel.'

'I've changed my mind.' She struggled to raise her voice above a whisper. 'Take me home again.'

He shrugged and turned over the meter. 'Your money.'

Tyres screeched as he pulled into the traffic. The aroma of chicken curry mingled with the cab's smell of vinyl and stale chewing gum as she huddled back in the seat. She'd never felt so cold and there was a horrible grinding pressure building in her chest.

She was naïve enough to think their relationship had changed. *You're mine.* To Carissa, those words exchanged the night he'd come back from Melbourne had been more binding than their marriage vows.

He'd been distant since she'd come home from the hospital; coming home late, up and gone before she woke. Now she knew why. He'd tied himself to her and now he regretted it. He didn't know how to tell her, or perhaps he didn't intend to—as she'd requested. Something shattered inside her.

She let herself into the house. Her legs seemed too heavy as she walked through the dining area with its cosy table still set for two with the remaining candle and vase of early freesias perfuming the air.

She dumped the basket on the floor. To calm herself, she broke open the bubbly and poured a generous glass. Only one, she promised herself as she set it on the piano.

She wanted a clear head when he got back. Despite the evidence, she wouldn't condemn him till she heard what he had to say.

He was right about one thing—a realist was rarely disappointed, but an optimist just kept coming back for more.

An hour later, she heard the crunch of gravel as the car pulled up. She closed the piano lid, picked up her glass and went to the kitchen to wait. Nerves were twisting her empty stomach into tight little knots as she sat down at the table. She wanted to hide in her bedroom, pull the quilt over her head and pretend she was asleep, but she stayed put.

She heard the front door open, shut. Heard his footsteps coming closer. Then he was there. A whiff of some expensive women's perfume floated on the air, taunting her.

'Hi. Something smells good.' He slung his jacket over a chair.

'I assume you mean the chicken curry,' she clipped. She willed her eyes to meet his. Clear, dark green, like secret pools in a dark forest. She could lose herself in those depths.

But she pulled herself from his captive gaze and focused on his jaw. No signs of lipstick, just the stubble she loved to touch. Right now she wanted to sock it. She ground her fists together under the table instead.

He gestured to the opened wine. 'You started without me.'

'I got tired of waiting.'

'I rang, but you didn't pick up. Guess you were in the shower.'

When she didn't enlighten him, he pulled out the

chair opposite hers and sat down. 'Carissa, I have something to tell you. I should have told you a long time ago but I was a coward. I was going to tell you over dinner and wine but I don't want to wait…' He leaned forward.

She leaned back. Misery slid through her body with an anger that had been building over the past two hours and now threatened to explode. That anger and pride kept her chin up, her eyes dry and her voice cold when she said, 'By all means, let's hear it.'

She thought she saw disappointment and something like panic flare in his eyes, then he shoved his chair back, slid his hands round the back of his neck. 'Perhaps I'll wait, after all. You don't appear to be in the right mood.'

'How do you expect me to be, Ben?' Without thought she tossed her last mouthful of wine at him, catching him squarely in the chest.

'Hey!' Frowning, he dabbed at the stain on his shirt. 'What the…?' Then he noticed the basket. 'What's all this?'

'*All this* is the special dinner I made for us.'

'I don't get it.'

Her lips twisted around a bitter smile. 'Oh, I think you *get it* all right, but it's not with me.'

'What the hell's that supposed to mean?'

She swiped at her eyes. 'When you called to say you'd be late I packed our meal and came by the Cove.'

'So why…? Ah, I wasn't there.' Oddly, she didn't see guilt on his face, but realisation. 'I told you I rang.'

'Why? To make another excuse? I wanted it to be special. I wanted us to…' She squeezed her eyes shut to stop the tears. 'Damn you, Ben Jamieson, I *hate* you. I'll hate you till the day I die.'

The silence was thick and tense and telling. Carissa swore she heard her heart breaking.

'That's a crying shame,' he said softly, so softly she barely heard. 'Because I love you.'

'I saw you with *her* and that…that little boy… If you want a divorce…' Then his words registered. Three little words that froze her in place. She stared at him, saw the emotions burning in his eyes. Honesty. Hope. Wariness? *Love?* A drum was pounding in her chest, violins were singing in her ears. 'Say that again. Slowly.'

'I said I love you, Carissa Jamieson. And if you'd waited long enough before crucifying me, I'd have told you. The *she* is a friend from Melbourne who called in after I rang you the first time. Her name's Jess and I invited her to tea tomorrow night. And no, thank you, I don't want a divorce. Not now, not ever. You're stuck with me.'

She pressed a hand to her mouth, cursing her verbal attack while she absorbed his words. How quick she'd been to condemn despite her intention to listen first and ask questions later. 'Ben, I thought the worst of you. I didn't give you a chance to explain. I was wrong, and I'm sorry.'

'No, I was wrong. I should have told you I love you a long time ago.' He reached over and grasped her hand in his warm one. 'I wasn't there for you when you lost the baby. All I could think was you'd married me for one reason, and that reason no longer held.

'I kept my distance to give you time to decide when you were ready to go your own way. I thought that's what you wanted. I should have asked you how you felt, but I didn't want to know the answer. I was so bloody scared it'd be the one I didn't want to hear.'

'I know how you feel because I feel the same way,' she almost whispered. 'I thought you'd no longer want me when you can have any woman you want.'

He squeezed her hand. 'Any woman? I only want you. You don't know how much I wanted to take you in my arms, how many times I turned to you in the night, wanting you, needing you. Loving you.'

Happiness and new hope blossomed inside her till she wanted to dance.

Ben turned her hand over, pressed a kiss to her palm, then pushed up from the table. 'I have to get something from the studio. I want you to go sit on our bed.'

She all but floated down the passage, grabbing freesias and candles on the way. She lit the candles so that a soft radiance filled the room, then she arranged herself demurely on the edge of the bed.

Ben came in with a guitar and seated himself on the dressing-table stool.

'A Segovia,' she murmured, running her hand over the smooth wooden surface. 'It looks new.'

'It is. I wanted to do this properly. I'm not a man who uses romantic words, Carissa. Maybe that's because I never needed them till I met you, but I do know music.'

They watched each other a moment as the beautiful notes he made washed over them. Then he seemed to turn inward, caught up in the melody.

The poignant piece he'd worked on in the shed.

He didn't need romantic words. He made love to her through his music. His heart and soul flowed through his fingers, filling hers with the passion of it, the magic of it. She wanted to weep for its sheer beauty. And for the man himself.

His eyes grew dark. The flickering light softened the sharp edges of his features, turned his hair to fire. She caught the drifting fragrance of approaching spring in the freesias, the lighter scent of sun-aired linen in the sheets. She knew she'd hold this moment in her heart for ever.

He let the last chord linger on the air before setting the instrument aside.

'That's the most beautiful piece I ever heard.'

'The inspiration's right in front of me. I called it *Carissa*. I want the world to know you're mine.' He rose and took her hand, tugging her up against him. 'I want us to start over. For us this time.'

'Yes.' Her hands weren't steady as she slid them up his still-damp shirt, unfastened the first button to explore the hard-packed chest covered in thick, springy hair.

She couldn't resist. She pressed her lips there, absorbed the taste of wine over the salty taste of masculine flesh. 'I love you, Ben.' And tugged at his belt.

'Carissa, wait…'

'No more waiting. I want you. Now.' She was shocked to hear the low, earthy demand in her voice.

'Are you sure it's okay?' He dipped his head, nuzzled her neck. 'The doc said—'

'Touch me, Ben.'

He eased those competent guitar-playing fingers over her cashmere sweater, down her sides, then leisurely up and over her breasts while he watched her. His lips were a sigh away from hers, his breath warm against her cheek.

'I once said you were a fantasy. You're any red-blooded male's fantasy. Now you're mine, only mine. I love you, Mrs Jamieson.'

He closed his mouth over hers. Even slow and dreamy, she felt the banked heat in the quiet contact. But this was how it should be tonight, a gentle celebration of loving.

Outside she heard a bird's call, the shifts and creaks as the old house settled. For a heartbeat she thought she smelled Gran's scent and knew she'd always, always remember this moment.

Fantasy and reality melded as they undressed each other then slipped between the cool sheets. *He loved her.* The words sang in her head. In her heart. And for the first time they were making love in the truest sense. She let herself soar on its wings.

Later, their bodies sated and entwined, she rested her chin on his chest and looked deep into his eyes. 'I know losing the baby hurt you too. But you know what? I think we were sent a little angel on loan for a few months to bring us together.'

She saw the emotion flare as his eyes misted over. 'An angel.' His fingertip caressed her cheekbone with infinite gentleness. 'I think maybe you're right. I have two angels in my life.'

Ben found her hand and squeezed and felt the emotions wrung from him over the past few hours pour into her. 'Carissa, you gave me back something I thought I'd lost. My belief in myself. My music dried up, but it came back, different. Better. I hear it with my soul now, not my ears. It's like tuning into the cosmos.

'But more than that, you gave me hope, lent me your strength, helped me heal. Even knowing that, I couldn't or wouldn't see what was right in front of me. A chance to build a new life, a new beginning with a woman who means more to me than anything or anyone that's gone before. I can't wait to show you off to Jess tomorrow night.'

'You've never mentioned her.'

'She's Rave's widow.'

A shadow crossed his heart, but that part of his life was over; it was time to move on.

'She's the woman you went to see when you first came.'

'How did you know?'

'A woman knows these things when it comes to her man.'

'We weren't married then.' He felt a rush of satisfaction and grinned. 'You were jealous.'

'I was not.' She sighed. 'Okay, maybe a little.'

'Ha.' He looked at her and knew he was opening doors to his life that up till now he'd kept closed.

'Let's play this scene again, starting with where you tell me you love me,' she said, trailing her fingers over his face, then down, over his chest and lower. 'And we'll move on from there.'

EPILOGUE

THE usual Saturday evening crowd buzzed in the Cove Hotel's piano bar. Ben Jamieson flicked a proprietary eye over the pianist and listened to her clever fingers on the keys. And this time she wore his rings.

Kicking back in the chair, he took a large gulp of beer and watched. That slinky sapphire number begged to be taken off. He wanted her, that was nothing new—seemed as if he'd wanted her forever. As if he'd loved her forever. No reservations, no holds barred.

As Carissa launched into another bracket of classics, her eyes collided with Ben's. Instant heat flooded her body as it always did when she looked at her husband.

Fifteen minutes later, Carissa closed the piano.

'Can I buy you a drink?' The familiar liquid voice with its hint of gravel made her smile.

'Sorry, management doesn't permit employees to socialise with guests in the hotel.'

'A walk, then.'

'Very well,' she said primly. She accompanied him past the bar, and across the foyer.

'Forget the walk.' He grabbed her hand. 'Let's break some rules and get straight to the good stuff.'

'Why, Mr Jamieson, I thought you'd never ask.'

His fingers tangled with hers. 'Do you know what I was thinking about while I was watching you play?'

'Getting naked and having your wicked way with me?'

'Got it in one.'

Then right there in the foyer, in front of all the guests and including George Christos, he lowered his lips to the resident pianist's. A sultry, body-temperature-elevating minute later he kissed his way to her ear and whispered, 'So what do you want to do about it?'

'The penthouse suite. And make it quick.'

At the top floor the elevator doors whooshed open. The scent of roses filled the air as they stepped out. Red rose petals showed the way straight to the king-size bed, already turned down and waiting. A bottle of bubbly chilled in a silver bucket.

'We'll start with a celebratory drink,' Ben said, undoing shirt cuffs and nibbling on her neck at the same time. 'And then we can get down to serious business. I've got this fantasy.' He worked his way to her ear lobe. 'You, naked but for stilettos and stockings. See what you can do while I pour the wine and I'll take it from there.'

'I'll stick to water, thanks.'

He took her shoulders and held her at arm's length. 'Since when did you refuse a hundred-dollar bottle of wine?'

'Since I learned I'm six weeks pregnant.' She planted an exuberant kiss on his mouth. 'I found out today.'

His smile was slow and devastating. 'In that case... You're a miracle, you know that?' He cupped her face with his hands and the kiss he gave her was heartbreakingly tender. 'I love you, Carissa. And just for that…'

He walked her backwards to the soft leather couch and sat her down. Tugging at the picture on the wall above their heads, he opened a safe and drew out a velvet box, then sat beside her. 'I was going to give you this when the baby was born. Then when…' He trailed off, swallowed. 'It worked out after all.'

He opened the box. A tear-drop sapphire glittered darkly against the flash of diamonds.

Carissa swallowed over the lump rising up her own throat. 'You bought this on our honeymoon. I remember the string of zeros on the price tag.' The fact that he'd bought it way back then, when their relationship had been so new and fragile, brought tears to her eyes.

'Sapphires for my blue lady.'

Much later, she rolled towards him as they lay sprawled on the bed where they'd first made love. Darkness lay like a blanket, the moon spilled through the window etching his face in silver. She kissed his chin. 'Ben?'

'Hmm?' He opened one green eye.

'This has been a beautiful night. The best. But if it's all right with you, I want to go home.'

He propped himself up on one elbow, a frown creasing his brow as he laid a gentle hand on her stomach. 'You're not sick or anything, are you?'

She smiled into the darkness. 'Not yet. I want to love you in our own bed. Let's come back here every year on Valentine's Day, and make it our other anniversary.'

'Are you sure?'

'Very.'

He kissed her slowly and purposefully in the moon-light while the scent of roses lingered around them. 'Then let's go home.'

Just Once

SUSAN NAPIER

CHAPTER ONE

'WHAT the hell do you want?'

Kate Crawford kept the polite smile pinned to her lips as she confronted the man who had wrenched his front door open with an impatient snarl.

Framed in the doorway he appeared intimidatingly large, his broad shoulders and muscled chest straining the seams of a well-worn grey tee shirt, scruffy blue jeans encasing his long, power-packed legs. His short-cropped hair stood up in untidy spikes, as if he had been running his large, battered hands through the dark brown thicket, and his deeply tanned face was chiselled into tight angles of hostility.

In spite of his obvious bad temper he was devastatingly handsome, a potent combination of classic male beauty and simmering testosterone. In fact, he looked more like a professional athlete than a best-selling author who spent a good portion of his time sitting at a desk.

'Sorry to disturb you, but I wondered if I could borrow some sugar?' she said, lifting up her empty cup and watching the shock that had rippled across his sculpted features congeal into a shuttered wariness. She was suddenly glad that she was wearing a casual sundress rather than the tailored elegance that was her signature in the city. The last thing she wanted to do was look as if she had dressed to impress. She hadn't even bothered with make-up. After all, she was now officially in holiday mode— the old-fashioned, do-for-yourself, bucket-and-spade, sand-in-the-sandwiches type of holiday, the kind that she had never had as a child.

'I've just moved in next door,' she explained pleasantly, affecting not to notice his stony silence as she waved her free hand towards the beach-front property on the other side of the low, neatly clipped boundary hedge—a small, ageing wooden bungalow, which was dwarfed by the modern, two-storeyed, architect-designed houses that had sprouted up on the two adjoining sections.

'I'm renting the place for a month, and thought I'd brought everything I needed with me, but when I went to make myself a cup of coffee I realised I'd forgotten one of the basics,' she continued with a rueful lift of her slender shoulders. 'I know there's a general store a few kilometres back but, well… I've just spent four hours driving down here from Auckland and I'd rather avoid having to get back in the car for a while. So, if you wouldn't mind tiding me over until tomorrow, I'd appreciate it; and of course I'll pay you back in kind…'

She kept her voice steady, confident that she looked a lot more composed than she felt. Although she was only a little taller than average, the willowy curves, elegant bone structure and haughty facial features that Kate had inherited from her undemonstrative mother helped project an air of cool sophistication and graceful poise, regardless of her inner turmoil. It had never mattered to her mother if the serenity on display was only skin deep. Strong emotions were ruinous to logical thought processes, and therefore to be discouraged. An ambitious criminal lawyer determined to be the youngest woman appointed to New Zealand's judicial bench, Jane Crawford had wanted her daughter to follow in her footsteps, but Kate had proved a severe disappointment on all fronts. A gentle and imaginative child, she had worked hard at school for only average results and had acquired neither the academic credentials nor the desire to compete with her brilliant, perfectionist mother. In quiet rebellion she had chosen to follow a totally different career path, one that had proved unexpectedly successful and wholly satisfying.

However, at times like this she was thankful for those chilly early lessons in rejection—they had built up her emotional independence and equipped her to face scathing criticism and hurtful rebuffs with a calm resilience that frustrated her opponents.

If she had been relying on the world-famous author to play the gallant hero to her damsel-in-distress routine she had obviously chosen the wrong man, she thought wryly. As a story-teller, his speciality was constructing tough, gritty, anti-heroes who were rude, crude and lethal to know—literally so where female characters were concerned. His creations, much like the man himself, were usually loners, alienated from society by their cynical mistrust of their fellow human beings and stubborn refusal to play by the rules.

Now that he had mastered his initial shock, the gorgeous, dark brown eyes were smouldering at Kate with angry suspicion.

No one was supposed to know where Drake Daniels sequestered himself to write his hugely successful thrillers. He lived mostly out of hotel rooms when he wasn't writing—partying up a storm, generating all the publicity his publisher could wish for on a merry-go-round of talk-shows, book-signings and festivals and special events—ostensibly enjoying his peripatetic lifestyle to the full. But sandwiched between the bouts of public hyperactivity were intervals of total anonymity. Every now and then he would drop out of sight for periods ranging from a few weeks to several months, and each year there would be a new novel on the shelves to delight his fans and confound his critics. To Kate's frustration, a lot of the readily available information about him had turned out to be cleverly placed disinformation. Even his publisher and agent had claimed not to be privy to where in his native New Zealand his private bolt-hole was located. It had taken a great deal of determination, cunning and several strokes of unbelievable luck to finally track him down to the sleepy fishing and farming community of Oyster Beach, tucked away on the east coast of the upper Coromandel Peninsula.

Kate raised her delicately arched brows along with the proffered cup in a gentle hint that she was still waiting for his response, but just as he seemed about to break his stony silence her complacency was shattered by the sound of a throaty feminine voice floating out from the cavernous hall behind him.

'Who is it, darling?'

Kate barely had time to glimpse the tall, voluptuous redhead in a short white towelling robe before the tall masculine figure turned away, blocking her view with his broad shoulders.

'Nobody.' As he spoke he kicked the door closed with his heel, leaving Kate blinking at the honey-gold panels of oiled timber.

For a moment she merely stood, stunned by his insulting dismissal, the blood thundering in her ears. Then she forced herself to walk away, her stomach churning like a washing machine.

Get over it. Move on.

She had done what she came to do. Fired the first shot in her personal little war. There was an old saying that a man surprised was half beaten, so by that measure she could consider herself well on the way to success. But now that she had sacrificed the element of surprise she needed to regroup her defences.

Her flimsy sandals crunched on the crushed-shell path as she retraced her steps along the side of the house with measured strides, resisting the urge to disappear in a cowardly short cut over the low hedge.

The few metres of sandy lawn between the sprawling rear deck of the house and the public beach seemed to take for ever to traverse, but Kate maintained her unhurried pace, acutely conscious of the burnished bank of tinted windows that angled around the back of the house on both upper and lower floors, affording the occupants a clear view of the three-kilometre beach as far as the mouth of the tidal estuary.

Were they watching her retreat, or had they already returned to whatever it was they had been doing before the unexpected interruption? The desire to look back over her shoulder was almost overwhelming, and it took an effort of will for Kate to cling to her feigned air of indifference.

As she reached the lip of the beach a slight, salty breeze riffled through her sun-streaked, caramel-brown hair, sending a few of the long, layered strands feathering across her slender throat. She paused to brush them back, tunnelling her hand under the rest of the silky-straight mass and flipping it free from the textured cotton bodice of her sundress to ripple down between her tense shoulder blades, welcoming the fan of air against the self-conscious burning at the nape of her neck. Her blue eyes narrowed against the splinters of late-afternoon sunlight reflecting off the shifting sea as she tried to gulp in some much-needed oxygen and ease the tightness in her chest. Boats rocked gently at their moorings out in the sheltered bay and, even though it was a glorious spring day and the tide was fully in, the narrow strip of beach was all but empty.

Oyster Beach was only just being discovered by the eager developers who had swallowed up large tracts of coastal land farther south and regurgitated them as fashionable beach resorts. With Auckland only a few hours' drive away, the cove was being promoted as the latest 'unspoiled' getaway for jaded city dwellers. Expensive new holiday houses sporting double garages and *en suite* bathrooms were starting to muscle in on the simple beaches and old-style family homes on their large, flat water-front sections and up in the sheltering hills 'lifestyle blocks' were being shaved off the fringes of productive farmland.

At present the permanent local population was only a few hundred, but that number ballooned to thousands over Christmas and New Year when the schools were out for the long summer break and the pressure on holiday accommodation and facilities was intense. Kate knew that her timing had been serendipitous because November was exam-time at New Zealand high schools and universities. If she had been a few weeks later she would have had little chance of finding anywhere in Oyster Beach for rent, let alone right next door to her quarry. Even the local camping ground was booked out several months in advance for the height of the summer.

At any other time Kate might have been inclined to linger and drink in the tranquillity of the scene in front of her, but at the moment all she could think about was making it back to the sanctuary of her temporary home.

Half-buried boulders wrapped in plastic netting shored up the grass bank at the edge of the beach, protecting the valuable, low-lying land along the foreshore from being eaten away by storm surges. Kate stumbled as she made the short jump down onto the powdery white sand and discovered that her knees were seriously wobbly. Her hands and feet felt cold and heavy at the end of her limbs and her ears had started to ring. She was, she realised with grim awareness of the irony, suffering some of the classic effects of shock—although she had been the one sup-posedly delivering the jolt!

She stepped back up onto the coarse, springy grass on her side of the hedge and huffed a sigh of relief when her shaky legs proved equal to the task. Moving a little more quickly, she sought the shadow of the creaking verandah and slipped in through the sliding glass door that she had left open to the fresh air.

'Gee, that went really well,' she muttered to the empty house, her fingers whitening around the empty cup as she relived those awful moments of hot hu-miliation when the door had slammed shut in her face. She had been tempted to storm off vowing never to speak to him again, but she was a mature, twenty-seven-year-old woman, not a sulky, self-absorbed teenager. She had questions to ask and a respon-sibility to uphold and, as her mother was so fond of telling her, failure was not a viable option!

She put the cup down on the kitchen table and flexed her angry fingers. Realistically speaking, what else had she expected? Drake Daniels had a reputation for freezing off people who became importuning and she had just doorstepped him like a crazed fan, or member of the despised paparazzi. Given his reclusive work habits, she should consider herself lucky that he had opened the door at all.

On the bright side, at least she now had confirmation that she was in the right place at the right time. When she had put her money down for the holiday rental she had been acting as much on gut instinct as on the elusive facts, although her instincts had certainly led her astray in one important aspect: she had not expected to have to cope with a mystery redhead as well as an angry author. Naively, perhaps, she had believed the myth that he crafted his compelling stories in total seclusion.

But that was what she had come here for, wasn't it? To separate the man from the myth? To explore his true character, not just the parts of him that he wanted people to see. Even if it was a truth she found hard to stomach.

She had to get a grip on herself, and not jump to hasty conclusions. Perhaps the woman was a visiting relative, although her research hadn't turned up any mention of living family members.

The slippery coils of nervous tension that had been shifting in her belly all day suddenly tightened, and a rush of saliva into her dry mouth gave Kate just enough warning to make it into the roomy, old-fashioned bathroom before vomiting up the small salad roll that she had made herself eat at a roadside café on the drive down. So much for thinking that it would calm her uneasy digestion!

Kate rinsed the sourness out of her mouth at the basin and dabbed a little refreshing cold water onto her face, dewing her cheeks. Without make-up to emphasis her ghostly silver-blue eyes and narrow mouth she should have looked pallid and uninteresting, but the age-spotted mirror above the basin was reassuring. One of the few positive legacies she had inherited from her irresponsible, absentee father was a honey-gold complexion that only needed a slight touch of the sun to deepen to a tawny glow. New Zealand was experiencing an unseasonably hot spring, and the meteorologists were predicting more of the same warm, dry weather in the coming weeks, so, if this holiday proved a disastrous mistake in every other way, at least she could return home with a tan that would be the envy of her work-bound housemates, Kate thought wryly.

She flicked her layered fringe aside from its central parting, smoothing it down from her temples to rest alongside the high cheekbones that gave her pale eyes their faintly feline tilt. She accepted that she wasn't beautiful, like her glacial blonde mother, but her sharply etched features were nicely symmetrical, and some men found her unusual eye colour attractive rather than off-putting. Her smile was her secret weapon; when genuine it bestowed a warmth that vanquished the natural aloofness of her expression. She practised it now, to give her wavering spirits a cheerful boost. *If you look confident, you'll act confident,* was another of her mother's bracing maxims, along with aggressive creed, *Don't get mad, get even!*

Purged of her energy-sapping queasiness, Kate suddenly found herself feeling peckish. She fossicked amongst the fresh supplies she had unloaded into the fridge and ate a pottle of yoghurt and some hummus and rice crackers while she waited at the bench for the electric kettle to boil. As she tried to keep her mind from fretting over her next move her gaze swept around the clean but shabby, open-plan kitchen, a far cry from the upscale, central Auckland town house she shared with her friend Sara, and Sara's cousin Josh. The appliances here were all basic models, functional rather than stylish, probably installed when the house was built. The green clocked wallpaper, faded Formica bench and patterned vinyl flooring looked original, too, but what would have seemed highly trendy three decades ago were now sadly dated. She had barely given herself time to unpack before she had trotted out on her abortive begging expedition, but her impression was that the whole place could do with a facelift. The three-bedroom weatherboard house was well-maintained but there was no sign of any attempt at expansion or renovation over the years, and Kate guessed that its present owner had inherited or bought it with the intention of keeping it as a landbank.

The kettle burbled and Kate occupied herself with the mundane task of making a cup of tea. She discarded the sodden tea bag in the sink and added a splash of milk, stirring it in with unnecessary force as her thoughts returned to the complicated tangle her life had become. Choices that had once seemed clear and simple were now fraught with danger, she thought, staring out the kitchen window at the gnarled pohutukawa tree whose grey-green leaves blocked out the concrete palace that was in the final stages of completion on the other side of the chain-link fence. She hoped that she wasn't about to get strangled in the web of deceit she had been busily weaving.

She raised the steaming cup to her lips for her first sip when a sudden, intangible sizzle of tension in the air made her stiffen. She jerked around, her heart leaping up into her throat as she realised she was no longer alone.

Standing silently in the arched opening between the kitchen and the living room, looking no more friendly than he had a few minutes earlier, was Drake Daniels.

She hoped he put her little choke of dismay down to the hot tea that had spilled onto her fingers. 'What are you doing in here?' she demanded, switching hands to shake off the burning droplets, disgusted to hear that her voice was high and breathless rather than cool and clipped.

'The door was open,' he said, jerking his head in the direction of the verandah. 'I took it to mean that you were expecting me to follow you…'

'It's open because the house is hot and stuffy,' she snapped. She knew she should play it cool, but the sarcastic words came spilling from her lips before she could stop them: 'What the hell do you want?'

His dark eyes glinted. He placed a small plastic container down on the Formica table, centring it with a mocking precision. 'I brought you the sugar you said you needed.'

'Oh.' Kate hugged her tea defensively to her chest as she wrestled with her conscience. 'Thank you,' she said begrudgingly, knowing full well that his meekness was a sham.

Sure enough, as soon as she had humbled herself, he unsheathed his sword.

'So, tell me: are you going to leave when you find out you're wasting your time here? Or is it going to take men in white coats and a restraining order to get rid of you?

'Are you stalking me?'

CHAPTER TWO

'STALKING you?' Kate widened her eyes in amused disbelief. 'You do fancy yourself, don't you?'

Her teasing tone made Drake's mouth thin. 'Stop playing games, Katherine,' he growled. 'How did you find me?'

She sipped her tea and mused on the question. 'I've always found you to be borderline paranoiac, and now it looks like you've inched over the line. Maybe the men in white coats should be coming for you…'

'Very witty—and very evasive.'

She might have known that he'd notice. Words were his business, his strength and his talent…interpreting nuances and assigning subtle layers of meaning to every line of dialogue and paragraph of prose. He would tie her up in verbal knots if she let him. Her best chance was to make simple statements that could be neither proved nor disproved, and then just stick to her guns. Or better still, say nothing at all.

'You're surely not going to claim that it's just pure coincidence that you turned up on my doorstep?' he accused, taking an aggressive stance, legs astride, hands fisting on his hips, a poster-boy for one of his disaffected heroes. 'What's going on, Katherine?'

A tremor of weakness shimmered through her bones. *Oh, if only you knew!* She looked into his moody countenance and felt the familiar, powerfully seductive tug of physical attraction that was the source of all her current turmoil. She still found it amazing that such a bold, passionate and charismatic man had reacted with such intensity to her ordinary, unremarkable self. That it had also taken him by surprise was evident from his hypersensitivity to any hint of possessiveness, and his thinly veiled restlessness whenever they had been together for any length of time. Sophistication had been the name of the game, and for a while she had actually carried it off.

She caught herself up before she could begin to wallow in bittersweet memories, her determination hardening. Oh, no, she wasn't going to let herself fall back into that trap! She was no longer that woman— willing to pander to his genius at the expense of her own needs and goals.

'What's going on is that I'm taking a long-overdue holiday,' she said firmly. 'I've accrued so much extra leave over the past two years that my boss was forced to point out a clause in my contract that says I have until next month to use it or lose it—'

'Marcus?' he interrupted sharply, latching onto the notion that his New Zealand publisher was involved. His eyes kindled with fury at the treachery. 'Enright sent you to find me?'

'Nobody sent me to find you—Marcus has no idea where I am,' she insisted with perfect truth. Her reputation as a dedicated employee who could always be relied upon to work above and beyond the call of duty to support good client liaisons had taken a knock with her abrupt decision to take all the accumulated weeks owing on such short notice, and it had dived even further when she had rejected Marcus's belated offer of a compensatory bonus if she sacrificed the accrual. Enright Media was a very tightly run ship, and it had entailed a lot of fast juggling of favours to get others to take on her responsibilities as well as their own while she was away, but as a researcher she was in a good position to know where the bodies were buried, and how and on whom to apply pressure. A disgruntled Marcus had been forced to concede that he had no legal grounds for insisting she break up her holiday allowance into smaller units, particularly as it meant she would be on deck over Christmas, when staff with young families were clamouring to jump ship.

'I told you, I'm on a holiday. That's when normal people take a break from their workaday lives to rest, travel or zonk out on a beach somewhere.'

'And you expect me to believe that of all the holiday homes in all the beach resorts in all the world, you walk into this one?' he demanded, his deep, velvet-smooth voice steeped in sarcasm.

The paraphrase of the famous line from *Casablanca* struck a painful chord. It had been Kate's ability to recognise quotes from old movies and obscure film noir classics that had captured his attention two years ago, when they had met at one of Marcus' champagne-drenched book-launch parties. They had spent the early part of the evening trading one-liners, Drake's fierce competitiveness challenged by her phenomenal memory for trivia and cool capacity to carry a bluff. Their feuding banter had become increasingly provocative as the night had worn on and Kate had shocked everyone, herself included, by leaving on his arm.

'Coincidences do happen,' she pointed out, relaxing deliberately back against the bench and taking another sip of her tea.

His handsome face rearranged itself into sharp angles of contempt. 'If I tried to use that tired old cliché in a book it would be laughed off the shelves.'

'Which is why they say that truth is stranger than fiction,' she said lightly, regarding him over the rim of the chunky mug. For once she almost felt in control of the relationship as she watched him vibrate with frustration. She was aware of a repressed violence in his nature, but for all his physicality she had never felt threatened by his considerable strength. At thirty-three, he had the maturity and experience to handle his inner demons. Whenever he exploded, it was with clever words rather than crude muscle.

'The strange truth being that less than four weeks after I leave Auckland you "just happen" to choose Oyster Beach for a sudden holiday and then you "just happen" to rent the place next door to mine?'

'Well, gee, I don't usually bother to check out the

ownership of neighbouring properties wherever I go, to make sure I'm not inadvertently going to intrude on your precious privacy,' she said, matching him for sarcasm.

His eyes narrowed as he pounced on the perceived slip. 'Then how do you know I'm the owner?'

'The rabid territorialism you're displaying is a dead give-away,' she said drily. 'Given your reclusive writing habits and erratic timetable, I doubt that you'd feel comfortable working anywhere but your own space. Someplace where you can come and go at will without attracting notice. And it's not as if there's a big choice of long-term rentals if you want something right on the beach...or so the travel agent told me,' she added swiftly.

'So how did you find out about this one?' He jerked his beard-roughened jaw at their surroundings. 'Internet? Newspaper ad?'

She almost agreed before she saw the potential trap. For all she knew the rental had never been actively advertised.

'Serendipity?' She smiled limpidly. 'I read a magazine story about some people who camp at Oyster Beach every Christmas, and then asked around. I am a researcher, you know.'

His jaw tightened. 'And something of an actress, too. You didn't even show a blink of surprise when I opened my door; almost as if you were expecting to see me. Yet you appeared not to recognise me.'

'I was shocked,' she said truthfully. The little electric pulses that zipped through her veins every time she saw him had intensified rather than faded with time. Her hyper-awareness was simultaneously exciting and inhibiting.

'So you just went ahead and trotted out your cheerful little spiel as blandly as if I was someone you'd never met before rather than the man you've been sleeping with for the past two years.'

Colour touched her haughty cheekbones. 'We've never actually slept together,' she corrected him with a crisp exactitude that would have made her mother proud. 'And in the rather awkward circumstances, I thought you would prefer me not to presume on our relationship—'

'Presume?' he echoed incredulously, dropping his hands from his hips. 'Am I really that much of a ogre?'

'Quite frankly, yes,' she punctured his scornful amusement. 'You made it very clear from the very beginning that there are situations and subjects which are strictly off limits between us—'

'I thought that was a mutual arrangement,' he cut in roughly. 'We're two very independent people, and, as I remember it, you're the one who's uncomfortable with the idea of us sleeping together. You never want to stay in my hotel room and you've certainly never invited me to spend the night at your house...'

Behind her back, Kate's hand gripped the sharp edge of the bench, using the small, cutting pain in her palm as a means of controlling the larger pain. Did he think that she hadn't been aware of the conflicting signals he had given out in those first few weeks? The reckless rush of passion that had precipitated them into an unlikely affair had caught them both off guard. Drake had been between books at the time and making the most of his freedom, and Kate had thought that once he plunged back into his creative cycle his interest would inevitably wane. Not having his experience in the etiquette of conducting casual romantic liaisons, Kate had quietly taken her cues from him. She had seen the way he shied away from gushing, clingy women, had noticed that, although he had a large circle of acquaintances, he had few real friends. He was quick to charm but slow to trust, so she had been very careful never to step over the invisible boundaries that his own behaviour had marked out, or to demand more than she was certain he was prepared to give. The reward for her restraint had been to hold his interest far beyond the usual few months his well-publicised affairs generally lasted. The price of loving Drake Daniels, she had discovered, was not to love him.

She smothered the hot words of protest that tingled on her tongue.

'We're getting off the point—'

'And what is the point?' He cocked his head. 'Oh, yes, that's right—your ridiculous pretence not to know me just now.'

If that wasn't the pot calling the kettle black!

'Maybe I was simply scared you might jump to the arrogant conclusion that I had followed you down here, and accuse me of stalking you! A normal person might shrug it off as just one of life's little amusing quirks, but with you there's no assumption of innocence; no, "Hi, Kate, great to see you—what on earth are you doing in this neck of the woods?" Your paranoid obsession has to build it into some big conspiracy theory centred solely around yourself.'

Temper kicked up a brooding storm in his eyes as he realised she had deftly outmanoeuvred him. 'That was what you meant by "rather awkward circumstances"?'

She hesitated, and lightning comprehension flashed in the storm-dark eyes. 'Ah…I suppose that was a reference to my being with Melissa…?'

Kate cursed herself for giving him the opportunity to torture her with more self-doubts. She was not going to betray the slightest interest in his half-naked companion.

She tilted her chin and gave him a coolly uncomprehending look. 'I meant the fact that I know you hate any interruptions while you're writing—' *Except by the mysterious Melissa,* an evil voice whispered in her ear. 'But if nobody knows where you are, I don't see how they can be expected to know which places to avoid. Perhaps if you were less secretive you might find out that people actually want to avoid you.'

'If you want to avoid me, Katherine, there's an easy solution. Pack up and go elsewhere for your holiday. If the rent isn't refundable I'll reimburse you. Hell, I'll even book you in at a five-star resort somewhere.'

Anywhere but here—he really was desperate to get rid of her! Kate smiled through a thin red veil of rage. 'Thank you, but I've never accepted expensive gifts from you before, and I don't intend to start now. I've already settled in and I'm quite happy with my choice,' she said, safe in the knowledge her bulging suitcases and bags were hidden behind the closed door of the master bedroom, where she had flung them before hurrying next door. She strolled over to sit down at the table with her tea, letting him know that she was unworried by his looming presence. 'I'm looking forward to being able to step out of the house straight onto the beach every day…'

'That's if it stays fine. You're a city girl, you'll get bored here by yourself. There's nothing for you to do if the weather turns—no shops, no cafés or restaurants, no entertainment—'

'Luckily I brought along my own brain,' she said drily, 'an essential accessory for the modern single woman. I'm sure I'll be able to keep myself amused. And I doubt the rest of the local community will be as standoffish as you. Perhaps I'll meet a handsome young fisherman who'll offer to show me the sights,' she added flippantly.

A muscle flickered alongside his compressed mouth. His restless eyes fell to her cup and his dark brows formed a straight line. He sniffed the air like a hound on a fresh scent. 'Is that tea? I thought you said that you were making coffee.'

Her stomach gave a commemorative lurch as another lie come home to roost. 'I changed my mind.'

'I didn't know you drank tea.' He frowned.

'There's a lot you evidently don't know about me,' she pointed out.

'So it would seem.' His gaze shifted to her face and subjected her to a darkly probing look. 'Well, since I brought you the sugar, perhaps you could offer me a cup?'

She barely stopped her mouth from falling open. 'I beg your pardon?'

'But not tea—I'd rather have coffee.' He began to prowl around the kitchen. 'Where are your beans?' He opened the fridge to inspect the shelves. 'God, this all looks depressingly healthy—where's all those lovely, full-fat soft cheeses you're so addicted to…and there's no wine, or stash of chocolate. Prunes? Who takes prunes on holiday? Don't tell me you're on one of those new faddy diets you said your mother is always suggesting you take. What is it this time—South Pacific Colon? Kidney-cleansing Vegan?' He closed the fridge and headed for the pantry.

'Do you mind?' Kate got there first and whipped out the small jar of coffee, pushing it into his chest before he could see the full container of sugar that had been sitting behind it. She shut the cupboard and stood in front of it with folded arms.

'Instant?' He looked pained as he cupped the jar in his big hands. 'What about fresh ground?'

'It's all I've got. Take it or leave it,' she said tartly. At home she had always made sure she had the blend of beans he liked and had taken pains to brew it to his personal taste.

'What in the hell is this? "Decaffeinated?"' he read off the label, as outraged as if he had discovered her keeping a dead body in the pantry.

'It's gentler on the stomach.'

'That's a contradiction in terms; coffee is supposed to kick you like a mule. Is this part of the new diet—some form of aversion therapy?'

'Well, it certainly seems to be working so far,' she muttered, glaring at him in dislike.

His dark head jerked up, eyebrows notching. How could a man who wrote such thrilling, emotionally dense prose be such a blind, insensitive swine? Kate could feel delayed reaction biting deep into her fragile self-control. Next thing he would be wanting her to invite his flame-haired companion over for a bonding drink!

'So I take it you won't be staying for that drink after all?' she said smoothly, sitting back down to her steaming brew.

Still holding her gaze, he unscrewed the lid of the jar, broke the new seal and inhaled the aroma, wrinkling his patrician nose.

'I suppose your tea is decaffeinated too?'

Her hands curled possessively around the mug, drawing it towards her. 'No. But I didn't make a pot, I just used an ordinary tea bag.'

His snobbish palate ignored the blatant discouragement. 'Well, I suppose that'll have to do, then.' She watched in dismay while he snagged a mug from the row of hooks under the cupboards and dropped in one of the tea bags from the open cardboard box on the counter.

'Make yourself at home,' she commented sarcastically as he re-boiled the kettle.

'Thanks. I am,' he said, filling his cup, his quick grin of genuine amusement setting off alarm bells. What had made him so good-humoured all of a sudden?

Kate wished she hadn't made it so obvious that she wanted him to leave, for now it seemed he was going to punish her by lingering.

'Any biscuits?' he asked, returning the milk to the fridge and scooping a teaspoon out of the cutlery drawer.

'No. I thought you were anxious to get back to—' She broke off as he dropped into the chair opposite, his long calves brushing her bare legs under the table, sending a shiver of goose-pimples scooting up her inner thighs. She quickly crossed her legs, swivelling her hips sideways so that she was well away from his unsettling touch, tucking the short, flared skirt neatly under her bottom.

'Back to Melissa?' he completed her question helpfully, heaping sugar into his tea.

Kate's face ached with the strain of not reacting to his casual twist of the knife.

'To your writing,' she said. 'I know you've got deadlines to meet.' She was pleased to see that her hand was rock-steady as she raised her cup to her lips.

'Is that what Marcus told you?'

'Sorry, I don't talk shop while I'm on holiday,' she said coldly. Let him believe that she was here at someone else's behest, if that was the way his mind was tracking. It would take some of the heat off her and, in reality, it was close enough to the truth not to cause her undue guilt.

He blew across his tea, wreathing his dark head in curls of steam: the devil in a domestic setting. 'Then what shall we talk about?' he invited in the deep voice that haunted her dreams.

Her stomach tightened and she lowered her lashes to hide a violent upsurge of emotion. 'What do we usually talk about?'

'Everything.'

And nothing... They never spoke about the disjointed nature of their affair—the weeks of passionate closeness interspersed by months apart, with little or no contact. In a mutual conspiracy of silence they could argue the state of the world, but never the state of their own feelings.

The only place their communications were truly uncensored was in bed, where actions spoke louder than words and their bodies were perfectly attuned to each other's needs. Drake was a generous lover, and Kate found a fierce rapture in his arms that helped carry her through the long, lonely periods of empty yearning.

The things that she ached to say to him were suddenly dammed up behind a thick wall of resentment. He didn't really want to talk, he simply wanted Kate to answer his questions...questions that she didn't yet have answers for herself!

'Nice weather we're having for the time of year,' she said.

'It is indeed...and you're obviously taking full advantage of it,' he agreed, taking up the challenge, his eyes stroking across the honey-coloured skin of her shoulders exposed by the spaghetti straps of her sundress.

Kate was suddenly conscious of the pull of the cotton bodice where it was cut straight across the slope of her breasts, notched in the centre of her cleavage by a V-shaped slit. The flower-splashed, chain-store dress was a comfortable old favourite of hers, despised by her mother for its cheerfully *déclassé* origins. She had never worn overly casual styles in Drake's company, knowing that it was her classic, understated elegance that appealed to his sophisticated tastes, and set her apart from the trend-setting flamboyance of more beautiful rivals for his attention.

She stopped breathing as Drake's gaze drifted down to the sliver of pale skin revealed by the straining V. Nor did she usually go braless when she was with him, preferring the protection and provocation of a lacy bra to enhance her slender curves. She hadn't worn this sundress since last summer, and was suddenly uncomfortably aware of a slight tugging at the side seams, a tightness pressing up under her arms that crowded her breasts forward against the strict cut of the fabric with an unaccustomed boldness. Thankfully the contrasting double-fold of colour that banded the top of the low bodice masked the crushed outline of her painfully sensitive nipples, and allowed her the semblance of indifference as he continued to rudely stare.

Was he making unflattering comparisons…or thinking that she had let herself go? Kate felt faint at the thought. Then she realised that she was still holding her breath and let it out in a little huff of relief, sucking in a fresh supply of oxygen to chase away the dizziness. The sudden reinflation of her lungs caused her breasts to further test their close confinement, and she was mortified to feel a stitch pop.

It wasn't only the dress, it was her own skin she no longer felt comfortable in, she tormented herself. And if he dared to ask if she had gained weight since he had last seen her, he was going to get a faceful of hot tea!

Perhaps he sensed her violent impulse because he rocked back on the hind legs of his chair with a lazy, placating smile, taking a long, leisurely gulp from his mug before resting it on his chest.

'Bright, splashy colours suit you rather well in this setting. That dress makes you look very much the part…' he trailed off suggestively and she obligingly snapped at the bait.

'What part?'

'The young, frivolous holiday-maker out looking for trouble.'

'I've never been frivolous in my life,' said Kate, offended.

He compounded the offence with a mocking grin that creased the sunfolds at the outer corners of his eyes. 'Sorry, perhaps I should have said "carefree"…'

A lot he knew! 'And I'm not "looking for trouble", either,' she added, far less sincerely.

'No? What about your handsome young fisherman?'

'What?' She took a moment to trace the origins of his *non sequitur*. 'That was a joke.'

'Was it?'

His cynical response make her hackles rise. 'You know it was!'

'Do I?' He lowered his chair with a thud and leaned forward on the table, the amusement wiped from his face. 'Because it's not as if there's anything to hold you back from experimenting. We never promised each other total fidelity, did we, Kate?'

Her heart stuttered. Experimenting? Was that what he was doing?

'We never promised each other anything at all,' she forced out evenly. 'But I think at the very least we owe each other a certain degree of respect and consideration.'

'You mean we should be discreet about our indiscretions?' he commented drily, his dark eyes intent on her still face. 'I thought I was…' His shrug encompassed their surroundings. 'A cosy little hideaway "far from the madding crowd's ignoble strife"…how much more careful can a man be?'

Trust Drake to frame a paralysing statement in a poetic quotation, but Kate was inured to his clever verbal games. She battled the crushing pain in her chest to try and work out what he was playing at, because there had to be an angle. He was brutally honest, but rarely deliberately cruel—and never towards Kate. However, she had never breached the unwritten rules of their relationship before...

It was almost as if he wanted her to be furious with him, to rant and rave like a jealous fishwife and insist on being the only woman in his life. Ah, yes...that would give him the perfect excuse to push her away, to end their affair before it threatened to become anything more complicated.

It struck her that a cosy little hideaway was the perfect place to commit a discreet murder!

'Well, you could do your—experimenting—offshore,' she advised, visualising him sinking to the bottom of the bay with an anchor slung around his neck. The satisfying mental picture brought a chill smile to her pale lips.

He shoved away his cup and got restlessly to his feet. She could see that her contrived calm was having the desired effect. 'Aren't you going to finish your tea?'

He looked down at her, his heavy-lidded eyes burning with frustration, his mouth smudged with sullen temper. 'No, thanks. Melissa's probably waiting for me.'

With or without the robe? Kate nodded understandingly. 'Right. You'd better hurry home to reassure her, then. You wouldn't want her to think you were over here firing up your Bunsen burner for an alternative study.'

His eyelids flickered.

'Of course, I'm sure you've already made it clear to her that she's not unique or in any way important in your life. It's always best to be up front about these things, isn't it, Drake?'

Tension pulled the skin tight over the bones of his face. 'We agreed, right at the beginning, that we didn't want any messy emotional scenes—' he grated.

'I'm not the one making a big scene,' Kate cut him off before he said anything irrevocable. She got up and began rinsing out the mugs under the running tap, speaking to him over her cold shoulder. 'I just asked for some sugar, remember? You were the one who came haring after me bristling with ridiculous suspicions and flinging out all sorts of dramatic allegations. You should chill out, Drake, and stop making such a big deal of it. Instead of wasting all that energy worrying about what I'm doing just go back to living your own life. We'll be neighbours for a month, that's all. I'll be as quiet as a mouse...you'll hardly even know I'm around...

'And if you wouldn't mind leaving the rest of that sugar—I think I feel like pancakes for dinner!'

CHAPTER THREE

'MUMMY, look at me!'

The chain on the swing squeaked as Kate swung higher, rocking her small body on the splintery wooden seat to get more speed, stamping her shoes against the hard-packed ground on the down-swing to propel herself up into the wild blue sky.

'Look at me, Mummy!' Her white dress fluttered, her hair spraying out around her head as she rushed through the air, her excited squeals mingling with the squeak and rattle of the chain as she went higher and higher towards the impossible goal—doing a complete loop over the steel support bar. What would happen when she was upside down, she wasn't sure, she only knew that her mother would be proud of her for doing something that only the big boys dared to try.

'Mummy!' She looked for her mummy's proud face but she couldn't see her against the blur of scenery. She suddenly couldn't see any of the other children or mummies and daddies, either—she was all alone in the big, empty park and it was getting dark. There was no one cheering or clapping her brave effort, only the rusty squeak of the chain to accompany her hysterical cry as she realised that she was going too fast and there was no one there to catch her if she fell, or to stop her from flying off into space and being lost for ever. 'Mummy? *Mummy!*'

Kate jerked into wakefulness, her eyes flying open, her hands clutching for the dissolving chains and finding only wrinkled sheets. Morning sunlight filtered in around the dark curtains, painting bright stripes on the faded wallpaper. The breath rattled in her chest and the haunting squeak from the disturbing dream still echoed in her thick head.

She groaned. She didn't need a psychiatrist to interpret the meaning of *that* little vignette. Her accidental conception hadn't stopped her mother from ruthlessly applying herself to her studies and graduating from university with first class honours. Money had been very tight and, except for during term-time lectures, there had been none to spare for day-care. Childish demands for attention had often been greeted with impatient dismissal or an instruction to play extra quietly. Before she'd even known what exams were Kate had learned to dread their approach. Her earliest memory was of lying under the bed in their cramped, one-roomed apartment whispering stories to herself because Mummy had been studying for something more important than silly games.

Kate rolled her head on the pillow, trying to rid herself of that haunting squeak. Except it wasn't coming from inside her head, she realised, but rising up from the skirting-board where it ran along behind the bed. And it wasn't a hard, metallic kind of squeak, either; there was a certain warm *furriness* about it that suggested some form of rodent. She grimaced at the thought of mice scampering around the house while she slept. She listened for the tell-tale scuffling of tiny feet in the woodwork, but the squeaking was too loud. Far too loud. More like...

Rats!

Kate shot bolt upright in the bed, too late remembering that she should have moved with more care. She grabbed at the package of crackers she had left open on the bedside table and stuffed one into her mouth, but even as she chewed she knew what was coming and, showering a trail of crumbs, she fled into the bathroom.

For the second time in just over twelve hours she inspected the hazed porcelain of the toilet bowl at close quarters.

Kate was never sick. Never. Until a month ago her biological mechanisms had been in perfect sync with her busy lifestyle. Then she had bought that wretched little box in the chemist and her world had gone haywire.

'Damn you, Drake Daniels,' she moaned, in between retches that produced little but burning bile. 'This is all your fault!'

If only it were, she might be able to work up a decent case for hating him. But the truth was that Drake had always been absolutely scrupulous about using birth control. Even though Kate had started on the pill the day after their first time together, he had insisted on using a condom every time they made love. 'No contraception is one hundred per cent perfect,' he had told her bluntly, 'so if we use two methods with optimum effectiveness we lessen the chances of a malfunction.'

Well, Kate was certainly malfunctioning now!

She cleaned up and staggered back to bed.

At least she seemed to have frightened away the mystery squeaker, she thought, lying flat on her back and nibbling cautiously at another cracker, glad to be able to push aside at least one of the problems in her life.

She put a hand on her flat stomach. Here was a problem that wasn't going to go away any time soon. In fact it was growing bigger by the day, although it was still only very tiny—less than half the length of her little finger, according to the books she had read.

How incredible, to have something so physically minuscule yet so all-encompassingly large invading her life! The shock, the dismay, and the sheer, blind panic that had first assailed her when she had stared at the plus sign on the home pregnancy test strip had long since changed to awe.

It was an awe that she could be fairly certain that Drake wouldn't share. He didn't want children. Not ever. He didn't want any physical ties that would compromise his emotional independence. He needed to be alone to write, he had told Kate when they had first met, and nothing and no one took precedence over his writing. As a researcher at Enright Media,

Kate was ideally placed to understand the demands of his particular genius. Caught up in the thrill and excitement of being desired by such a fascinating and complex man, she had walked into the affair with her eyes wide open. She had accepted that Drake was not the marrying kind. As their affair had matured into an ongoing relationship she had known that if she objected to his periodic disappearances or acted concerned by his restless comings and goings she would have been rapidly shunted out of his life. So even as she had fallen ever deeper in love with him she had persuaded herself that she was content with the status quo. She was a realist—a practical, self-sufficient, modern woman. She had a fabulous lover, a demanding job with a good salary, and plenty of friends to pal around with when Drake was out of town. No ties suited her just fine. And up until now she had been far too absorbed in her career to even think about having babies…

Dry flakes of cracker stuck in her throat, forming a lump that refused to budge.

Drake had been in Auckland for three whole months prior to taking off to work on his new book— the longest continuous period they had spent together. Kate had dared to hope it indicated that they were reaching a new level of trust. At first she had put down her persistent feeling of nausea after he had left to depression, then to the remnants of a late bout of winter flu combined with a rush-job involving a biographer who needed help reconstructing hand-copied notes that a drunken ex-wife had tried to flush down the toilet. But her weight gain and the tenderness in her breasts were less easy to dismiss and when she'd counted back and realised that she was ten days overdue she had rushed out and bought a test-kit from the pharmacy. Her hands had been shaking so hard when she'd used the dipstick that it had taken a while to confirm the earth-shattering truth.

She was pregnant with Drake Daniels' baby!

She had stopped taking the pill immediately, but it had taken days for the reality of her situation to sink in, and when it had she had set about tackling it with her usual pragmatism. She'd worked out that she was unlikely to be more than a few weeks pregnant. Unlike her mother, who had married a fellow university student for the sole purpose of exploiting a loophole in the student allowance scheme, Kate had discovered her accidental pregnancy early enough to give her a full range of options.

She had made herself carefully consider them all, before choosing the only one that was ever going to be acceptable to her woman's heart.

She was *not* going to have an unwanted child.

This baby was already an indivisible part of her, a symbol of her love, a triumph of hope over pessimism. Her baby had conquered almost impossible odds to be conceived; it was now up to Kate to take over the fight for the best of all possible futures.

She didn't fool herself that Drake was good father material. But he *was* going to be a father, and she had to decide whether she wanted him in her baby's life. She had suffered too much from her own parents' selfishness to want to burden another child with the pain of constant emotional rejection. Until she had made that decision she vowed to tell no one of her condition, her confidence in her ability to be a good mother still too fragile to risk exposing it to the opinions of the wider world.

So she had tracked Drake down to his lair in a desperate attempt to try to establish a better understanding between them before her secret was exposed by her burgeoning body. She had to decide when and how to tell him about the pregnancy, and discover just how much involvement he might want—and she could bear—after the baby was born.

The morning was cool but with the promise of later heat, so Kate pulled on a gauzy skirt and loose tee shirt and caught her hair up into a jaunty pony-tail. She ate a dry piece of toast with a smear of honey and, when she was confident it was going to stay down, indulged the sharp onset of hunger by slicing up a banana and a kiwi fruit into a bowl and spooning over a generous dollop of low-fat vanilla yoghurt. Carrying the bowl in one hand and a cup of green tea in the other, she wandered out to the verandah and perched on the step to eat a leisurely breakfast. The water out in the bay was like shimmering glass, the only movement the gentle ripple of wavelets over-turning at the edge of the beach and the swoop and splash of a pied shag arrowing into the water and re-emerging with a squirming fish, which it swallowed with a few flicks of its long neck before flapping off to dry its wings on a rocky outcropping. Licking the last of the yoghurt off her spoon, Kate left the bowl on the step and strolled down to the beach with her green tea. The sand was cool under her bare feet and the crystal-clear water shockingly cold as she paddled out to ankle depth.

As she turned to wade back to shore she saw a lone male figure standing on the upper deck of the house next door. He was shirtless, his dark mahogany chest smooth and glossy in the sunlight, his tapering torso cut off at the waist by the solid balcony wall, making her wonder if he was fully nude. Drake didn't own any pyjamas and was totally unselfconscious about his body when he wasn't intent on using it for pleasure. The first night they had made love she had been shocked by his lack of inhibitions, and very aware of her own hesitancy in flaunting her nakedness. She had tried to disguise her embarrassment, but to her amazement he had been powerfully aroused by her reticence.

If she hadn't had a few more drinks than usual at the book launch, she probably wouldn't have had the courage to accept Drake's invitation back to his hotel room.

She felt an electrical tingle in her veins at the memory of the weight of his hand on the small of her back as he had unlocked the door to his room. Once inside she had drifted out of his reach, surveying the huge, split-level suite with assumed amusement that had hid a glittering rush of nervous excitement.

'Rather over-the-top for one person, isn't it?' she commented, eyeing the polished black marble pillars, jewelled rugs and luxurious furnishings.

He grinned, tossing his black leather jacket over the back of an antique chair and snagging her evening purse to drop it on the seat. 'Marcus works a great contra-deal for me with the international owner, who's a big a fan of my books.'

'You mention his hotels in your books in exchange for free rooms?' asked Kate dubiously.

'Bite your tongue, sweetheart; I don't play the sap for no one,' he sneered, in a passable Bogie imitation. Given his reputation for laughing criticism to scorn, she was surprised when he added: 'Contrary to what the intellectuals say, I do have some artistic ethics. I don't abuse my readers with subliminal advertisements buried in my text. It's an up-front arrangement—I do all my press conferences and interviews in his hotels worldwide, and I autograph first editions for him. And the rooms aren't free, I still pay something—but nothing like the rack-rates, so why not enjoy the best on offer? I happen to like the extravagant contrast to the austerity of my other life—my writing life,' he added when she tilted her head quizzically. 'The months when I shrink my world to the size of a keyboard and screen and live like an ascetic. That's why I need to let off steam every time I emerge from my monastic cell—to reduce the risk of a creative meltdown.'

'Writers have a much higher than average occurrence of mood disorders, especially depression,' Kate murmured, wondering whether she was being naïve to hope she was more than just a convenient escape valve. Not that it mattered. In the space of a few hours the intense euphoria she felt when they had briefly shaken hands during their introduction had developed into a relentless craving; a single, stolen kiss in an empty corner of the crowed room merely confirming her addiction.

'Do we really?' he drawled.

She smiled sheepishly. 'Sorry—occupational hazard for a researcher.'

'You must have a great deal of interesting information squirreled away in odd corners of your brain, waiting to spring out of your subconscious,' he said, his brown eyes narrowing in a fleeting moment of abstraction that made her feel totally invisible.

'Yes, but it's what you do with it that matters,' she said with a wry shrug. 'A lot of it is very esoteric or trivial. Don't confuse memory with intelligence.'

His attention snapped back with uncomfortable intensity. 'What makes you think you're not intelligent?'

She thought of her endless struggles with hated school exams, and her mother's coruscating lecture when Kate had secretly interviewed for a job instead of applying for university.

'Not unintelligent…' That was what had so infuriated her mother. She had viewed Kate's abysmal marks as a wilful act of rebellion. 'Just…um…intellectually unfocused.' This was definitely not the time to be worrying about what her mother might think! 'I suppose I tend to be a Jill of all trades and mistress of none,' she finished lightly.

His smile took on a wickedly sexy smoulder. 'Ah, an intellectual slut…my kind of woman!' he growled.

Kate's nerves skittered at the bizarre sexual imagery induced by his phrase. She didn't know whether to be insulted or flattered.

'I thought we were here to settle an argument about who played Velda in *Kiss Me Deadly,*' she said, glancing at the wide, flat screen hanging on the wall above a sleek, electronic box. 'You said we could watch it here on DVD.'

'I have a better idea,' he said, walking towards her.

'Oh?' Her tongue darted out to moisten her dry lips, heat beginning to flush through her belly and breasts at the fierce expression in his eyes. He hadn't kissed her in the taxi coming over, but he had wanted to, and his restraint had made his desire all the more exciting.

'We both know Maxine Cooper was Velda, so let's forget the movie and I'll show you the real reason I always stay in this particular penthouse...' he purred, taking her hand and beginning to lead her towards the spiral staircase in the corner of the room.

Oh, God, what height of decadence was he about to reveal? A solid-gold bed with sheets of red silk? A black marble spa pool filled with champagne?

But they kept climbing up past the sprawling main bedroom and stepped out through folded shutters into a magical scene, shaded lights around the high walls illuminating a lush green jungle of plants and a riot of heavily perfumed spring flowers.

'The roof garden...for my exclusive, and very private use...' he said softly, allowing her to walk ahead of him across the dense fan of green grass that divided into winding pathways of creeping ground-cover curving around enclosed thickets of soft ferns and spiky palms.

'It's fantastic,' she murmured, her high heels sinking into the turf as she paused by a shrub smothered in starry-white flowers and inhaling the heady night-perfume of Mexican orange blossom.

'That's what I think. Whenever I'm here in town and I start to feel like a victim of my own success, I skip out on the crowds and come up here to mellow out for a while. It's the perfect cure for mood disorders...a little piece of Eden. And now it has its very own Eve...' She heard a faint activating beep and turned to the sound of soft music rising from hidden speakers.

To her shock Drake had shed his footwear and his white silk shirt and was stripping the belt from his dove-grey trousers. At her gasp his hands stilled.

'Have you changed your mind?'

It was on the tip of her tongue to claim that he was assuming way too much. But they would both know it for a lie.

'No, but— I...should we? Out *here*?'

'Why not? It's warm, the grass is soft and the air is sweet, and we're literally closer to heaven than anywhere else in town. But if you're worried we might get buzzed by a police helicopter...' He picked up the remote control he had used to operate the sound system from the glass table beside him and pressed a button. With a low rumble a curved roof of tinted panels extended from the far end of the walled garden and eclipsed the distant stars, finally clicking home against the granite side of the building.

When Kate looked down from this fascinating piece of engineering Drake was stepping out of the last of his clothes, exposing himself without false modesty to her wide-eyed gaze, his large hands, curled into loose fists, hanging quietly at his sides, the angle of the lights painting intriguing shadows in the hollows of his sculpted perfection.

'I want to make love to you now,' he told her with arrogant confidence.

'So I see,' she said shakily, trying to look and sound blasé rather than panic-stricken by his impressive proportions, the thick nest of dark hair in his groin framing a magnificence that would put any one of his highly sexed heroes in the shade.

He shifted restlessly, the muscles bunching in his thighs. 'Aren't you going to reciprocate?' he murmured, nodding at the classic, sleeveless 'little black dress' that she had dressed up for the evening function with cropped blue jacket of oriental design.

Not quite sure how to begin, Kate automatically did what she would normally do at home when preparing for bed, and reached up to pull the pins out of her smooth chignon and let her hair flow like warm caramel through her fingers, shaking her head to fan out the remaining kinks. Then she hesitated, biting her lip as she wondered where she was going to put the pins.

'That's it?' he rasped tightly. 'That's all you're going to do? You're not even going to take off your shoes?'

She thought he was angry, impatient with her nervousness. 'Uh, no, I—' The pins fell from her fingers, spearing silently into the grass around her feet as she realised he wasn't angry at all...far from it! If it was possible, he appeared to be even more aroused than before, prowling towards her stiff-legged, his eyes gleaming black in the muted light, the tension in his voice purely sexual.

'You playing the tease, Katherine?'

'No, of course not!' she denied breathlessly, hypnotised by the fluid play of light and shadow across the shifting planes of his hard body as he continued his hunting prowl across the grass, masculinity personified. As she watched he unfurled a fist, and showed her a palm full of little foil packets. So many? She felt a thrill of exquisite apprehension tingle through her bones, her confidence overpowered by his physiological perfection, her own physical flaws suddenly magnifying themselves in her mind. She instinctively wrapped her jacket across her breasts as he came to a halt, his body crowding hers.

'No? The blushing virgin, then?' he said, tossing the handful of foil to join her scattered hairpins.

She blushed.

'Hardly!'

'You've been around, then?' he said slyly, plucking at the lower edge of the jacket where it poked out below her folded arms.

She tilted her nose up at his deliberate crudity. 'No, I have not "been around",' she sniffed. 'But I have occasionally been in the vicinity,' she admitted with a prim dignity that made his teeth flash white in the darkness.

'Not *my* vicinity, sweetheart, or you wouldn't be acting so cool.'

Cool? She was practically burning up!

'It's just—' She felt something warm—something hard yet invitingly soft—kiss her belly button through her skirt, but she didn't dare look down for fear of losing what little remained of her self-control.

'Just what?' he goaded. 'Just that you're getting cold feet?'

Damn it, if he backed off now she would kill him! She forced her arms to loosen. 'No!'

'No,' he echoed with gritty satisfaction. 'So it must be that you're just too prim and proper to get naked on a first date,' he taunted cockily, his heavy hands settling on her bony hips, his long thumbs massaging the slippery fabric over the smooth skin of her lower belly. 'You've already decided on letting your hair down with me...' he leaned forward to brush his face through the shiny curtain veiling the side of her neck, and inhale the subtle scent of her shampoo mingled with the faintest trace of musky feminine arousal '...mmmm...but the lady obviously wants to be warmed up a little before the main action. You don't want to take them off, ergo you want me to make love to you with your clothes on...'

Her silver eyes widened. 'You can do that?' she blurted foolishly.

Her scepticism made him purr like a sexy tiger.

'Oh, baby, I can do anything you want...'

His big hands slid caressingly down her flanks and slipped under the knee-length hem of her dress, raking up the skirt with his forearms as his hands stroked slowly back up her legs to span her hips.

'Hmm, stockings…that makes things easy…' he discovered on the way up. 'Oh, no…*stay-ups*,' he corrected himself as his fingers found the delicate band that encircled the silky-fine skin of her upper thighs. 'Even easier…'

He sighed when he found the narrow strip of lace drawn tight over her hip-bones. 'Rippable?' he murmured wistfully, winding one stretchy ribbon around a questing finger, drawing the whisper of satin passing between her legs ravishingly tight against her moistened core.

She squeaked and he laughed, pulling her flush against his scalding nakedness, letting her feel the urgent insistence of his arousal, the rough thicket in his groin catching against her smooth panties. He widened his stance, cupping her bottom as she trembled in a fever of eagerness. 'Never mind, we'll work around them,' he promised in a throaty growl, gathering her tight between his hair-roughened thighs, tipping her off balance as he lifted one of her legs and draped it around his hip. 'I love a challenge…'

He ducked his head and nuzzled aside the jacket to find the outline of her bra against the smooth fabric of the dress, navigating his skilful way to the press of her nipples.

Kate tilted her head back, closing her eyes as she felt the rake of his teeth through the cloth and the simultaneous hot slide of his hardness rocking against her creamy centre, unable to believe this was really happening… She was allowing herself to be ravished by a naked stranger on a rooftop—and she was loving every wicked moment of it!

In a night of glorious firsts she learned that Drake Daniels was very much a man of his word. He delivered on his sensual promise, making love the same way he wrote his books—with fierce concentration and meticulous attention to detail, and a dedication to delivering a climax worthy of his wildly thrilling build-up!

After they had made love several times under the stirring palms they moved inside to the palatial bedroom, and later down to the main part of the suite where they fuelled their sensual excesses from the lavishly stocked bar fridge, and resumed their sexy badinage through a much-interrupted viewing of *Kiss Me Deadly*.

Neither of them slept and in the morning Kate was staggering slightly as she fumbled into her crumpled clothing, aware that having to go home to change was going to make her horribly late for work.

Sitting in the middle of the bed, his lower body swathed in a white sheet, looking very much like a dissipated Greek god, Drake followed her preparations to flee with hooded eyes. His watchful silence made her even more self-conscious.

'I'm never late,' she muttered, stuffing her laddered stockings into her purse and sliding her feet into her grass-flecked heels, uncertain of how to stage-manage a graceful exit.

'This was *not* a good idea…' She meant lingering

over-long in his bed, but to her dismay Drake took up her theme.

'Neither of us was thinking—it was nothing to do with choice, it was pure sexual chemistry,' he said abruptly, the dark growth of beard giving his face a saturnine look. He braced himself on one arm, the folds of the sheet pooling in his lap. 'Don't worry, it's like fireworks—dazzling but essentially ephemeral. If we let it alone it'll fizzle out.' The melting brown eyes hardened with cynical resolve. 'But you're right—this can't happen again. It would be a mistake to try and turn it into something that it's not. As it happens, I'm off to LA the day after tomorrow, for an extended book tour across the States...'

Kate disguised her sudden pallor by turning to the full-length wardrobe mirror and raising her arms to fold her hair into a neat self-knot at the nape of her neck in the absence of most of her pins.

He was telling her not to make any plans that included him. They had no future together.

Out of the corner of her eye she could see Drake's partial reflection past her bent elbows. He was rubbing the centre of his chest with the heel of his hand, as if massaging an ache. He wasn't half as relaxed as he looked, she decided, noting the tension in the set of his head and the fist at the end of his braced arm. Perhaps he expected her to throw a tantrum at his frank rejection of any emotional connection between them, or, worse, to pout and insist on a long-drawn-out discussion of their feelings.

She wasn't going to give him the satisfaction of

knowing that she *had* believed they had something special.

Lesson number two in dealing with the unpredictable Drake Daniels:

Never give him what he expects.

She brightened her expression and turned around. 'Right. A mistake. Well…I'll be off, then. See you around. No, don't bother to get up and see me out.' She waved a casually dismissive hand as he made a sharp movement under the sheets. 'I'm quite happy to make my own way. I've been doing it for some years now,' she pointed out with only the barest hint of sarcasm.

'Oh, and if you find yourself in need of another chemistry lesson…feel free to give me a whistle.'

Before he could recognise that vague allusion she had reached the spiral staircase, where she paused to look provocatively back over her shoulder, and hit him square between the eyes with a husky rendition of classic exit-line.

'"You know how to whistle, don't you," Drake?'

It was almost worth the pain of leaving to see his expression, an instant, ungovernable blaze of lust mingled with baffled admiration.

Almost…

CHAPTER FOUR

A MONTH later Kate had answered her cell phone in the early evening to a distinctive, deep velvet voice that had made her heart jump.

'To Have and Have Not.'

'Ernest Hemingway,' she murmured automatically, tamping down a dangerous flare of hope.

'I'm flattered, but actually it's Drake Daniels,' he said with typically brazen cheek. Did he really think that picking up exactly where they'd left off was going to make her forget the intervening weeks?

'I know who it is,' she said coolly, her heart still fluttering in her throat. Tucking her personal card in the pocket of his black jacket as she left his hotel room had been a wild gamble she'd thought that she'd lost. Even if he hadn't found it before he'd jetted off to America, he knew where she worked and she was in the phone book

Her eyes darted around the almost empty office and she slumped lower in her seat so her head slipped below the level of her flat-screen display, giving her the illusion of privacy. She had endured a lot of ribbing from colleagues who had seen her leave the party with Drake, especially after her unprecedented late arrival at work the next morning. Luckily, none of them had really believed the fastidious Katherine Crawford capable of getting down-and-dirty on a first date with a serial womaniser, and their interest had rapidly faded on hearing that Drake had left the country.

'I thought you might have forgotten me.'

Fat chance of that, with the reception area plastered with blow-ups of his latest book-jacket! Every morning when she came to work she was greeted at the door by his sexy grin and mocking brown eyes.

'I have an excellent memory for trivia,' she reminded him.

'Ouch!' he said, with the vocal equivalent of a rueful shrug. 'I suppose I should be grateful that it's your passion, then, as well as your profession.'

She found her toes curling inside her delicate pumps. How magnificently he turned his guilt to flattery. 'Most researchers have university degrees— I got lucky when I did a work experience with Enright's just as they were setting up their own PR department,' she found herself telling him. 'Marcus noticed how much I enjoyed reading and how good I was at ferreting out interesting facts for people, and offered me on-the-job training if I stayed. It turned out to be a perfect fit. I like being able to come up with things that surprise and intrigue people.'

'So, I guess you already know that although Hemingway and Faulkner were included in the writing credits for the movie, a lot of the dialogue in *To Have And Have Not* was actually improvised on set.'

'Which goes to show that even great authors don't always get it right,' she shot back, feeling exhilarated and alive again for the first time in a month, but unwilling to let him entirely off the hook. She cupped a hand over her phone as the last of her co-workers in the open-plan office switched off his computer and began loading his briefcase. 'Why are you calling, Drake?'

There was a brief pause during which she visualised him smiling with that irresistible twist of self-derisive arrogance.

'I've forgotten how to whistle,' he drawled. 'I thought you might bring your lips over to remind me.'

Hope burned incandescent, even as she cautioned herself to wariness. Drake was never going to fit into the mould of a conventional lover.

'To New York?' Enright Media subscribed to a multimedia clippings service for all its clients. In spite of her pretence of indifference in front of her colleagues, it had been impossible to resist snooping through the press reports of his trip. He had been last spotted at a famous nightclub in the Big Apple, with the usual phalanx of eager acolytes.

'I'm back in Auckland…at the penthouse.'

She closed her eyes at the powerful memories invoked by his words. 'And obviously at a loose end,' she said wryly.

'I have plenty to do. I'd just rather do it with you,' he said with seductive simplicity. 'There's a party

I've been invited to tonight—I thought you might like to go.'

Yes! He wasn't just calling her for a quick sexual fix!

'And afterwards we could come back here…'

Her nipples hardened against her blouse. 'Let me guess—you have a DVD of *To Have And Have Not* for us to watch,' she murmured, giving a weak waggle of her fingers to her colleague as he headed out with a casual reminder of the usual after-work session at a trendy local watering hole.

'Well…that, too, of course…' he said, and she could hear the sexy amusement in his voice. 'Although, tradionalist that I am, I was going to suggest *Casablanca*.'

He would. Romantic but ending in a bittersweet parting—yes, that would appeal more to Drake's cynical nature than the hopefully upbeat ending for the wise-cracking hero and heroine of *To Have And Have Not*.

'As long as you understand I can't stay the night—I have to start work early tomorrow,' she warned him, drawing her definitive line in the sand. She was never going to risk reliving the painful awkwardness of that first morning-after. She inhaled a deep breath and took the plunge. 'After all, we don't want to make this into something it's not…'

There was an edgy silence. 'You're a devil for matching the quotation to the moment, aren't you?' he said. 'Agreed.' His voice deepened to that spine-tingling drawl that made her feel weak as water. 'I'll just have to make sure that we cram everything in before the witching hour…'

And cram they did. For two years their affair had been a case of feast and famine, with neither side willing to admit to any vulnerability. Had they both been so busy protecting themselves that they had wrecked any chance of building a real relationship?

Kate shaded her forehead with the flat of her hand as she stared up at the lone figure on the balcony. That wary stillness was so characteristic of Drake, the watchful vigilance of a man who had to constantly guard himself against the world. He never spoke about his childhood except in the vaguest of terms, but there had to be something there that had warped his ability to trust...particularly women. He sloughed off praise and criticism with equal ease, using his cynical brand of humour to appear open and gregarious, while in fact revealing little about himself that wasn't already in the public arena.

How long had they been standing there staring at each other, separated by more than just the physical space between them—Drake perched on his high, lonely pedestal, Kate grounded in the ordinary, everyday world he had left behind?

On impulse Kate lifted her hand and waved. For a moment she thought she saw his hand twitch on the shiny aluminium rail as if he was going to wave back, but then she saw Melissa move out from the shade of the house onto the sunlit balcony, and put her hand on his bare arm. He turned to accept the cup she handed him, sliding a brown arm across the back of her dazzling white top as they both retreated inside the house.

At least they weren't having breakfast in bed! thought Kate savagely, letting her hand drop to her somersaulting belly.

'It's OK, little one, I won't let that wicked witch keep your stupid daddy walled up in his ivory tower,' she soothed.

Her green tea had gone cold, and she was tipping it onto the sand when she noticed what was happening to her abandoned breakfast dish.

'Hey!'

She chased up the bank and snatched at the bowl just as it tipped off the side of the step and shattered on a stone that edged the straggly garden.

'Now look what you've done!' she told the big, lolloping dog that peered at her with mournful eyes through its long, matted fringe of mottled grey. It was quite the ugliest animal she had ever seen, looking like a lanky cross between a foolish Afghan and giant poodle on a bad-hair day, with a ridiculous tail that curved lopsidedly over its back in a soggy flag of defiance. It smelled strongly of seaweed and wet wool. 'Give me that!' she said, tugging the spoon out of its gummy mouth, pulling a face at the skein of drool that came along with it.

'Yuk!'

She could have sworn the dog grinned at her before starting to slaver at the pieces of china, rattling them against the stone.

'Don't do that, you'll cut your tongue,' she scolded, pushing at the sandy grey coat. The dog staggered aside and she was horrified to see that it only had three legs, the right rear one ending in a woolly stump at its bony hip.

'Oh, you poor thing,' she said, scooping up the broken bowl and scratching the dog between its floppy ears. It responded with an ecstatic squirming and cheerful caper that showed her it had well adapted to its handicap.

For all its size it was pathetically scrawny under the shaggy fur and she wondered if it was a stray, until she saw a glimpse of black collar buried in the shaggy ruff around its neck.

'Come here and let's see who you are,' she said, but when she tried to slide her fingers under the black webbing the dog pranced away, returning to duck and snuffle at her sandy toes, skittering away again as she squealed with ticklish laughter at the rough swipe of its tongue.

She put her hands on her hips and tried a stern, 'Heel,' but the hairy head merely cocked in momentary puzzlement before it loped over to give a doggy salute to a stunted shrub at the corner of the house, a performance greatly facilitated by not having to cock a leg. Then, with a loud 'wuff' that made her jump, it lunged at the ventilating grate in the base of the house, its claws rattling against the concrete blocks, and Kate remembered the rats.

'I don't suppose you're available for a job as a hired assassin?' she murmured above the excited whines, knowing that her tender heart would never want even a rat to die anything but a humane death.

But her three-legged visitor had already revealed

a sad lack of interest in gainful employment, giving one final bark as it dashed off to investigate a screech of scavenging seagulls fighting over stolen booty further along the beach.

After wrapping up the fragments of china in newspaper and making a note of the breakage for the rental agent, Kate did the rest of her unpacking before deciding the sun was high enough in the sky to be suitable for basking.

She changed into her new bikini, quite modest in terms of coverage but in a vibrant, eye-catching purple piped with lime-green that the shop-assistant had assured her would make heads turn. One in particular, she hoped. Since there was a slight breeze she draped herself in the matching see-through, lime-green sun wrap that had cost even more than the exorbitant bikini.

Dragging the light, powdered-aluminium sun-lounger from the 'games cupboard' in the garage out onto the back lawn, Kate unfolded it and positioned it carefully to take advantage of the sun's rays, while making sure it was angled in full view of next door's wrap-around windows. She had originally intended to go down onto the beach, but decided that she would be more visible on the elevated flat of the section.

Stashing a drink bottle where it would be in the shade of her body, along with her sunscreen and a few emergency crackers wrapped in a paper towel, Kate spread a thick beach towel over the woven plastic bed of the lounger and adjusted the back to a comfortable angle. Then she settled down, sliding her sunglasses onto her nose and plopping her purple straw hat on her head. Hefting the glossy library book she had brought with her, she propped it open across her hips.

She would have liked to have read one of the instructional baby books or pregnancy manuals she had hidden away in the bottom of her suitcase, but that would have been a rather obvious give-away, even to an insensitive jackass who was too busy breaking hearts to recognise a good woman when he had her cradled in the palm of his hand...

Kate leafed to page one.

'Simon Macmillan traded in blood and diamonds.'

She had read Drake Daniels' first novel more than once before, but then she had been reading for pleasure—and pride. Now she was reading for research. All authors put something of their real selves into their books. Somewhere in these pages were traces of the man she was trying to understand. Perhaps the skilled researcher in her would be able to sort out some sober facts from the thrilling fiction.

If not, well...she knew it would be a cracking good read, and Mac would turn out to be an undercover good guy who destroyed a dirty deal in conflict diamonds while losing his double-crossing rebel girlfriend to treachery and torture.

Psychological subtext: women are not safe to trust.

At first Kate twitched and shifted and was uncomfortably conscious of her exposed position, but gradually she became engrossed in the familiar story and forgot about ulterior motives, or that she was not supposed to be reading for sheer kicks.

Roused from her trance when her legs began to tingle with warmth, she got up and lowered the back of the lounger so that she could lie down on her stomach, placing the book flat in front on the grass and propping her chin in her hands, wriggling her hips to flatten out the slight sag in the plastic that had been hollowed out by her bottom. Occasionally a midge would perform a crazy loop-the-loop across her field of vision or an annoying fly trickle across the back of her leg, but eventually the drugging combination of sun and sea and weeks of nervous tension took their toll, and before Mac had even kissed his deadly African princess for the first time Kate had drifted off to a light doze, her nose buried in the crook of her elbow.

She was disturbed by a chill shadow across her upper body and surreptiously wiped the drool that had gathered at the corner of her sleep-slackened mouth on her arm before she lifted her head to smile at her visitor. Shades of that ramshackle dog!

All her cleverly rehearsed phrases zipped out of her head, her smile lingering as a polite rictus when she saw that the figure looming over her was not the tarnished hero of her life but his deadly Titian princess, dressed neck-to-toe in white. Although the hair was more carroty than artistic auburn, decided Kate in an inward yowl, and the lady was definitely pushing thirty, at the very least. That alabaster brow was positively botoxical, and those luscious lips—that *had* to be collagen!

'Hi,' Kate said wittily, pushing the comforting shield of her sunglasses up her nose, while simultaneously trying to untwist the wrap that had got trapped under her side as she tried to gracefully roll over on the uncooperative sun-lounger. The aluminium frame made an ominous creaking sound as her elbow slipped through a gap in the webbing, but she finally managed to wrestle herself free and sit up in reasonable dignity.

'We haven't met, have we? I'm Katherine Crawford.'

She held out her hand. Politeness, she had learned from her lethally charming mother, could be very empowering.

'Melissa Jayson,' came the clipped reply and some minuscule part of Kate relaxed. *Not* Melissa Daniels, then. She crossed one nightmare scenario off her list.

The jade-green eyes that went with the brilliant hair glittered like glass as the politely proffered hand was rudely ignored.

'I don't know what you think you're doing here, but why don't you just get out and leave him alone?'

'I *beg* your pardon?' Kate said, sitting bolt upright, Lady Bracknell in a bathing suit.

'He doesn't *want* you following him. He comes to Oyster Beach to get *away* from the smothering attention of people like you. You can't possibly understand his needs. Give him some space, why don't you?'

'Let me guess, you and Drake are graduates from the same school of etiquette?' said Kate drily, when she had got over the sting of the lightning attack.

Under the silk top the over-inflated bosom heaved, revealing a gap between the scalloped hem and the low-rise white jeans, and a strip of winter-pale skin sporting the sparkle of an impressive navel ring. Diamonds, no less…probably from Sierra Leone, thought Kate darkly.

Thinking of navels made her think of her baby and she pleated the folds of her wrap over her tummy. By her calculations she was barely two months along, and the books said it would be another two before her baby bulge began to show, but even now she felt a responsibility to shield her son or daughter from negative experiences in the womb.

'Drake and I have known each other since before *you* were around,' the other woman flung at her. She smiled, but only the muscles around her mouth moved. 'He's told me all about you, but you have no idea what he and I are to each other, do you?'

Kate's hormones staged a dangerous mood swing. On the other hand, perhaps it would be good to communicate some fighting spirit from Mama!

'What are you, his mistress or his muse?' she dared to ask bluntly. 'Because I know you can't be both—Drake doesn't trust women enough to allow any of them dominance in more than one compartment of his life.'

'You don't know him as well as you think you do,' came the contemptuous reply. 'You may think you're special but you're really no different from any of his other groupies. You like sharing the limelight with a famous author and helping him spend his money, but you have no idea what it takes for him to create his works. Why don't you stop distracting him and let him get on with his writing—?'

'While you ply him with cups of coffee and mop the creative sweat from his brow?' said Kate, watching the green eyes flicker and the collagen lips flatten. '*Am* I distracting him?' she added innocently. 'I've only been here one day. If *I'm* a distraction, why aren't you?'

She regretted the rhetorical tag when it was rewarded by a nasty little smile. Melissa looked down, manicured red fingernails flicking an invisible speck off the pristine white jeans. 'Let's just say that Drake has a particular need that only I can fulfil for him. And we keep each other *extremely* well satisfied between the sheets...'

Kate's hand, tucked in her lap, balled into a fist. *This one's for you, kid!*

'Let's not say that. Let's try and be discreet and respectful of each other's feelings, and not start an undignified cat-fight in public.' Her quiet voice stepped up a decibel. She was used to being a mediator in arguments, not an instigator. Confrontation was not her style, but she had witnessed from the cradle how it worked. 'Otherwise I might be tempted to say you're a grade-A, gold-plated bitch who thinks she has the right to run roughshod over other people to get what she wants. But this isn't about you or what you want. Your shame-and-blame tactics aren't going to make me run away with my tail between my legs. I wonder if

Drake knows you've snuck over to try and bully me out of his life?'

The redhead stiffened, her elbows tucking into her sides, her jaw clenching as she half turned away, her white sandals acquiring a freckle of dust from the dry grass. 'I suppose you're going to run crying to him telling tales!'

Kate blinked, suspicion curdling in her sour stomach at the subtle body language.

'*Does* he know?' she asked sharply.

'He has been a victim of a stalker before, you know. She wrote him hundreds of letters—a pathetic woman who thought five minutes of conversation and his personal autograph to her in the flyleaf of a book meant they were soul mates.'

She *hadn't* known, but the evasive reply had the red flags snapping briskly. 'How tragic. I've never even sent Drake a postcard, but if I get an overwhelming urge to buy stamps in bulk I'll be sure and check myself into a facility. Now, if you wouldn't mind moving out of my light, I'm trying to get a suntan.'

'You—'

'Melissa?'

The older woman spun around and saw Drake stepping around the end of the hedge. She immediately walked jerkily back the way she'd come, the two of them exchanging a terse word as they passed each other on the grass without stopping.

Kate took a long pull from her drink bottle and stood up as he came to a halt at the end of the sun lounger. He wore the same disreputable blue jeans

that he had worn the day before, with battered
workman's boots and a checked shirt with the sleeves
rolled up. The decadent, city-dwelling Drake Daniels
who wore expensive designer-casual with careless
flair was nowhere in sight. Until you looked into his
cynical eyes—then the rumpled, down-home, easy-
going country-boy was revealed to be the sham. Or
perhaps the double life he lived had actually split him
off into two distinct personalities. In which case,
both of them were in the doghouse with Kate!

She took off her sunglasses to blister him with her
naked scorn. 'Next time do your own dirty work.'

'I beg your pardon?' His Lady Bracknell wasn't
a patch on hers, she thought.

'Either you sent her over, or you primed her to go
off in my direction,' she accused.

He tipped his head down, scowling. 'What did
she tell you?'

She gave him a brittle smile. 'That you were fantastic in bed, but since I knew that already the conversation sort of stalled out.'

A trace of discomfort shifted in the dark eyes.
'Kate—'

She didn't want his pity, or his remorse. 'Oh, don't
ruin the callous, two-timing image she sketched out
so vividly. Just be grateful that I know you don't
really believe I'm a bunny-boiling psychotic, or you
wouldn't have let your trash-talking girlfriend come
within a mile of me. My own father is mooching his
life away on a dot in the Pacific because he couldn't
handle the responsibility of a relationship with me.

You needn't worry that I'm the type to slit my wrists just because a man I respected turns out to be a self-absorbed idiot and coward to boot—'

His face paled, eyes burning in their sockets. 'Don't even say it!' he said harshly, grabbing her arm and jerking her into silence. 'Look, if Melissa went too far, I'm sorry—she thought she was helping…'

'Helping herself to you,' she joked warily, easing her arm out of his painful grip as he seemed to go into physical lockdown.

He looked sick as he watched her massage the blood back into the pale streaks his strong fingers had left on her forearm. She had hormones to blame for her disruptive urges; what made his behaviour so strangely contradictory? For a moment she had had a brief awareness of his potential emotional depths, and realised for the first time that perhaps this journey was going to be more painful for him than it was for her.

In the midst of her own turmoil she felt an irresistible urge to make him smile, to banish that disquieting bleakness from his eyes.

'Gee, and to think Oyster Beach came across as such a pleasant little backwater when I was planning this holiday,' she mused. 'Who knew it would be such a hotbed of passion and intrigue? Inspiration must bite you at every turn—lucky you have your best writing-boots on.'

His mouth twitched, his eyes falling automatically to his feet, which unfortunately brought the book she had been reading into his purview. Face up on the grass, the cover blared its author's first mega-seller in its third reprint. With seven books published in the last six years, in a multitude of languages, each successive blockbuster had guaranteed a surge in new sales for his backlist.

His mouth relaxed into a knowing grin. 'Been reduced to finding your thrills vicariously these days, have you, Kate?' He bent to pick it up, and frowned when he turned it to read the classification code on the spine. 'You got this from a *library?*'

'Don't say it as if it's a dirty word, libraries are wonderful. They're one of the foundations of civilisation—'

'I thought you said you *had* all my books,' he interrupted her, staring broodingly at his younger image on the back cover. 'You work for the publisher, for God's sake. Bloody hell, you could have asked me if you wanted a copy! What happened to the one you had?'

He looked so annoyed that she wasn't going to tell him that her own Drake Danielses were far too precious to her to risk taking to the beach. Better to lose or damage a library book than one of her own first editions, all of which had his slashing signature on the title page, thanks to Marcus' practice of asking every one of his authors for a dozen signed copies to distribute around the office.

'First novels often aren't worth keeping. They're too disappointing when comparing them with an author's later, more refined techniques at work,' she murmured glibly.

For a glorious moment she thought he was going to fall for it. At least the healthy colour had returned to his face, she thought as he teetered on the edge of an explosion. Then he caught himself.

'Why, Kate, you never complained about my lack of refinement before,' he said, arranging the placement of the book back in her hands so that she had two pairs of identical brown eyes drilling her with their sexy mockery. 'In fact, I thought you liked it. I certainly don't ever recall you saying you found my technical skills disappointing.'

'I know how sensitive you artists are to criticism,' she said acidly, and this time he did laugh out loud.

They both knew his professional ego was bullet-proof. He made no secret of the fact his formal schooling had been spotty and at eighteen he had been working as a labourer to save enough money to begin years of travelling. He had worked his passage from port to port around the world on short-haul cargo ships, stopping off to do unskilled labour wherever he could pick up a job, living and working in dangerous environments because they always paid the best money. Curious and observant, he had kept journals throughout his travels, using them as the basis of his first novel. After it had been snapped up for publication he had continued to write because he had stumbled on the purpose of his life. He'd discovered that he had a natural talent for tapping into the popular imagination of millions of people from all cultures and all walks of life, an instinctive gift for words that could make grown men weep and ladies brawl.

'If this is a library book, you must be expecting to be back in Auckland fairly soon?' His eyes ran up and over her, but to her chagrin he didn't seem to notice the knockout bikini, partly because she was hugging his book against her chest, but mostly because he was too busy running through his mental checklist.

'Knowing how much your mother's daughter you are when it comes to the letter of the law, I can't see you deliberately flouting the rules and running up a fine, even if it's only a library fine, so maybe you never planned on staying the whole month here after all,' he worked out, with the convoluted logic of a highly creative mind. 'Maybe you expected to be able to do whatever you came here to do fairly quickly, and be back in town in time to return the book.'

Kate could have told him she had far more pressing concerns weighing on her conscience than late library books. 'That's a bit of a stretch, isn't it, even for you? The loan is for three weeks and you can renew at least twice by phone or online—'

He brushed aside her argument, too intrigued by his paranoid fantasy. 'You don't even have a phone connection in the house, let alone wireless coverage, and the cellular signal is erratic at best. Your mind is far too tidy to leave things like that to chance…no, there's got to be something—'

'For goodness' sake, this isn't the middle of the Gobi Desert, Drake,' she cut in with exasperation, not sure whether he was serious, or simply winding her up. With Drake's sardonic sense of humour it was sometimes difficult to tell. 'I *could* just stroll next door and ask to use *your* internet connection. And don't tell me you don't have one, because you email your manuscripts and revisions.'

He folded his arms over his chest, his smooth jaw set at a stubborn angle as he moodily toyed with the suggestion. 'So you could. Maybe that's the whole idea—access to my computer. I told Marcus there was a good reason the first few chapters are late. He knows I'll deliver the goods. Is he throwing the panic switch already just because I'm not answering his emails? Did he put the squeeze on you to do him a personal favour?' He snorted. 'Threaten your job if you didn't use your leverage with me to find out what's going on with the new synopsis, and why I haven't sent the partial? Because if he did any of that, you can tell him that he's violated our confidentiality agreement and he can kiss goodbye to any more books from me.'

'What a shame, and you two have been such loyal friends through all these years, and had such a wonderfully successful run together—you've stuck with Enright Media, even though you must have been wooed by every big publisher in the business,' said Kate, her voice dripping with false compassion at his outrageous threat. 'It seems you just can't trust anyone these days, can you?' Then she clapped her hand to her cheek. 'Oh, that's right, I forgot—you never *do* trust anyone, anyway. How nice it must be to have proof that your lack of faith in your friends has been justified.'

He cooled off instantly. 'I haven't proved anything,' he growled defensively.

She gave him an oozing smile, destined to trigger

every warning instinct in his wary nature. 'Just out of interest, why *haven't* you sent him the partial?'

He momentarily froze, and then let out a shuddering breath, running his hand over his head, raking his hair into disturbed peaks. 'Hell, Katherine, rub it in, why don't you?'

'Thank you, I will.' She relished the chance to take her revenge. 'If you really believed that farrago of nonsense it's a short step to thinking that Marcus might have introduced me to you at that party two years ago as part of his long-term strategy of betrayal. I could be a mole.'

'I don't think moles go in for sunbathing, and certainly not in purple bikinis,' he murmured, showing that he was not as impervious as she had supposed. 'They're very solitary, dark-loving creatures, with powerful appetites…'

'That sounds familiar. Maybe *you're* the mole,' she suggested.

'With what mission—to betray myself?'

'Well, it would cut out the middle man.'

A flicker of amusement in his eyes indicated a mocking self-awareness—but as usual when their conversation threatened to breach his invisible walls he deflected her attention away from himself. 'At least we've narrowed down the list of possible motives for you being here. The process of elimination will eventually bring us down to the truth.'

'"You can't handle the truth!"' The angry quote from *A Few Good Men* floated into her mind and tripped off her tongue before she could stop it.

'Not been around long enough to qualify as a classic yet, Kate, but it was Jack Nicholson playing Colonel Jessep. And he was wrong, wasn't he? Because people are constantly having to adjust to newly revealed truths…it's called *living*…'

'Some people are too busy crying wolf on their friends or looking for reds-under-the-bed to fully engage in living,' she said, suddenly feeling on the brink of tears. She wasn't going to be stampeded into telling him about their baby in a burst of anger at his wilful lack of understanding. 'Or, in your case, perhaps I should say reds-*in*-the-bed!'

In a flutter of iridescent green she turned to flounce back into the house, but was halted as he grabbed a piece of handkerchief hem.

'Melissa's a freelance editor.'

Kate stilled at the revelation, but didn't turn around. After a moment, he spoke again, his voice rusty with reluctance. 'She's worked on nearly all of my books. I pay her to read the manuscripts for me, give me an overview and correct punctuation and grammar before I send them in. Why do you think my manuscripts are so polished when they land up at Enright's?'

Kate turned slowly, tethered by his fistful of green gauze. She had heard that he only ever required the occasional line-edit. 'But doesn't the editorial department usually do all that stuff?'

He hunched his shoulders. 'I don't get a say at who Marcus employs—I don't like people I don't know taking over and changing things. But I had to do something after the nightmare I went through over the editing on the first book. I have a mild form of dyslexia and never paid much attention to formal English at school so I have two strikes against me. But it is *my* story to tell—and I want to give the nit-pickers as little excuse as possible to tinker with my intentions.'

The light bulb went on inside her head. Of course. This was a Drake Daniels she knew very well. He would do everything he could to minimise the exposure of his weaknesses to others. It was all about *control*.

'But you let Melissa tinker,' she said, eaten up with a jealousy that was far more than sexual.

'We go over it together. She's good at what she does. I know she'll fix the technicalities and throw in a few criticisms and leave the final interpretation to me.'

'Does Marcus know?'

'He doesn't need to know.' He shrugged. 'He doesn't care about the process; all he cares about is that I deliver him a saleable book at the end of it.'

Kate stared at him. She shouldn't be so surprised. *Need to know*. He operated his whole life on that basis.

His fist tightened, putting tension on her wrap as he misinterpreted her long look. 'I suppose now you're wondering if she's more a ghost-writer than an editor.'

It had never even occurred to her. Knowing Drake, she would bet that Melissa had a major battle on her hands with every altered comma.

'Actually, I was wondering how long you two have been together.'

'We're not *together*,' he rejected instantly. 'I send her chunks of the book to read and she comes here to work with me on the edit, that's all. It never takes more than a few days.'

'She calls you "Darling".'

'She calls everybody "Darling".' He clenched his teeth. 'Melissa and I have never slept together.'

His statement fell starkly between them. 'But she obviously would like to,' said Kate.

'A lot of women want to sleep with me; that doesn't mean I do,' he snapped impatiently, hitting on a source of increasing agony for Kate.

'Why not? What's to hold you back?' she gouged viciously at the open wound.

'For God's sake, Kate, I'm not interested and Melissa knows it. Nor is she. That was all an act! She makes a mint off her contract with me, she wouldn't ever want to jeopardise it. Apart from anything else she's *married*.'

'That's no barrier these days.'

His head reared up at the splash of acid in her voice. 'It is for me.'

She would concede that. Too many messy complications.

'What if she got a divorce?' prodded Kate.

'I'm not going to sleep with her, Kate, not even to justify your jealousy.'

He was so smug! 'I'm not jealous!'

He flipped his wrist, winnowing the thin fabric, wafting warm air around her bare thighs and midriff. 'You look pretty green to me!'

His sly humour struck her on the raw. 'Green also happens to be associated with harmony, growth and fertility—' She stopped, stricken. He continued to hold on, his eyes alert with sharpening curiosity, and with a little gasp she rotated quickly away in a balletic twirl that shed her gauzy cocoon, leaving him holding an empty snatch of nothing as her bikini-clad figure disappeared into the house, a sharp click of the latch signalling that her tantalising flight was not an invitation to pursue!

CHAPTER FIVE

KATE was still alive in a state of angry embarrassment a few mornings later when she backed her car out of the garage to head down to the wharf and see if any of the fishing boats she had seen coming in were willing to sell some of their catch from the boat.

The anger was mostly with herself for being a wimp. After coming all this way to challenge Drake, she was now ducking and diving to avoid being seen until her chaotic hormones stopped her leaking tears at inappropriate moments, skulking around inside the house with the doors locked, taking long walks up the beach to find a hidden spot in the sand-dunes where she could do her sunbathing, and driving up into the hills to explore the nature trails.

The embarrassment followed a very uncomfortable second encounter with Melissa Jayson at a local roadside vegetable stall, where Kate had paused on one of her carefully timed walks to buy a bunch of leafy green silver beet, a brown bag of crunchy sugar-snap peas and a large head of broccoli. The stall was

a little wooden shed at the entrance to a long
driveway heading down into the bush along the
estuary shore, the method of payment an honesty
box with a large, rusting padlock attached. Kate had
been fishing in the lightweight fanny-pack clipped
around her waist for the coins to post in the slot when
the crunch of tyres and whirr of an electric window
had made her turn her head.

'Hello,' Melissa Jayson called from the driver's
seat on the far side of the late-model station-wagon.
She was in a figure-hugging dress with full make-up
emphasising her striking features, but this time all
Kate could see was the wedding ring prominently
displayed on the finger tapping the steering wheel in
time to the beat on the stereo. 'Would you like a lift
back to the house?'

'No, thanks, I'm going in the other direction. I'm
walking for fitness,' Kate said quickly as her coins
clinked into the box.

'Are you sure?' Kate could hear her scepticism. It
did seem rather unlikely that she would carry a large
bouquet of vegetables around to wilt in the hot sun,
when the logical thing would have been to buy them
on her way back.

'I'm sure.' Was this an olive branch or a prelude
to more backbiting? Should she apologise for calling
her a Grade-A bitch? According to Drake the poor
woman had only been trying to guard her client's
back, or protect her investment, even if with ques-
tionable vigour.

'Would you like me to at least take the vegies for

you? I could put them in our fridge until you've finished your walk.'

Our fridge? It was ridiculous how much that casually possessive little word grated.

'No, thanks. Really, I'll be fine. I haven't got that much further to go.' For all Drake's protestations that there was nothing between them, Kate was still picking up a vibe that suggested a more than simply professional interest on the redhead's part.

'Well, OK, then, if I can't persuade you…'

'No, but thanks for stopping,' she made herself say.

The Other Woman laughed wryly. 'Really? I bet you wished I'd kept on driving—straight on down into the estuary.'

'The thought did cross my mind,' Kate admitted.

'Well, if it's any consolation, darling, Drake was in a furniture-chewing mood when he came back to the house the other day. He practically got out the thumbscrews to find out what we'd said to each other.'

'Did you tell him?'

This time Melissa's laugh was genuine. 'Are you kidding? After he prowled about like a cat on hot bricks when you arrived, moaning that he wasn't going to be able to write a word while you were breathing down his neck, and then acted as if I'd violated one of the ten commandments by telling you? Let him stew! I gather you didn't tell him much, either—just enough to set him marinating in his own juices. Once he's done he might go well with that broccoli.'

Damn! thought Kate as the car roared off. I wanted to keep hating her and now she won't let me.

Sharp, pushy, but up front and funny... Kate could see why Drake might find her good to work with.

It was all his fault. If he hadn't primed both women to resent each other with his manipulative behaviour, she and Melissa might even have been friends. But, of course, Drake wouldn't want that to happen, she brooded—the two opposite sides of his life meeting instead of keeping to his rigid lines of demarcation...

And there was still one good reason to resent Melissa, she reminded herself. She was obviously great at her job. Her position with Drake was highly valued and secure, whereas Kate's was already shaking on its flimsy foundations. Drake would have no trouble finding another lover, but first-class private editors were extremely thin on the ground.

Knowing that she was letting her fears for the future paralyse her will put Kate even more out of sorts. Procrastination had the effect of concentrating her mind on safely trivial concerns, like the fact that every time she set foot outside her door the three-legged dog would dash out of nowhere, drool a greeting over her toes, and hang about with a lugubrious expression until she fed it a few biscuits or a bowl of yoghurt. Or the elusive rodent whose phantom squeak was bothering her at odd times of the day, as well as spooking her at night. She had found an old mousetrap pushed to the back of the cupboard under the bench in the kitchen, still baited with a rock-hard lump of old cheese, but it looked a bit flimsy for the task. Judging by the volume of the squeak her unwanted house-guest was not your average house-mouse.

It occurred to her that she could ask Drake if he was any good at rat-catching. Perhaps it would be a face-saving way of re-approaching him, with the added bonus of being genuine, so if he rebuffed her with the name of a local exterminator she would still have gained something. And if he did offer to personally crawl under her house with a torch and a rat-trap, well…this time she would make sure she didn't let her hormones run riot!

Her sudden craving for a nice piece of fish scotched the rat idea by suggesting a more mature approach. They did say the way to a man's heart was through his stomach and according to her reading the waters around Oyster Beach were famous not only for oysters and a teeming variety of fish, but for particularly plump, juicy scallops.

Drake was a sucker for a scallop.

He had always declared his own cooking skills to be rudimentary, and since there was nothing so glamorous as a restaurant in the small community, and she doubted the take-away joint next to the gas station ran to Coquilles St Jacques, perhaps offering him a feast of his favourite meal made with delicacies fresh off the boat would create the right atmosphere to re-establish communication. If she also had to invite Melissa for the sake of politeness, well…so be it. It might even prove ultimately more informative than just having Drake by himself. After all, it was thanks to Melissa she was now in possession of a few more intriguing facts…about the way Drake worked, about the dyslexia that might very well be inherited by his son or daughter. She was rapidly coming to understand that even if Drake *wasn't* emotionally involved in his baby's birth and upbringing, there were lots of ways in which he would critically influence the child's life.

Arriving back from the wharf with a bulging plastic bag of scallops, kindly dug from their shells by the grizzled fisherman for no extra charge, Kate swung into her driveway. Halfway back into the garage she remembered she would need mushrooms, too, for the Coquilles. She might have to go as far as the store for those, unless there were some available from roadside stalls on the way. She shifted the car into reverse and put an impatient foot on the accelerator. As she shot back down the driveway in a burst of revs she glimpsed a whisk of mottled grey out of the corner of her eye as it scooted behind the car. She instinctively swerved and jammed on her brakes but there was a jarring thud and high-pitched yelp as the rear wheel ran up onto something and bumped down again.

Kate was out of the car and kneeling beside the back tyre within seconds, scraping her hands on the decorative rocks that lined the drive as she braced herself to peer underneath. Wedging the mud-flap against black rubber tread was the ubiquitous three-legged dog, no longer irritating her with its foolish antics but lying lax, and ominously still. Grateful that the wheel wasn't actually resting on the dog, Kate scrambled back into the idling car, and with shaking hands slowly drove it forward until she estimated it was well clear of the fallen victim.

This time when she knelt on the driveway beside the dog, she was relieved to see its side shuddering and its head lift briefly before thumping back onto the rough concrete with an accompanying low whine, the stump of the missing leg twitching pathetically, the ridiculous tail limp and streaked with a dark stain she feared could be blood.

'Oh, God—' Stricken with guilt, she tentatively touched the trembling coat, wary of causing any more damage to broken ribs. 'It's all right,' she said shakily, daring a few, butterfly-light, pats. 'You'll be all right once we get you to the vet…he'll fix you up…'

She knew there was no way she was going to be able to lift the heavy animal into the car by herself, nor did she have any idea if there was a vet anywhere close. Murmuring foolishly to the dog that she'd be back in a moment, she ran around into Drake's paved front yard and hammered violently at his door. It seemed to take an age for him to open it and as soon as he did she gabbled wildly:

'I've hit a dog with my car. I think it might be badly hurt, but I'm not sure. It's just lying there, whimpering, and I don't know who owns it or what to do. Is there a vet around here, or a doctor I could take it to for help?' But in her panic she didn't think to wait for an answer, she was running back, anxious not to leave the dog injured and alone. If it died she didn't want it to die alone.

By the time she got there Drake was beside her,

cursing under his breath when he saw the animal, crouching down and running his large hands over the hairy hide, running explorative fingers through the thick pelt, eliciting a feeble flicker of the tip of the foolish tail.

'It was my fault—I mustn't have looked properly,' Kate agonised. 'It ran behind the car when I was backing. Thank God it wasn't a child!' The thought made her feel ill. 'I can't have been going very fast but I think maybe it went under the wheel—'

'Him,' said Drake tersely, cutting off her semi-hysterical spate of words.

'What?'

'It's a "him", not an "it". He's obviously a male,' he said, his face oddly desolate and blank of expression as he gently manipulated each of the three big paws and quieted the broken whines with an indistinct murmur.

'Oh, I wasn't sure…with all that hair,' Kate quavered, grateful to cling to a steadying fact in a sea of wretched uncertainty. 'He's been hanging around ever since I got here, but I don't know where he comes from. Do you think he'll be OK?' she asked anxiously.

'I don't know. I can't feel anything broken but we need to get him to a vet as soon as possible in case he's bleeding internally. There's a clinic about thirty kilometres away, near Whitianga—it covers a big rural area as well as the town, but they always have more than one vet on call.'

Internal bleeding! Kate's stomach twisted as

Drake continued, 'The only visible sign of trouble I can see is this graze on his muzzle.' He withdrew his hand from the dog's mouth and turned it over to show her the bright red splodge of blood on his palm. Kate's senses swam and she turned away and was promptly sick on the edge of the grass.

'Sorry…shock,' she mumbled, taking the hand-kerchief he thrust at her and wiping her mouth.

'You didn't hit your head?' he asked sharply, his face pale and set, his mouth grim.

He looked more shaken than she had ever seen him, fighting some inward battle for calm, and she realised he must be worrying about concussion. She put her hand over her belly, freshly aware of the fragility of life, and grateful for her habit of caution.

'No, I was wearing my seat belt, of course, and anyway, as I said, I wasn't going that fast—'

He shifted his crouch, leaning forward to slide his arms under the dog's recumbent form, smoothly straightening his legs in order to rise to his full height without jolting. As Kate suspected, the big-boned dog was even heavier than he looked and the strain on Drake's neck and shoulders was clearly visible as he adjusted his unwieldy burden against his chest. Kate winced at the pitiful yelp that the move elicited, and hurried to open the rear door of the car, but Drake was already moving in the opposite direction.

'Where are you going?' she cried, almost tripping as she hastened on his heels.

'He's obviously not going to fit in your car lying

down. I have a four-wheel drive with very good sus-
pension—he'll be less likely to be cramped or jostled.
Go and get my keys from Melissa, and tell her to call
the vet—the number's in the red index on my desk.'

By the time she had breathlessly returned Drake
had the dog lying full length on a tartan rug on the
wide back seat of his battered grey Land Rover. He
grabbed the car keys from her hand and hefted
himself up into the front seat.

'Wait!' said Kate, scrabbling at the back door
handle as he gunned the ignition.

He frowned impatiently at her through the open
window. 'There's no need for you to come. I know
where I'm going—'

Kate's shaking hands succeeded in getting the
door wrenched open. 'Of course I have to come,' she
said, shocked he would think otherwise. 'I injured
him; I'm responsible for him. I can't just abandon
him for others to look after!'

'Nobody's accusing you of abandoning him. You
got help, that's as much as you could do.' He swore.
'Damn it, I don't have time to argue—'

'So stop arguing and start driving,' ordered Kate,
climbing in behind him and shutting the door with a
snap. She eased herself down on the bench seat by
the dog's head and squirmed her way into the seat
belt, being careful not to entangle the animal.

'What if something happened on the way?' she
pointed out as Drake pulled onto the road. 'You have
to concentrate on your driving. The poor thing is
probably scared out of its wits as well as being in

pain. He could hurt himself again if he starts to panic. He might not be used to travelling in a car.' Her tight voice dropped into a croon. 'Someone's got to be here to hold your paw, don't they, boy?'

The dog was lying on its side, and its panting breath moistened her bare thigh below her khaki shorts. She fondled a floppy ear and brushed the woolly strands of fur away from the single visible eye, which glistened dolefully, making her feel even more guilty. For once she was grateful when he gave her leg a disgustingly gooey swipe.

'Oh! He licked me. Do you think that's a good sign?' she said hopefully.

'Licking you is always a sign that something good's about to happen,' came the mocking response.

Kate's glare drilled into the back of his head above the headrest. 'How can you make jokes at a time like this?'

'What better time to try and deflect thoughts of doom and gloom?' he said harshly. 'Humour in the face of adversity is a very useful human defence mechanism.'

Of course it was, and particularly so for Drake, she realised. The dry wit, flirtatious wordplay and entertaining anecdotes with which he avoided intrusive questions were the perfect distraction from his real feelings. Didn't she do exactly the same thing when trying to shield herself from caring too much?

She looked over at his hands on the wheel, and noticed them shifting with a rapidity and frequency that wasn't necessary for the control of the vehicle.

He was fighting frustration, charged with adrenalin-fuelled urgency that he had to control for the sake of driving them safely on the narrow, winding roads.

She felt a movement against her leg, the dog trying valiantly to shift its heavy head into her lap, as if attempting to comfort her with its trusting forgiveness. She squirmed closer so that she could help him lift his grazed muzzle across her thigh.

In between croonings she speculated about his ownership, undeterred by Drake's clipped responses.

'I wonder who owns him. Do you know? A dog with three legs...he must be well-known in the neighbourhood—'

'He certainly strays around—'

Kate was quick to cut him off. 'He's not a stray! Are you, boy?' she soothed the dog. 'He's got a collar, but every time I try to twist it around to look for the tag, he cringes. He has to belong to someone. Someone who doesn't look after you properly, eh, boy? I don't think he can be fed very much, he's always pestering me for titbits—'

'If you bend over him in that purple bikini I can understand why.'

She met his eyes in the rear-vision mirror above the dash. 'Drake! I'm being serious. He always seems to be ravenous.'

'He's obviously a hardened scrounger.' His eyes flicked carelessly back to the road.

'Don't say that; he can hear you!' said Kate, putting a hand over the dog's ear. 'I told you he has a collar. If his owner's not caring properly for him he's got no choice but to scavenge. He can't very well hunt for himself with only three legs.'

'He seems to have managed to track down your bleeding heart.'

She frowned at his apparent callousness. 'His coat seems very messy,' she said, picking out a burr. 'He could do with a brush.'

He lifted his chin to bring the dog into his line of sight. 'Probably been rolling in the dirt. He's a mutt, not a show-pooch.'

'I wonder if he's ever groomed? Owners like that should be shot!'

'I thought you were a proponent of non-violence?' His narrowed eyes met hers for a brief challenge before swerving away again.

'It's just a turn of phrase,' she said impatiently. 'Pet owners have a responsibility.'

'He's more like a nuisance than a pet.'

Now she was truly shocked. 'It's not his fault. He shouldn't be allowed to wander.'

'Maybe he *needs* to roam.'

Kate gritted her teeth at his stubborn refusal to share her sensible concerns. How could she love such a hard-hearted man? And how could such a hard-hearted man ever make room in his petrified organ for the love of a child? She leaned across the dog's head, her tee-shirt tickling its nose into a messy snuffle. 'But it's dangerous—'

'This is the countryside; risks are assessed differently in remote areas,' he said as she quickly leaned back again. 'People here don't keep their dogs penned up.'

'But he could at least be kept in a fenced yard—'

'Oh, for God's sake—get real!' He looked daggers at her in the mirror. 'He hates being shut in. He goes berserk if you try to tie him up or keep him behind the fence; he nearly kills himself trying to get loose.'

Kate's hands stilled their restless stroking, her eyes widening as the certainty hit her like a freight train.

'He belongs to you!'

His eyes whipped back to the road. 'He's a stray.'

It all came together. The shocked curse. The grim examination. Having the vet's phone number handy on his desk. And, most telling of all, the hard carapace of flinty self-control.

'Maybe he was a stray, once. But he's your dog now, isn't he?'

'Nobody wanted a hopeless mongrel like him.' He shrugged. 'He would have been put down.'

She took that as a yes. 'Because he only had three legs?'

'He had all four when he first landed on my doorstep,' he said drily. 'He lost his back leg when he practically shredded it ripping his way through a chain-link dog-fence I put up to keep him "safe".' He glanced back just long enough to see her wince. 'Which of course only made him even more unattractive to your average dog-lover who either wants a purebred or something useful or cute.'

'So when did you adopt him?'

'I didn't adopt him.' He sounded as if she had

accused him of an iniquity. The muscles at the back of his neck stiffened. 'The vet says he was probably abused in a confined space as a pup—which makes him very much of an outside dog. I've never owned an animal, but said I'd let him hang around at my place until something could be arranged that didn't involve a lethal injection. That was five years ago, just after I built the house. Unfortunately no one ever answered the ads, and I'm still stuck with him.'

And still deep in denial about it!

He had built the house with the proceeds of that first book, she realised. Prior to that he had been a wanderer, spending his money as he went. But as soon as he'd had the means, he had made a place for himself, and, although he might categorise it purely as a place to write, a temporary refuge, it was more than that— it was *home*. He had been secretly putting down roots.

'What happens to him when you go away?' she asked curiously. 'If he hates being shut up he obviously can't go into a kennel.'

'I usually drop him off with a mate of the vet's, who has a lifestyle block up in the hills. In the shorter term I pay a local to come and live in the house,' he admitted gruffly. In other words he firmly kept a foot in both camps—the dog owner and the rootless wanderer. And, of course, he also had his town mistress on a completely separate string!

'Doesn't he pine?'

'Not noticeably. He likes company but he's not particular. He doesn't like to be owned. Mostly he needs the freedom to come and go.'

He could be talking about himself, thought Kate, struck by the stunning psychological similarity. They both had attachment issues. She had often wondered about Drake's family background, but he had never responded to her tentative comments, and she knew only the vague details—that he had been orphaned as a teenager by the death of his mother, and had no contact with his father. She suspected abuse, but had known better than to ask.

She did have one more question, however, that did urgently require an answer: 'So what's his name?'

'He didn't come with a birth certificate.'

'You must have given him a proper name.'

'Since he never comes when I call him, it seems a bit pointless.'

'So what is it?' She could see he was relishing her frustration at his evasions. She could also see that his hands were more relaxed on the wheel and the muscles in his jaw were no longer clenched. 'Let me guess.' She pretended to think. 'Rumpelstiltskin!'

He almost smiled.

'No? How about Rover? Very appropriate to his nature.'

There was no response from dog or man.

'Spot? Montmorency de Waverley Assortment?'

That got her a human snicker. She raised her eyebrows and he gave in to her persistence, his worried eyes wary as they reflected his surrender.

'Prince.'

'Prince,' she repeated. There was suddenly a huge lump in the middle of her throat. It could have been a mocking appellation, but from his shifty expression she guessed otherwise. It was the wry and wistful choice of a boy for his first dog. Drake had called his shambling, shabby, shock-haired goof 'Prince', and now at least something about the woolly hound would have the dignity that genetics had cruelly denied him.

She looked down to hide the sting of tears. Drake might act as if he had no desire for commitment, but the existence of Prince suggested that at some level he *did* want to establish emotional ties in his life. He may not *choose* to love, but he *could* and *did* love.

And if one love could force its way into his well-guarded heart, why not another?

'I'm very sorry I hurt Prince,' she said quietly. Would he ever be able to forgive her if she caused the death of his dog? 'I should have been more careful.'

He didn't rush to absolve her with soothing lies, but he did offer her comfort to ease her guilt. 'So should he. He makes a sport of pretending to chase cars. He's been knocked about before. It was an accident, Kate.'

He sounded fatalistic, but Kate knew better. He had simply internalised his fear. 'I hope he's all right.'

'We'll soon find out. The clinic is just up ahead.'

The white-coated vet who came out to greet them with a metal gurney was a tall, thin man about Drake's age, with a long-suffering expression on his bright and humorous face. 'You're lucky I hadn't gone out on rounds yet, Drake. At this rate I should get a royal warrant to stick on my door. What on earth has Prince done to himself now?'

'Not him—me—' Kate began, only to have her explanations pre-empted by Drake's terse account as he lifted the whining dog onto the gurney. The vet's friendly air didn't dilute his brisk professionalism and he kept up his patter as he pushed the gurney through the doors and past the reception desk in the waiting room.

'We'll take him straight through to the surgery and I'll assess whether he needs a scan. But we'll start off with the cheap option.' He cast a smile into Kate's anxious face. 'That's me. Hands and eyes are a vet's most valuable tools.'

'I'll be paying, so I don't care how much it costs,' she blurted. 'Just do everything you can—'

'Don't be ridiculous,' Drake said roughly, stroking the dog's head. 'I can afford any treatment he needs—just send the bill to me as usual, Ken.'

'But—'

'For God's sake, Kate, stop making it such a drama. I don't need your guilt money!' he snapped as they paused for the vet to open the surgery door.

Kate's hand fell away from the gurney. She knew it was fear making him lash out, but it still hurt to hear him declare he wanted nothing from her, and she had to steady herself against the wall.

'Are you all right?' said the vet, his eyes suddenly sharp on her pale face.

She stared at the name badge pinned to his coat as she fought for composure.

'Ken Cartwright B.V.Sc.' the black lettering said as it moved briefly in and out of focus, making her feel as if she were standing on shifting ground. 'I'm just a little dizzy,' she excused herself.

'She threw up before we left,' added Drake unnecessarily.

Ken's sharp gaze became speculative as it ran over her from head to toe. Oh, God, she hoped that vets didn't have any special instinct for detecting early pregnancy in humans!

'Perhaps you should sit down for a few minutes—Christy!' Ken called out to his receptionist. 'Would you get a glass of water for Kate here, while Drake and I see to Prince?'

'Oh, really, I'm fine...' she murmured, but Ken was already disappearing into his surgery with the gurney, while Drake hesitated outside.

Kate braced herself, but when he frowned it wasn't to issue another rejection. 'Are you sure it's only dizziness? Are you feeling sick again?' He glanced restlessly over his shoulder at the closed door and back at Kate, his eyes black with inner turmoil, clearly torn.

Drake never vacillated. He always knew what his priorities were and was never afraid to make harsh decisions.

'Go,' she urged, freeing him from his agony of choice. 'I don't need you—Prince does. Go and find out what's happening to your dog.' And when he still hesitated, she gave him a physical push. 'For God's sake, go! I have to go to the bathroom, anyway, so there's no point in your hanging around here. Go!'

And having given him the freedom to follow his

heart, she went off to find her glass of water and have a short, but deeply satisfying cry in the toilet cubicle, under the beady eyes of six fat hamsters crowded onto the veterinary products calendar on the back of the door.

CHAPTER SIX

IT SEEMED an age, but it probably wasn't much more than twenty minutes before Drake came back out into the waiting area.

Kate took one look at his shuttered expression and dry eyes and her heart sank. His body seemed tautly bunched under the woven cotton shirt and stonewashed jeans, simmering with unexploded tension, his mouth hard enough to chew nails.

Ken Cartwright, who was steering him with a consoling hand on his shoulder, was more relaxed—although he must face this sort of situation fairly often in his professional life.

'Well, that's it. I've done all I can. I think you'd better take this guy home and give him a stiff whiskey.'

He thought alcohol the best way to handle grief? Kate's heart swelled in her chest.

'Oh, Drake,' she said helplessly, sharing his misery, 'I'm so sorry. Your beautiful dog!' She burst into tears and threw her compassionate arms around his neck, burying her wet face in his chest.

His arms came up to clamp around her shaking body, his strong, encircling arms almost muffling out the sound of the vet's next words.

'Beautiful? She surely can't be talking about Prince—his ugly mug would win the booby prize at Crufts!'

Kate stiffened, her head bumping Drake's chin, unable to believe her ears. She could feel the chest under her wet cheek silently vibrating...oh, God, was he actually *crying*?

She turned her head and gave the grinning Ken Cartwright B.V.Sc. a blistering look.

'You call yourself a vet? What kind of thing is that to say to a man who's just lost his dog?'

'Prince is lost? Are those tears of relief?' Ken grinned over her angry head at Drake. 'You should be so lucky!'

Kate's jaw dropped. 'Someone should report you to the—to the—'

'The place where people report vets for making really bad jokes?' he supplied. 'I'm sorry, Kate. But it looks like Drake is going to have that ugly mug around for the foreseeable future.'

'You mean he's still alive?' She jerked her head back to look up into Drake's face through tangled wet lashes.

'He's more than OK. He's perfect.' The smile he was wearing was even bigger than Ken's. It hadn't been dammed-up grief, but fierce relief that he had been fighting to control when he'd walked out!

'Is he?' she sought professional confirmation from the man she had been vilifying only seconds ago.

'A bouncing box of birds.'

Kate blinked at his cheerful alliteration and pulled her hands from Drake's neck to swipe the wetness from her cheeks. 'But there was blood—'

'Rubbed a bit of skin off his nose, that's all.'

'I felt the bump, I felt the car go over him—'

'No sign of any crushing, or marks on his coat. Are you sure it wasn't something else you ran over?'

'No…at least, there were some rocks along the side of the driveway…' she faltered, remembering how the steering wheel had seemed to jump out of her hands when she had swerved to try and avoid the dog '…but he was lying there up against the tyre, whimpering and whining—'

'Yes, fancies himself a bit of a Hollywood star, does our Prince. Wouldn't surprise me if you gave him a bit of a nudge and he decided to fall over and ham it up. For all he's skittish he likes attention, especially from a tasty woman.' He winked.

'He travelled all the way here with his head buried in her lap,' said Drake drily.

'Lucky dog!' chuckled Ken, making Kate pinken. 'Here I thought he was some kind of giant schnauzer-cross and he turns out to be a ladies' lap-dog. 'Nuff said!'

Kate suddenly realised she was still snuggled up against Drake, her stomach pressing into the buckle of his jeans, her breasts squashed into the narrow space between their upper bodies. She wedged her elbows against his chest and shoved herself out of his entangling arms—with difficulty because he seemed reluctant to cooperate. Probably because he knew what she was going to say.

'You knew I thought he was dead! And you were laughing at me!' she shouted.

'Not at you, sweetheart—*with* you,' protested Drake, acknowledging his utter defencelessness to the charge.

'You insensitive pig!' She scrubbed again at her cheeks to make sure all trace of her sympathy was gone. Unfortunately, so were her chances of appearing aloof in her displeasure. 'You and that—that...scrofulous hound deserve each other. I bet he was laughing at me too,' she said, remembering the lolling tongue.

'Is she always so volatile?' asked Ken.

Drake's eyes darkened as he looked down at her, curiosity mingled with a dawning new awareness. Kate tensed, sure he was going to say something witty and suggestive.

'I'm not sure,' he said slowly. 'She's rather difficult to get to know.'

'*I'm* difficult!' Her momentary speechlessness gave the vet time to step in by smoothly suggesting that his assistant had had time to give the dog his antibiotic injection by now.

'I don't think there's any chance of infection to his nose, but I'll give you some antibiotic cream to take with you, Drake, just in case. Come and get Prince and I'll give you a sample box from the surgery.' He smiled at Kate. 'It was nice to meet you, even in this roundabout fashion. The mouth-trap here doesn't give up much, but I won't pretend not to know who you are…we get given lots of gossipy magazines for the waiting room here. I hope this doesn't put you off your visit..?'

He was blatantly fishing, and Kate ignored Drake's restless movement to cruise by the bait. 'Oh, I'm not staying with Drake. I've rented my own house on Oyster Beach…'

'Next door to mine,' Drake chipped in, only to be totally ignored by his so-called friend.

'Oh, really?' The blue eyes twinkled at Kate. 'Ever been out on a racing catamaran?'

'No, she hasn't—she gets seasick in the bath. I thought you were going to get me that prescription? You have a sick tortoise over there who's been waiting long enough.'

'Mmm, he does look a bit green,' said Ken, with a glance at his next patient, clutched to the chest of an old man who looked not unlike a wrinkly tortoise himself.

Kate bit off a gurgle as Drake glared at her. 'You wait here,' he said sternly.

Ken pointed towards the chairs, using the same tone of voice. 'Yes, sit, girl, sit!'

Christy was on the phone and Kate hovered by the desk for a few moments thinking to ask her if she knew anything about rats. But the receptionist seemed to be getting into an argument about a bill, so Kate moved to a discreet distance, inspecting the various posters on the walls.

She was standing in front of a glossy chart

showing the life-cycle of the blowfly complete with close-up photographs of the rear ends of maggoty sheep when a gravelly voice said: 'Revolting little devils, aren't they? And fancy having to live in a sheep's bum! Give me a good, old-fashioned, lusty leech any old day.'

Kate turned to find herself the target of a pair of vivid green eyes deep-set in a pale, intense face. For a brief moment she was distracted by the mop of flaming red hair, unpleasantly reminded of the woman who had given her so much cause for discomfort, but then her senses responded to the very male impact of the unshaven chin and sexy mouth, the lazy, white-lidded gaze and the lean, tapering body encased in a black tee shirt and jeans. His face said he was somewhere in his thirties, but the decadent eyes were much, much older.

'Oh, I don't know,' she said, consciously trying to act normal. It was difficult when he looked so fascinated by her own eyes, but perhaps that fathomless gaze was just part of his technique. 'Some maggots have a useful side, too. Like leeches, they're being used medicinally in some hospitals—to help remove dead tissue in and around infected wounds. They're supposedly more effective than surgery because they don't excise any healthy flesh.'

Oh, yes, have a conversation with the man about rotting flesh—very normal, Kate!

He received the lecture in flattering silence, moving around to lean a casual shoulder against the wall. 'I'll never swat a fly again,' he vowed, hand on his heart. 'But I still prefer blood-suckers to scum-suckers. Leeches seem like they might be more fun to hang around with at parties…'

'You would know,' she murmured, and bit her lip, thinking that might have been a bit rude.

His eyelids drooped, his trade-mark, world-weary smile hiking his sensual mouth. 'OK, now we both know that you know who *I* am,' said Steve Marlow, former bad-boy rock-star, now New Zealand's—and one of Hollywood's—most sought-after composer of movie-music. 'Am I allowed to know who *you* are?'

'Kate.'

'Tell me, Kate…' he jacked one black-booted foot over the other as he trotted out one of the most hoary old clichés in the pick-up business '…do you come here often?'

Her heart didn't even miss a beat. 'Only in the maggot season.'

He laughed, his attractively harsh voice project-ing off the walls. Shaking his head, he looked around the now-empty waiting room. 'Are you here to pick up an animal?'

'I'm here with a friend.'

'So am I. My nephew's pet rabbit who has been losing some of his rabbity-bits in order not to over-populate his hutch.' He placed his hand on the wall above her head and leaned confidingly closer. 'Has anyone told you what absolutely stunning eyes you have?'

'Yes. *I* have,' said Drake, striding across the floor

to slip his hand under Kate's elbow and tug her away, her feet stumbling as Prince blundered eagerly between them to head-butt Steve Marlow in the thigh.

'Ouch! Can't you keep this damned dog of yours under control?'

'I am. He's trained to attack tired, old, talentless has-beens who sleaze around younger women desperately trying to relive their faded days of glory!'

'I still can't believe you said that,' a mortified Kate was repeating as he encouraged Prince to jump up into the back seat of the Land Rover and settle down on his tartan rug. 'You just insulted a Kiwi icon. It's a wonder he didn't punch you in the nose, like he did that music critic backstage at the Oscars!'

'He'd have to pump up those skinny arms first!' sneered Drake, hustling her around to the front passenger door.

Just as she was getting in, Steve Marlow came out of the clinic with a carry-cage, and walked over to a black convertible parked near the door.

He looked across the gravel parking yard at them, and lifted up the cage to show Kate the sluggish white behemoth squatting within. 'Hey, Drake!' he called, in his famously husky voice. 'Are you still on for our usual Friday-night pool session?'

The mocking lilt made Drake stiffen. 'Why wouldn't I be?'

The bright green gaze went pointedly to Kate's sun-burnished head. 'Oh, I don't know...Ken and I just thought you might have found more exciting things to do...'

Drake made a growling sound deep in his chest. 'You and Ken are gossiping old women! I'll be there, with bells on. The both of you can prepare to go down in a screaming heap—*as usual*.'

'What about Kiss Me Kate with the sexy silver eyes—will she be coming, too?'

'She doesn't play pool.' Drake slammed her door with unnecessary force and got behind the wheel.

'She could hold our beers!' The gravelly yell that had sold a million albums degenerated into a burst of coughing as the Land Rover did a sharp turn past him, kicking up a cloud of dust into his face.

Drake pulled his arm back inside the open window and turned onto the black tarmac.

'Did you just make an obscene gesture at him?' said Kate disapprovingly.

'He did it first.'

Sure enough, as she looked out the back window she could see Steve Marlow's black-clad figure extending a crudely upthrust finger at the departing vehicle.

'He looks just like the cover of his breakthrough album,' she laughed.

'Poseur!' snorted Drake.

Kate hid a smile. 'I didn't know you two were friends.'

She held her breath but to her delight he didn't shy away from her obvious curiosity. 'We knew each other for a while as kids. We've kicked around a bit since we met up again several years ago. Why would I boast about it?'

Why indeed? He never gossiped about others, or

name-dropped to impress. He didn't have to—he was quite impressive enough on his own account.

'Goodness, Oyster Beach is turning out to be quite the Celebrity Central,' said Kate, settling back in her seat.

'You won't run into Steve at the beach,' said Drake, sounding smug about it. 'He burns like a vampire in the sun. The Marlow family have a holiday place way back in the valley,' he said with deliberate vagueness. 'Steve's only there now and then, in between shuttling back and forth to the UK and the States.'

'I suppose having to protect his skin from the sun is what keeps him looking so boyishly young,' Kate mused, unable to resist feeding his evident irritation.

'More likely a decaying old painting riddled with corruption stashed away in his attic!' he grunted.

'I thought he seemed very nice,' she said demurely.

'*Nice?* He's a fire-born hell-raiser from way back! He's dangerous. Stay away from him.'

As if she had a choice! She knew very well that Steve Marlow had just been idling away a few minutes of his time. It was the arrival of his friend that had truly piqued his interest. And Drake had played right into his hands.

'He's obviously not the same person he was when he was with the band—'

'But he's done it all…booze, fags, tattoos—sex, drugs and rock'n'roll. Who knows what perversions he's into now to give his jaded senses a kick? You can do practically anything you like in Tinseltown. He's not someone you want to know.'

He sounded as pious as a priest. 'I thought you liked him, I thought he was your friend?' she said, bewildered.

He hunched over the wheel. 'I do. He is. That doesn't mean I'd let him date my sister,' he muttered.

Her mind stuttered to a stop as she swivelled in her seat to stare at him. 'You have a *sister*?'

His profile hardened. 'I don't have any family; I was just using the word metaphorically,' he grated. 'We're talking about you.'

She recoiled. 'And you think of me in a *sisterly* way?'

'Of course not—you know what I mean.' He cast her an accusing look. 'You're too good for him.'

'You mean I'm a goody-goody,' she said resentfully. She wound down the window to cool her cheeks in the rushing air. It was true. Becoming Drake's lover was the baddest thing she had ever done, she brooded. Of course, having an illegitimate baby was about to put paid to that goody-goody image for ever!

'Well, I happen to think his music has always been terrific,' she said defiantly. 'Even when he was with Hard Times. They produced some classics of the hard-rock genre—'

'Yeah, and thanks to that he has enough groupies hot on his tail. He doesn't need you drooling over him, too.'

That was the second time in a few days she had been insulted by the same accusation. 'I am not a groupie!'

'No? What is it with you, then? Have you started giving off some pheromone that announces you're available? You never even *notice* other men when you're with me, but all of a sudden you're flirting with everything in pants—first Ken, then Steve—'

'Flirting?' Kate spluttered. 'I was attempting to engage in normal conversation with two men I'd never met before. If there was flirting going on, your friends were the ones doing it. And that was only because you were bristling like a dog around a bone. You're so jealous you can't even see—'

'Jealous!'

She gasped as he suddenly swerved, and pulled into a rest stop carved out of the bush-covered cliff at the side of the road, no longer trusting himself to drive. He yanked on the brake and cut the engine, turning to confront her across the console with a savage face. 'That's rich, coming from *you*.'

She tried to dial back her anger in the face of his, realising that her not-so-innocent prodding had stirred up a hornet's nest, but determined to stand up for her rights. 'Oh, I see—it's all right for you to dangle another woman under my nose and accuse *me* of being jealous, but when the shoe's on the other foot it's a different matter.'

'Don't ever accuse me of being jealous,' he spat at her.

'Why not? It's not a dirty word.'

'It is to me,' he said, so thickly he could hardly get the words out.

'But—*why*?'

He gave her a look of impotent fury. Neither of them heard Prince whine in the back seat. 'I'm not that person,' he said through his teeth.

'What person?' And when he remained silent, she nudged him: 'A little bit of jealousy is usually considered healthy in a relationship.'

'In a healthy relationship, yes. In an unhealthy relationship it can be dangerous for everyone involved,' he said rawly. 'It can eat a person up from the inside and be hugely destructive.'

She felt a frisson of fear. That sounded very like personal experience talking. 'What do you classify as an unhealthy relationship? Is that what we have?'

He angrily pushed away the past, his eyes hot as they slammed into hers. 'No, of course not, because we know how to control it, we don't let it control us—we're equals.'

'And what if I don't want *control* any more?' she challenged recklessly. 'What if I want something different?'

The heat in his eyes turned molten. 'Is that what the matter is, Kate? Is life getting too tame for you when I'm away? Can't get any satisfaction? The lack of sex making you edgy and restless...sending you out looking for diversions?'

He leaned over, flipped open the clasp of her seat belt and dragged her against his chest, pinning her hips across the central console. 'Well, here's a diversion for you!'

His hot mouth sealed over hers, his hand tunnelling up under her shiny mass of hair to cup the back of her delicate skull, tipping her head to give him deeper access to the moist, satiny cavern. His tongue stabbed, stroked, enticed...the slight roughness of his jaw scraping her chin, his musky male scent teasing her nostrils, filling her with a familiar sense of heady abandonment.

His mouth slid around to her ear, his teeth nipping then sucking suggestively at the tender lobe.

She shuddered, her hands clenching on his shoulders, fingers digging through his shirt into hard muscle, and his hot breath fanned the sensitive nerves behind her ears as he laughed roughly. 'Oh, yes, you like that, don't you? I know all the things that turn you on…' He used his tongue to stroke the delicate little nub of flesh, sending fresh quivers through her body. 'You like the things I do to you, because you know I can give you exactly want you want…'

The hand pressing on the middle of her back moved around to shape her breast through the soft tee shirt, cupping the soft weight and his thumb stroking her stiffening nipple through the intricate lace of her bra as he kissed his way across her throat to tease and play with the dainty lobe of her other ear.

'For instance, I know that when I'm doing this, you're remembering about how it feels when I suckle that other, even more exquisitely sensitive little bud…' he whispered roughly. 'You know the one…the secret one that's tingling right now between your legs, making you long to bite and claw and scream for me, the way you do when we're in bed…'

Kate's hips writhed helplessly against the hard console as she squeezed her thighs together to try and ease the forbidden throb intensified by his taunting words. His hand tightened on her breast, compressing the pleasure into an even greater density, drawing at her thrusting nipple in a rhythmic counterpoint to his softly suckling mouth.

'Drake—' Kate groaned, her hands sliding from his shoulders to the neck of his shirt, lusting for the feel of his bare skin against her seeking fingers.

'Yeah, baby, it's me,' he said, lifting his head to look down into her silver eyes, drowning in blind desire, before breaking open her kiss-stung lips with his teeth to feast once again on her voluptuous surrender. 'Who else could it be? Who else knows how to turn you on so hard, so fast? You can be cool and standoffish with other men, but not with me, never with me…'

It was true, and the fact that he knew it and yet still withheld the essence of himself from her should have been humiliating, but it wasn't, for she could hear the exultation that overlaid the taunting passion in his voice. Something deep and powerful and primitive within him wanted her to be for him, and him alone, regardless of what his private demons were telling him.

A deep rumble tore from his chest, vibrating through her fingertips spread over the warm hollow at the base of his throat, and the big hand holding her head shifted to her shoulder blades, keeping her still as he worked impatiently at the front catch of her bra through the folds of her tee shirt.

Just as Kate felt the plastic clasp give way, they were wrenched from their mutual absorption by a roar and brief, blaring toot.

Kate jerked back, her dazed eyes following Steve

Marlow's black convertible as it swept out of sight around the corner.

'Oh, God!' she said, pushing away his hands and fumbling to do up her bra, not half as deft as he at conquering the small clip through the masking material.

'I bet he got an eyeful!' said Drake, with a hint of malicious gratification.

'Did you know he was going to be coming this way?' she paused in her pink-cheeked struggles to ask suspiciously.

'The valley road turn-off is a few kilometres further on, but I didn't plan this, if that's what you're thinking.'

'I wouldn't put it past you.' She frowned.

'Well, I didn't. Which is not to say I'm not pleased he saw us.' He met her glower with a mocking shrug. 'It's a guy thing… Here, let me help you with that…' He put his warm hands up under her tee shirt and boldly drew the cups of her bra together, his fingers brushing her taut nipples a little too often for it to be accidental as he eased the lacy fabric into place around her breasts and neatly snapped the clip into place. 'There,' he said thickly, adjusting her breasts for one final time in their snug cocoon, his hands reluctantly trickling away down her quivering tummy. 'Maybe we should take this into the back seat,' he murmured, watching her black pupils expand even further into the silver irises.

She cast a guilty look behind them, struggling to find a reason to resist his alluring suggestion. 'Prince is there,' she remembered with a relieved gasp, prompting the dog to lift his head at the sound of his name and loose an ear-splitting 'woof'.

'There's plenty of room. He can scrunch up, or hop into the front seat and watch...'

'I don't think so,' she began repressively. Her honey skin became even more flushed under his sultry gaze as she realised he was only teasing. He had never meant her to take his suggestion seriously. She tried to hide her chagrin by adding smoothly, 'He might be traumatised for life.'

'*I* might be traumatised if we don't,' muttered Drake, rolling his hips and tugging at the denim to ease the constricted front of his jeans. To her embarrassment Kate realised that he hadn't even undone his seat belt...she was the one who had been doing all the writhing and squirming.

'I should have remembered you don't like making love where there's any chance of being caught *in flagrante*,' he continued to needle, 'but I thought you said you wanted something different. Now I see you're all talk and no action.' He switched on the engine and put his hand on the automatic gear-shift, shifting it out of park in preparation to pull back out onto the road.

Trust him to reduce her demand to the lowest common denominator—sex. Two could play at that game!

Kate stopped fishing under her bottom for the end of her seat belt and grabbed the collar of his shirt, jerking his head down and around so that she could stretch over and plant a deep, soulful kiss on his unsuspecting lips, using her tongue to glide her way into the slippery recesses of his hot mouth.

At the same time, she ran her flat hand firmly down the front of his shirt to the buckle of his jeans. She felt the tension in his stomach and knew he thought she was going to keep on sliding her hand down until it cupped the bulging denim pushing out the zip. Instead she increased the pressure on her hand and thrust it between the denim band and loose hang of his shirt, reaching into the tight space between jeans and skin at the apex of his strong thighs. She felt an electrifying jolt go through his entire body, his shocked jaw sagging open to her exploring mouth as she fanned her fingers out over the silky distension in his briefs, tracing the rigid tip of his erection, feeling it pulse against her circling thumb.

He groaned, his hips lifting, the lunging twist of his chest towards her engaging the locking mechanism of his seat belt, trapping him at the mercy of her exploring touch. He was about to wrench himself free when she cruelly broke off the kiss.

'What I want different is for *me* to dictate the choices,' she purred. 'And what I choose now is to go home and have a cheese and pickle sandwich for lunch, so—carry on, driver!' And with one last, wicked little tease of his straining manhood she was withdrawing her hand from his pants when another car tooted past, briefly slowing as it drew alongside, this time a big, sturdy, dust-laden four-wheel drive with the personalised number-plate VET KEN.

When Drake had finished cursing a blue streak at her actions he looked over at Kate, buckled into her seat belt and sitting primly upright looking serenely ahead, her hands folded in her lap.

'You're as red as a poppy,' he discovered.

She could imagine. She could imagine far too much, that was her trouble, she thought, smoothing her hair nervously behind her ear.

'His seat was so high up...do you think he could see what I was doing?' she couldn't help asking.

Drake laughed so hard that Kate refused to speak to him all the way back to Oyster Beach, but it was hard to act cool and dignified when you had been spied with your hand down a man's pants! It didn't seem fair that her foolish attempt at revenge had rebounded so embarrassingly on herself. Or that she had found it so unexpectedly arousing to toy with Drake in that scandalous way on the open roadside. If Kate was hauled up on a charge of public indecency her mother would have fifty fits—and probably recommend hard time in the slammer!

Even Prince seemed to be having a sly laugh at her expense as he punctuated Drake's continuing chuckles with an occasional wuffle, and he added insult to injury when he leapt out of the car at the other end and raced around as if he'd just undergone a day at a leisure spa rather than prompted a mercy dash to the clinic to save his life.

Kate apologised stiffly to Drake for the disruption to his day. 'I hope I haven't put you and Melissa too far behind in your schedule by dragging you away from your writing for so long,' she said, and beat a hasty retreat as his lingering smirk turned to a moody frown.

It wasn't until she'd forced down a cheese and pickle sandwich in order not to make even more of a liar of herself that she remembered the scallops she had left in the front seat of her car.

She went to fetch them and stowed them on the bottom shelf of the fridge. Then, worried they might have already gone off by sitting for more than an hour in the hot sun, she took them out to put them to the sniff test. They seemed fine, but to risk eating spoiled seafood was foolish when any toxic reaction had the potential to hurt her baby. Anyway, she had gone off the idea of a dinner party, she thought as she wrapped the scallops in news-paper and placed them in the rubbish bin outside the kitchen door.

So she was stunned when, later that afternoon, Drake knocked at her door and asked her over for dinner, hastening to add that he wasn't doing the cooking.

'Melissa's going to do scallops—she always insists on doing the cooking when she's here; it's the only way she claims she can get a decent meal,' he said, unknowingly rubbing salt in her wounds.

'I don't think I—'

'It's in the nature of a farewell dinner. Melissa goes back home tomorrow.' The casualness of his words were belied by the sensuous awareness in his eyes. Tomorrow one source of upheaval between them would be gone. Melissa would go back to her husband and Drake would…what? Retreat? Or advance?

'She'd really like you to come,' he said, strolling

back to the verandah steps and turning to say, 'And so would I.'

'The two women in your life at the same table?' she said drily, following him out.

'I quail,' he admitted, but with a slight smile that was infinitely reassuring.

So much so that Kate decided to take the gamble: 'Or are there perhaps a few other women in your life that we should invite, to forestall any future confusion about who fits exactly where?'

'Well, there's always your mother,' he replied lightly. 'You could say she fits around the fringe of my life—by way of producing you.'

He and her mother had only met a few times when their paths had crossed socially, and to Kate's secret relief they had cordially disliked each other. Drake didn't like the way that her mother tried to dominate him with her relentless, battering logic, the way that she had hectored Kate as a child and still continued to denigrate her hopes and dreams as an adult, and Jane Crawford had hated that she couldn't influence his opinions or command his attention and respect and thus prove her superiority over the male sex. As a consequence she had been contemptuous of Drake's success, expressing cold disappointment that Kate should let her silly public infatuation for a 'chain-store novelist' destroy any hopes of her being taken seriously as a career woman.

But if Drake had been the kind of man to kowtow to her mother, Kate wouldn't have fallen in love with him.

'No, thanks.' She used the mocking offer as the springboard for her retaliation. 'But I am sorry that I'll never get the same chance of inviting the woman who produced *you* to dinner,' she said, just as lightly. 'That might have been interesting.'

His mouth twisted. 'No,' he said tightly, 'it wouldn't.'

'Of course not,' she sighed, half turning away to watch a dinghy being rowed out to one of the moored motor yachts.

'Because she only had one topic of conversation.'

'And what was that?' she asked carelessly, looking back at him, still expecting to be greeted by one of his usual witty evasions.

'Her husband. He was everything in the world to her, quite literally. Even though he dumped her for another woman when I was six—walked out, divorced her, moved overseas to remarry and never contacted her again—she still clung to the fantasy that he was going to come back. She loved him therefore he must love her, and when the truth began to seep through the cracks of her obsession she blotted it out with drugs. She committed suicide when I was a teenager, not because she wanted to die, but because, according to the twisted reasoning in her note, she was proving to *him* how much she loved him, by showing that she couldn't live without him…'

It was a shock to hear the ugly story laid out so casually on a sunlit step. His almost clinical detachment made it sound as if he were discussing a plot in one of his books, but the underlying bleakness in his voice exposed it for the painful truth. No wonder he didn't like to talk about his childhood.

'I'm sorry,' Kate said, carefully reining in her sympathy. She looked out at the yacht, rocking now as the dinghy tied up alongside, fighting down her desire to pepper him with questions, trying to act as if his personal revelations were an everyday occurrence. 'I had no idea.'

'Few do…fortunately I'd legally changed my name as soon as I was old enough, so my past stops there. The press find PR rumours more interesting anyway; no one cares about tracing some kid called Richardson.' He shrugged, following her gaze to the activities of the oarsman in his bright orange life-jacket. 'You know what the real kicker was?' he murmured, after a moment.

She remained silent, afraid of stemming the dark tide of words.

'When her husband left her, my mother thought that she could use me to keep him tied to her for ever. But instead he simply cut his losses, and immediately had another son, to replace the one he'd left behind. While my mother was telling me to set a place for Daddy every night, he was creating a whole, shiny new family for himself in Australia—two boys and a girl. So when he finally found out his crazy ex-wife had killed herself he wasn't interested in being foisted with the product of her tainted love. And since there was no one else to claim me, I went into the foster-care system…'

'Her husband'… She noticed how he never said 'my father'—and Kate couldn't blame him. Since her parents had separated even before she was born she had not been a witness to any emotional carnage. At least she and her genial, happy-go-lucky father had had some contact with each other over the years— mostly letters exchanged behind her mother's disapproving back, and the occasional visit to the islands when she had been old enough to afford to pay, since Barry Crawford was chronically short of money and could rarely be bothered to bestir himself from beneath his beloved palm trees. Her father hadn't wanted the rights or responsibility of custodial parenthood, but he hadn't ignored her whole existence!

She darted a look at the chiselled perfection of Drake's profile, her heart aching for him, and for her baby. No longer did it surprise her that Drake had always been so bitterly opposed to having a family. In his experience love and marriage were associated with obsession and abandonment, with children merely pawns or weapons in their parents' hands.

He turned his head, capturing her sideways glance, and raised a quizzical eyebrow.

'Shall we say six o'clock for dinner?'

'Yes, all right,' she murmured, taken off guard by the sudden switch from the momentous to the mundane.

'We keep country hours here in Oyster Beach,' he said, and strolled away while she was still grappling with her new perspective on his life.

Had that little bout of unaccustomed openness been a bribe or an enticement? she wondered as she watched him go. A warning or an invitation? Either way he must know he had her hooked.

She approached his house that evening with some trepidation, but, to her surprise, Kate enjoyed the dinner, and the company. After some slight initial stiltedness the atmosphere had relaxed as the conversation had inevitably turned to books and become wide-ranging and general. Drake looked askance at her when she refused a glass of wine, but he readily accepted the excuse of her illness earlier in the day, and when her offer to help Melissa in the kitchen was snapped up he seemed bemused.

'I didn't know you could cook,' he said as she expertly whisked up a sauce for the vegetables.

'You never asked.' He knew damned well that he had been careful to steer well clear of cosy, domestic settings. They had always dined out or at his hotel when they were together. 'Actually, I'm a superb cook.'

She was slightly smug when she saw that Melissa had taken the easy way and crumbed the scallops but the meal was delicious and her compliments sincere.

By the time she wended her way back home under a star-pricked sky she was well pleased with her performance. She had played it low-key with Drake and not made any attempt at intimacy, conspiring tacitly with Melissa to keep the conversation away from the personal and firmly focused on more entertaining issues.

After dinner, instead of sophisticated banter they had engaged in an argumentative game of Scrabble in which Kate had been ignominiously crushed by the two fiercely competitive professionals. However, a round of

Trivial Pursuit had given her the chance to trounce them both and restored her buckled self-esteem.

The perfect ending to a slightly traumatic and wholly enlightening day.

CHAPTER SEVEN

THE next week was a curious mixture of good and bad. For two days after Melissa left Kate didn't see hide nor hair of Drake, but she did see a great deal of his hairy companion.

'What's the matter, Prince, is he ignoring you, too?' she asked on the third morning, putting down a plastic bowl with the meagre trimmings of the meat she had cooked the previous night, mixed with some boiled rice.

After finding the light rubbish bin outside the kitchen door tipped over and the scallops chewed out of their newspaper wrapping and left scattered on the grass, she had roundly scolded the dog, who had managed to look so downcast at being accused of the crime that she had relented and started feeding him more substantial snacks.

If Drake objected to her suborning his dog he could come over and complain about it but, as he had pointed out, Prince was a shameless scavenger and was probably fed by locals up and down the beach.

Since she had always lived in places with restrictions on owning animals Kate had never had a furred pet, but she was determined her child would have more than a goldfish to cuddle and love. Not an energy-sucking giant like Prince, but something suitable for a small yard. Trained to be careful with money, Kate had saved up more than enough for a deposit on an older do-up in one of the outer suburbs, or a town house with a back garden in one of the newer intensive-housing developments. She knew she couldn't expect emotional or financial support from her mother, and she still had no idea what to expect from Drake. Things might be tough for a while if she had to go it alone, but she would cope.

'You should tell your owner that all work and no play makes Drake a very dull boy,' she suggested to Prince as he wolfed down the food in two bites and overturned the bowl to make sure he hadn't missed anything.

She wondered if she had made a mistake in thinking that Drake's confidences of the other day might herald a promising new phase in their relationship.

'But dull is relative, I suppose,' she told the dog.

No doubt Drake was deeply engaged in some death-defying heroics via his latest alter-ego. His thrillers weren't written as a series linked by the same central characters, as many other, highly successful thriller-writers chose to do. Drake rebuilt his world from the ground up with every book. Each featured a new cast, new country, new conflict…and a new girlfriend to betray the hero, or to be kidnapped, tortured, murdered or otherwise threatened in an attempt to subvert his desperate cause. Innocence was no defence in Drake Daniels' novels. It always seemed to presage disaster for the woman when any of Drake's cynical heroes began developing tender feelings towards her, and making plans for the future.

The way he dumps his girlfriends in real life when they start getting too close, and demanding too much of his attention, she mused.

'Perhaps I'm better off with him being wary and suspicious,' she said to Prince. 'Do you think I should just tell him about being pregnant and brazen it out, or lead up to it gradually and risk him accusing me of trying to trick him?'

Prince thought she should wear a plastic bowl on her head and roll around on the grass, and then dash down to the beach and dig holes.

Kate declined, but she did allow him to tag along when she went for her afternoon walk, and on the way back around the flat, rocky point she met Drake coming towards her.

'So this is where you are!' he declared, halting. He was wearing faded khaki hiking shorts and a Hawaiian shirt hanging open over his tanned chest, the sheen of perspiration on his skin indicating that he had been walking briskly.

'Are you talking to the dog, or to me?' said Kate, looking up at him from the shade of her straw hat. 'I thought you were busy working.'

'I've been working since six a.m. I'm taking a

short break.' He picked up a stick of driftwood and threw it towards the sea. Prince sat and watched it arc over and hit the wet sand just in front of the waves, then trotted over and gummed it up, delivering it back to Drake with an air of patient long-suffering that made Kate snicker.

'I've never seen a dog be sarcastic before. I didn't ask him to come, you know, he just followed me,' she said, warmed by the thought that he had missed either of them.

Drake turned and fell in beside her as she picked her way through the scattered stones. 'You don't "ask" Prince to do anything, he'll do just what he damned well pleases—how do you think he got his name?'

She knew from the offhand warmth in his tone that 'Prince' was a term of affection, not derision.

'I thought it was because of his regal bearing,' she said, as Prince 'wuffed' into a pile of rotting seaweed, his three legs scrabbling madly as he skated on the slimy mass.

Drake laughed. 'You wouldn't believe it now but he can actually look almost respectable when that coat has just been groomed. The problem is, it only lasts five minutes—until he can find the nearest pile of dirt.'

'That's because he doesn't want to be respectable, he wants to have fun.'

'Don't we all?' said Drake with a silky nuance, sliding his hand down his bare chest in a way that reminded her of that day in the car. Her temperature shot up and she failed to look where she was going.

'Careful!' Drake caught her elbow as her sneak-ered foot skidded into a rock pool.

'Oh!' Kate lifted her dripping foot and then looked into a pool. 'Oh, look—hermit crabs.' Her sundress fluttered around her knees as she crouched down for a closer look at the tiny creatures, humping their houses on their backs. 'They remind me of you,' she teased, testing one with her finger and watching him retreat back into the depths of the spiral shell.

'Clever, adaptive survivalists?'

'Hard-shelled and soft-centred.'

'You think I'm soft-centred?' He sounded as if he didn't know whether to be amused or appalled, his hand remaining on her elbow as he tugged her back to her feet to resume their walking.

'You must be, or you wouldn't need such a hard shell,' she teased. 'Well, semi-soft, anyway,' she amended to hide the shock as she realised the stunning truth of her words. As cynical and tough as he made himself out to be, at his core Drake felt himself vul-nerable; that was why he erected so many defences.

'Actually, at the moment, I'd class myself as semi-hard,' he said, pointedly looking at the sway of her breasts against the low-cut dress.

'Drake!' She looked furtively around the beach, resisting the urge to place her hands across her chest like a Victorian maiden.

'Oh, look, cat's eyes!' He diverted her from her confusion, stooping to pick one of the convex shells up from a shallow pool, holding it for her to see the iridescent trapdoor at the bottom pulling into place, before gently putting it back in the water. 'It reminds me of you,' he mimicked her teasing tone.

She wrinkled her nose. 'Great, I'm like a sea-snail.'

'Beautiful and functional, what more can you ask?'

'I'm not beautiful,' she denied. 'Not like my mother.'

'No, thank God—she's like a perfect line drawing, sharp and flat, whereas you're like a watercolour—delicate and subtle, yet vibrant with colour and life, with deeper shades of meaning than appear at first glance.'

'You are quick with your similes this afternoon,' she said, trying to prick the dangerous bubble of joy that threatened her determinedly casual façade. 'Does that mean you're still working? I hope you brought your notebook with you.' She tilted her head back to see and laughed, because—sure enough—there was a tell-tale rectangle outlined in the back pocket of his shorts.

His fingers intertwined with hers, giving them a faint punishing squeeze.

'You don't like being compared to your mother, do you?'

'We're all a product of our parents; I suppose we can't avoid it,' said Kate, her voice softening as she thought of their baby. Was this the moment to broach the subject?

'But, as Shakespeare said, "comparisons are odorous"—'

'I thought they were odious.' Kate was pleased to have caught him out, still smarting from her drubbing at Scrabble.

'That was John Donne, not Shakespeare,' he topped her for smugness. 'He actually said: "She, and comparisons are odious", which sums up your mother even better!'

'For someone who's dyslexic, you sure read a lot,' she complained, unoffended. She remembered an interview where he'd said that, when working way out in the boonies, reading had been one of the few forms of safe entertainment, the only other options for a bunch of misfit males thrown together for the duration of a dirty job being drinking, gambling and fighting. He'd seen a few men die from their choice of amusement.

He grinned. 'I cheat. I have a book of quotations lying on my desk. Some of my heroes have fought some very erudite villains,' he informed her.

Kate laughed and he continued, after a slight pause, to say offhandedly: 'I never had any help with my dyslexia as a kid—we moved around too much, and after the drug-taking started my mother never bothered whether I was at school. But when I was older I found out for myself how to get around the barriers, and I read whatever and wherever I could.'

'Is your dyslexia inherited from your mother or your father?' she asked without thinking.

There was only a brief falter in his stride. 'I have no idea.'

'I'm sorry; I didn't mean to pry,' she said, feeling the mental shutters start to come down.

'I don't remember being read to as a child, if that means anything,' he said abruptly. 'But there were plenty of other explanations for that—my mother always scurrying around, frantically making sure we had everything *just so* for her husband, so that he wouldn't lose his temper when he got home, tired out from work and found that everything wasn't perfect—or, rather, he was tired out from his *mistress* as my mother found out on the day he left—' He came to a dead stop in the sand, stiffening, and Kate thought he was angry at having said more than he had meant to and was about to storm off, but then she saw he was watching Prince, who had rushed into the chilly sea to snap at the small rush of waves generated by the wake of a passing launch, and was now heading back towards them at a rolling clip.

'No, Prince—!' he ordered sternly, dropping her hand and stepping forward as the floppy ears started to rotate, but it was too late and the dog's whole body went into violent convulsions, the shaggy wool letting fly a hail of cold sea water mixed with gritty sand that made Kate shriek.

'Damn dog!' cursed Drake, mopping down his spattered chest with the corner of his shirt.

'He was only doing what comes naturally.' Prince's inherent instability had toppled him backwards into a heap on the sand and Kate started forward to help him up. 'Oh, you poor—'

Drake flung up a barring arm. 'Don't—you'll hurt his pride,' and they watched the dog roll over and bounce up as if falling over had been his intention all along.

Kate looked at him wryly. 'Don't tell me—it's a

guy thing!' She brushed at the grainy wet spots on her dress and took off her hat to shake it out.

'You look as if you have freckles,' said Drake, running his thumb across her bare collar-bone, smearing a row of dots. He bent and put his mouth where his thumb had been, his tongue dipping into the sensitive crease between her collar-bone and slender throat. 'Mmm, you taste much saltier than usual.'

'What are you doing?' Kate shivered, pushing his head away, his dark hair silking against her palm.

'Trying to help you clean up,' he said innocently, his eyes anything but innocent. 'Why don't you come up to the house and I'll dry you off properly?'

She had been so absorbed in their conversation she hadn't realised that they had walked all the way back.

'Thank you, but I have a perfectly adequate towel at my place,' she said, clutching her hat to her breasts.

The sultry look in his eyes kindled into wicked amusement. 'I wasn't thinking of using a towel.'

She gave him a haughty look. 'I know, and, as I said, I can look after myself. You need to get back to work and I—I—have things to do.' He had said he was taking a short break and she didn't want to give him any further excuse to accuse her of being disruptive to his writing routine. She knew from his own description of his methods that he worked in sustained bursts of intense concentration. It was important that he know *she* knew the difference between her presence being distracting and being destructive. Then he might even start to see that she could be a positive, supportive element in his working life...

'What things?' Strong legs planted in the sand, arms akimbo, bright shirt flaring around his gorgeous bare torso, he was an almost irresistible temptation. She firmly beat it down. For all she knew, this seductive teasing might merely be a test on his part, to see how much of his attention she intended to demand.

'Just…things. *Female* things,' she added cunningly—words to make most men blanch and run.

He didn't budge, his eyes on her hands, nervously scrunching her hat. 'Are you *afraid* of me, Kate?' he murmured, half curious, half taunting.

She decided on the truth. 'Yes,' she said, shaking her hair back behind her ears and replacing her slightly crumpled hat, like a warrior putting on a defensive helmet. 'I don't *know* you—'

He was *en garde* even before she had fully unsheathed her words. 'You know me well enough to make love to,' he pointed out.

'I—it's different here…*you're* different,' she said, trying to marshal all the things she wanted to say in the right order.

'I thought you said you wanted something "different",' he said sarcastically. 'Have you changed your mind again?'

'Yes, I mean no—'

His patience snapped. 'Well, when you *do* decide to make up your mind, let me know!'

This time he did stump off, and she thought he might disappear into himself again for another few days, but to her surprise and subdued delight, the next afternoon when she went walking at roughly the same time he appeared again, and the next...each time a little earlier in her walk until by the end of the week they were setting off together.

Walking and talking was certainly much more productive than sitting and talking, the relaxed surroundings and lack of watchful eyes making Kate realise how proscribed their lives had become in the city.

Most of their talk was idle and unthreatening, but inevitably they touched on weightier subjects and Kate began to amass more pieces of the puzzle that made up Drake Daniels. Like the fact that when he had shed the name of Richardson he had also sloughed off his Christian name, Michael, and had deliberately chosen a name that had no connection with either his father or his mother—one that was sufficiently different to satisfy his hunger to be unique, to be more than the nobody his parents had reduced him to by their destructive indifference.

Drake had been a defiantly swashbuckling name to his younger self, he admitted wryly, and Daniels had been the name of the only adult whom he had respected, a high-school English teacher who had seen a special spark in the troubled youth that no one else had bothered to nurture, and whom he had attempted to encourage, challenge and inspire in the short time that they had shared a classroom, advising him to travel as far and widely as he could to expand his human experience for his future writings.

They occasionally met other people on their strolls, who either casually greeted Drake by name or failed to recognise him at all, and Kate learned that the ebb and flow of tourists at Oyster Beach dictated his puzzling annual schedule—summers for travel and research and roughly drafting out ideas, the rest of the year fitting in periods of intensive writing at Oyster Beach in a way that avoided both school and public holiday breaks.

One afternoon at low tide, after they had walked in the other direction to the mouth of the tidal estuary, they came across three shrieking little boys digging trenches in the wet sand near the waterline.

'They don't look old enough to be out here on their own,' said Kate, estimating them to be no more than five, one of them a toddler still in nappies. She glanced up at Drake, who was staring broodingly at the sandy trio. 'And don't tell me things are done differently here in the country.'

'I wasn't going to.' He was scanning the straggle of houses tucked into the trees behind the low dunes and then out to sea. 'Ah…' He pointed to a lone female figure lying up in the dunes, nestled into a hollow by a log, protecting the pages of her book against the ruffle of the light breeze.

'I hope she's paying more attention to the children than she is to her book,' worried Kate. 'Young children can drown very quickly in only a few centimetres of water.'

She went over to talk to the trio about their endeavours and felt better when she saw the woman instantly put her book aside and sit up, responding to a reassuring wave by relaxing back on her elbows, but not resuming her reading until Kate moved away, hurrying to join the man who had dawdled on ahead.

'Can't be one of my books—or she wouldn't have been able to put it down so easily,' jibed Drake as Kate fell into step beside him.

'Why didn't you come down and say hello? They would have liked a man to admire their work.'

'No, thanks. I told you, kids aren't my thing. Why do you think I always come back to town during school holidays?'

'I thought it was to avoid all their parents. It's not as if the little ones know or care that you're the great Drake Daniels. They're completely unpretentious. That toddler was so cute the way he tried to copy his brothers—'

'A total pain in the neck, if you ask me,' he said tersely.

'How can you say that?'

'Drop it, Kate,' he ordered, but then he was the one unable to leave it alone. 'Since when were you so keen on ankle-biters, anyway? I thought you agreed with me that they don't fit in with a career-orientated lifestyle.'

'But lifestyles don't always stay the same throughout people's lives,' she argued. 'They're constantly being modified by changing circumstances, like having children...'

'If people *want* to change. Some people should never have children,' he said flatly. 'Especially when they don't have the time or inclination to care for them, or because social pressures and vanity or self-interest— or simply pure carelessness—come into play.'

Kate's heart staggered. 'At that rate neither of us would have been born,' she said, desperately trying to put a positive spin on his words, 'and think what the world would have missed...'

He didn't respond to the opportunity to use his usual amusing wit. 'And think of all those parents who buy into the perfect baby fantasy and then find the day-to-day reality turns them into abusive monsters!' he grated. 'Call me a heartless bastard, but I don't ever want to add any kids to the list of my mistakes.'

No, not heartless—but maybe one who cared too much, thought Kate shakily. In spite of what he said, she didn't believe it was solely a matter of preserving his highly enjoyable lifestyle. Drake seemed convinced that he would not be a good parent. He was an intelligent man—he must know that he wasn't doomed to perpetuating his parents' weaknesses and failures, yet it appeared that he wasn't prepared to put himself to the touch.

Kate had far more trust in him than he did in himself. She knew that, whatever happened, he would never punish an innocent child for an adult's mistakes. Although cynicism ran strongly through his books, they were essentially heroic stories of men who found personal redemption in a worthy cause. She only hoped that Drake would find it worth redeeming himself for the sake of his own child.

She could have let herself be depressed by his vow to eternally shun fatherhood, but by the end of the stroll her natural resilience had reasserted itself, boosted by Drake's relentless flirting. Because she had fallen eagerly into bed with him the first time they had met, she realised that she had missed out on the seductive excitement that she was now experiencing as with a look, a word or a touch Drake attempted to evoke reminders of the powerful physical attraction that existed between them. She had deprived herself of the delicious torment of the should she/shouldn't she nervousness and the romantic thrill of the chase the first time around, so why shouldn't she enjoy it to the full in the precious little time she had left?

Her only previous serious relationship had been with a newly qualified lawyer who had sought her out at a party just after her nineteenth birthday, and laid gentle siege to her reserve. Brett had been flatteringly devoted for long enough to make her start to wonder if they might get engaged, but when she had finally been persuaded to reluctantly introduce him to her mother he had been off like a shot, resurfacing a few weeks later as one of Jane Crawford's new crop of hotshot legal protégés.

At the time she had thought Brett the height of romance, but he had never made her bones melt and her flesh quicken, as Drake could do with a single, smouldering look.

It was slightly disconcerting to discover in herself a streak of cruelty that took pleasure in his frustration as she continued to keep him at arm's length.

When he offhandedly suggested on their Friday walk that Kate might like to come to the planned pool game that evening after all, he clearly expected her to be instantly charmed by the idea.

'Will the others be bringing women, too?'

'Not that I know of—what's that got to do with it?'

She lowered her eyelashes demurely. 'Well, I wouldn't want to start a fight.'

He snorted.

'I thought I was supposed to stay away from Steve Marlow in case he dragged me into a life of degradation and crime.'

'Maybe I over-stated the case a bit,' he admitted.

'Are you going to win?'

His diffidence disappeared. 'Of course! They're rank amateurs—they just like to think they're hustlers!' he said, oozing male hubris.

'And you want me along to provide the applause for your victory?' she teased, touched by the notion that he wanted her to see him as the conquering hero. Or maybe he just wanted to prove to them both that he wasn't jealous. 'Do I get to pin my favour to your sleeve?'

'Not unless you want me to get beaten up. It's a pub not a jousting ring.'

'Will I be able to play…since you told Steve Marlow that I couldn't? Or will I have to stand around holding your beer?'

'*Can* you play?' he asked, looking so surprised she was tempted to lie simply for the pleasure of seeing his face.

'No, but I can learn.'

He looked vaguely hunted. Obviously his impulsive invitation was becoming more complicated than he had planned.

'Or if you think you might need help, I could just

wear something short and low-cut and lean on the table whenever the others line up their shots,' she offered sweetly.

His eyes creased as he imagined the graceful Kate Crawford vamping it up as the local pub tart. 'Or you could just wear nothing at all and we'll forget about going to play pool,' he murmured with a wicked grin.

He grinned again when he saw the prim white shirt and blue trousers she put on to go to the pub, her white sandals showing off small feet with innocently unpainted toenails. 'That's my girl,' he chuckled.

Am I? Kate wanted to say. *Am I really?*

It was a rowdy night unlike any she had ever spent and she really enjoyed it once she had stopped being polite and simply shouted like everyone else, to be heard over the local band rocking the rafters and the bawling exchanges, catcalls and shouts of laughter. There were lots of jeans and flip-flops and more men than women, but the atmosphere was buzzing and Kate quickly discovered that a locally made, no-alcohol spiced beer was the choice of brew for designated drivers and wowsers alike, for very good reason.

She was on her second delicious glass when Ken and Steve arrived—minus partners but hugely amused to see Kate tucked up to Drake's side—and they all listened to a few songs from the band while waiting for the pool table they had booked to become free. Although there were a few grins and knowing hails from the crowd, mostly aimed at Steve, it was all very laid-back, and there were no intrusive approaches or fuss about the fame in their midst. Everyone was just there to enjoy themselves at full volume. It was a little quieter in the back room of the pub where the pool tables were, but that changed when Steve kept feeding coins into the jukebox in the corner, ordering Kate to pick the songs most guaranteed to annoy Drake. So she chose dreamy, romantic ballads punctuated with the occasional head-banger to appease the good-natured groans from around the room.

In spite of Drake's earlier boasts, his two friends made him work for his wins—mainly because they kept ganging up to ruin his concentration when he was playing one or other of them. Remembering her comments about leaning on the table, Kate enjoyed looking at the provocative pull of Drake's faded jeans as they stretched across his tautly muscled backside when he bent to use his cue, and when he had a difficult shot facing her she made sure he knew she was staring down the open neck of his shirt, her own fingers playing suggestively in the V of her collar. However, he got his own back when chalking the tip of his cue, and she hurriedly primmed her mouth and pretended not to understand his sensual stroking and the deliberation with which he held her eyes while he gently blew off the excess chalk.

In the interests of fair play, Kate declared herself strictly neutral in the cheerfully insulting male byplay over the game and ferried cardboard tubs of hot chips and battered fish, jugs of beer and bottles of soft drinks to the protagonists, fascinated by the easy camaraderie between the three men, despite the fact that, as Steve pointed out, they were rarely all in the area at the same time. She enjoyed watching the differences in their play and chatting with each as they sat out games, but finally the series came down to a single match between Steve and Drake, while Ken kept up a hushed commentary that had Kate in fits of laughter.

Her sides were still aching when they drove back through the black, shadowy hills to the beach. Drake turned on the CD player and Kate was content to lie back and dream impossible dreams to the caress of some moody blues and the humming vibration of the Land Rover's engine.

Wrapped in a sensuous cloud of happy imaginings she was almost dozing when Drake murmured that they were home, and insisted on walking with her to her door.

'Enjoy yourself?'

'You know I did. I like your friends.'

'I noticed,' he said, but without any heat. 'They liked you, too.'

She sighed with a strange contentment. 'Steve said the three of you don't get together very often any more,' she said, unlocking the front door. A lot of Oyster Beach people didn't bother to lock their doors, at least in the off-season, she had been told, but Kate's cautionary habits were too deeply ingrained.

'No, but when we do it's always as if we only saw each other yesterday. The group dynamics are such we can just pick up where we left off. Some friendships are like that.'

'That's what we do, too, isn't it? Pick up where

we left off,' she said, turning in the doorway. But not any more, she thought wistfully.

'Aren't you going to ask me in?' he suggested softly as she switched on the light and blinked at him like an owl, her silver eyes still hazed with dreams. 'Offer me a nightcap?'

'I don't have any alcohol in the house,' she said, hypnotised by his slow smile.

'A coffee, then.' He reached out and stroked her hair behind her ear, his thumb briefly brushing the lobe. 'Isn't that the way the two of us usually end a night out?'

No. They usually ended it in bed, making love. Her eyes dilated with betraying speed, her pink lips parting, her breasts rising and falling against the white cotton shirt.

'Coffee keeps me awake,' she croaked.

'That's good. Awake is good,' he murmured, slowly lowering his head, his thighs bumping against hers as he shuffled her back against the wooden panels of the open door. 'I wouldn't like you to be asleep when I did this…'

His kiss was warm, soft, sweet and sensuous…a delicate tasting of her resistance, with no aggression to trigger her alarm, just a gentle teasing of her lips, a whisper-soft stroke of his firm, velvety mouth.

It was so sweet and so soft it left her wanting, and as he began to draw back her arms slid around his waist and folded across his strong back, holding him secure while she went on tiptoe to try and increase the pressure against her yearning mouth.

He didn't make the mistake of swooping inside with his tongue, instead he withheld himself, luring her to seek her own pleasure and move ever deeper into danger.

His legs shifted, his knee bending as his denim thigh eased between hers, rising up to fit snugly into the notch of her body, his hands on her hips tilting her pelvis into the cradle of his and then stroking around to trace the outline of her panties through the thin fabric of her silk trousers. When he began to softly knead the rounded cheeks of her bottom, moving her rhythmically against the rigid muscles of his thigh, she uttered a tiny, shivery cry that broke on the still night.

'Ask me inside...take me to your bed,' he whispered, sipping the cry from her bee-stung lips. A clever glide of his fingers slipped a few of the pearl buttons on her shirt and she felt the delicate swirl of his fingertips on the silky swell of her tightening breast. 'You know you want to, Kate. You won't even have to ask, you just have to want me...I'm yours for the taking...all of me is yours...' He moved his hips in a slow rotation that rubbed the thick bulge between his legs against her feminine mound, teasing her with the memory of the turbulent ecstasy his heat and hardness could provide.

For a moment they both thought the faint squeak was her whimper of surrender, but then Kate groaned and turned her cheek to the door, her arms dropping away. She could feel Drake's rigid body drawn so tight it was trembling, then he uttered a harsh sound and let his forehead rap on the door behind her averted head, leaning it there while he said thickly:

'I can't take much more of this. I thought we were lovers, Kate. What's happening? Why can't we make love?' He lifted his head, temper seeking a safer outlet. 'And what the hell is that infernal noise?'

Now the enchanted spell was well and truly broken. 'A rat, I think,' she said. 'I told you about it, remember.'

'You've told me so many things…except, apparently, the one thing that really matters.' He pushed himself away from the door, breathing deeply, half turning away to hide the painful state of his body. 'Just tell me this, at least: have you fallen in love with someone else, Kate? Someone who makes it impossible for you to be with me?'

'No!' She fumbled with the buttons on her blouse. 'I— No— There's only ever been you these past two years. Please, just give me a little more time,' she begged.

'You haven't been raped, have you?' he rasped.

'What? *No!*' she said, her eyes rounded in shock. 'You're letting your imagination run away with you.'

'That's what I'm paid for,' he growled. 'You still want what we have, Kate. Stop fighting it. Whatever it is that's bugging you you'd better sort it out soon. Or I will.

'And first thing tomorrow I'm going to sort out that damned rat of yours!'

CHAPTER EIGHT

WHEN Kate walked into the house the next afternoon her heart jumped to find Drake standing barefoot in the middle of her kitchen, looking rumpled and gorgeously surly in the same shirt and jeans he had worn the previous night.

'I thought I locked up when I left; how did you get in?' she said breathlessly, setting down the cardboard box and large plastic bag she was carrying by the leg of the table.

'The rental agent gave me a spare key for emergencies,' he admitted, eyeing her grumpily.

'You mean you could have come in here any time you wanted?' she said faintly, thinking of *1000 Tips For A Healthy Pregnancy,* which she thought she might have left open in the bathroom.

'I could but I haven't— *I* respect people's personal privacy,' he said pointedly, as if reading her mind. 'I haven't been pawing through your secrets. But I told you I'd be over to help you with your pest problem, and when you didn't answer your door I thought something might be wrong…'

'What—like something out of *Curse Of The Rat People*? Did you think I might be lying chewed up on the floor?' she said sceptically, hugging herself with the knowledge that he worried about her in her absence. So it wasn't entirely a case of 'out of sight, out of mind'...

'Besides, you said you'd be here *first thing*. It's now after lunch.' She toned down her sarcasm as she took in his slightly bloodshot eyes, and dissipated expression. 'Are you all right? You don't look so great.' Which was a lie—Drake always looked terrific, whatever his physical state. And she had never known him to be ill. He either had the constitution of an ox or, more likely, he downplayed and concealed his illnesses the way he did the rest of his vulnerabilities.

He ran a hand through his hair and scratched his grainy chin. 'I was up all night writing.' He glared at her with a mixture of accusation and bewilderment. 'I didn't crash out until six a.m. I've only just woken up.'

Oh, so maybe she *had* been out of sight and mind for a while...

'That's not my fault,' she defended herself from his look. 'I didn't order you to go home and write yourself into a coma.'

'No, you just wound me up, pumped me full of adrenalin and kicked me loose. What else did you expect me to do?'

She looked quickly away, smoothing back her hair and composing her face into a cool expression. Not quickly enough, however, for he suddenly chuckled knowingly.

'Why, Kate, is that what *you* did last night? Go to

bed and dream a little wet dream of me?' he taunted. 'What a waste, when the real thing was right there for the asking.'

'But then you wouldn't have got all those pages written,' she told him stoutly, fighting to keep the heat that suffused her body out of her face.

'Maybe I wouldn't have minded the sacrifice,' he said silkily.

'Well, *I* would—I don't want you to *sacrifice* anything for me,' she said with haughty pride. 'People who feel forced to surrender something they value for the sake of someone else generally tend to get bitter and twisted if things don't work out the way they planned. My mother says she sacrificed her valuable time and money to give me a good education, which I've wasted, and she never lets me forget it. So, no, thanks, don't make any grand gestures on my behalf…'

'Wow, I did hit a sore point, didn't I?' he murmured. 'I was only kidding. Once I'm in the grip of writing fever I just have to keep going until it runs its course. It's a very anti-social tendency so it's actually quite useful when inspiration strikes in the middle of the night.'

'I saw a light on up in your office when I got up for a glass of water some time around three,' she confessed, revealing her own somewhat restless night. 'I thought you had probably just forgotten to turn it off.'

He had shown her his office the night of their scallop dinner—a large, book-lined, high-ceilinged room upstairs in the back corner of the house, with folding doors that opened onto a balcony shared with his bedroom, facing directly out to the beach. There was also a window on the other external wall, which overlooked Kate's holiday haven and the north-eastern end of the beach, but it was fitted with reflector glass and motorised tilting shutters, which he usually kept closed. He didn't like to feel claustrophobically shut in when he was working, he said, but he needed the security of walls and at least the illusion of total privacy.

'It's probably still on now. When I get in the zone I don't even think about practicalities like light, heat, food, sleep. I work and drop. It can make me a bit of a bastard the next day, though.'

Crudely, but aptly put. 'Is that an apology?'

'No, an explanation. Which is more than you've given me.' He left her to digest the wider implications of his comment as his eyes fell to the carry-box by her feet, which had begun to shudder and squeak.

'What in the—?' His eyes shot back to her face. 'You caught the rat yourself!' His surprise had a tiny suggestion of chagrin—St George deprived of his dragon.

She smiled wryly. 'Sort of.' She bent down to unfold the handles and reef open the top.

'You're not going to let it go after all that—?' Drake lapsed into silence as he noticed the Vet Clinic's stamp on the flap of the box in the same moment that a ball of furiously squeaking fur bounced out onto the faded floor and resolved itself into a small, glossy black kitten with a white breast and underbelly, and four white paws that immediately scampered into motion.

'A kitten? You went and got *that* little thing from Ken to catch a rat?' said Drake incredulously as he watched the creature skitter around a table leg. 'I hate to tell you this, sweetheart, but you've been suckered—it'll be eaten alive.' The kitten turned in response to the deep rumble of his voice, approaching his bare feet with the little black tail held high, wagging eagerly back and forth, and the squeaking redoubling in volume.

'That *is* my rat,' Kate told him with a rueful look at her night-time nemesis. 'I didn't get it *from* Ken; I took it *to* him.'

It had been a very uncomfortable trip, too, with the kitten squeaking in protest at being cooped up in the semi-dark again, poking a pathetic white paw through the tiny ventilating gap she had created in one of her suitcases by loosely tying the two zip fasteners together.

She watched the black tail start to wag even faster as Drake scooped up the kitten in one big hand, and cupped it level with his face, inspecting the small, triangular face with the yellow eyes and tiny white moustache angled crookedly under a black nose.

'When I opened the door under the house to shine the torch in, she came rushing out, squeaking to beat the band. Ken said she's not as young as she looks— several months at least—but she must have been hiding under the house and coming out at night scavenging for food, and then got trapped under there somehow in the last few days. He says she's lost a little bit of body weight, so he's given me some supplements to add to her food.' She nudged the plastic bag with her sneakered foot.

The kitten suddenly lunged forward and began swiping her piquant little face back and forth against Drake's nose, nuzzling his mouth in between squeaks.

'I think she likes you.' Kate laughed as Drake emerged from the flurry of friendliness spitting strands of black fur and hastily set the kitten back down on the floor to resume her exploration of the kitchen.

'Why can't she miaow like other cats?' he mumbled critically, still picking fur off his tongue. 'You'd have rescued her much sooner if she'd had the decency to behave like a proper feline.'

'I don't know, but I think it's cute,' she said defensively. 'Ken says not all cats vocalise in the same way—he said it could be physiological, or because she hasn't been around other cats who miaow. He said she must have been in good condition when she got trapped under the house or she wouldn't still have fat stores left in her body, so she's either a very good hunter or someone's pet, but no one had been asking about missing kittens.' She smiled as the animal made a daring pounce on a patch of sunlight.

'Ken seems to have said an awful lot,' he remarked, eyes narrowing on her softened face as he crossed his arms across his chest. Her gaze jumped to his. 'So how come *you* still have the cat and not him?' he pressed. 'Didn't you take it to the clinic to hand it in?'

Kate's gaze slid away from his and she busied herself unpacking the plastic bag. 'Well, yes...but Ken gave Koshka a thorough check-over and all the tests, and there's nothing actually wrong with her— the nurse gave her a good brushing and she doesn't even have fleas!' She darted him a triumphant look that was met with lowered brows.

'Koshka? You've given her a name already?'

'It's Russian for cat. Ken was calling her Kitty—I had to give her something prettier than that!' she insisted.

'Oh, yes, he knows all the right triggers.' His voice dripped with sarcasm as he shook his head. 'Don't tell me he persuaded you to adopt it?' he growled. 'What's going to happen when you go home? You're not allowed pets in your town house.'

'I know that. I'm not keeping her—just foster- ing for a few weeks, until I leave, or Ken can find her a home...'

Drake rolled his eyes. 'Where have I heard *that* one before?'

'He said she'd be kept alone in a cage if she stayed at the clinic, whereas here she can prowl and play, and we'll be good company for each other,' she hastened to add.

'You already have company—me. Not to mention my faithful hound.' His mouth took on a malicious curl. 'I guess the problem will be solved soon enough. Koshka won't be more than a single gulp for Prince.'

Kate gasped, and even though she knew he was joking she protectively snatched up her little charge, cuddling the warm, squirming body into the curve of her neck, laughing softly when a raspy tongue began to lap at the side of her jaw. She didn't notice the bloodshot brown eyes darken with a moody bleakness as Drake watched the tender byplay.

'We won't let that big goof get you, will we, Koshka?' she crooned, tickling a white chin and letting small, sharp teeth gnaw at her scratching finger, the wagging tail beating a light tattoo against her breast. 'Mummy will look after you.'

'Foster-mummy,' corrected Drake. 'You'll get attached—how are you going to feel when you have to give her back?'

'I'll cross that bridge when I come to it,' said Kate, letting the cat scamper free to investigate the hall, jogged by his abrupt tone into remembering that he, too, had been fostered. She hoped that after the horror of his mother's suicide, he had passed into loving hands, but the indications were unfortunately otherwise. He obviously had no trust in maternal figures.

'What do you know about caring for a cat?'

'Not much, but I bought a book at the clinic, and I'm sure it's largely a matter of practical common sense. I have plenty of that,' she reminded him.

'She'll shed all over your clothes. You'll hate that. You're very fastidious.'

'I'm not compulsive about it, and cats are fastidious creatures, too—they're always cleaning themselves. Anyway, who cares about a bit of stray fluff when they're on holiday?'

'It'll get on the furniture, too. The landlord might object.'

'She's a short-hair so it shouldn't be too much of a problem, but I did buy one of those sticky rollers from Ken's receptionist just in case,' she admitted.

'Boy, they really saw you coming, didn't they? How many cat toys did you buy?' he said, moving over to peer into the top of the bag.

'A few,' she said, batting away his hands and scrunching it closed to hide the embarrassing profusion of balls, catnip treats and clockwork mice. She gave him a very cool look. 'They're educational.'

'She's a cat; you're not going to turn her into Einstein in a few weeks. She might wag her tail like a dog, but the similarity ends there. You can't train cats the way you can train dogs.'

'You mean *some* dogs. Your dog doesn't seem to be very well trained.'

'Oh, so we're reduced to insulting each other's pets now, are we? Prince is a supreme individualist— he knows what he's supposed to do, he just doesn't want to do it.'

'Like master, like pet,' she told him cattily.

'So, I guess that makes you cute and soft and cuddly, then,' he said, with an insinuating smile. She tossed her head at him and he laughed, banishing the last of the brooding shadows that had hung around him. 'You bristle just like a cat, too. I always thought of you as a cool, sinuous, haughty Siamese and now I'm finding out that you're a cosy little bundle of mixed-breed mischief. You even squeak when you're excited. You know, that little sound you make when you—'

'Oh, go write a novel, why don't you?' Kate said, shoving him towards the door. She had never blushed so much in her life as she had this last week. It had to be the over-excited hormones running riot in her bloodstream, upsetting her normal levels of biological self-containment.

'Thanks, I think I will.' He grinned, his eyes briefly shifting to focus on something in the middle distance, in a familiar sign of mental abstraction.

But just as she was resigned to having been eclipsed by his soaring imagination his gaze focused back on Kate's flustered face, and he hooked her around the waist, arching her lissom body back over his arm for a long, lush, lascivious kiss. He hadn't shaved or showered—he must have staggered straight out of the house from his bed—but Kate loved the sexy scrape of his jaw and the earthy male ripeness exuded by his hard body beneath the rumpled clothes. It made her think of long, sweaty nights of passionate exuberance and torrid delights.

'You said you haven't been with anyone but me since we met,' he murmured, his warm breath feeding into her mouth as he reminded her of the words she had blurted out last night. 'Was that true?'

'Of course it's true,' she sighed, knowing that to deny it now would be a gross self-betrayal. If the truth of her fidelity made him gloat it would at least show him capable at some level of enjoying normal human possessiveness without confusing it with pathological obsession. And if it made him feel nervous or trapped by the implied commitment on her part, then he would just have to deal with it!

'Quite a pair, aren't we?' She felt his smile shape her lips. 'Free to do what we please—and what we do is please each other so well that celibacy becomes an active pleasure when we're apart.' He broke away from her mouth and saluted her stunned brow with a departing kiss. 'I didn't stop looking at other women the night we met, but I certainly stopped wanting them—it's surprising how sexy a stretch of celibacy can be when you know what's waiting for you at the other end, or should I say *who*…?'

Having made his stupendous admission with breath-taking nonchalance, he cruised out the door, careful to close it against escaping felines.

Kate felt winded—and perversely betrayed. Her proud portrayal of serene indifference to all the gossip and rumours about other women had been a wasted effort. Drake *had* been faithful to their relationship despite the no-strings caveat he himself had insisted upon. For months…*years*…she had forced herself to accept his tacit policy of 'don't ask, don't tell' *when there had been nothing for Drake to tell*!

It was typical of Drake to slip her a life-altering revelation about himself under the guise of flippancy, and even more typical of him to disappear afterwards. The characters in his books might be dissected to within an inch of their lives, but in reality Drake preferred his own character armour to remain firmly in place and to dole out psychological insights with miserly reluctance. He knew that knowledge was power and he was very careful not to put the balance of power in any hands but his own. He had just handed a little more over to Kate. He would now pull up the drawbridge until he felt comfortable with what he had done.

She wasn't in the least surprised when she didn't see him for another day, and when he did reappear he made no reference to their previous conversation, dropping back into the safe realm of daily walks, teasing arguments and sexy banter and the occasional shared meal. There was a new physical awareness between them, however, unrelated to sexual tension that was always there in the background, and Kate knew that the next step was hers to take. She was in no hurry to make it, knowing that it could destroy the painstaking trust that they had been slowly building up, and take him away from her for ever. From attempting to seduce her at every turn, Drake was now playing a waiting game and she was slightly chagrined to recognise that she had half wanted him to take the decision out of her hands and use his sexual dominance to *force* her to tell him what he needed to know.

Drake continued to also hold himself aloof from Koshka's eager pursuit of his affections and after a few days of keeping the cat indoors, on Ken's advice, Kate was amused to see Prince as disdainful as his master of this pretender to the throne of her attention.

Koshka, however, wasn't in the least oppressed by her failure to charm, the disparity in their sizes, or the supposed natural enmity between cats and dogs. Tail wagging, she would greet Prince with friendly squeaks whenever he appeared, trotting curiously in his shadow and ignoring his gummy show of yellow teeth when she tried to steal the scraps that fell from his food bowl. When he snored in his favourite shady spot beneath the hedge she would prowl over, batting at a floppy ear or sleepy twitch of the tail, and when he grandly ignored her teasing she would curl up beside him in a sunny spot of grass for a quick catnap before wandering off to find some fresh, feline challenge.

It was Koshka's habit of making sudden, thundering sprints up and down the house for no apparent reason that was the reason for Kate's literal, and figurative, downfall a few days later.

She was carrying her sun-lounger, book and water bottle down the verandah steps when a glossy black ball of lightning shot out of the house behind her and streaked between her feet, tripping her up and pitching her head first down the stairs. Her flailing hand made a frantic grab for the wooden hand-rail, but only her fingernails made painful contact with the splintered paint, throwing her at an angle over the side of the steps. Seeing the rocky garden edge looming up she desperately tried to twist and protectively curl up her body, missing the rocks but landing heavily on top of the metal bar of the sun-lounger, which had hit the ground sideways, unfolding as it fell.

She lay, dazed and breathless in a tangle of bent metal and canvas, the bar that had painfully folded her in two still jammed into her bare abdomen. It took her several attempts to struggle free but she eventually managed to roll over onto her back, weakly pushing away the wreckage of the lounger, wincing at the long scrapes she could feel on her hip, elbow and thigh. Her bikini top had been dislodged and she twisted it back into place, tiny beads of perspiration jumping out on her forehead as she became aware of an ominous, cramping pain low in her belly.

Koshka returned to nuzzle at the shiny pool of hair flared out around her head, and discover the delicious, salty moisture at her temples, and Kate raised her head to escape the gentle rasp of her abrasive tongue, bracing herself on one arm to start pushing herself upright.

Then a big hand was there, cupping her neck, a strong arm supporting her shoulders.

'My God, Kate—that bloody cat! I had the shutters open—I saw the whole thing. You could have broken your neck!' Drake knelt down beside her, shooing Koshka away as he helped her sit up, curving her against his supporting chest, brushing the dirt and grass clippings from her damaged side, anxiously tilting up her white face and examining her dazed eyes beneath the damp fringe sticking to her forehead, looking rather grey-faced himself. 'Just sit here for a moment; don't try to get up until you feel a bit steadier,' he said huskily. 'A knock like that can really take it out of you. Thank God you fell on that lounger and not on your head. Anything broken, you think?'

'No...' It was as much an answer as a thread of protest as he gently unfolded the arm that Kate had tucked protectively across her middle.

'Shall I carry you inside?'

'No, I want to stand up…I need to stand up,' she insisted shakily, hoping against hope that when she stretched out she would find that she was just experiencing a muscular spasm from the shock of the fall.

Murmuring reassurances, Drake helped her to her feet, letting her lean on him as she tested her ankles and gingerly flexed her shoulders and wrists. To her relief the pulling pain in her stomach started to fade away, just as she'd hoped it would, once the blood started pumping freely around her extremities again.

They took it very slowly going back up the stairs, and when she limped back inside the house Drake made her lie down on the couch for a few minutes with her feet propped on a cushion. She accepted an offer of sweet tea when the alternative seemed to be having him hover over her or pace up and down. When Koshka wandered back inside innocent of all the commotion she had caused, Kate petted her forgivingly as she sipped her tea, covering the little ears to block out Drake's dark threats of discipline.

When she felt a little less fragile, she persuaded him to let her go and pull on a tee shirt over her bikini, but when she emerged from her bedroom she was white-faced again, fully dressed, wearing shoes, and carrying her purse.

'I think you'd better take me to the doctor,' she said thinly to Drake, who was standing in the kitchen stirring sugar into a mug of tea for himself.

'Why? What's the matter?' He put the mug down abruptly and strode over. Before he reached her side she went even paler, biting her lip and blinking hard as she dropped her purse and pressed both hands to her stomach.

'Oh, God—' she choked.

'What is it?' He slid his hands over the top of hers, feeling their icy tremor, fearing she was sliding into delayed shock. 'Come on, Kate, tell me,' he ordered harshly, to jolt her consciousness. 'Don't fade out on me—do you think you've hurt something inside?'

'Yes.' She looked at him, her silver eyes wild and tormented. 'The baby…I think something's happening to the baby!' She caught her breath on a frightened sob. 'I feel this pain in my side and all around my middle, like a tearing…I think I must have hurt my baby when I fell. Oh, God, what if I'm losing it? I don't want to lose my baby—'

'Baby? You're *pregnant*?' He looked as if he had been hit in the face, but his stunned bewilderment only lasted a split second and then he was as white-lipped as she, his eyes burning black holes in the stony mask of his face as he made all the right connections. 'You're carrying a child? *My* child? *That's* why you came to Oyster Beach?' He read the truth in her agonised expression. 'You want to have the baby and keep it? *Damn you all to hell, Kate!*' he exploded. He spun, slamming his fist against the wall.

She put her hand on the sleeve of his polo shirt, feeling the iron muscle underneath quivering with tension as his fist continued to grind against the caved wallboard. 'Please, can we talk about it later?' she begged his averted profile. 'I need to go to a doctor now and I suppose the nearest medical practice is in Whitianga—I don't think it's safe for me to drive. Drake?'

He didn't move and her fingers curled into the unyielding muscle. 'Unless you *want* your baby to die!' she cried in panicked desperation, shaking at his rigid arm. 'Maybe you're thinking that if you delay long enough you can force me into a miscarriage—get rid of the baby and save yourself some grief!'

He tore himself from her grasp and away from the wall, his handsome features for once ugly. 'If you believe I'm capable of murdering an innocent child for selfish gain, then what in the hell made you think I'd ever be any kind of fit father?' he said savagely. 'No, don't bother to answer that—you were going to sucker me into playing Daddy to your kid and now you know better than to even try,' he added with incandescent fury. 'Where are your keys? We'll take your car—it'll be quicker.'

He stopped, not looking at her as he demanded harshly; 'Are you bleeding?'

'No,' she said, breathing shallowly, 'but I have these sharp, low-down, stabbing pains...'

This time there was no supportive arm around her shoulders. He escorted her out and into the car without touching her, or even glancing at her until she temporarily emerged from her desperate anxiety to remember, 'Oh, could you make sure that the kitchen window's open before we go, so that Koshka can get out when she needs to—there's plenty of water and dry food down but no litter box inside...'

With a curse and a black look of angry incredulity, he got out of the car again with violent, jerky movements and slammed into the house. When he came back he jammed the key into the ignition and grimly started to drive.

Wrapped up in her pain and fear for her baby, and the bitter knowledge that her sins of omission had caught up with her, totally damning her in her lover's eyes, Kate hugged herself in silent despair until Drake's question pierced her mental anguish.

'How pregnant are you?' he asked with ferocious reluctance, the words seemingly torn from deep in his chest.

'I think about eight or nine weeks by now—'

'You think? What does your doctor say?'

She didn't want to tell him she hadn't seen a doctor yet. She knew her GP didn't handle pregnancies so she would have to ask him to recommend a specialist or midwife as her lead carer. She hadn't been ready to take any of those official steps—not until she herself had felt ready to accept the giant changes that it would immediately bring to her life.

'I—it must have happened just before you left—'

'*Happened?* A pregnancy doesn't just *happen* when you take the kind of serious precautions we do! At least I *thought* we were both on the same page about contraception. When did you stop taking the pill?'

She had known he would accuse her of trying to trap him, but it was still a blow. 'I *didn't*—not until I missed my period the week you left, and the pregnancy test came up positive...*twice*,' she emphasised,

twisting to look at him and biting her lip against
another sharp spasm of pain. 'I might have occasionally missed taking a pill, but never deliberately, and
you always use condoms, so tell me how I could
have planned this. And why would I, knowing how
you feel about children—?'

'You don't know how I *feel*,' he said scathingly.
'You only think you do. But you made a big mistake
if you thought you could talk me round. You're not
going to con me into bearing the responsibility for
your decision—'

She felt as if he had stabbed her in the chest. 'If
you're talking about a decision not to terminate, I
don't need anyone else to take responsibility for that,'
she said sharply. 'I don't care what you or my mother
say, I'm not getting rid of my baby just because it
doesn't fit the image of a sophisticated career woman.'

He stiffened at the wheel. 'Your mother told you
to have an abortion?' He cast her a violent look. But
was he any better?

'I haven't told her—I wanted you to know first,'
she said, turning her head to stare blindly out the
window. 'But I know that's what she'll say I should
do. She would have aborted me, if she could have
done it legally…even back then she was thinking
ahead to what would best serve her professional reputation. I grew up in a one-parent family so I know
how tough it can be, but I can do it, I could even
afford a house and take in boarders to help with the
mortgage and child-care if necessary. There are
always plenty of overseas university students looking

for quality long-term home-stays. My mother will be furious and scathingly disappointed in me, but then that's nothing new…'

The thick, condemning silence descended again, re-inforcing Drake's message of brutal uninterest, and this time it lasted until they arrived at the group practice on the outskirts of Whitianga. While Drake parked the car Kate walked inside and explained matters to the practice nurse on the desk, who immediately said she'd show her into an examination room to await the first doctor to become free. As she was leading the way across the hall Drake came striding up to them, eyes raking over Kate, and the nurse hesitated.

'Oh! Does your hus—um…your partner want to come in, too?'

'No!' said Kate firmly, before Drake could open his mouth to say anything hurtful. 'And he's not my partner. He just gave me a lift. You can stay in the waiting room,' she told him with dismissive coldness that blew directly off the frozen wastes in her heart.

She was feeling both hot and cold fifteen minutes later as she stared at the kindly, middle-aged female doctor in a mixture of anger and disbelief.

'But the test was positive both times I did it,' she repeated, 'and it said on the packet that it was ninety-seven per cent accurate.'

The doctor shrugged. 'Done correctly, yes, but there are a number of things that could give a false-positive result—for instance you may have let the test sit too long before you read it, or, if it happened twice, the kit might have been expired or faulty, or if you'd had a urinary-tract infection you were unaware of at the time, that could have compromised the test—'

'But I've also had all the signs since then,' protested Kate. 'I've missed two periods, and I've been nauseous, and having to go to the toilet more frequently, and my breasts have been sore…'

The doctor's voice was gentle, but inexorably firm. 'Well, I've done the internal exam and tested your urine and you're definitely not pregnant. The pain you're feeling is probably a pulled muscle from your fall, or possibly a little tear—an anti-inflammatory will soon settle that down. I'll do the hCG blood test for you but I'm sure that'll just confirm my diagnosis. You said there was some spotting a couple of weeks after your first period was due? You could have had what we call a chemical pregnancy, which is a very early miscarriage.'

'But I missed another period after that and—and I was so *sure*…'

'Have you been under any emotional stress at work or in your private life recently?'

'Well, yes, but no more than usual.' Kate grimaced. She had always found Drake's arrivals and departures very stressful—trying to act normal and carry off the appearance of cool acceptance of his wanderings while she was dying inside. Whenever he left she would wonder when they would see each other again, and when he returned she was never certain how long he would stay.

'You wanted this baby very much, I take it?' the doctor murmured, as she gently dealt with the splinters embedded in the hand with which Kate had grabbed at the rail.

'Yes,' Kate whispered. 'I did.' As soon as she had watched that test strip change she had eagerly embraced the miracle, the long-forbidden hope. She had wanted Drake's baby more than anything else in the world...except his love...

And now she had to face life with neither.

'Well, sometimes, when we want or believe in something very, very much the mind can cause the body to produce signs and symptoms that can fool a woman into thinking she's pregnant...'

Fool! Kate repeated to herself as she left the doctor's office, hollowed out by grief and the shameful knowledge of her own devastating self-betrayal.

She knew now why she had convinced herself there was no rush to have her pregnancy professionally confirmed. At some deep level of her subconscious she had known the truth and not wanted to face it. The phantom pregnancy had been a way for her to break out of the prison of her 'no strings' affair with Drake, to force herself to take action and challenge the very nature and balance of their relationship.

To make a horrible situation worse, when she got back out to the reception desk she found that she had left her purse lying on the floor back at the house, and had to ask Drake to pay for her consultation.

'Well?' he said curtly as they walked to the door.

She swallowed. She wasn't going to parade her guilt and shame in front of a roomful of interested patients. 'Quite well.' She stretched her mouth into a meaningless smile. 'The doctor said I must have pulled a muscle in my fall.'

Drake stopped outside the doors. 'So the baby's all right, then—it wasn't hurt?' he said, his voice tight with hostility at having to ask.

Kate's dry eyes ached. *Fool!* She lifted her chin. 'It was all a stupid false alarm,' she forced herself to confess.

'In that case, here.' Drake stunned her by slapping her car keys into her hand.

'You want *me* to drive home?'

'I don't care where you go. As long as I'm not there. I can't do this. I'm out of here.' He turned on his heel and headed along the pavement towards the township.

'But— I have to explain— We need to talk—' she called after him.

'No, we don't. There's nothing you could say that I want to hear. Anyway, they say actions speak louder than words.'

And with that he walked away.

CHAPTER NINE

KATE was building a sandcastle on the beach when the little girl whose lopsided lump she was busy turning into a fairy-tale structure complete with flying flags of fuzzy pussy-willow grass suddenly popped her thumb out of her mouth and extended it in a skywards spike.

'Man!'

Kneeling in the hard-packed sand just below the high-water line, Kate squinted against the low angle of the sun in the direction indicated by the moppet's soggy salute and sat back on her bare heels with a little breathless grunt of shock.

Drake was back!

Her sandy fingers unknowingly clenched, scrunching a hole in the side of a tower and endangering the route of the heroic fairy prince she had been explaining to the child was about to clamber up to rescue the enchanted maiden, aka a pod of seaweed whose green hair owed its inspiration to Rapunzel.

'Hah!' Her little companion seemed to think it

was all part of a new game, and cheerfully bashed
down another of Kate's painstakingly crafted towers
with its pretty mosaic of shells.

'Oh, no, darling, we're building them up, not
pushing them down,' choked Kate, hastily blinking
away the tears she blamed on the needle-sharp jab of
the sun and spreading out her hands to protect the
flank of her castle from an enthusiastic little fist.

The man, who had been padding steadily along
the beach towards them, came to a halt at the edge
of the shallow moat on the seaward side of the castle,
crouching down to survey the damage, his knees
splayed, the dark trousers that had been rolled up to
his calves pulling tight across the tops of his thighs,
his long bare feet melting into the wet sand.

'Looks like you could do with some help,' he said,
pushing up the sleeves of his pale grey knitted-silk
sweater, revealing the golden brown hair on his
tanned forearms.

'No, thanks, we're doing fine without you,' said
Kate, just as another tower got a smashing makeover,
sending a spray of damp sand into her mouth and
down the top of her scoop-necked top.

'Hey, sweetheart, how about you and I fill this
bucket with some more sand?' said Drake, picking
up the bright plastic pail with its turret-shaped base
lying by his feet and holding out the matching spade.

To Kate's disgust the little girl trotted obediently
over to his side and began digging, while Drake
scooped up mounds of sand with his cupped hands
and rapidly filled the pail.

'You'll get your clothes dirty,' said Kate sourly, wiping the grit from her mouth with her arm, noting that it definitely wasn't beachwear he was sporting. Who had he dressed to impress? she wondered.

'Like yours?' he said, his mouth curving as he looked at her sand-clogged striped top and water-stained shorts.

When she didn't smile back, his own faded, his brown eyes unflinching as he weathered her wintry stare.

'It'll all come out in the wash,' he commented, sinking down onto his knees and turning his attention back to his task, smoothing over the compacted sand in the bucket and inverting it to produce a smooth-sided release from the bucket with a sharp rap on the top, far more perfect than Kate had obtained.

The little girl clapped her hands.

'More!'

Drake obliged until there was another square of perfect towers, which he joined up with mounded walls. Kate doggedly worked on the original castle as he and his helper dug a moat and filled it with buckets of sea water.

'I think I need to hire a decorator,' he said to Kate, noticing her sneaking sidelong glances at the expansive grey walls. 'Would you like to help?' He picked up a single strand of pussy willow from the bunch of grasses she had gathered in the sand-dunes earlier and held it out to her, the delicate, pale golden catkin at the end of the stalk quivering and dancing in the gentle sea breeze.

It was too reminiscent of an extended olive branch and she opened her mouth to coldly refuse, but then she saw the girl's innocent blue eyes, alight with eagerness, fixed on her face.

She reached out to reluctantly accept the offering.

'I suppose I could.' Her voice was like broken glass but the little girl listened to the words, not the jagged tone, and as Kate poked the stalk into the top of one of the new towers she began pulling her precious collection of shells from the sagging pocket of her shorts and handing them over one by one for Kate to press into the base of the walls.

Watching her crawling around on her hands and knees, Drake said with a curious edge, 'Should you be doing that? What about your pulled muscle?'

She didn't understand his concern. After all, he had been the one to turn his back on her grief-stricken admission. He must have realised how shocked and upset she was, how devastated by her humiliating mistake. He hadn't cared *then* what she was going through.

'The doctor gave me an anti-inflammatory. The pain relief was pretty well immediate.'

He frowned. 'Don't those things have harmful side-effects?'

'I'm sure the doctor wouldn't have prescribed it if it was dangerous,' Kate told him tartly. 'But if you were so worried about it perhaps you should have asked me about it at the time instead of running off like that. But then, that's fairly typical behaviour for you, isn't it?'

She hadn't meant to let that slip out, but when she

saw the skin tauten over his cheekbones she was glad. There was no reason now to hold back, no secret baby to protect. She was on her own.

'Oh, yes, that's a pretty one, isn't it, darling?' she said as the little girl poked a small paua shell with its pearlised blue and green interior under her nose.

'Here, Kristin, put it in your bucket,' said Drake, handing it over with the spade tucked inside, startling Kate with his use of the girl's name.

'You know who she is?'

'Of course I do, they're locals. Look, Kristin—your mother's getting ready to take you back up for your tea.'

The woman whom Kate had briefly spoken to earlier had repacked her beach bag and was shaking out her towel. Seeing them looking towards her, she waved, yelled out a greeting to Drake and her thanks to Kate, and called to her daughter, who skipped off without a second glance at the result of all their hard work when she heard the words 'spaghetti' and 'ice cream' floating on the breeze.

'There's gratitude for you,' murmured Drake as she got stiffly to her feet. 'Never mind, the tide's still on its way out and the local school kids should be getting off the bus about now. Your monument will get plenty of admiration before the sea comes back to demolish it. Here…' He sought and found a stick from amongst the heaps of seaweed strewn along the high watermark and wrote 'Kate and Kristin did this' in large capitals alongside the crenellated towers.

Kate found it interesting that he had added the little girl's name without prompting, but not his own.

'For someone who doesn't want any children, I'm surprised you're so good at handling them,' she said, unable to curb her resentment. 'Most people who haven't had much contact with children find it hard to relate to them.'

Herself included. She had never been interested in babies or young children until she had thought she was pregnant, then they had turned out to be the subject of a profound, and hitherto inadmissible fascination. Again she felt that deep, wrenching sorrow, the sense of loss that she had no right to feel. She began to walk quickly back along the beach towards the house.

Drake had tensed at her words. 'In the kind of group homes I was in there are always plenty of kids coming and going.' He shrugged, turning to follow her, easily keeping up with her swinging strides. 'It's supposed to be part of the "family experience" to get the teenagers to help look after the younger ones.'

His voice petered out, as if he expected her to interrupt with a question, but Kate merely quickened her pace, the breeze against her face making her eyes sting as she pulled ahead.

'I came back, didn't I?' he said roughly, digging his feet into the sand to regain her shoulder. 'That must count for something.'

'You think?' she said sarcastically.

'I was only gone a couple of days.'

Eternity times two. He was very efficient at his disappearing act, though, for he had even arranged for a man in a pick-up to come and collect Prince and lock up the house. When Kate had seen that happening she had wished that falling in hate was as easy as falling in love. At least she had still had Koshka to stroke and to hold, and to lick away her tears. The little cat had slept on her bed, curled up on the turndown of the sheet, her soft motoring purr a comforting reassurance that Kate had not been left entirely alone in the world.

'Yes, that's quite a record turn-around for you. I thought you'd be away much longer,' she said truthfully. 'But I forgot that you have a work in progress. You had to come back for that—you have a lot of writing to do. And of course that always takes precedence over everything else!' She could hear herself getting shrill and was relieved to see her front lawn. She almost broke into a run.

'Kate— That's not why I came back.' He leapt up on the grass and shadowed her to the scene of her fall. 'I only went as far as Craemar—the Marlows' holiday place—Steve put me up there—'

'Oh, I see, and I suppose you told him all about me,' she said with one foot on the step. 'Cried into your beer and gave chapter and verse on how I almost tricked you into having to behave like an ordinary human being—'

'God, Kate, *no*,' he said, snagging the sleeve of her top to hold her back, 'it wasn't like that—his whole family were there—'

She had thought her humiliation was complete; now she discovered there was fresh reason to cringe. 'You mean *they* all know about it, now, too?' she cried in horror.

'I haven't told *anyone*, Kate. I didn't go there to get drunk and rave; I just needed to get away to *think*.'

She pulled her sleeve out of his grasp. She didn't know what to believe any more. She didn't trust him—or herself—to know what was really true. 'Excuse me, I think I'm going to go inside and be sick,' she flung at him, and rushed up the stairs, hoping that would be enough to make him think twice about harassing her with his unwanted attention.

Unfortunately her words had the opposite effect and after scarcely a moment of hesitation he charged into the house behind her, following her trail of sandy footprints right into the sanctuary of her bedroom where she had fled to shed bitter tears.

'What are you doing in here?' she said thickly, backing away from him, glad that she hadn't yet succumbed to the building pressure behind her eyes.

'You said you were going to be sick.'

Just as the doctor had predicted they would, the physical symptoms of her pregnancy had vanished, so she couldn't blame her savage burst of fury on a hormonal mood swing.

'And you wanted to what? Enjoy watching my misery?'

'I thought you might need some help.'

She was infuriated by his strained gentleness. 'You haven't been much help so far—why start now?'

'Calm down, Kate, it isn't good for you to get all wrought up over trifles.'

Trifles? Kate's mouth fell open at his sheer gall. He looked around the room, which was in a defiant mess very different from her normal, fastidious requirements, and frowned.

'Are you packing?'

She recovered from her momentary speechlessness. 'You wish! Unlike you I don't choose to run away from my problems.' No, she ran *to* them. That was *her* problem!

'Then what's all this?' He nudged a foot against a stack of carrier bags by the door.

'Just some things of mine I'm putting out for the rubbish.'

One of the packages slumped, spilling out books, and he bent to tuck them back in the bag, jerking upright as if he had been burnt when he saw the colourful titles.

'You're throwing out your books on child-care?'

She gave a bitter laugh at his fierce frown. 'Well, I won't need them now, will I? Do you think I should give them away to charity? Feel free to take as many as you like.'

His body took on a dangerous lean. 'What do you mean you won't need them, now?' he said warily.

He wasn't usually so obtuse. 'Well, if I'm not going to be a parent, I don't need to read books on how to develop good parenting skills,' she choked.

Did he think she would want to keep the reminders of her foolishness around for next time she thought she was pregnant? She was twenty-seven, and in love with a man who had brutally rejected the very essence of her womanhood—at this rate there would never be a 'next time'.

His wariness gave way to stark tension. 'What are you going to do? Give the baby up for adoption?'

Kate gasped, shaking her head helplessly.

His face greyed. 'God, you haven't decided to go for a termination after all?' He heeled his chest with his hand, as if massaging the flood flow through his heart. 'Kate, you're not thinking straight. You can't abort your baby...you'll never be able to live with yourself. It's not the right decision for you—'

He didn't know!

Kate stood frozen, inwardly reeling with shock.

He didn't know there was no baby! She'd thought he had understood—outside the clinic when she'd told him it was all a false alarm—she had thought he'd realised that she meant the whole pregnancy. But he had obviously thought she meant the threatened miscarriage!

He still thought that she was pregnant.

And he didn't want her to abort his baby.

No, not *his*...'your baby', he said, not 'my baby' or 'our baby'. He was firmly separating mother and child from any connection with himself.

'But it is my decision,' she said cruelly. 'Unless you want to go to court and fight over the right to the foetus—drag out our past, present and future for the world to gloat over...'

He flinched, but stood his ground, the muscles grinding along his jaw. 'Kate, don't make any decisions on the basis of the hurt and anger you're feeling right now. Believe me, I know how badly that goes—

how irrevocable some acts of bitterness can be. Every life is precious, because life is so fleeting we have to treasure it while we can…I came back because you're important to me, and this baby doesn't change that.'

Again, it was 'this baby' not 'his', thought Kate, growing icier with every word.

'The fact that it was unplanned by either of us doesn't have to be a disaster.'

So he was prepared to concede that she hadn't tried to trap him with the oldest trick in the book. How generous!

'I'm a wealthy man, I can set up a trust fund to support you and the baby for the rest of your lives, so there'll be plenty of money for child-care if you want to continue your career.'

Ah, there it was, the pay-off!

'And we can buy you a house, one with plenty of room that you won't have to share.' He was growing uncharacteristically nervous at her silence, speaking more quickly and persuasively. 'It'll be much more convenient than your town house and more private than my hotel—no need to be self-conscious if you ask me to stay overnight…'

If? That big, fat, horribly pregnant 'if' sent a huge chunk of fractured ice shearing off her glacial heart.

Now he was prepared to take on her and the baby, albeit stashed in an expensive love-nest somewhere? Now, when it no longer mattered! If he had once mentioned love instead of ticking off his convenient boxes she might have reacted differently, but this was too little and too late.

She marched out of the bedroom and threw open the front door in a furious gesture of repudiation.

'Get out!'

'Kate, I'm only trying to make you see—'

'Get *out* of my house!' She would have liked to have told him that she wanted him to never darken her door again, but as well as being horridly clichéd it would have been a lie.

He hesitated and she thought that if he pointed out that it wasn't actually her house she would hit him, but fortunately he brushed past her, turning on the doorstep to warn her.

'OK, I'm going—but I'm not going away, Kate. Not again. And you're not leaving Oyster Beach, either, until we work things through. Sooner or later you and I are going to have to deal with the consequences of our actions—*together*, rather than individually. Our baby is as much a part of me as it is of you, because, after two years, *you're* part of me…'

He couldn't have said anything more calculated to play on her conscience.

After vowing to be honest in all her future dealings with him she had just been vindictive and cruel. She had let him go away thinking she was holding his baby hostage in her barren womb.

Kate paced the house as the sun sank lower in the sky, running her hands constantly through her hair, as if she could brush away the sticky tendrils of guilt clinging to her mind and disordering her thoughts. She couldn't stomach the idea of food, but since her strange cravings and loathings had vanished with the baby she made herself a good, strong, black and bitter cup of instant caffeine.

Taking her coffee out to the verandah, she couldn't help glance wistfully up at Drake's shuttered office window. The light was on and the shutters were slanted open, a motionless black silhouette standing, staring down at her through the tilted slats, a lonely, brooding figure who sent a hot needle of pain searing through the ice encasing her emotions.

A boy who had been abandoned by his father, suffered the ultimate fatal rejection from his mother; shadowed by a teenager who had been bounced from pillar to post in foster care; shaded by a man who had never had—or permitted—anybody but a mangy dog to possess a piece of his soul. How could she condemn him to mental torture for merely being the product of his environment?

Leaving her half-finished coffee steaming on the kitchen table, Kate put a bowl of canned cat-food down for Koshka and walked around to Drake's front door.

Her knock was answered so quickly she realised he must have seen her coming. She also realised that she was still barefooted and wearing the sandy, salty clothes she had worn to the beach whereas Drake had obviously not been brooding so hard that he hadn't taken the time to shower and shave, and change into clean jeans and a short-sleeved white linen shirt.

'Come in,' he said, his deep voice quiet and inviting as he stepped back and to one side, but she didn't move.

'There is no baby.' She could hardly hear herself over the thunder of her heart in her ears.

'I beg your pardon?' He greeted her bald announcement with a puzzled tilt of his head, as if he thought he hadn't heard her correctly.

'I'm not having a baby. That doctor confirmed it. I'm not pregnant. That's what I meant when I told you it was a false alarm.' She lifted her chin when she saw a red flare in his eyes, an instant before they turned as black as pitch. 'So you see, you can stop worrying—there are no consequences for us to deal with after all,' she continued in a steady monotone. 'I just came over to tell you that—'

'Oh, no, you didn't,' said Drake, grabbing her around the waist as she turned to leave. He hauled her inside the door and slammed it shut, engaging the dead-bolt.

His arms caged her against the door on either side of her sun-flushed shoulders, his face a series of jagged angles under the flare of the overhead light in the vaulted entranceway, his velvet voice as abrasive as sandpaper in his bewilderment.

'I don't understand. Explain it to me, Kate. Are you saying the initial test was *wrong*? And that your own doctor never noticed?'

So she was forced to drag it out, to tell him all the gory, embarrassing details that had been picked over by the doctor in Whitianga, including the damning fact that she had never consulted her own doctor.

Mired in her guilt, she waited stoically for a celebratory cheer of relief, followed by a justifiable outburst of anger and contempt, but Drake's response was so muted it could have been called a non-response.

'So you *could* have been pregnant a few weeks ago, but we'll never really know,' he said quietly when she had mentioned the chemical pregnancy theory.

She shrugged, her bare shoulder blades rubbing against the wood of the door. 'The doctor said that apparently around half of first pregnancies end in a miscarriage, sometimes so early that the woman doesn't even know about it.'

'But *you* knew,' he said, dropping his arms and straightening up.

'I *thought* I knew,' she said, free to move past him into the big, unlit living area where she could safely avoid his all-seeing gaze. Someone had lit a bonfire at the far end of the beach and through the big picture windows she could see the fiery sparks leaping up into the sky, reaching out for the cool sprawl of stars that were just beginning to prick through as dusk teetered on the edge of night. 'As it turns out I was only pretending...'

'I'm sorry.' His voice was soft as the night as he came up behind her.

The breath shivered out of her lungs and she wrapped her arms around herself, wishing she were one of those sparks, dancing up into nothingness. 'Why? You never wanted the baby—'

'Not for the baby. For you. For *your* loss. Because it was so much more than a pretence for you, wasn't it, Kate? For weeks you thought you were having my baby...'

She bit her lip, but the self-inflicted pain didn't help banish the tears that stood in her eyes, blurring the dance of the sparks. She opened them wide and blinked, but then a strong pair of enfolding arms slid around and over hers, chasing away the chill, drawing her gently back against a warm column of hard flesh, and the tears spilled over her cheeks and dripped down into the crease of a tanned elbow.

The arms tightened and she felt Drake's square chin skim over her shoulder at the nape of her neck, his head dipping and turning so that he could push his face into the side of her throat, his hard forehead nudging up under her jaw, his lips moving against her soft skin.

'Ah, Katherine…I'm sorry…' He began to rock her from side to side, his big hands compressing her upper arms, his hips directing but also passively supporting the sway of her willowy body.

A sob burst from her chest and she briefly struggled against his unbreakable grip.

'Kate…' he whispered against her throat. 'Katie…'

It was the first time he had ever used the sweet diminutive of her name and that he should do it now just seemed too much. A second sob tore loose, and then another, and then the tears just wouldn't stop. When she stopped fighting his hold he slid his arms down to her hips and turned her around, pulling her hands around his waist, drawing her head against his chest and rubbing the knuckles of one hand up and down her spine, continuing to rock her in rhythm to her sobs.

'I don't know why I'm crying; there's nothing to cry about,' she wept, her voice muffled in the folds of his linen shirt. 'It's not as if I've really lost a baby…just a silly delusion… What made me think I could be a good mother, anyway? I suppose you think I'm totally mad—'

'Shh, Kate,' he soothed, 'you're the sanest woman I know—you're the one who anchors *me* to my humanity.' He rested his cheek on the top of her tousled head. 'You lost something precious to you this week, and even if it *was* just an illusion, why shouldn't you be allowed to grieve for it?'

Her fingers clenched into his shirt, the beat of his heart against her jaw reverberating through her bones. 'You don't really care,' she choked, lifting her head. 'You're happy that your life can go back to the way it was before…'

'Not happy…sad.' He tilted her chin up so that she could see the truth of his words in his sombre face. 'In all the time I've known you I've never seen you cry, except at a movie. That made me feel safe. I don't like to see you hurting.'

She looked up at him with drowned eyes, a ghostly silver in the half-darkness. 'Then *why*… why did you walk away from me like that?' she said rawly.

He brushed back the hair from her forehead, dislodging several grains of sand, which he stroked away from the top of her furrowed brows. 'Because I'm a flawed human being, sweetheart. Sometimes I let the past get in the way of my better instincts. But I do learn from my mistakes and I'm here for you now, so you don't have to bear this alone.'

He pressed his lips to her crumpled forehead, smoothing it out with a string of gentle kisses that drifted to the corner of her damp eyes, and down to her salty cheeks and bite-swollen lips. His soft murmurs of tender reassurance and the rocking cradle of his arms, the feather-light touch of his mouth stroking her reddened eyelids closed, and the achingly sweet brush of his cheek against hers both lulled and enticed her into a dreamy state of contented acquiescence.

So that when she found herself upstairs in Drake's luxurious grey and blue bedroom, being divested of her clothes, she was only mildly curious.

'What are you doing?' she murmured through tear-thickened vocal cords as Drake's comforting arms withdrew so that he could pick up a remote control to draw the blue silk drapes and dim the squat bedside lamps to an intimate glow.

'Getting comfortable,' he said, pulling the white shirt over his head without undoing the buttons, and discarding it carelessly on the thick silver-grey carpet. He did the same with her top and was deftly drawing her salt-stained shorts down her legs when she bestirred herself to weakly protest.

'I haven't had a wash. You can't look at me; I'm all grubby—'

'I don't mind. Hop out,' he ordered and threw the shorts on top of the pile of clothes when she unthinkingly obeyed.

'I do. I always have a shower before I see you,' she fretted, trying to hide herself behind her arms. 'I need to feel that I'm clean, and look my best, and smell beautiful...'

He took her hands, gently saluting the one that still showed signs of bruising from the extracted splinters, and placed them over his shoulders, spanning her slender waist with his big hands and nuzzling her pouting mouth with more of those butterfly kisses. 'You're just as appealing to me au naturel,' he murmured reassuringly. 'You smell like a real woman; I like that better than any artificial fragrance...a woman of the sun and sea and beach.'

He licked at the tracks of her tears on her face and she gave a sad, salty chuckle.

'You feel like Koshka, only your tongue is softer.'

He gave her some more of his soft tongue, and took advantage of her distraction to unfasten her bra, letting out an exclamation as a thick crust of dry sand fell away with the cups, leaving her bare breasts coated with a fine dusting of pale grit, the minute grains of quartz sparkling in the lamp-light.

'I need a towel, I'm all sandy,' she said self-consciously, wrinkling her nose and trying to ineffectually brush away the grittiness.

'Fairy dust from your fairy castle,' he said huskily. 'Here, let me be your towel...' He replaced her hands on his shoulders and used the tips of his fingers to whisk delicately over and around the soft mounds, stroking his thumbs where the sand clung stubbornly to her milk-white flesh. He bent his head to blow gently at the recalcitrant grains, watching her breasts rise and tauten, the soft pink nipples puckering at the caress of the warm, moist zephyr. He pushed her to sit on the bed and picked up his shirt, kneeling in front to her to tenderly buff around the ruched peaks with the butter-soft linen, his eyes darkening as she flinched and gave a sudden gasp.

'Oh, a button.'

He looked at the balled shirt in his hand, its pearlised buttons gleaming amongst the folds of fabric. 'Did it catch against you?'

She nodded.

'Like this…?' He deliberately turned the shirt and scraped a smooth, hard button against her sensitised nipple.

'Oh…' She shuddered, her eyes widening, her head tipping back, and he did it again, scraping the little disc back and forth across the swollen peak until it deepened from pink to mauve, then according the same delicious punishment to her other breast.

'Oh…they…oh, don't,' she gasped unconvincingly as the blood thinned in her veins, rushing into her breasts and pooling between her thighs, easing her sorrowing heart of some of its coagulated heaviness. She closed her eyes and groaned, racked by a piercing yearning.

'They're almost clean now,' she heard him murmur throatily. 'I just need to…' and suddenly the fabric was replaced by his warm breath again, and then his mouth, licking around her areolae, suckling gently but firmly at the twin peaks.

'Would you have nursed our baby like this?'

Her eyes flew open with shock to meet his hot

gaze, smouldering at her through his thick lashes, his lips still drawing tautly on her nipple, enfolding it inside his mouth in the hot curl of his tongue.

She plunged her hand into his hair and pulled his head away. 'How can you ask that?'

He looked at her pointed breasts, cleansed of sand but glistening with the evidence of his possession. 'I don't want you to be afraid to talk about it. I don't want you to think you have to pretend it never happened. You would have been a good mother, Kate, never doubt it.'

The reminder made her feel guilty all over again. 'We shouldn't be doing this...'

'But it's making you feel better, isn't it?'

She quivered with confusion. 'I'm not going to have sex with you,' she said fiercely. Men always reduced everything to sex!

'All right...we'll just get into bed and cuddle together—you'd like that, wouldn't you?' he suggested persuasively, reaching over to fold back a corner of the blue silk counterpane and show her the crisp white sheet. 'You'd never let us do that before. You'd allow the requisite few minutes for a post-coital cuddle, but as soon as there was any danger of either of us drifting off to sleep you'd be up and moving about, suggesting things to do or getting dressed to leave.'

'I thought that was what you wanted...' she said, bewildered and intrigued by this seductively tender alien who had apparently taken over Drake's body.

'Well, you were wrong. I like having you close. I

wanted to make love *and* be able to fall asleep to the feel of you in my arms.' His eyes had fallen to her filmy white lace panties, and his finger began to toy with the elastic at the top of her leg.

She clamped her legs together to halt a molten gush. What if he found sand in her panties?

'I'm not taking them off...' she said weakly.

His finger hooked under the fabric. 'I think you should,' he advised. In contrast to hers his deep voice was compellingly certain. 'They're a bit tight, and you want to be comfy...' And before she could blink, or accuse him of calling her fat, they were whisking through the air.

'All right, but you have to keep your jeans on,' she warned, her white bottom flashing as she scrabbled hastily under the covers and peeped out at him, using the sheet to cover the beginnings of a smile.

He looked disappointed but contented himself with merely unsnapping his top button to relieve the pressure behind his zip.

He climbed into the bed facing her, snuggling tantalisingly—but not crushingly—close, his hot chest just far enough away to rub her breasts with every indrawn breath, his big hands stroking her back, his heavy thigh lying over the top of hers, the centres of their bodies pressed together, the springy curls at the base of her belly catching against the rough denim bulging tightly in his crotch.

Their heads nestled on thistledown softness, their noses almost touching at the sloping intersection of their luxury pillows.

'This is nice, isn't it?' he said, one hand moving down to cup the globes of her bottom, adjusting her more securely against his lower body, and she felt his voice in the hard tips of her breasts where they fenced with his flat nipples.

'Y-yes…' she said uncertainly, feeling the familiar throb of excitement pulse in her veins.

The longer she lay there, the worse it got. She didn't want him to want her only for sex, she realised restlessly, but their thriving sex life was a healthy expression of their intense mutual attraction, and, as such, was an indivisible part of her love.

As her temperature rose she could feel his skin absorb and radiate more heat until it began to get uncomfortably hot under the covers. And yet still he made no move to acknowledge or ease the growing tension in their bodies. In spite of his earlier seductiveness, Drake was going to refrain from any sexualised affection because she had insisted she wanted it that way. He was showing that he respected her wishes above his carnal desires, when what she really wanted was not restraint, but reckless proof of life.

Kate impatiently kicked off the smothering covers. 'You can make love to me now.'

Drake reared up on his elbow. 'Are you sure?' he asked tensely.

She dug her nails into his arms impatiently. 'Yes, I'm sure…Drake, I want you—I want you to make love to me here, *now*!'

He didn't need a third invitation. Nor was there any long-drawn-out foreplay. He tossed off the covers and swivelled them sideways on the bed, tugging her hips to the edge of the mattress, sliding backwards until his feet struck the floor. Propping himself over her on one braced arm, he opened the fastening of his jeans and pushed himself deeply inside her, uttering a thick, guttural sound of satisfaction as she lifted her hips to guide him home. With a twisting jerk of his hips he seated himself even more tightly between her spread legs, the muscles in his thighs rippling under the denim as he braced his feet against the floor, bent his hungry mouth to her breasts, and began the deep, hard, thrusting rhythm that they both urgently needed, bringing them quickly to a mutual, violent convulsion of groaning ecstasy.

Twice more he racked and then wrenched her body with convulsive pleasure before turning off the lights and finishing with a long, slow, sensual loving that left them panting and weak with sweet exhaustion. Then he pulled the sheets firmly back around them, arranged her to his satisfaction…facing away from him with her bottom spooned by his hips…and tucked his arms around her, sealing her back to his smooth chest.

'And now,' he informed her with yawning satisfaction, 'now we cuddle up and go to sleep together like all good lovers do!'

CHAPTER TEN

Two weeks later, Kate tiptoed up the hall to stand outside the firmly shut door to Drake's office, pressing a warning finger to her lips as she looked down at Prince, trailing at her heels, who looked to be winding up for an inquiring 'wuff'.

She raised a hand to knock and dropped it again, chewing at her lip. The door shut meant that Drake wasn't to be disturbed—they had arranged that all-important signal right from the start. If she came over and his door was shut, she went away again.

Except in dire emergencies. Which this wasn't—well, not as Drake would class it, anyway…

'I can hear you thinking!'

Muffled by the near soundproof door, Drake's voice made her jump.

'Woof!' yelled Prince at the sound of his master's voice, clearly letting her off the hook. Or so she thought.

'You may as well come in, Kate.'

She cracked the door open and poked her head in, pushing Prince back with a firm hand.

'I wasn't going to knock,' she told him. 'I was going to wait. Have I wrecked your train of thought?'

He angled his head down and looked at her over the top of his narrow spectacles. She had been charmed to discover that he wore the neat, gold-rimmed reading glasses when he worked for prolonged periods at his desk. She had teased him that it made him look like a 'proper writer', but he had got her back by wearing them the next time they made love, and forcing her to admit that they made him look incredibly sexy.

'Do you want the polite answer, or the truth?'

'The polite answer, please,' she said, pushing the door wider.

He threw down the gold-topped pen with which he had been correcting pages and took off his glasses.

'You're looking rather frazzled.'

'I'm frizzled *and* frazzled,' she said, fingering through her salt-laden locks. I don't seem to have any water.'

'Low tide classified as an emergency now, is it?' he asked, but his brown eyes were amused as he rocked back in his chair, lazily stretching his arms before tucking his hands behind his head. 'If you wait twelve hours I'm sure it'll come back in again.'

'I mean at the house. I went to have a shower and nothing happened. None of the taps are working, either. The rental agent said to phone a plumber, but apparently he doesn't work weekends in Oyster Beach…unless you have too *much* water. He'll come for a flood but not a drought. Would you mind if I used your guest shower?'

He gave her an impatient look. 'You know you don't have to even ask, you can shower here whenever you like—or have a soak in the spa.' His eyes glinted. 'I know you like a long, leisurely bathe, so that your skin is soft when you stroke on those silky body lotions.'

He was reminding her that more than once he had applied them for her, revealing a wicked talent for erotic massage...

'Thanks,' she said in an effort to stay focused on her errand. 'I've been down on the beach all morning and I think I've brought half of it back with me.'

He looked approvingly at her glowing colour. 'Aren't you glad I persuaded Marcus to give you an extra month's holiday?'

'Persuaded? Blackmailed, more like!' she laughed.

Impossible to believe now that she had initially rejected Drake's suggestion that she spend a few more leisurely weeks at the beach, but he had been very persuasive and hadn't hesitated to use her area of greatest vulnerability.

'You've just gone through a very emotionally draining experience; you owe it to yourself to fully recover before you plunge back into the fray,' he had lectured. 'Didn't the doctor say something about your stress levels helping to send your hormones all out of whack? Marcus will work you into a nervous break-down if you're not careful. I know he regards you highly but that doesn't mean you should let him persuade you that you're completely indispensable—that's just his way of cracking the whip and making least-work for himself. Another month isn't too much to ask when you've worked for him continuously for so long, and your health is at stake. I bet you've hardly had a day of sick leave in your whole career. He owes you a long-service sabbatical at the very least—'

'Well, I suppose I could phone and ask…' she said uncertainly, tempted by the thought of a few more stolen weeks alone with her lover, and yet at the same time mistrustful of her current state of blissful irresponsibility. This was her healing time and she and Drake were consciously living it from moment to moment, taking each day as it came and carefully putting aside any reference to the future.

'Don't ask him, *tell* him!' And when she baulked at that he shrugged and seemed to give up.

But when she finally borrowed Drake's phone to make the toll-call, she found Marcus strangely affable, chuckling fatly in her ear and reassuring her that her job would be waiting for her however long she decided to stay away, that she was worth her weight in gold and that any research she wanted to do for a private client while she was away was okey-dokey with him.

'You went behind my back!' Kate confronted Drake as soon as she'd hung up the phone, trying hard to be angry.

'It was for your own good. Someone had to play hard-ball on your behalf.'

'How would you like it if I negotiated one of your contracts without telling you?' she demanded.

'Be my guest, sweetheart, I hate all that hoopla,'

he drawled, taking the wind out of her sails. 'I could fire my agent and save myself twenty per cent!'

The next tussle between them was that Drake had decided it was silly for her to continue to pay her holiday rental when she was sleeping nearly every night in his bed. 'Since you're spending so much time over here you may as well stay for the next few weeks,' he tossed out casually. 'With the high season coming, I think you'll find you won't be able to renew your rental for another month, anyway.'

'I think it's better if I keep my own space. If I can't, and there isn't another rental somewhere nearby, I'll just go home,' said Kate with firm finality, her heart in her mouth as she rejected his offhand invitation. But she wasn't going to make any more life-changing decisions based on foolish assumptions. She knew all too well how dangerous wishful thinking could be, and Drake's offer had been only for her to stay, not to move in with him. There was a subtle, but enormous difference, particularly when the phrase was used by a man whose business was subtle shades of meaning.

'Besides, I know how vital your privacy is to you when you're working,' she reminded him. 'So, thanks for the offer, but it's better this way for both of us.'

Fortunately, when she contacted the rental agent, he shuffled his files and came across a note about the unexpected cancellation of his next booking, so to her relief she and Koshka were able to settle in for the duration.

'Why don't I come and see what the problem is

with your water,' he said now, switching off his
computer monitor and lunging out of his chair.

'But your door was shut,' she said guiltily, following him downstairs with Prince.

'And it would have stayed shut if I hadn't been stuck
in a rut. A bit of he-man stuff on the side might kick
something loose,' he said, fetching a few tools from his
garage and stuffing them into his jeans pockets.

'Is it going badly, then?' she said sympathetically.

He gave her a slightly defensive sidelong look.
'No, actually, in general it's going rather well.'

Which was more than could be said for her shower.

'Do you know anything about plumbing?' she
asked dubiously as she watched him tinker and curse
at the shower head.

He bristled as if she had challenged his manhood.
'I helped build irrigation systems in the desert—what
do you think?'

She threw up her hands in surrender. 'Just asking.
Er…I'll leave you to it, then,' she said, hurriedly
backing out of the bathroom as he pinched the skin
between thumb and forefinger in the wrench and
swore even more viciously.

Some time later he sought her out in the lounge,
where she was reading with Koshka dozing on her lap.

'It's no use. You're not going to have water any
time soon. Your pump has packed up.'

'What pump?' asked Kate, depositing the sleeping
cat on the couch.

'You're on bore-water here. The pump sucks it out
of the ground and then pumps it from a tank through

to your pipes. It may be a major job to fix it. Even if the plumber gets onto it right straight away he'll probably have to wait for parts.'

'Oh, so what do you think I should do?'

'There's nothing you can do at the moment. You obviously can't stay here without water. Unless you fancy ferrying a bucket from next door every time you want to flush your toilet,' he added sarcastically as he watched her open her mouth to protest.

Within an hour he had her packed up and installed in the large, ground-floor bedroom at the front of his house, looking on with folded arms as she hung her clothes in the big walk-in closet.

'This is only temporary—until the pump is fixed,' said Kate, turning to place a stack of her folded underwear into the chest of drawers and catching the quiet look of satisfaction on his face.

'Of course.'

She looked at him sharply and he responded with a smile of devilish smugness. 'Well, I guess I'll be getting back to work. You know where everything is by now. Make yourself at home...'

She knew where the smugness came from when she met the laconic plumber who after several post-ponements was frustratingly vague on an estimate of exactly when she could expect to have running water again, and over a week later she was still totting up the amount of the refund that she would be owed by the landlord.

And loving living with Drake.

At first she was restless and edgy and very conscious of the need not to encroach, but that feeling eased when he casually asked if she would mind doing a little research for him and she plunged eagerly into the task of combing his extensive library and using his extra laptop to pull down information from the internet on the geopolitical history of the Balkans. He was first amused by her enthusiasm, and then taken aback at the speed at which she synthesised the facts.

'This is duck-to-water stuff for you, isn't it?' he murmured when he sat down to lunch to find yet another concise fact-sheet sitting by his plate. 'This'll save me a hell of a lot of reading. I'm sorry if I've turned this into a bit of a busman's holiday for you.'

'I'm happy to sing for my supper,' she told him readily.

His brown eyes glowed. 'You do that already, in much more exciting ways.'

Colour touched her cheekbones. 'I'm glad you like my cooking,' she said primly, deliberately reading an innocent meaning into his provocative words. 'Perhaps I should be charging *you*—Marcus did suggest I might take on a private commission.'

'Maybe that's because I hinted to him that I could benefit from your expertise,' he admitted with laughter in his eyes. 'He practically fell over himself at the thought he might get a book out of me a second sooner. And if you want to hear me sing, sweetheart, you only have to touch me the way you did last night…'

She loved the nights even more than the days, and not just for the intimate dinners and excitement of his love-making, but for what came afterwards, when they would lie in each other's arms in the dark, talking.

That was when he gradually expanded on the details of his life with his mother, and the jealous possessiveness that had grown like a cancer, distorting her love into the sick obsession that destroyed her life, turning him from a son into a whipping boy for the man who bred him, and then into an enemy as he had tried to fight against her long slide into drug-addiction.

It was in the still of the night that Kate's unspoken love and serene acceptance were rewarded by the secrets of his guarded heart. He seemed to find it easier to talk in the dark and she certainly found it easier to listen.

One evening he came back from a trip to the store with a package under his arm.

'It's from Marcus,' he said, sitting on a stool at the breakfast bar to slit the large envelope and extract a note and a smaller, striped airmail envelope.

Kate froze in the act of slicing vegetables for dinner. 'I thought he didn't know where you lived?'

'He does now—at least he knows about the post box at the store,' he murmured, studying the writing on the front and the back of the envelope.

'Well, he didn't find out about it from me,' she said quickly.

'No, from me.' He glanced up and smiled ruefully at her expression. 'Part of our trade-off for your extra month: satisfying his curiosity and making myself a little less inaccessible.'

Kate was stunned. 'I thought all the arm-twisting

was the other way around. And so you just *told* him?'
she said, her heart swelling. 'For me?'

He shrugged as if he had dropped a damp squib
rather than a bombshell. 'It was inevitable I'd tell
him soon, anyway. I'm thinking of getting off the
merry-go-round and moving down here permanently.
Now that I have a solid backlist and financial security
for life, I can concentrate more on the writing and
scale back on the tours and the high-profile personal
publicity.'

He was thinking of moving to Oyster Beach! Kate
felt the shock of it move through her body. Where
would that leave her?

'When are you thinking of moving?'

'I haven't got that far in my planning,' he said,
with discouraging brevity.

Her eyes fell to the envelope he was turning over
and over in his hands.

'Why don't you open it?' she asked.

'Because I know who it's from.' He tossed it down
so that she could see the return address. It was from
Perth, Australia.

James John Richardson.

Richardson?

She raised her eyes to his face. 'Is that—?'

He smiled grimly. 'I'm sure there's more than one
James John Richardson in the world, but Marcus
says that this particular one claims to be my long-lost
father. He sent Enright's a letter asking for this one
to be passed along.'

'Do you think he is?'

'I know he is. I made sure I always knew where the bastard was, and that he never knew who I was.'

'Are you going to read it?'

He stood up, his body stiff with rejection. 'He's nothing to me. I have no interest in communicating with him—ever.'

'But it could be important—'

'No!' He turned on his heel. 'You read it if you're so interested. I have work to do....'

Kate contemplated the envelope for a long time after he left before she picked it up and ran her knife along the flap. The letter inside was a single sheet, typed.

When she went up to his office, Drake was standing on the balcony, looking over the beach, his arms braced against the solid rail. He didn't look at her as she quietly came up beside him, the letter open in her hand.

'He wants money, of course,' he told her harshly.

She had done his research, now he needed her précis. 'He said he saw your photograph in a bookshop and knew who you were because you look just like his other sons. He did some digging and says he thinks the press would be very interested in the pitiful story he has to tell, if you won't help him out of his financial difficulties. He says you owe him for putting up with your mother's craziness long enough to have you. That you're rich enough for a few hundred grand not to make any difference to you. How did you know?'

'Because it was never going to be a letter of re-conciliation and remorse.' His smile was a rictus of bitterness. 'He never had any remorse for what he did. He can rot in hell for all I care.'

'But if he sells his story—?'

'Let him,' he ground out. 'All publicity is good publicity according to Marcus—right? The scandal might even sell me a few hundred more books.'

'Drake—' She put her hand on his shoulder and he shrugged away her sympathy with a violent jerk of his body.

'My name was Michael James Richardson. I was taught to be very proud of my father, to do everything I could to be a good son. But not good enough. Because after he left my father had another son, and he christened *him* Michael James Richardson. He took even my identity from me, wiped me out as if I didn't exist. So I wiped him out. Let him bring on the world—he's getting nothing from me!'

That night, he took her with an almost painful ferociousness and afterwards, their bodies spooned together, his palm resting heavily on her belly, he told her about his little brother, Ross, who was born when he was nine.

'I don't know who the father was, but it was probably one of my mother's dealers, I suppose—she was taking everything she could by then and would do pretty much anything for a fix—or one of her coke-head friends. She claimed James had come back and wanted her to have his baby, and that made her try to clean up for a while, but it didn't last much past the birth. So I was the one who looked after Ross. I fed him and changed him, lied to the welfare and stole to get him clothes.' The darkness made Kate super-sensitive to the rising tension in his body and voice and she closed her hand around his strong wrist, anchoring him to her warmth as she realised what must be coming. 'Only I couldn't be there all the time,' he said thickly, 'and when he was four he got sick and my mother was too high to notice anything wrong. By the time I got home from school it was too late; he had a big rash that turned out to be meningococcal disease. He died the next morning.'

Kate felt the first tremor and rolled over, wrapping him in her arms as he buried his face in her hair.

'God, Kate, it happened so fast.' She felt the wetness on her neck, the echo of agonised bewilderment in his voice. 'One day he was there, the next he was gone as if he'd never existed. Just like my father. Just like my mother when she killed herself six months later. Ross had had one chance for life, and that was me, and I wasn't there for him. I was his surrogate father and I let him die. Do you wonder that I couldn't cope with the thought of being responsible for another child?'

Kate held him in her arms as he silently wept, whispering her love in her heart, and perhaps, in her effort to give him solace, she might even have whispered it into the dark hair that brushed against her cheek as he bowed his head on her breast. It was no time to point out that Ross might have died anyway, that meningococcal was a fast and ruthless killer that even medical personnel sometimes failed to recognise in time.

In his mind he knew that but his heart still harboured that thirteen-year-old's bitter grief. Drake had taken the guilt upon himself and it had petrified over time into a stony barrier to love, pushing out anything that might threaten to make him revisit that traumatic sense of loss.

Kate didn't know whether the night was cathartic for Drake, for he was already up and working when she woke the next morning, but for her it made her next action essential.

There was one thing they hadn't ever touched on in the past few weeks, and that was their first, cataclysmic coming together upstairs in his bedroom, when Drake had violated his most fundamental rule.

Just once.

Perhaps Drake still didn't realise his inexplicable oversight, or had forgotten or blocked it from his mind, but for Kate the lapse had begun to loom increasingly large in her thinking. And now it had assumed a critical significance.

Which was why she sloped off to Whitianga under the guise of a shopping trip, to re-visit the doctor. She still had not had a period, and this time she was leaving nothing to chance. At the risk of making a fool of herself she was going to get herself thoroughly checked out.

Just once.

Just once without a condom or any other form of contraception. What were the chances for a woman whose over-stressed body had already stopped menstruating? she lectured herself on the road. Minuscule.

At best. She had turned out not to be pregnant last time, and this time would be no different.

Just once.

Just once she would like to feel that she wasn't at the mercy of some malicious fate that took delight in ransacking her life.

Just once.

Yes, the doctor agreed cheerfully as she handed over a prescription for prenatal vitamins. It only took once. That was why there were so many teenage pregnancies.

'At least that gives you an exact date to work with—some women like that because it helps give them ideas for the baby's name,' she told Kate briskly, obviously not sure whether to be amused or sympathetic at her patient's shell-shocked reception of the news. 'You're only four weeks along so it's early days yet, but there's no reason to think that this pregnancy won't progress normally. You must be pleased after what happened last time—you did say that the baby was very much wanted.'

Kate looked at her blankly and burst into tears.

Many tissues and much embarrassment later Kate slunk out of the clinic, congratulations ringing in her ears. Still in a daze she drove into the centre of town, hardly even aware of the light bustle of lunchtime traffic, and did the shopping that would provide the excuse for her trip. All in a strange state of suspended emotion.

Fortunately, when she arrived back and used her front door key to sneak in, it was to discover a note from Drake to say he'd received a reminder to take Prince for his annual vaccination, so she was relieved to find herself with some valuable breathing space. Time to calm down and recover her composure.

She carried her shopping bags into her bedroom and put them on the bed, frowning at the unexpected profusion. Had she really bought so much?

Koshka, whom she had found squeaking at the front door, prowled in and jumped up on the cream bedspread to nose into the interesting crackle of a brown paper bag.

'Oh, you want to have a look, do you?' Kate up-ended the bag and showed the cat the pale lemon-and-white striped top and leggings and the knitted hat that went with it. 'That's because we don't know whether it's a girl or a boy,' she said, carefully folding up the tiny outfit, size 0000, and putting it aside to dive into another bag. 'But I do have one or two pinks and a few blues…'

Soon the bed was awash with baby clothes and Koshka was lying down with her tail thumping back and forth on the bedspread looking mightily bored with the colourful array. Unable to resist, Kate pulled a cute little bobble hat over the velvety black ears and laughed at the squeak of offended feline dignity. She began to feel it…that long, slow, fizz deep inside, the inner fuse that was about to release an explosion of feelings.

'I suppose I did go a bit mad,' said Kate, whisking off the hat as the cat rolled over on its back. 'A lot mad,' she corrected herself, stacking everything into piles. She fetched an empty suitcase from the bottom of the walk-in wardrobe and unzipped it on the bed. 'Totally insane, in fact.'

'Kate?' The call coincided with a door slamming somewhere in the house, and by the click of claws on the kitchen tile.

Kate gasped in horror. Quickly she scooped up everything on the bed and stuffed it into the suitcase, slamming the lid shut and turning her back on it, just as Drake burst into the room.

His eyes immediately went to the suitcase. 'What's that? What are you doing?' he said hoarsely.

'Nothing,' she said quickly, for fear he would try to look.

His eyes flashed back to her face, seeing the lie. 'Packing your bags? You're leaving, Kate?'

'I—'

'Leaving me? Just like that? No discussion…no right of reply?' he said savagely. 'What were you going to do, prop a Dear Drake letter on my desk?'

'No—'

'How could you? After last night? After what I told you?' His face changed, went as flat as his eyes, his beautiful voice: 'Or is that it? Are you afraid I might have inherited my mother's mental instability?'

'*No*—'

'Or my father's sheer, cold-blooded inhumanity?'

'No, Drake, it's nothing like that.'

He grabbed her hands and pulled her away from the bed to face him. 'Then tell me. What is it? What have I done wrong?'

She sighed. 'Nothing. You haven't done anything.'

Her sigh seemed to alarm him more than anything else. He laced his fingers through hers, securing her more completely to his cause.

'Don't go. Whatever it is, Kate, don't leave me,' he said, sending a piercing arrow of sweetness through her heart. She had never heard him plead before. Even last night, raw and bleeding with emotion, he had not spoken with such fierce desperation. 'Talk to me. Please. Just tell me what I can do to stop you. I've let you know the worst of me, but you can't judge me solely on what I've been. I can change, Kate...haven't these past few weeks shown you that? I let you into my life; don't turn around now and shut me out of yours! You can tell me anything. What is it you think I can't handle to hear?'

'That I love you, for one thing,' she said, taking her heart in both hands.

He looked stricken. 'I know. You told me that last night. But that's not the only thing, is it?'

It was her turn to be stricken. 'You know? *That's* all you have to say?'

His fingers tightened on hers as if he feared she was going to snatch them away. 'I'm not good with words—'

Her eyes widened. 'Drake—you're a *writer*.'

A muscle flickered along his jaw at her gentle scorn. 'I mean at *saying* them...to you. Other people don't matter.'

His discomfort made her heart stutter, then soar. 'You're also famous for your wit.'

'Wit is a weapon. Love is... It's dangerous...

loving people,' he said, twining and re-twining their fingers.

'I know, but sometimes you have to do it anyway.'

He hunched his shoulders, his face flushing. 'For God's sake, Kate, you must know well enough by now I love you,' he admitted roughly. 'I told you I won't want any woman but you, and I've practically been doing handstands to impress you all month. You're the only woman I've ever wanted to have permanently in my life, to live with. You like it down here at Oyster Beach, don't you? We could move here together, you could freelance and I could write, we could be free—you and me…'

'And baby makes three,' she murmured, expecting the inevitable recoil.

He looked down into her upturned face. 'Are you saying that you won't marry me if I don't give you children?'

'I— Marry?'

'That's what people who love and trust each other do, don't they?'

'I—I didn't think you were the marrying kind,' she stammered.

'You've been wrong about me before. Don't you trust me to love and to cherish you for better and for worse? Why were you seeing the doctor again today, Kate?'

Her eyes dilated. 'You saw me?'

He shook his head. 'Ken's receptionist. You're living in a small town, sweetheart. Why didn't you tell me you were going? Was it too private?'

She tried to escape his hold, but he wouldn't let her go.

'Don't be frightened to tell me. Are you pregnant, Kate?'

She sucked in her breath. 'What makes you say that?'

'Because I was naked inside you that time you cried in my arms. My first time being with a woman like that,' he admitted, sensuously stroking her cheek and tracing his finger around to the sensitive nerves behind her ear. 'I forgot myself, until I was inside you, but I liked it far too much to pull out. I never knew it would be so intense. I felt myself come uncontrollably inside you and I loved it, but I knew you weren't on the pill and after what you had just gone through I knew I had to look after you. I've been counting the days and you haven't had your period since. And you glow, Kate...you don't see it but you *shine*, from the inside out...'

She was confused by his pride, his deep satisfaction. 'I—I thought you said you didn't want children.'

'That's because I didn't know what a powerful healer love is... Yes, I'm afraid of the huge responsibility, the mistakes I might make, but with you beside me, to share the worries and the burdens as well as the rewards...you make me feel strong, Kate. You give me faith in myself that I never had before.

'Unless...' he faltered, looking very un-Drakelike in his uncertainty '...unless you're worried because you think I might not be able to commit to being a good father... I don't have a very good role model, or track record in the commitment department, do I?'

'Nor do I, come to that,' said Kate. 'And you told me you thought *I* would still be a good mother. As soon as I get my refund from my landlord I'll buy you a whole library of books on how to be a good father,' she attempted to tease him back into his usual arrogance.

He looked at the ceiling. 'Actually, you won't be getting much of a refund, because your landlord thinks you and your cat have been shamelessly sponging off him all along.'

She looked at him uncomprehendingly, then the light dawned.

'*You* own the house next door?'

'I own several houses in Oyster Beach.'

'You knew that I was coming?' she accused.

'I knew the place was rented, but I don't keep up with the details. I didn't know until you arrived who the tenant was. I was angry at first, but only because you make me feel too deeply—you always have. I found myself wanting you too much. But once you were here...well—' he gave her a devilish grin of triumph '—it was just too good an opportunity to miss.'

'You could have had me thrown out at any time,' she said wonderingly.

'You had a water-tight rental agreement,' he said glibly 'And...uh...speaking of water.'

'The bore pump was never broken?' she guessed.

'A fifty-cent seal and it'll be good as new,' he said without an iota of regret.

'*You*—' she jabbed him in the chest '—are a very devious man…'

'Then it's just as well that I'm marrying a very shrewd and managing woman, isn't it?' he said, winding a lock of her hair around his finger and gently tugging her into his kiss. He nudged her knees back against the bed, his mouth slanting on hers, his tongue sliding against hers, his hands spanning her hips, stroking the stomach that harboured his baby, rising to cup the breasts that were designed for nurture and pleasure, only to freeze in mid-caress as he turned his head.

'What's that?'

'What?'

'That squeaking. In the suitcase.' He gave her an incredulous look. 'Don't tell me you were even going to pack the cat.'

'Oh. *Oh!*' She must have gathered Koshka up with the baby clothes. Her hand hovered uncertainly as she remembered the embarrassment of riches within, but Drake beat her to it, throwing back the lid and watching Koshka's head pop out of her cosy nest of clothes. He picked a white bootee off the lashing black tail.

'I've been shopping,' she said weakly, smoothing over the rest of the contents as the cat leapt from the case and shot out the door.

'So I see.' Drake fitted the tiny bootee over the tip of his thumb and waggled it at her. 'For our daughter?' he asked softly.

'Or our son.' She looked at his grave face, misty

with memory, wistful for all the love that was yet to come. 'We could call him Ross, if you liked...' she offered, her eyes stinging with tears.

He slid his arm around her waist and tumbled her with him to the bed to kiss away her sorrow and replace it with laughter and love.

'And if it's a girl we can call her Joy, after you. Because that's what you bring me, sweetheart.' He made it a kiss and a vow. 'Joy for now and for always.'

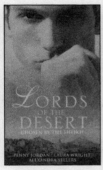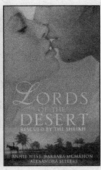

THE O'CONNELLS DYNASTY

Passion and seduction guaranteed!

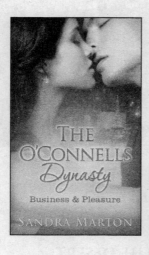

The O'Connells
Dynasty:
Business & Pleasure

Available
15th January 2010

The O'Connells
Dynasty:
Conveniently Wed

Available
19th February 2010

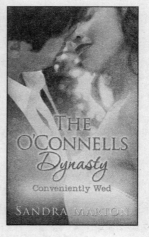

millsandboon.co.uk Community

Join Us!

The Community is the perfect place to meet and chat to kindred spirits who love books and reading as much as you do, but it's also the place to:

- Get the inside scoop from authors about their latest books
- Learn how to write a romance book with advice from our editors
- Help us to continue publishing the best in women's fiction
- Share your thoughts on the books we publish
- Befriend other users

Forums: Interact with each other as well as authors, editors and a whole host of other users worldwide.

Blogs: Every registered community member has their own blog to tell the world what they're up to and what's on their mind.

Book Challenge: We're aiming to read 5,000 books and have joined forces with The Reading Agency in our inaugural Book Challenge.

Profile Page: Showcase yourself and keep a record of your recent community activity.

Social Networking: We've added buttons at the end of every post to share via digg, Facebook, Google, Yahoo, technorati and de.licio.us.

www.millsandboon.co.uk

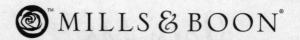